T0012806

DEATH
Comes to the
COSTA
DEL SOL

ALSO BY M.H. ECCLESTON

The Trust
Death on the Isle

DEATH
Comes to the
COSTA
DEL SOL

M.H. ECCLESTON

HEAD
of ZEUS

An Aries Book

First published in the UK in 2023 by Head of Zeus
This paperback edition first published in 2023 by Head of Zeus,
part of Bloomsbury Publishing Plc

Copyright © M.H. Eccleston, 2023

The moral right of M.H. Eccleston to be identified
as the author of this work has been asserted in accordance with
the Copyright, Designs and Patents Act of 1988.

All rights reserved. No part of this publication may be reproduced,
stored in a retrieval system, or transmitted in any form or by any means,
electronic, mechanical, photocopying, recording, or otherwise,
without the prior permission of both the copyright owner
and the above publisher of this book.

This is a work of fiction. All characters, organizations, and events
portrayed in this novel are either products of the author's
imagination or are used fictitiously.

9 7 5 3 1 2 4 6 8

A catalogue record for this book is available from the British Library.

ISBN (PB): 9781803280424
ISBN (E): 9781803280400

Cover design: Ben Prior

Printed and bound in Great Britain by
CPI Group (UK) Ltd, Croydon CR0 4YY

Head of Zeus
5–8 Hardwick Street
London EC1R 4RG

WWW.HEADOFZEUS.COM

For my family.

One

The bar had seen better days. A crack, as wide as a pencil, wandered between the ceiling beams. There was a film of dust on the chrome coffee machine and the bottles of red wine in the rack by the wall. It was a cool place though – typically Spanish. A dozen tables, none of which matched, were set out on the black and white tiled floor. At the far end, double doors opened on to a courtyard with more tables, shaded by a large fig tree. A fountain gurgled in an alcove. There was nobody around.

She looked down the copper counter. Blinked. George Clooney was staring back at her. A picture of him, at least – propped up against a stack of white cups. It was an advert for a brand of coffee. He was wearing a tuxedo, with a black bow tie – the kind you tie yourself – dangling from his open collar, a tiny coffee cup raised halfway to his lips. There was an enigmatic expression on his face, as if he was just about to wink at her, or sneeze.

Astrid's mind drifted while she waited for a bartender to appear. What if her father had moved to Italy rather than Spain, and she'd been sailing around Lake Como instead of the Costa del Sol? Perhaps she'd have some kind of emergency on the boat – *a toaster fire, maybe?* – and have to dock at Clooney's waterside villa and ask for help.

He answers the door in the same unbuttoned shirt. 'Are you alright?' he says, ushering her inside.

Then he makes coffee for both of them, and while Astrid sips hers at the marble kitchen island, he starts fumbling with his bow tie.

'Never could get the hang of these things.'

'Another awards ceremony?'

'I'm afraid so.' He looks up with those liquid brown eyes. 'All I want to do is crash on the sofa and watch some TV.'

'Like *Dogs Need Homes*?'

He gasps, then steps forwards. 'I love *Dogs Need Homes* – it's my favourite show.' He takes Astrid's hand and slowly leads her to the TV room and—

'*Hola!*'

Astrid snapped out of her daydream. Behind the bar stood a man who could, if she squinted, be George Clooney's sadder, less successful brother. The stubble, and his light blue shirt, which was frayed at the collar, told the same story as the crack in the ceiling.

'Sorry.' She read his confusion. 'I was miles away.'

He was still staring at her.

Astrid sat up, and in a low and steady voice said, '*Lo siento, he estado*—'

'It's okay,' he interrupted. 'This is the Costa del Sol. There is no need to speak Spanish.'

'Got it.' *Really? Four weeks trying to learn Spanish on the sail over here – that was a waste.*

He stared at her again.

'You alright?' Astrid asked.

'I apologise. You remind me of someone.' He clapped his hands. 'Now – what can I get you?'

Astrid glanced at George Clooney. 'Coffee?'

The man's shoulders sagged. 'Sorry, the machine is broken.' He held up a finger and smiled. 'I have something you'll like.'

Without waiting for her to answer, he went down the bar and started preparing something out of sight. She heard the chopping of a knife on a board, and the rattle of ice cubes. Astrid studied the framed posters on the wall of Spanish movies and famous flamenco dancers, and the curled banknotes from around the world that were pinned to the beam above her head.

The bartender returned with a tin jug and a tumbler the colour of sea glass. The ice crackled as he poured out a pale-yellow liquid.

'Rosemary lemonade.' He pushed it across the counter.

She drank it slowly, the scent of the lemon and rosemary making her feel light-headed. She knew that if she'd ordered it back in England, it wouldn't be the same. Here, in a lonely Spanish bar on a hot day, with the foothills of the Sierra Bermeja shimmering beyond the fig tree, it was perfect. 'Delicious. Thank you.' She pushed the glass back across the bar.

The bartender refilled the glass and introduced himself. His name was Eduardo. He'd owned this place – Bar Finca – for twenty years. He lived upstairs with his two children, a boy and a girl, both young teenagers. 'They're good kids,' he said. 'Not so good at school, maybe. They like swimming and riding their bikes too much.' He laughed, then caught himself. 'I'm sorry, I've talked too long. Tell me what brings you here?'

Astrid told him she'd sailed down from the Isle of Wight to

spend some time with her father, who'd lived here for a while. 'Peter Swift. He lives on this road. Peter and Jennifer?'

He shook his head a couple of times. Then slapped the counter. 'Yes! That is who you remind me of. Red sports car.' He mimed wrestling a steering wheel. 'Very fast.'

'Yep – that sounds like him.'

'I know him now.' He nodded over to the double doors. 'Sometimes I see him walking on the hill trails.'

She took a draw on the lemonade, the sprigs of rosemary tingling on her lips. Then she checked her watch. It was time to go and see him – she couldn't put it off any longer. This was what she wanted, more than anything. So why was she so nervous?

'When was the last time you saw your father?'

'Two years.' *Two years… how has so much time slipped away between us?* But she knew the answer – it was Jennifer.

'That's a long time.'

'It is.' She opened her purse. 'How much do I owe you?'

'Two euros.'

She passed the coins across the bar. He took the money and put it in his pocket, instead of the till. 'Good luck.'

'Thanks.' She slipped down from her bar stool.

'Because—' He paused, not wanting to interfere, but knowing it was worth saying. 'Because family – that's all there is. Without family, who are we?'

She tried to force a smile, but couldn't – he was right, this was why she was nervous. Her father – he was the only family she really had. If this didn't work out, then what? Where else would she go? 'Yes – that's very true, Eduardo.' Then she thanked him and told him she'd come back, and he said he'd be pleased if she did.

★ ★ ★

Outside in the street, she checked the address on her father's last letter – she was close. There were only a dozen houses before the road came to an end. They were big houses – two or three storeys. Each one was a different style, from whitewashed villas to rust-coloured forts that looked like Foreign Legion outposts.

Her father's house was the second to last on the road. It was a peachy cake of a building. A terracotta tiled roof jutted out, throwing a slim blade of shadow down orangey walls. A purple bougainvillea rambled over a wooden front door pitted with black diamond studs. Impressive. It was good to see her father was doing well for himself, she thought. For *both* of them. Chances are, Jennifer was around. If so, she'd be polite. Keep it civil.

There was a convertible red Triumph sports car in the drive. *Must be his car*. A pair of tan driving gloves neatly folded on the dashboard. *Definitely his car*. She strode forward and rapped on the front door, straightened her dress... and waited. But nobody came.

She went over to the side of the house and carried on down an alleyway, past a green recycling bin that was full of empty wine bottles, round the corner and out into the bright sunshine again.

In front of her was a well-tended lawn with cactuses and agave plants lined up against white boundary walls. Below the lawn was a lower tier of paving. A pool was set in the middle, like a baguette-cut sapphire. Beyond the pool was the Sierra Bermeja. It was majestic. Few mountains were this big, this close to the coast. She'd used the peak as a marker to sail into the Mediterranean yesterday – watching it rise up to meet the sky, its lower ridges splayed out like the paws of a sphinx, guarding the town of Estepona huddled below it.

There was a scuttling noise from inside the house, and something shot out from the open patio doors. Astrid jumped back. *What was it? A dog?* It took some close inspection to be sure. It was like a small cloud of fluff propped off the ground by four spindly legs. Round and round it circled, its claws *rattering* and *tattering* on the stone path. Astrid knelt down. She could just make out some features hidden in the fluff – two gleaming black eyes and a black button nose. It stalked towards her, its jaw dropping to reveal a row of teeth like a tiny picket fence.

Astrid reached for her phone and bent down. 'Hullo, Furball,' she whispered, taking a close-up picture. She wasn't sure why, exactly. Maybe just to have a record of it – in case someone asked her what was the strangest creature she'd ever seen. The dog made a few high, furious yaps. Then it wheeled round a couple of times, darted its eyes back to the house and started yapping again. Louder this time.

Jennifer appeared at the doorway. She flipped her sunglasses down from her forehead and shook her head in disbelief. 'Is that you, Astrid?'

'Sure is,' Astrid called over.

Jennifer wrapped her leopard-print beach dress tight around her, knotting the silk belt at her waist. 'I can't believe it.' She slipped her feet into a pair of flip-flops by the door and wandered down the steps. The little dog stood up on its back legs and did a couple of pirouettes, whimpering in short bursts. Jennifer leant down and bundled the dog up, bringing it close to her face. 'Yuss, yuss, baby,' she cooed. 'You're safe with Mummy now.'

The little dog began licking Jennifer's face, its sharp tongue dabbing at the corner of her mouth, streaking her lipstick across her cheek.

'That's got to be unhygienic, don't you think?' Astrid realised she was *that* close to adding 'for the poor dog'. *That close*. She held her breath. *Steady, Astrid. Don't ruin this*. But there was something about Jennifer that made her bristle. No, not something – *everything* about her was annoying.

Jennifer gathered up the dog and whispered in her ear, 'Ooo… don't worry about this strange lady. You go and have a little nap, baby.' She put the dog down between them. Viewed from above, it was almost spherical, like thistledown.

'Come on… hop it, Furball,' said Astrid. The dog peered up, curled its black gums at the corner of its mouth and trotted back into the house.

'It's Lulu… not Furball,' said Jennifer.

'I'll try and remember.'

'Sorry, I forgot. You're not really a dog person, are you?'

'Actually—' Astrid squared up. 'I really like dogs. I had a little dog for a while – Sheepdip.' *That felt sad*. She realised it had been almost two months since she'd left him in Dorset.

'A dog?' Jennifer raised an eyebrow. 'You?'

'Yes, I like dogs. But it's like people, isn't it? You get some nice ones… and some annoying ones.' She kept a straight face and sidestepped Jennifer on her way to a table on the patio which was shaded by a large parasol. She sat on the seat at the end, glad to be out of the searing heat.

Jennifer caught her up. 'So, um… this is a nice surprise.'

She fixed a watery smile. 'Did um… did Peter know you were coming? He never mentioned it.'

'No, I finished a job on the Isle of Wight, and I thought I'd just sail over here. Spur of the moment kind of thing.' Astrid glanced at the open patio doors. 'Is he around?'

'He's in his office – day trading. It's his new money-making scheme. Don't ask me how it works though.'

'Okay, I won't.'

Jennifer looked at the gold bangle-style watch on her wrist. 'He should be finished in a minute. Most of the European markets shut down about now, then he'll switch off for the day.'

Astrid placed her bag by her feet. 'That's fine, I'll wait.'

Jennifer smiled again – an even weaker smile this time – and headed into the house. Astrid waited for about five seconds. Then she tried out a few of the seats. Facing the house, facing the garden – imagining which was the best seat to get up from to greet her father. She'd thought about this moment for so long and she wanted it to be perfect. Dramatic, even. Just her and her father, who she was sure would be surprised and delighted. So far, it had been Jennifer, surprised and mildly appalled, plus her mutant dog.

Eventually, she heard footsteps in the gloom beyond the patio doors. There were whispered voices. Her father strode out into the sunshine, a large glass of red wine in one hand, the other tucked into the pocket of a pair of sharply creased khaki shorts. The outfit was rounded off with a white linen shirt and a cream Panama hat. Jennifer was close behind, carrying a tray on which was balanced a jug of iced water and some glasses.

Astrid stood up quickly, bumped her head on the crossbar

of the parasol, shouted 'Fugg...' – and when she'd composed herself, her father was awkwardly drawing back his outstretched arms and settling into his seat. She'd missed the big father and daughter moment.

'Are you alright, Astrid?' Jennifer buzzed in, scooping a chunk of ice from the jug.

'I'm good, thanks,' said Astrid, rubbing her head.

Her father crossed his legs and rested his hands on his knee. 'Astrid... what are you doing here?'

She wanted to say that she'd missed him. That when she'd nearly drowned at the Isle of Wight it was him, only him, she'd thought about. And that she'd thought about him across five hundred miles of fickle sea. But that moment had sailed too. So she just shrugged and before he could say anything, Jennifer said, 'How long are you planning to stay?'

Lovely. She'd barely arrived, and Jennifer wanted to know when she was leaving. 'I've booked into the harbour for a couple of weeks, so at least that long.'

Her father took off his hat, placing it carefully on the table. He always wore the same type of hat when the sun was out or the cricket was on the radio, even if he was still in his pyjamas.

Jennifer tipped her head to one side and looked mournful. 'Can we say how sorry we are to hear about you and Simon splitting up?'

'I'm fine.' Astrid felt an acidy tickle low in her throat.

'If you want to talk about it,' added Jennifer, 'I'm here to listen.'

Astrid thought that she was more than happy to talk about it – how Simon's affair had imploded their marriage. Just not with Jennifer. It wasn't the kind of advice she needed. 'I'd rather not, thanks.'

'I understand.' Jennifer paused. 'But for the record, we think it's for the best.'

Astrid crossed her arms. There had been a lot of use of the word 'we' so far, although her father hadn't offered an opinion on the subject. 'I didn't realise you'd both discussed it.'

'Of course.' Jennifer looked to Astrid's father. 'Peter and I discuss everything.'

Her father smiled benignly. He was looking well – tanned and lean. At least she didn't have to worry about his health. 'Yes, I read her your letters, Astrid. I was sure you wouldn't mind.'

'They were very entertaining,' chipped in Jennifer.

'Entertaining?' coughed Astrid. 'The collapse of my marriage was entertaining?'

'Gosh, no,' said Jennifer. 'All those eccentric characters you met in the village.'

'They're my friends.'

'Well, whatever they are, they sound delightful.' Jennifer set out a glass in front of Astrid and tipped the jug of water. Astrid raised her hand and told her she was okay, even though she had a rasping thirst. Jennifer's hand had been in the jug to get the ice cube and she'd been clutching Furball only a minute ago. 'Sorry, I forgot. You probably want something stronger. Wine, isn't it?'

Youch! Had they been discussing her alcohol consumption too?

Her father raised his glass. 'As long as the sun is over the yardarm – that's what I say.' He made a chinking motion of his glass in the air. 'And somewhere in the British Empire, the sun is always over the yardarm.' He took a swig and gazed out at the Sierra Bermeja, capped by the first golden light of the evening. 'Although the concept of the British Empire is unpalatable in some quarters at the moment—'

'Dearest.' Jennifer stroked his wrist. 'Perhaps this isn't the best time for one of your speeches about the British Empire. Why don't we hear all about Astrid's news? We haven't had a letter for weeks.' She took out a leopard-print scrunchie from a side pocket and tied her hair back. The outfit complete, she sat back and waited for Astrid to speak.

Astrid wasn't in the mood to go into much detail. She sketched over her trip down to Spain on the boat, which had thankfully been uneventful. Plain sailing, apart from a handful of days anchored up because there'd been too much or too little wind. Even though it only took a couple of minutes to explain, it felt like forcing up cold soup. She wanted to tell her father all about the murder she'd solved on the Isle of Wight. She wanted to ask *him* about Uncle Henry. Why had he fallen out with his brother? A rift so deep that when Uncle Henry died, he left his beloved boat, the only thing he owned, to her. 'Anyway, enough about me,' she said, winding up the story. 'What have you been up to, Dad?'

'Oh, well…' Her father breathed out in a low whistle. 'It's been hectic. The day trading has been keeping me incredibly busy.'

'Peter went on a seminar in Marbella, didn't you?'

'I did. It was most informative,' said her father.

'And I've been super busy too – with my salon.'

'Salon?' said Astrid.

'Yes, Classy Costa Cuts. It's a hairdresser's in the town. British customers – tourists and expats.'

Astrid cheered up slightly. Maybe this explained why they hadn't visited her in London for a couple of years.

'Yes, we've both been working flat out,' said her father. 'Although we did manage to have a weekend in London at Christmas.'

Maybe not. 'Sorry… you were in London at Christmas? Why didn't you visit me?'

Jennifer refilled her glass. 'Whistlestop tour, I'm afraid, Astrid.'

'I needed to pick up some things from Marks and Sparks – cords, slippers,' added her father. 'And Jennifer wanted to see *Jersey Boys* again.'

'*Jersey Boys*? Again?' Astrid choked.

'It's a musical,' said Jennifer. 'About the sixties band, The Four Seasons.'

'Yes, I know what it's about,' Astrid snapped. There was no excuse. They'd seen a musical – *again* – instead of her. 'The point is…' Her voice cracked. 'The point is… if you were in London, you could have just dropped in and said hi. Just an hour.'

'Sorry,' said Jennifer. 'We didn't have the time.'

Astrid's neck was burning, even though she was in the shade. She got up. 'You know what, I think I'd better go.'

'No, no.' Her father stood up. 'You don't have to.' Jennifer tapped him on the arm, and he quickly sat back in his seat.

'I've come all this way to see you, Dad, because I was worried about you. And it's…' A tear began to prickle at the corner of her eye. 'It's been a waste of time.'

'Assstrid,' soothed her father.

That's all she heard as she walked away. That and Jennifer muttering something like 'Just leave her, Peter', although she couldn't be sure.

Two

Usually, when making a grand exit – and she'd flounced out of a few work meetings in her time – Astrid had realised exactly what she should have said just after she'd left the room. The door would shut, and the killer line would spring to mind. This time, she'd said exactly what she wanted to. It was simple – coming here had been pointless.

She took one of the side roads that drained down to the sea, her mind toiling back and forth over what had happened. She'd tried to talk to her father, but Jennifer had got in the way. Hovering about. Finishing his sentences. Telling him what he couldn't say. It wasn't a relationship – it was Stockholm Syndrome with better weather.

At the bottom of the hill, the road faded into a dirt track that curled down to a pleasant beach. It ticked all the holiday postcard boxes. A wide scythe of golden sand. Rows of sun loungers laid out under straw parasols. Knots of wind-battered palm trees. A sign said 'Playa del Cristo'.

She sat on the sand next to an orange kids' climbing frame and gazed over the water. The Rock of Gibraltar was a grey thumbprint jutting out into the Mediterranean. On the Moroccan side was a mountain about the same height – Jebel Musa. Astrid remembered the story from classics at school.

When Hercules arrived at the Atlas Mountains, he decided to take a short cut. Instead of climbing over the top, he used his strength to smash it in two. Good for him, thought Astrid. Showing a bit of initiative – presumably there wasn't a Mrs Hercules tugging on his arm and telling him to sit down. Jebel Musa and the Rock of Gibraltar were supposed to be what's left of the mountains – the Pillars of Hercules. Between them lay the Strait of Gibraltar – seven nautical miles at its narrowest, funnelling some of the trickiest currents Astrid had to navigate on the whole trip. She'd come a long way to connect with her father. But how could she, with Jennifer getting in the way?

She pushed her heels into the sand, her mind tracking ahead. He might seem happy – but he was bottling it up. He had to be. And how long before he snapped? Was it going to be like those reports you see on the TV news? The opening shot – blue flashing lights. Yellow-and-black crime-scene tape drawn across the path of a suburban house. The shocked neighbours wander out and tell the reporter the usual things – 'They seemed like such a good couple' and 'He was such a quiet man, always said hello in the morning'. As if that was relevant. Maybe it wasn't heading that way, exactly. But everyone had their limit. Didn't they?

Astrid was about to get up when her phone buzzed. A text. She read it, an eyebrow slowly arching.

It was from her father.

Where are you? I need to talk about Jennifer.

Three

Astrid had just enough time to get to a beach shack near the kids' climbing frames, grab a bottle of water and meet her father's red Triumph as it glided to the end of the dirt track. He took off his driving gloves, folded them on top of the dashboard, and explained he'd only had one glass of wine – before she asked. Then he led the way to a low wall by the beach, dusted the sand off with the back of his hand, and sat down. She sat down next to him, warm embers smouldering in the pit of her stomach.

He looked dead ahead. 'If I tell you something, can you keep it to yourself, Astrid?'

'Of course.'

'Right…' He took off his hat and put it on the wall next to him. *The hat's off – this is serious.* 'There's something I have to tell you about Jennifer.'

'Go on.' The embers glowed.

'Someone has been sending her messages on The Twitter.'

'It's just called Twitter.'

'Is it?'

'Yes, Dad.' It felt good to call him Dad.

'Amazing, isn't it? The way people can get in touch these days. I remember when we had red phone boxes.' He mimed picking up a phone receiver and ratcheting his finger round a dial. 'And if you ran out of coins you had to reverse the charges. A lady would come on the phone and put you through.' He rolled his eyes skywards. 'Now everyone can call, text, Twitter away to their heart's content. Where did the time go, Astrid?'

'I know,' she said softly. This was another conversation – a bigger one. Where had the years gone? *Later*. Right now, she needed to get him back on track. 'Anyway, Dad… these messages. What did they say?'

'It's actually the same message. It simply says, "I know your secret".'

'Secret?' She bit down on her lower lip, determined to keep a straight face. 'Okay… and what is her secret?'

'Does it matter?'

'I guess it might be relevant,' she said calmly. 'I mean… do you know what it is?'

'No, and I haven't asked her.'

'Why not?'

'Because if she wanted to tell me, she would.'

'Uh, okay.' She half yawned, at the same time wondering how long she could keep up the illusion of being uninterested – when she was dying to know what Jennifer's secret was. A secret too awful to reveal to her father. A past crime? A second family somewhere? It happens. She'd read about people who lead double lives for decades – shuttling between two families, each clueless that the other existed. Imagine – all those direct debits.

'The thing is, Jennifer is dreadfully upset about this.' Her father crossed his legs and huffed out a breath. 'She just wants it to stop. Me too – you know what I always say?'

She did.

'Happy wife, happy life,' he said.

Ironically, she noted, it was a phrase he'd used a lot during his first marriage, and there had been little happiness in that. They sat in silence for a while, watching the people on the beach. There were only half a dozen families. The kids were splashing around in the shallows or clambering on the climbing frames while their parents slept on the sun loungers or dabbed at their phones.

'Listen, Dad.' She hopped down from the wall and turned to face him. 'Why don't I try and find out who's behind this?'

He straightened up. 'You'd do this for us?'

Astrid nodded solemnly. She told him that she had some free time on her hands and wanted a challenge. 'I'll crack this for you – you'll see, Dad,' she said, working her fist into her palm.

He looked her up and down and smiled ruefully. As if he'd seen something new in her or remembered something about her that he'd forgotten. Then he went over the few details he had. A couple of weeks ago, an anonymous Twitter account called The All-Seeing Eye sent Jennifer a message saying they'd discovered her secret. She ignored it, hoping they'd go away. But they didn't. Since then, they'd said the same thing, in public this time – they knew her secret, and they were going to expose her. That's all her father had. There were no clues to who was behind it. 'You think there's a chance you can get to the bottom of this?'

'I don't see why not,' she said confidently.

'Thank you. Jennifer is very stressed by all this.' He pushed himself down from the wall, gratitude written across his face.

For a moment, it looked like he was going to step forward and hug her. But he stumbled at the last second and ended up sort of patting her high on the shoulder and muttering 'Good, good', before striding off towards the Triumph.

She watched him slip on his driving gloves and start the engine. Then he turned it off, got out and waved her over.

When she got there, he'd opened the boot of the car and was reaching for something inside. 'I almost forgot,' he said, shaking his head. 'I thought you could help me out.' He lifted out a package wrapped in brown paper and string. It was flat and square, about twelve inches across. 'It's a religious piece. Renaissance – Perugino.'

'An original Perugino?' She let out a sharp gasp.

'I wish it was.' He chuckled. 'It's just a copy of one of his famous works. One of his apprentices in his workshop in Florence would have knocked it up. But I'm very fond of it.' He shut the boot of the car and explained what was needed. The painting was damaged – there was a tear in the canvas. Nothing major, and seeing as she was 'a first-class conservator', maybe she could fix it.

She didn't hesitate. 'Of course, Dad. I'll give it my best shot.' He passed the package over and said he'd pay her hourly rate. She wafted his offer away. 'Forget it – I'll accept wine.'

'Sounds good,' he said, stepping round to the driver's seat. She waited for his car to roar over the brow of the hill, her excitement dropping from vigorous boil to a light simmer. This, she thought, could work well. Her father was delighted with her. She was going to sort out his painting *and* track down Jennifer's tormentor. It would mean spending more time with him – keeping him updated with her findings. And in the process, Jennifer's secret might just slip out... whatever it was. Maybe it was so bad she would have to go back to the UK. *Adios*, Jennifer.

By the time she reached the end of the beach, her conscience had overtaken her and was waiting for her at the next bench. She slumped down. Was she really going to reveal Jennifer's secret? Recently, she'd been so chilled and positive – at peace with the world. Digging around in Jennifer's private life felt negative. Cruel even, and that wasn't who she was.

A few minutes later, she was back at the marina and heading up the pontoon towards her boat. She'd made her mind up. No, it was fine. This was her chance to get to know her father again. Her last chance, maybe. There was no going back. And if Jennifer did have a secret, her father should know about it. It was settled.

There was only one problem – she had no idea how Twitter worked.

Four

Astrid hurried below deck, propped the package in the corner and filled a tall glass of water at the sink. With all the walking in the heat – which she wasn't used to – she hadn't drunk nearly enough. Her thirst extinguished, she went back up on deck and untied the bike. It was time to explore the town.

At the back of the marina, she took the promenade that ran alongside the town beach. It was wide, with pinkish flagstones, and ran in a gentle smooth curve out to the east. She'd caught Estepona in a good mood. People seemed happy and relaxed. It was the start of the town's own long holiday. Nearly all the tourists, which were mostly families, had gone back to wherever they'd come from – Britain probably, if the dual languages of the signs above the beach restaurants were anything to go by. *Mariscos – Seafood. Pescados – Fish. Carnes – Meats.*

She cycled slowly. The restaurant staff were working in a lower gear too. At the first place she passed, a man in a white shirt was idly snapping the elastic bands off the corners of the tables. Another was replacing the paper tablecloths with white cotton ones. At the next place, the menus were being changed in the wooden stand by the street. The olive trees in their pots were being pruned and watered. The restaurants were getting a spring-clean at the start of autumn. The first chance in months for the waiters to speak in Spanish to the locals, who were claiming their favourite tables and their town back. Or at least sharing it with the expats.

Astrid carried on down the promenade for a mile or so until the sand ran into a rocky outcrop. Then she turned back, choosing a line nearest the road. There was shade there, from a canopy of sails stretched out over white metal frames, or in the small gardens of palms with bright beds of orange and yellow marigolds at their base. Halfway along the promenade she cut north into the town up a broad avenue. She found a Carrefour supermarket a few hundred yards on the left.

It was cool inside, with wide aisles and everything you might need on the shelves and big cardboard boxes in the corners that said *Super Precio* on the side. As she was on her bike, she only got a few things. A metal water bottle, a ring-bound jotter, a pair of blue and white stripy espadrilles, more sun cream and a wide-brimmed straw hat. She put the hat on outside the supermarket and headed back to the boat.

In the past, when someone asked her if she was 'on Twitter', Astrid would say 'no' while thinking 'why?' Why would you want to broadcast your every thought to random strangers? It was like shouting at the traffic: best left for the drunk and deluded. Now, sitting in a chair on the deck, laptop on her knees, finger poised over the 'create a new account' box on Twitter, it still felt like a bad idea. It had to be done, though – she knew that, if she was going to keep an eye on Jennifer's troll.

A boat eased into a mooring a couple of spaces down, setting up a ripple that made her grip the laptop by both sides. It was an impressive yacht – one of the best in the marina. Gleaming white, with black smoked-glass windows and doors. A tall man, late forties, with a tidy goatee beard, was at the helm. He was wearing a Hawaiian shirt in electric blues and yellows and a baseball cap. He gave a jaunty salute. Astrid saluted back. Then she cracked her knuckles and typed in her personal details.

Next, she had to choose a name for her new Twitter account. It turned out there were quite a few Astrid Swifts out there, and many of them had got wind of Twitter before she had. It took until @AstridSwift14 before she felt special again, then she began to explore.

The rules were simple, as no doubt half the world already knew. You have a 280-character limit to say anything you want. Anything at all, whether anyone might be interested or not.

I'm thinking about making a sandwich, said @grubmaster29.

Others had already prepared sandwiches, and cakes, and salads, which they'd taken photos of and added 'Nom, nom, nom' underneath and a line of emoji faces with their tongues lolling out. There were lots of pictures of food. And babies, and cats, and dogs – usually asleep – and cars, and weird cloud formations, and patio furniture, and a tyre in a ditch, and a single brown shoe, and smooth grey pebbles stacked up in a tower, and some Harrods bags on a duvet. Just about anything people had tasted or looked at that day. It was like rewinding through the mind of a hyperactive child who'd stolen a credit card.

There were people complaining about the weather, and the bad service they'd had on trains, or commenting on TV and films, and moaning about politics, and the state of their nails, and asking multiple-choice questions. Polls were a regular feature.

@thetastymuffin13 wanted to know – *If you were a potato, how would you like to be cooked?*

The options were mashed, baked, boiled and sauteed. Astrid hit 'sauteed'. It was the least popular choice with 11 per cent of the votes. Incredible, thought Astrid. We're living in a golden information age with the entire knowledge of humankind available at the tap of a screen. And somehow, people would prefer to spend their time establishing the consensus on the best way to be cooked if they were, by some quirk of fate, a potato. But then of course she realised she'd just clicked the poll herself. *Oh, the irony.*

After only twenty minutes on Twitter, her brain had been sauteed. Or mashed (39 per cent). There were just too many ideas and images flashing up. Too many jagged gear changes between the banal and the tragic. It was disorientating. The question now was – what was going to be *her* first tweet?

She looked up from her laptop. It was a pretty scene. The sun was setting out to the west, throwing a soft light over the peaks of the Sierra Bermeja. Shadows folded over the villas on the hill and the cream apartment blocks behind the road. In the foreground was the blue and white harbour complex. It was an unusual building. An octagonal white tower with bright blue details, more Greek than Spanish. A skirt of awnings shaded the offices and cafés around its base. Yes, she'd take a photo of that. There were a lot of sunset photos on Twitter – people must like them.

She took the picture and uploaded it. Then she paused, thinking about what she could say about the picture. It was a sunset. The sky turned orangey when the sun went down.

What more information could she add? *Best not overthink it, Astrid.* She wrote 'Sunset over Estepona Marina' and sent it off into who knows where.

Now to find out what the internet troll had been up to. It didn't take long to get to *@JenniferClassyCostaCuts*. There was a headshot of Jennifer – her hair neatly combed. Her make-up perfect. The 'bio' below said: 'English-speaking owner of a traditional British hair salon in Estepona. Pensioner discounts.'

Astrid scrolled down Jennifer's timeline for the past couple of weeks. She'd posted a tweet nearly every day – friendly messages, special offers. And every time there was the same reply from an account called *@TheAllSeeingEye7*.

I know your secret

Sometimes there was a GIF attached. A golden eye burning in the night sky. A child from a black-and-white movie drawing a line across their throat with their finger. Or there was a string of emojis – bulging eyes, a flame, and laughing faces being the favourites.

Astrid sat back, not sure where these replies could take her. That's all there was. There were no hints about what this secret might be, or how it might ruin Jennifer. She checked her own photo of the sunset. No likes. *I guess it takes a while*, she thought.

When she looked up again, the man in the Hawaiian shirt was approaching her boat. He had an ice bucket in one hand. A green bottle and two glasses were nestled in among the ice cubes. The fingers of his other hand were fanned out under a round plate, which he held delicately at shoulder height.

'Permission to come aboard?' he piped. Then, without waiting for an answer, he stepped nimbly over the rail and on to the deck.

Astrid pulled open a chair for him. The man put the ice bucket on the floor between them and sat down with the plate on his lap. She held out her hand. 'Astrid Swift.'

He shook her hand, a pleasant smile pushing up his tanned cheeks. 'Nelson.'

'Right, Nelson… as in the admiral or Mandela?'

'Mandela, of course.' He took off his baseball hat, revealing a ruffled mat of straw-coloured hair, and placed the hat at his feet, his hand moving on to the bucket to pluck out a glass. He passed it over to Astrid. She'd been planning to have a week off drinking – after that barbed comment from Jennifer. *Maybe start tomorrow?*

He filled both glasses and clinked his against hers. 'Down the hatch.'

'Cheers.'

He studied her as she swirled her glass and took a sniff. 'Go on then… take a guess. What is it?'

Astrid swirled the glass again and took a deeper sniff. 'Okay, there's grapefruit… nectarine.' She took a sip, the coldness gliding over her tongue. 'Dry. High acid… yup, it has to be an Albariño.' She may not have had good wine for a while, but she still remembered what it tasted like. And Albariño was one of the best wines in Spain.

Nelson had his palm flat to his chest and was gasping theatrically. 'Fantastic! You got it in one. As soon as I saw you, I knew you were sophisticated.'

'Thank you – do you like your wine too?'

This turned out to be a rich seam of conversation. Nelson

was in fact both a 'wine buff' and a bit of a 'foodie'. That was the main reason he and his wife, a divorce lawyer, had moved down here. Spain's wine and cuisine were, he insisted, superior to France's. Halfway through his eulogy, Astrid stole a look at her phone, which she'd tucked down the side of her chair. There were still no likes for the sunset.

Nelson refilled her glass and ploughed on with his story. He'd retired early after a successful career as a psychotherapist – couples therapy, usually. 'If I didn't fix their relationship, I'd sling them over to my wife,' he laughed, rolling smoothly into the next chunk of his CV. They'd then cashed in their house in Colchester, bought the boat and set out for a new life in Estepona. His wife, Talia, who'd also retired early, spent half her time with him on their boat. The rest of the time she was back in the UK, where she looked after her ailing mother. He missed her, he said, but he was good at keeping himself busy – 'pottering around the coast' or scouting out restaurants for his regular review slot in a local English online newspaper. 'Guess what it's called?'

Astrid didn't hesitate. 'It's Nelson's Column. Right?'

'Yeah... that's it,' he said, a little deflated.

Astrid then told him a bit about herself – a rough sketch of how her art conservator career accidentally turned into a sailing tour. Minus the grisly details of solving two murder cases. 'I'm over here to see my father and stepmother, Peter and Jennifer.'

His eyes lit up. 'Yes, yes, I know them. It's a small world. All of us expats know each other.'

'Are there still a lot of expats here?'

'Umm...' He sucked in some air, thinking about how to order a long answer. 'Yeah, since Brexit, numbers have dropped a bit. But there's still around sixty thousand Brits living on the Costa del Sol. That's the official figure – the people who are on the Padrón.'

'Padrón?'

'The town hall register. That's how the authorities know you're here.' He topped up their glasses. 'Then you have the swallows.'

'Swallows? There's a lot of jargon, isn't there?'

'Sure is – the swallows are the Brits who fly in for the winter. You used to be able to stay for six months without a visa. Now you have to shuttle back and forth. Unless you have a Golden Visa.'

'Golden Visa?'

'Yeah – if you invest five hundred thousand euros in Spain, usually property, then you can stay for good. You're golden – it's the visa people would kill for.' He stretched back in his chair. 'Anyway, one way or another the Brits are here to stay.'

Astrid sneaked another look at her phone. Still zero likes.

'Now, have I got a treat for you.' He tapped the edge of the plate on his lap. 'Let me introduce you to my favourite Spanish cheese.' On the plate were a dozen large cubes of ivory-coloured hard cheese. There was a stack of cocktail sticks on the edge. He stabbed a cube and passed it over. 'This is a Manchego. The finest sheep's milk cheese in the world.'

She closed her eyes. It was delicious. Nutty, with a buttery smoothness that lingered on the palate.

'It's the kind of cheese…' Nelson paused for inspiration. '…that will lull you to sleep with the sound of sheep bells echoing around the high plains of La Mancha.'

'Ooo… I like it. Very poetic.' She took one more peep at her phone. No likes. Nelson spotted her grimace.

'Bad news?'

'Err... not really.' She fished out her phone. 'Listen – can I show you something?'

'Of course.'

She showed him the photo of the sunset on her Twitter page. 'That's a nice sunset, right? People should like it?'

He took the phone and examined the photo. 'It's a gorgeous sunset – who says it isn't?'

'Uh, everyone on Twitter apparently.' She told him that she'd just joined up and this was her first tweet. And how it felt curiously sad to be ignored – 'brushed aside... by millions.'

'Oh, for goodness' sake, Astrid,' he laughed, checking her account again. 'You have no followers.'

'No followers? This is getting worse. I don't know if my self-esteem can take any more of this.'

Nelson calmly explained how this was no reason to panic. After signing up, you're supposed to pick other accounts to follow. People then follow you back if you sound interesting. So having zero followers was the problem, not her photo. 'It's like...' Nelson rubbed some cheese crumbs from his goatee. 'It's like you're at this amazing party. That's what Twitter is – a party full of colourful, wonderful guests. A few idiots, or course,' he added. 'But you, Astrid, have gone into the bathroom, locked the door and started talking to the mirror.'

Astrid brightened. There had been no reason to take the snub of the sunset picture personally. Nobody had seen it. For the next ten minutes, Nelson added a list of Twitter accounts she might find useful. Art galleries, museums, restaurants, and useful contacts for British visitors to Spain. He finally added his own Twitter account – proudly announcing he was 'honoured' to be her first follower. 'There you go... you have eleven followers less than Jesus. One hundred and thirty-four million less than Barack Obama.' He passed her phone back. 'Now you just have to do something about your bio. It's blank. You need to sound irresistible and thrusting. And a decent profile shot, please. Nobody follows an anonymous egg. Except bots.'

'Good advice,' she said, not understanding what half of it meant. She switched off her phone and slipped it into her pocket.

They chatted for a little bit longer, then both turned in for the night. She'd had an exhausting, emotional day. Nelson had to dash off early to check out a food market down the coast. She went straight to sleep, although it was stifling hot in the cabin, even with all the portholes open. No cheese-induced orchestra of sheep bells. Or lovers' whispers. Just a very satisfying thought that she was now on Twitter. The battleground of the poison tweeter, whoever they were. She'd sort this case out too. Like she did the last two. Her father would be pleased with her, and everything – huge yawn – would be alright with the world.

Five

Classy Costa Cuts was down a quiet side street off the Avenida España, the road that ran alongside the promenade. The side street was lined with drab offices and shuttered garages. The hand-painted sign, *Classy Costa Cuts – British Hairdresser's*, bookended by two bright metal butterflies, was a rare splash of colour.

Astrid pushed aside the beaded curtain and stepped inside. There was a coat stand by the door, next to one of those 'magic eye' posters on the wall. A tired black leather sofa slouched under the window and, in front of it, a low glass coffee table heaped with British magazines. Against the side wall were three black and chrome revolving chairs facing three mirrors. Each had a small white sink underneath. Between the mirrors were two paintings – a dolphin leaping out of the water across a full moon, and a portrait of a young Prince Charles and Lady Diana.

It was silent, apart from low whirring coming from the far corner. It took Astrid a few seconds to work out what it was. Someone was sitting in a chair reading a magazine. Her head, from the chin up, was wedged into the dome of an old-fashioned salon hairdryer – the kind you only see in archive TV footage. Jennifer swished through another beaded curtain at the back of the room, a cup of tea balanced on a saucer. She switched off the hairdryer and lifted back the dome to reveal an elderly woman with damp white hair. The woman thanked her and took the tea.

'Oh, hi, Astrid.' Jennifer came over.

'Is this a good time?'

Jennifer said it was and sat down on the sofa, patting the space next to her for Astrid to do the same. Astrid was about to tell her why she was there, but Jennifer already knew.

'Thank you so much for doing this. I'm, I'm,' she stammered, 'I'm a bundle of nerves.' She reached up and twisted a clump of hair. 'Look, my hair – it's lifeless. I'm losing my sparkle, Astrid.'

'Try not to worry, Jennifer. I'm sure I can sort it out.'

'I hope so,' she said, looking around the empty salon. 'It's going to be pretty quiet from now until next Easter.'

Like the rest of the tourist businesses in the town, Jennifer was adjusting to the low season. Now that the schools were back, the families with young kids had disappeared. Except, she said, the ones that were happy to take their children out of school during term time. 'You'll see them for the next couple of weeks, looking a bit sheepish.' Jennifer veered back to the threatening messages. 'Anyway, these messages – they have to stop,' she said tearfully. 'The bad publicity... my business might not survive.'

'I thought my father's day trading was doing well?'

'Oh, yes – it is.' She hesitated. 'But I love my little salon.' She gazed round the room again. 'This is my dream, Astrid. And my lovely customers. I don't know what I'd do without them.'

The woman finished off her tea and eyed Astrid and Jennifer impatiently from the far end of the room. Jennifer hurried over and took the customer's cup, placing it to one side. Then she waved Astrid over and introduced them both. This was Vera from Doncaster, one of Jennifer's 'regular ladies'. She'd retired and moved out to Estepona twenty years ago, and she had no intention of going back to the UK.

'You can't take it with you.' She beamed. 'The sun, that is.'

'No, you can't,' chirped Jennifer.

Vera turned to Astrid. 'There's even a big Lidl.'

'What more do you need?' said Astrid.

Jennifer picked up a *Chat* magazine and thrust it into Vera's hands. 'There you go. A copy of *Chat*. It's a French magazine for people who like cats.' She winked.

'Huh?' said Vera.

'Don't worry, Vera, just my little joke.' She carried on talking over Vera's head. 'I like to have a bit of banter with my ladies. It relaxes them.'

It was a pretty good joke, Astrid admitted to herself. Even though she'd resisted laughing out loud. A bit corny, but Jennifer did have a better sense of humour than she'd remembered. 'So, listen, I don't want to get your hopes up at this stage, Jennifer.' Astrid paused. 'At the moment, there's only a few tweets from this troll to work with.'

'What troll?' Vera piped up.

In one fluid motion, Jennifer dropped the dome of the hairdryer down over Vera's head and switched it on at the side. 'Carry on, Astrid.'

'Right... um, to start with...' she whispered, pointing at the dome of the hairdryer.

'Don't worry, it's pretty powerful. She won't hear a thing.' Jennifer tapped on the side of the dome with her knuckle. Vera didn't move.

'Okay, then I'd like to ask you a few questions.'

'Before you do,' Jennifer smiled, 'I just want to say how touched I am that you're doing this.'

Astrid felt a stab of guilt in her chest. She knew a big part of why she was investigating was to discover Jennifer's secret. 'It's fine, Jennifer.' Astrid wafted her thanks away. 'Alright, first things first. When did these messages start?'

'About two weeks ago.'

'Okay – and is there anyone who might want to damage your reputation? A rival business, maybe?'

Jennifer shook her head. 'There are other hairdressers in town. But they're Spanish owned. I'm the only salon catering to the Brits, so I'm not much competition.'

'And from your past? Any enemies?'

She thought for a few seconds, then gave a firm 'No'.

Astrid studied her. This was the bit she liked. Asking questions. Listening carefully. Panning for that nugget of gold – an incriminating stumble. Ideally, she'd like to be conducting the questioning in a back office of a regional police station. Where she'd get to switch on an old tape recorder on a Formica table and say something like 'This is Detective Superintendent Astrid Swift, the time is' – checks basic clock on wall, sips tea from polystyrene cup – '3.20 p.m. I'm starting the interview—'

'Are you alright, Astrid?'

'Sorry? Yes... um.' Astrid composed herself. 'Okay. Have you noticed anyone behaving suspiciously at the salon or near the house?'

'No.'

'Friends... relatives behaving differently?'

'The thing is, we have a lot of friends – but relatives...'

Jennifer took a breath. 'Peter, well… it might sound a bit sad, but he's my only family.'

It did sound a little sad. But then, thought Astrid, she hardly saw her sister Clare, or her mother. So her father was her only family too. And she was there first. 'This secret, Jennifer? What do you think they're referring to?'

Jennifer looked blank. 'I've no idea.'

Astrid asked her a couple more times, but Jennifer held her ground. She insisted there was no secret. Astrid detoured off on a few other questions. Had she noticed anyone following her? Any unanswered calls? All 'no'. Then she circled back for one last try. 'The thing is, Jennifer…' She leant over the hairdryer. 'I hate to be nosy, but if there is a secret and you tell me, it might help identify who might have got hold of that information.'

Jennifer shook her head. 'No, honestly…' She sniffed the air. Astrid did too, inhaling a sharp burning smell, a bit like a bonfire of dried leaves.

They looked down. Vera's hands were tightly gripping the armrests of the salon chair, her knuckles whitening around a range of gold rings.

'Oh, good heavens!' Jennifer blurted, quickly switching off the hairdryer and cautiously drawing the dome back. Vera's hair was a white frizzy ball. A haze of smoke settled on the crown.

'Christ, that's a powerful blower.' Beads of sweat were rolling down Vera's pink cheeks. 'We done?'

'Almost.' Jennifer furiously waved her hand over the top of Vera's hair to clear the smoke. But it only fanned the singed ends back into life, making them glow and crackle. More smoke began to drift up from the back of Vera's head.

'Hang on.' Astrid noticed a plastic spritzer bottle on the side, full of water. She grabbed it and passed it over to Jennifer, who aimed it at the source of the smoke and began pumping at the trigger. There was a sizzling sound as the smoke turned into steam, and a long sigh of relief from Jennifer.

Throughout this, Vera didn't budge. She just sat there, flipping through the *Chat* magazine, stopping at an article that seemed to be about a woman who married a ghost.

The small hair-fire extinguished, Jennifer put the empty spritzer down. She wiped Vera's forehead with a towel and did her best to sound calm. 'Right then, Vera, almost there.' She reached for a large gold can of hairspray and whirled it round Vera's head with one finger on the nozzle. A fine acrid cloud settled on Vera's hair. 'There... perfect,' she said, her voice wavering.

It wasn't perfect – it was awful. There was a halo of scorched hair just above Vera's temples – as if someone had laid a wreath of burnt grass on her head. Vera got up, and before Jennifer could step in front of her, she checked her reflection in the mirror. Her hand slowly reached up to touch the burnt hair.

Jennifer stood next to her and spoke into the mirror. 'Listen, Vera... can I just—'

'Ooo, that is gorgeous,' Vera gushed. 'It's not what you usually do, but I love it. Thank you.'

'What? I mean, great,' stuttered Jennifer. 'It's a new style I read about. I thought you'd like it.'

Vera gathered her bag by the coat rack and pulled out her purse. She plucked out a neatly folded five-euro note and passed it over. Jennifer refused to accept it. 'No, I couldn't.' She closed Vera's hand over the note and told her to put it away. 'You look so beautiful, Vera, this one is on me.' Vera smiled and shuffled out through the beaded curtain. Astrid and Jennifer hurried to the door and watched her wander down the street, stopping to admire her hair in a shop window. When she was out of view, Jennifer leant back against the wall and breathed out. 'Astrid?'

'Yup?'

'Can we pretend that never happened?' Jennifer giggled, and Astrid found it impossible not to join in this time. She got her stuff together and told Jennifer she'd do her best to find out who was behind the poison tweets. Again, Jennifer told her how grateful she was, and Astrid said goodbye and stepped out into the street. She'd only got ten yards down the street when Jennifer called after her, then hurried to catch up. 'You know, I forgot to say something. About these messages.'

'Go on.'

'I'm not the only one who's been getting them.'

'Sorry… there are others?'

'Oh, yes,' she said matter-of-factly. 'I should have mentioned it.'

'What?' Astrid's jaw dropped.

'Yes, there's quite a few of us. Including our lovely neighbours, Bridget and Sebastian. They're renovating a farmhouse at the end of the road. She's very concerned.'

'And they've received the same message?' asked Astrid.

'Yes, the same message. "I know your secret".'

'Well, if it's a trolling campaign, don't you think you should all go to the police, rather than have me sort it out?'

'No, no,' fussed Jennifer. 'We don't want to involve the police.'

'Okay,' she shrugged. 'And these other people – you know all of them?'

'Oh, yes,' she said. 'We all meet up in Shakespeare's.'

'Shakespeare's?'

'Shakespeare's Bar and Grill. It's a British-themed restaurant near the marina. I go there a lot to catch up with the other expats. The food isn't too bad. Cheap and cheerful – pub grub, really. Generous portions. And they do a knockout jug of sangria. And on Mondays—'

'Don't worry,' interrupted Astrid. 'I can get the full Tripadvisor review from you later. Let me just get these facts straight first.' She started to count each point down on her fingers. 'There are a number of people on the troll's list?'

Jennifer nodded.

'Who socialise in Shakespeare's?'

'Yes. You'll be able to work out who from the troll's account. They're a super bunch. Oh.' She raised a finger. 'But if you do meet them, be careful of Morgana.'

'Why's that?'

'I mean, she's lovely. Runs a stall selling bangles and things. But she's a bit of a talker. Doesn't let anyone get a word in edgeways. Chatty. Yes, chatty – that's the word. You know the type?' Astrid was about to agree, she knew exactly the type. But Jennifer had a full head of steam. 'And she has this long tragic story she tells anyone who'll listen. I must have heard it a dozen times. Lovely lady, as I say, but—'

'Yes, sorry,' Astrid interrupted. 'Final question. Does anyone else have any idea who is behind this?'

'No.' Jennifer finally paused to catch her breath. 'We don't have a clue.'

Six

A strid strolled along the promenade, head down, admiring the square pinky flagstones and the way her blue and white espadrilles flashed across them. Astrid had forgotten how much she loved espadrilles. They always put you in a good mood – they were the sort of shoes you find at the back of the wardrobe when it's wet and wintery outside and you're jolted back to summer, and beaches and sand. It was the same with the smell of suntan lotion, or that hyper-lemony ingredient they put in mosquito repellent.

She'd decided to take a detour along the beach, to let the conversation with Jennifer sink in. This was a much bigger trolling campaign than she'd thought. Not just Jennifer, but a list of expats – whoever they were. It was a lot more work, but there was no way she was giving up. It was quite exciting. Who knew what skeletons were about to come tumbling out of the closet? And one of them belonged to Jennifer. *Let's not forget that, Astrid.*

The beach was nearly empty. It was midday – the ragged stands of palm trees on the sand didn't cast a shadow. Most people had packed up and gone to find some shade. Nearby, a man was slowly sweeping the sand with a metal detector. He stopped now and then to go carefully over the hollows left by the sunbathers. She waved at him. He gave a half-hearted wave back, tightened his bum bag and carried on.

At the boat, she sat at the table and took out her phone – her heart gave a bump. Her Twitter account had woken up. There was a little bell symbol with a '15' inset into it, which, after some fiddling about, she worked out meant fifteen people had noticed the account.

Eight of those were 'likes' for her sunset picture. 'Knew it,' she breathed, exhaling pure vindication. It was a very good sunset picture, after all. The other seven interactions included news that Nelson had retweeted the picture – recycling it with his followers. Which would explain where she'd got the 'likes' from.

Then there were five new followers, all random men. Their profile pictures showed them sitting on the bonnets of sports cars, or drinking cocktails by the pool, or lifting weights. Finally, there was one message – from *@godfearingexmarine457*.

Hey Astrid – my DMs are wide open for love connexions. U in?

Astrid shuddered. Had she accidentally joined a dating site? She went to the sink and washed her hands. Then she settled in at the table again and focused on what she needed to do – find out who was on the troll's list.

It didn't take long to work it out – even with her limited skills at navigating Twitter. Digging deeper into the *@TheAllSeeingEye7* account, she could see the replies they'd made to other people. She took out her jotter and smoothed down the first page. Then she wrote down the accounts they'd been hounding. In ten minutes, she had a list of names: six individuals and two married couples.

Jennifer
Bridget and Sebastian
Terry
Declan
Zhang
Wonderful
Roger and Charlotte
Morgana

All of them had received the same 'I know your secret' reply, along with the usual emojis and ominous GIFs. There was no explanation why. She stared at the list, even though she knew an answer wouldn't magically leap off the page. For any more clues, she'd have to meet them all – as soon as possible. A generous portion of 'pub grub' was now the order of the day.

Shakespeare's Bar and Grill wasn't easy to find. She circled round the harbour complex a couple of times, staring at her phone, trying to work out how she'd missed it. She was directly at the blue pin on the map. Eventually, the man with the metal detector on the beach wandered past. She stepped out in front of him. 'Hi, do you know where Shakespeare's is?'

'Shakespeare's? Yeah, I know where it is,' he said, eyes trained on his Crocs. She was looking at them too. They were lime green and matched with white sports socks that came to different heights at his ankles.

'Would you mind telling me where it is?'

There was an awkward pause. He stood there, his shoulders slumped. His expression, she thought, wasn't exactly sad...

just a bit lost. Then he said 'Up the steps,' pointing to a flight of concrete stairs to her right.

'Thanks,' she said. He didn't reply. To fill the silence, she asked. 'Do you ever go there?'

'Shakespeare's? No, not much.' He knitted his fingers together. 'People... they're um, they're not my thing.' He picked at a streak of dirt on the front of his Hobbit T-shirt. 'Conversations, you know? Can't seem to say the right thing.' He was about forty. Maybe a bit taller than Astrid if he straightened up.

'My name's Astrid,' she said, holding out her hand.

'Is it?' he said, his eyes dropping to his feet again. 'Right, I'll be off.' Then he hitched up his bum bag, made a deliberate two steps to the side, one forward, like a knight moving in chess, and carried on down the pavement.

Astrid took the flight of stairs. The man, whoever he was, was right. Shakespeare's was up there, on a broad terrace looking south. There was nobody around. She took a seat at one of the half a dozen tables out front and admired the view, which was fabulous – an uninterrupted panorama from the lighthouse to the east, to the Rock of Gibraltar in the west.

Around the low white walls were big terracotta pots with a sculpted bay tree in each one. A length of patriotic red, white and blue bunting had been strung across the entrance. She studied a laminated menu. It was mostly British pub food. Pies, ploughman's lunch, 'all day breakfast', roast beef, chicken – mostly breadcrumbed, with the option of salads or chips. The chips had 'McCain' next to them, with a whole range of descriptions from 'crinkle cut' to 'chip shop'. The rest of the menu was seafood and a single vegetarian option

– a 'grilled vegetable wrap'. Although there was a disclaimer that the dish had been 'made in a kitchen where meat was also prepared so may be contaminated with animal products', thus making it sound so unappetising that even the most famished vegetarian might just order a bag of crisps – which, the 'snacks' section of the menu revealed, were also available. Astrid ran her finger down the menu, slaloming it past a streak of dried ketchup.

'You eating?' There was a rasping voice behind her.

Astrid turned to see a woman sitting with her chair up against the white wall. She wondered why she hadn't seen her before. Perhaps, given the depth of her tan, a dark brown that might be described as 'teak' or 'Tudor oak' in a fence paint, she'd mistaken her for a piece of furniture. She'd also been sitting perfectly still. Like a lizard on a wall, conserving its energy.

Her eyes darted to Astrid. 'If you are, I'd avoid the steak and kidney pie.'

'Is that right?'

'Yeah. I had it once. It disagreed with me.' Astrid had a hunch that a lot of things, people mostly, disagreed with this woman. 'It went through me like the Cresta Run.' She brought her hand to the midriff of her pale-yellow blouse and grimaced. 'The calamari's not much better. Very chewy.' She made a slow circular motion with her jaw, as if tasting it again. 'Like eating a puncture repair kit. 'Orrible...'

A waiter hurried out from the open glass doors of the building and slid between Astrid's table and the seated woman. 'Thank you, Pearl, for your contribution,' he said, his back to her. He was mid-thirties, with narrow shoulders and a tense expression, however much he tried to smile. 'Pearl's on to her third Dubonnet and lemonade. It brings out the restaurant critic in her.'

'You know what?' Pearl chirped from behind him. 'You should have photos of the food on the menu. Then people know what they're getting. Lots of the restaurants in Benidorm do it.'

The waiter kept his back to her. 'Do you know... a long time ago, some Inuit cultures – when some members of the tribe got very, very old – the others left them out on ice floes. They just let them drift out there into the great blue yonder. Never to be seen again.' He brought out an order book from a cloth belt at his waist. Then a pencil. 'Of course, mercifully, they don't do that these days.' He glanced over his shoulder at Pearl and muttered, 'More's the pity.'

'I missed that,' Pearl snapped.

The waiter smiled to himself. Then licked the end of the pencil. 'Right then, what would you like?'

There were a couple of high squeaks from Pearl's plastic chair as she tried to edge round into sight. But the waiter shuffled sideways to screen her out until the squeaking stopped. Astrid ordered – a large glass of house white despite her promise to cut back (*next week, definitely!*) plus the calamari with 'curly fries', which she was cajoled into by the waiter.

Behind her, Pearl humphed. 'Going for the calamari then... that's brave.'

The waiter ignored her and introduced himself. His name was Roger. He was an ex-geography teacher from Milton Keynes and he'd been here for five months. This was his first holiday season running the restaurant. His wife, Charlotte, who'd also been a teacher, did the cooking and he took the orders because he was, he admitted, a terrible chef. 'I could burn a cup of tea,' he said proudly.

Astrid was feeling pretty pleased with herself. Roger was one of the people on the troll's list. It was tempting to imagine what his secret was. A teacher who'd packed it all in to run a bar in Spain? That was quite a career move. Maybe he was running away from something? But what? This was going to be a game for everyone on the list.

Astrid sipped her wine and chatted with Pearl who, like the other expats she'd met so far, launched into her personal backstory without prompting. For most of her working life, Pearl had managed a bed and breakfast in Blackpool. It had, she said, been a 'roaring success'. Great reviews. Local awards. Booked up every holiday season. Then the arrival of the budget airlines 'stuffed it up'. Her regular clientele drifted away to warmer climes in the holidays. Spain mostly. She said she didn't blame them. 'The Lancashire coast is lovely. But Easter? Do you want to be ringing down to reception for a hot water bottle, or sitting by a pool on the Costa del Sol?'

Astrid nodded her sympathy as she started on the calamari, which was remarkably good – not that chewy, with a satisfying crunch.

By now, another person had joined them on the terrace. He was wearing bright pink shorts. No shirt. A gold chain hung down to a shark's tooth that nestled in a carpet of white chest hair. Roger served him a pint of lager and steak and chips. They'd shared a joke, then he set his newspaper to the side of his plate so he could carry on reading the back sports pages as he ate his food. The way he spread out in his chair, lounging back between mouthfuls, knees apart, knife and fork pointing upwards in his fists – it was like he owned the place. Maybe he did?

Astrid decided she'd check out the rest of the bar. On the door was a poster of all the football games coming up on Sky TV. Next to it was a handwritten list of house rules. The top one said '*NO DISCUSSING BREXIT*'. Below that was '*Patrons Must Wear Shirts And Shoes*'. Then, '*Only Restaurant Food to be Eaten on the Premises*'.

Inside, the bar area was open and brightly lit, with two ceiling fans that ticked slowly round, recirculating a current of tepid air. Most of the space was taken up by a clutter of wooden tables, nearly all without chairs. They'd been drawn up to face a big-screen TV – probably for the Sky football matches – and not put back. A football theme was worked into the decor here and there – a framed England shirt. An old leather football in a case. Signed pictures of players.

The Shakespeare theme seemed to be an afterthought. There was a portrait of the playwright behind a well-stocked bar. That was it, as far as Astrid could see. Then there were some other more bizarre touches. They included a signed photo of Sean Connery having a drink on the terrace of Shakespeare's, and a picture of three Wombles riding on a monorail. It was all very British, in a way. Which was the point, of course. This was the hub for British expats – where they could grab some gossip and information. There was a noticeboard bristling with cards advertising English-speaking services: plumbers, school tutors, visa assistance and GPs.

The side door swung open. A man with dark buzz-cut hair wheeled in a trolley loaded up with three cardboard boxes with *Hula Hoops* printed on the side. He glided into the kitchen, where she heard Roger greet him warmly with, 'Hey, Zhang – just drop them over there.'

So that's Zhang – another tick on the list. Astrid went back out to her table to pay the bill.

As she rooted around in her bag for her purse, a large bulldog appeared from the alleyway. It was huge – as if someone had thrown a rug over a Shetland pony – with a ruffled face like a pile of wet gloves. It could certainly give Lulu a run for its money in the strangest dog contest. Not that this one was capable of doing much running. It waddled over to Astrid's table and began snuffling at the ground.

Pearl, who'd fallen asleep in her chair, came to life. 'Oh, here he is,' she grunted, pointing at the dog. 'The greedy beast.'

'What's his name?' asked Astrid.

'The Hound of the Basket Meals – that's what I call him, anyway,' she said bitterly. 'They call him The Beef. He just came in one day and now he's the bar mascot.'

Roger hurried out to the terrace. He saw the dog's bottom sticking out from under the table and started apologising. Astrid said it was fine, she liked dogs. He got down on his knees and started pushing the dog from behind. The dog locked its front legs, so Roger had to shove harder until it slid, inch by inch, out the other side. Pearl watched out of the corner of her eye, giving a running commentary. She disapproved – both as a customer and someone who'd maintained a five-star hygiene rating over forty years in the hospitality trade. It was, she said, 'unthinkable' for dogs to be in the dining areas. 'But then this is Spain, and well…' she added cryptically.

Eventually, Roger heaved The Beef out into the light. The dog snorted, then waddled over to the man in the pink shorts, flopped down at his feet and looked up expectantly. The man pinched a ribbon of gristle from his plate and tossed it on to the floor. He sucked his fingers then wiped them on a napkin, which he rolled in a ball and dropped on to the middle of the plate.

'Who is that?' said Astrid.

'That's Terry,' said Pearl.

Terry – name number four. And she was right about him being the owner. Astrid was now feeling very pleased she'd visited.

'It's his restaurant,' added Pearl. 'He's a pretty good landlord.' She looked at Roger. 'Just needs to improve standards in the kitchen.'

'You know what, Pearl.' Roger stiffened. 'If you have a problem with the standards at Shakespeare's, you're more than welcome to take your custom elsewhere.'

Pearl pursed her lips. 'I'll make do here,' she said. And there it was. However much she complained, she wasn't going anywhere. Shakespeare's had everything she needed. All the comforts of home – drinks, food, a menu in English and a beautiful view out over the marina. Pearl slipped a ten-euro note under the edge of her glass and hauled herself out of her chair. 'Right,' she said. 'I'm off to church.'

'Church?' Roger's voice went up an octave. 'This is new.'

'Not really – I've been going up to the Catholic church in the old town for months.'

Roger started wiping her table down with a cloth as Pearl walked away. 'Be careful of the holy water, Pearl,' he whispered. 'You don't want to get burned.'

Astrid wondered how long Roger had been in teaching. Quite a while, probably. All those years dealing with unruly kids had congealed into a sunny sarcasm. He'd become an expert at the tangy one-liner. The Parthian put-down. It was the much under-estimated skill of the veteran teacher.

Pearl stopped by the exit to the terrace. 'I heard that, Roger Cherry,' she said, not bothering to turn round. 'And I'm going to say a prayer for you.'

'Jolly good,' he called after her. 'Oh, and the deep fat fryer is on the blink. If you could put in a word.'

Pearl ignored him and carried on to the steps that headed down to the marina. Roger turned to Astrid. 'Don't worry, apart from Pearl, all the expats are very nice. We get on well.'

'Yes, I'm sure you do.' Astrid got up and reached for her purse. She paid the bill, adding a couple of euros tip.

He thanked her. Then added, 'We have to stick together, don't we? Us Brits abroad.'

She waited until Roger went back into the restaurant and Pearl had crossed the road towards the apartment blocks. Then she left. It had been a good start. She'd seen three people on the troll's list: Roger, Zhang and Terry. She could begin to add some notes to the jotter later – although there wasn't much to go on. There was no love lost between Pearl and Roger. Could Pearl be the troll? Unlikely. Twitter might be a bit high-tech for her. Anyway, razoring letters out of magazines and pasting them to a note would be more her style.

She stopped when she reached the marina. Seeing as she was on a roll, she might as well tick off another couple of names on the list – Bridget and Sebastian.

Seven

A hundred yards beyond her father's house, the tarmac gave way to a rutted track of baked earth, framed either side by two dry-stone pillars. There was no gate. No number. Ahead, in a dip, she could see the roof of a building that was half exposed beams, half terracotta tiles. She was in the right place – that must be the farmhouse that Jennifer had said Bridget and Sebastian were renovating.

She carried on over a rise in the track. Now she could see the whole plot. It was a flat piece of dusty ground about the size of a couple of tennis courts. On the edge, facing the sea, was a large caravan propped up on blocks of wood. There was a circular iron table out front, with a faded parasol poking out of the middle.

As she approached the caravan, someone peered out of the window, and a few seconds later the door sprang open. A woman, mid-thirties, wearing a cream shift dress, her auburn hair held up with a tortoiseshell clip, tiptoed down a metal step. She jumped the last bit, her Birkenstocks throwing up a puff of dust. 'Astrid?'

'That's me.'

She flung her arms open wide. 'How lovely. Jennifer said you might drop by. I'm Bridget.'

The woman gathered Astrid in and air-kissed her twice. *Mwuh, mwhuh.* These were the actual sound effects she made. Then she released her grip and immediately apologised for everything in sight. 'I'm sorry about the mess.' She did a full 360-degree turn, hands on hips. 'We've only just started the build and we're upside down at the moment.'

'Honestly, there's no need to apologise,' said Astrid. 'You've obviously got your hands full.'

'Tell me about it,' she sighed. Then she hurried back into the caravan.

Astrid looked over at the run-down farmhouse. It was surrounded by building equipment – a battered concrete mixer, wheelbarrows, a small generator. A couple of spades were sticking out of a pyramid of yellow sand. A man in a white T-shirt and khaki shorts was moving between the open beams. She watched him for a while, hammering the wood for a few seconds then descending the ladder, forgetting what he needed, and going back up again.

In the caravan, a heated discussion was under way. She couldn't quite make it out, but a girl, arms folded, was shaking her head at Bridget. The door swung open, there was some muttering from inside the caravan, and a teenage girl appeared in the doorway. She was slim, like Bridget, with short punky blonde hair. Bridget appeared from behind the girl and gripped her by the shoulders. 'And this is my daughter, Miller – she's very shy.' Bridget pushed her gently forward into the sunshine. 'Come on, say hi to Astrid.'

'Yeah... hi,' she said softly.

'Hi, Miller.'

The girl squirmed out of her mother's grip and stepped back into the caravan. Bridget watched her go. 'That's it, darling, you get on with your homework... um, yes, love you too.' Although for the last part, Astrid was watching Miller through the glass and saw that she hadn't said anything to her mother.

Astrid went over and sat at the table under the parasol. Bridget emerged a couple of minutes later with a silver tray of drinks and teetered over. 'Fifteen,' she said, her voice brittle. 'What a lovely age.' She put the tray down. In the centre were two glasses of orange juice on antique Spanish tiles. There was a straw and a slice of orange in each glass.

'Ooo... yum,' said Astrid, reaching out.

'Hang on.' Bridget pulled out her smartphone and took a few snaps of the tray of drinks at various low angles. 'Right,' she said, scrolling through the photos, nodding appreciatively, 'help yourself. It's freshly squeezed orange juice. We use the oranges from our own trees.'

Astrid wondered if she should be taking photos as well, so she could post one on Twitter later. The 'likes' for the sunset tweet had dried up, so she needed something for her next tweet.

Bridget was a good talker. Without pausing for a sip of her drink, she rattled through how they'd all ended up here in the hills above Estepona – 'all' being her, Miller, and her husband, Sebastian. He was currently doing all the renovation work on the farmhouse, which she called a 'casa de campo', not, as most people would say, a 'finca' – that referred to the plot of land. And Bridget would know, seeing as she was, by her own description, a 'Spanophile'.

Bridget loved everything about Spanish culture – the food, the architecture, the music. In fact, she had her own 'very popular blog' called 'Treading over orange blossom'. It was a celebration of Spanish rural life as seen through the blinking eyes of a new family from Barnes in London where, apparently, Sebastian had been 'high up in graphic design'. That was before they'd decided to cash in and create the perfect family home on the Costa del Sol. They'd been there for six months and, like all the other expats, were loving the weather. Bridget gazed out at the sea that sparkled below them.

'You can't bring the sunshine with you,' said Astrid, before Bridget got there.

'No, you can't. And you can't swim with dolphins in the Thames.'

'Actually,' – Astrid raised her finger – 'there were some dolphins that once entered the Thames. So technically, you could swim with them. But you might get hypothermia or dysentery, so it wouldn't be much fun.'

'Ugh.' Bridget gripped her necklace, which was made of hand-painted beads. 'And then there's the rats. I can't even bear to think about them. They say that in London, you're never more than six feet from a rat.'

'Yes… apart from in Hampstead. They asked them all to leave.'

Bridget laughed, unsurely. 'Anyway, we might be living in a building site now. But it's going to be marvellous.'

This opened up a conversation about how Astrid had left her job as an art conservator in London and settled for a life on a boat. Bridget was also a good listener and sat back taking it in. Not all the story, of course. It would be too much to give the whole story to every new person she met. And she'd be meeting a few people this week on her list. *The list…*

Astrid finished her orange juice and turned her chair to face Bridget. 'Listen, did Jennifer tell you why I'm here?'

'Yes, it's the internet troll. Jennifer said you were going to try and find out who they are. That you have a sharp mind, so are perfect for the job.'

'Oh, right. Well, I can't promise anything, but I'll do my best.'

'Thank you.' Bridget looked relieved. The threatening tweets, she said, had added even more stress to her life. She and Sebastian had ploughed all their savings into the renovation. Miller still hadn't found a place at a local school, so was taking online courses. Then Bridget had her blog to run, which was a lot of work. 'And now this internet troll turns up saying they know our secret. It's all so... so horrid.'

But then, thought Astrid, it wouldn't be so bad if Bridget and Sebastian didn't have a secret. Would it? The same for Jennifer. 'You don't have to tell me, Bridget...' Astrid shifted her seat nearer. 'But is there anything you think this person has found out about you?' She paused. 'That you wouldn't want out there in public?'

Bridget looked into the distance, shaking her head, as if trying to think of what it might be. Or pretending to. It was impossible to tell. 'No, I mean... I can't think of anything.'

'And enemies... is there anyone you can think of you've fallen out with?'

Again, she shook her head. But not as convincingly this time. 'I mean, you know...' Her voice petered out. 'There's nobody I can think of.'

'Nobody?'

'Hey.' Bridget got up. 'Why don't I give you a tour of the project?'

That was that, thought Astrid. For now, anyway.

Bridget set off past the caravan towards the farmhouse. Astrid trailed a couple of paces behind. The closer they got, the more run-down the building appeared. Here and there were missing sandstone bricks. A vine, as thick as a forearm, crawled up over the guttering. Sebastian had a huge amount to do before the place could be lived in.

Bridget stepped over an open trench with a thick yellow pipe snaking around in the bottom and ushered Astrid towards the front door. Not that there was a door. 'Welcome to Casa de los Olivos,' she drawled. 'The House of Olives.' She stood to one side for Astrid to go ahead.

Inside was a big open space, like a long barn. A handful of metal posts were propping up the roof beams. The front wall had been torn down, creating a spectacular view over the sea – the perfect 3:2 proportions for landscape painting. Astrid stood there for a while, soaking it all in. It was a perfect day. The sky was completely blue except for a feather of white cloud over the Jebel Musa.

'It's amazing,' said Astrid, taking a few steps forward.

Bridget joined her, hands on hips, eyes ahead. 'I know – stunning. Sebastian and I decided to just rip out the walls. Bring, as they say…' She gathered her hands to her chest, as if she'd caught a watermelon that someone had thrown to her. '…the outside in.'

Astrid looked up. Right now, there was a lot of the outside coming in. Only half of the roof was finished. When they'd decided they'd seen enough of the view – about thirty seconds of gazing and nodding – Bridget continued with the tour. At each open doorway she pointed into a gloomy room and said things like 'This is the master suite' and 'This is the breakfast room'. Although there was nothing in there but bare walls.

In one room, there was the sound of urgent banging coming from the roof. Sebastian must be up there, taking it out on the tiles.

Bridget finally led the way out to a dusty square that was open to the hills. 'And this is going to be the Moorish courtyard.'

'Impressive,' said Astrid. It was. If they had enough money and energy to finish it, this was going to be a beautiful home. 'You ever watch *Grand Designs* with... um, whatshisname?'

'Oh, my goodness,' Bridget gasped. 'Kevin McCloud. I love that show.'

'I love it too.' Astrid did. She'd never missed an episode when she lived in the apartment. Each week the presenter, Kevin McCloud, an expert on modern design, would follow a couple as they tried to finish a grand building project. Usually, it went very badly. That's why people watched it. The best episodes were huge follies, build on optimism and dwindling finances. Just before the last ad break, before they came back for the big reveal of how it all worked out, McCloud would stalk around the half-built house, shaking his head. He'd poke his finger into damp plasterboard. Peer into dripping pipes and mutter things like, 'If they don't get the roof on by Christmas, Reuben and Alice's dream of a new home will be in tatters.'

Of course, it usually worked out and the dream home did get finished. Kevin would then wander round, cooing his amazement. Which made the viewers who'd been hoping for disaster very annoyed indeed. And determined to tune in next week to see if the next couple royally botched it up.

'The thing is, with those TV shows,' Astrid continued, 'there's often a neighbour who complains. Tries to block the project. Do you think that could explain what's going on with the troll? You have a malicious neighbour?'

'I'm not sure.' Bridget wrinkled her nose. 'I mean, nobody really lives that close.'

'No problem… it was just a hunch.'

'And anyway, we have a *licencia de obra mayor*.' Bridget obviously knew her Spanish. 'It's the local planning permission, so it's a bit late for anyone to complain.'

Astrid tipped her hat back and scanned the surrounding land. There were a few white houses dotted in the hills above them. A handful across the valley to the east. The backs of the houses on the road she walked up, including her father's, were at least a couple of hundred yards away.

'The thing is,' said Bridget, 'social media can be a strange place, right? Good and bad.'

'Exactly. Mostly good, I'd say,' replied Astrid, knowing that she was offering less than twenty-four hours' experience of the subject.

'But it can turn against you. People throw dirt around – there's a pile-on.' She rubbed her beads again. 'My blog, well… it's doing fantastically well at the moment. It's a good revenue stream for us. I don't want anything ruining it.'

They carried on to the back of the plot as it rose into a stand of young olive trees. Below them, Sebastian stood up on the roof, put his hammer into his tool belt and waved. Bridget waved back. She said he'd been working extra hard in the past few months. Recently, it had been impossible to hire cheap builders. So, he was having to do all the building work himself. 'It's been a steep learning curve,' she said, sidestepping a pile of broken tiles.

Astrid surveyed the property one more time. They'd barely

started. It was going to be a huge task to get it finished on their own. 'I hope you don't mind me asking...'

'Go on.'

'Can you afford all this?'

Bridget turned her palms up and shrugged. 'I hope so,' she said. 'I mean, we're putting everything we have into this project.' She smiled feebly. 'I just hope it's enough.'

Kevin would love it. His voice-over would ooze: 'With budgets stretched to breaking point, is Bridget and Sebastian's Spanish dream about to turn into a nightmare?'

They walked back down the hill together in silence. Astrid said goodbye, and Bridget thanked her for trying to get to the bottom of the mystery. Then she said what a few people would tell her over the next few days.

'We can't go back now, Astrid... we just can't.'

Eight

Astrid put her bag down on the cabin rug. It was that slow part of the day – three thirty – when time slumped, like a dip in an old mattress. Not quite late-lunch. Not yet early-evening. The lazy two hours of the day, when taps drip slower and clocks tick louder. As good a time as any to take a look at the painting her father had given her.

She collected the package from the corner and placed it on the table. Carefully, she untied the string and peeled back the brown paper. The scene in front of her was one she'd seen many times before. It was an oil painting of *The Last Supper*, the most famous meal in art history. All the elements were there: Christ, centre-frame, his finger raised as he explains that one of the twelve Apostles at the table will betray him before sunrise. Either side, his disciples react in shock. John, on Christ's left, collapses on the table. Somebody among them is guilty and they don't know who. Well, Judas knows. He's the only person seated in front of the table, face turned to the viewer. The only one without a golden halo.

Astrid studied the table in the picture. Paintings of *The Last Supper* often had hidden clues and symbols. The food, along with the bread, would usually be lamb or fish, both references to Christ. Blue stripes to the tablecloth represented the Jewish people. Or Judas would be shown spilling a salt cellar. That was a nod to the saying 'betray the salt', which meant 'betray one's master'. She didn't notice any of these things in the painting – nor could she work out what they were eating, other than pieces of bread. It was a small copy of a much larger fresco Perugino had made in the mid 1490s, so some of the detail was lost at this scale.

The rip her father had mentioned was luckily high up on the painting, in a section of sky above the hillside background. It was less than an inch long, with a crossbar about half that length, so it formed – Astrid smiled at the irony – a crucifix floating in the air. She turned the painting over and checked the back of the canvas. The rip was all the way through. But it was small and shouldn't take too long to fix.

Turning it over again, she stood back and took in the whole scene. Her father was right – it was a charming piece, even though it was just a copy by an apprentice. There would be plenty of copies like this in circulation. *The Last Supper* was a big seller – monasteries would nearly always have one in their refectories. It wasn't worth a fortune, then. Not up to the standards of his gallery on the King's Road when things were going well and he could take his pick.

She wrapped the painting back up in the brown paper, a childhood memory ambushing her. There she was: twelve years old, standing in the headmistress's office, ready to face the music about some rule-breaking. She couldn't recall what exactly, and she wasn't too worried about the punishment ahead. It was an all-girls school in Hampton, to the west of London. Private, with school fees so high the pupils never got expelled. The school wasn't throwing that kind of money away.

She shuffled in front of the headmistress's desk. They were scanning the note her teacher had made her deliver in person. On it were the details of her crime. A large oil painting was hanging on the wall behind the headmistress. It was a still life – two beautifully painted mackerel with a cut lemon in the foreground. She'd seen it before, in her father's gallery. It wasn't in the same league as the big art dealers in St James's. But her father had good taste and enough rich, largely female customers – the 'merry widows of Mayfair', as he called them – to make a very good living. The headmistress looked up and saw Astrid was staring at the painting. 'Yes, it's one of *his*,' she said, without any more explanation.

The next time she was in the headmistress's office – another misdemeanour – she noticed two more paintings she'd seen before in her father's gallery. They were Scottish landscapes this time. The walls were filling up. Then around three weeks before the end of the summer term, she was idly gazing out of the window and saw her father's Jaguar swing into the playground. Ten minutes later, the headmistress tapped on the glass panel of the classroom door and spoke with the teacher in the corridor. When the teacher came back in, he casually walked up to Astrid and whispered that she had to get all her things together and meet her father in the car park. She packed up, and when she got to the car her father was angrily stuffing a painting back into the boot. 'Honestly,' he fumed. 'That woman wouldn't know a Raeburn if it kicked her in the shins.' He didn't discuss what had happened – on the way home in the car or ever again. But she knew – she'd just left her school, and she wasn't going back. From then on, she and her sister, Clare, were 'off to the local comp', as her mother said in an appalled tone that would equally work with the announcement 'You're being sent to Wormwood Scrubs'. There, with the teenage years yawning ahead of her, she had to start again. The swot, the outsider with the 'stuck-up' accent. Waiting for old friends to get in touch and new ones that never arrived. That's when she learnt how to fill her time on her own. To sketch and visit the galleries in London. To not fear loneliness.

Astrid checked her watch. Three thirty-nine. It was still early, but she felt tired. Not enough energy to push through the day. She decided to have a siesta. That's what you were supposed to do in Spain, wasn't it? Just a couple of hours to recharge the batteries.

Nine

Astrid woke up at five past nine with a dry mouth and a firm promise that if she was going to try the siesta thing again, she'd set the alarm on her phone. Even after a couple of glasses of water, she still felt a bit groggy. A walk in the cool evening air might see the rest of it off.

The promenade was the busiest she'd seen it. There were couples and families strolling in both directions. Mostly local – from the broken conversations she heard in Spanish. A few were tourists – they were the ones stopping to take photos of the sunset. Or they hovered around a couple of street vendors, tall African men who'd laid out their goods on a large square sheet on the ground. The first was selling sunglasses, which he'd lined up in rows. The other's sheet was covered in leather goods: belts, purses and bags with fake designer logos. Astrid was about to check them out when there was a high whistle from down the promenade. The two men jumped to their feet and hurriedly gathered all their goods into the sheets, then swung the bundles over their shoulders. And they were gone – shouldering through the bushes and over the road. A minute later, a man in black trousers and black gilet with *Policia* written across it sauntered into view, a baton in his hand. He looked around, slipped the baton back into a holster on his hip, and carried on up the promenade.

Astrid walked on until she found a jewellery stall. It was much more official than the African vendors'. There was a little table at the front, topped with a velvet cloth. It was covered with shallow trays of rings and earrings. Behind was a wooden stand with bracelets and necklaces hanging from a series of rungs. On the ground was a cardboard sign with a Union Jack flag on it, and the words 'Morgana's Jewellery'.

Another bit of luck, thought Astrid. One more name to tick off the list.

There was a woman sitting on the low wall next to the stall. She was wearing a floaty wrap with bright lemons on, a book in her hand. When Astrid approached, she folded down the corner of the book and put it on the wall. She had dyed red hair that fell in curls around high cheekbones. 'Hiya,' she said, in a crisp Welsh accent.

'Hi there.'

'You on holiday?'

'No, I'm sort of... I'm visiting my father for a couple of weeks.'

'How lovely.' Morgana got to her feet and opened up a small canvas chair that was leaning up against the table. 'Tell you what.' She patted the canvas of the chair. 'Why don't you grab a seat and I'll replace those hair braids of yours.'

'Oh, no. Don't worry – they're fine.' The few coloured braids were her only connection to her good friend Kath back in Dorset. She'd put them in five months ago, and they were still in good shape.

'Alrighty,' Morgana chirped. 'Why don't I give you a nice henna tattoo?'

Astrid flinched. She had nothing against tattoos, henna or real. Her mother did, though – she'd said they were the 'preserve of sailors and criminals'. Astrid didn't have strong feelings either way. Done well, they could be beautiful – she just didn't fancy one herself.

Morgana noticed her reticence. 'Are you allergic to henna? We use the natural stuff and we can test a dot on your hand.'

'No, it's not that. I just, um—'

But Morgana had gripped her shoulders and steered her on to the seat. She unfolded a chair for herself and sat down facing her. 'Do you want to pick one?' she said, passing over a laminated sheet. On it was a range of designs – some traditional Indian patterns, but mostly Disney cartoon characters, dolphins, rainbows and unicorns.

Astrid stared at the laminated sheet, her jaw slowly falling. 'They're all lovely, but I'd rather—'

'Tell you what.' Morgana plucked the laminated sheet from Astrid's fingers and tucked it behind the trays of rings. 'I'll do one of my specialities – a mother turtle. You're going to love it.'

There was no point protesting. Morgana had gripped Astrid's hand and was reaching for a small tube of henna with a fine point. Astrid slumped in the chair, reminding herself to google 'how to get rid of henna tattoos' when she got back to the boat.

Morgana chatted as she worked – about how the town had changed now the tourists had left and when the hot weather was going to break. Soon, she hoped.

Astrid waited until the outline of the turtle's shell and flippers had been piped out before she eased into the subject of the trolling campaign. She explained that she was Jennifer's stepdaughter, and she was going to try and get to the bottom of these 'I know your secret' messages.

As soon as she mentioned it, Morgana brought her hand up to her mouth and gasped through her fingers. 'It's terrible, isn't it? Just awful – I've barely slept since it started.'

'I'm sorry to hear that.' Jennifer, Bridget and now Morgana. Everyone on the list she'd spoken to so far was deeply upset about the troll. They all desperately wanted it to stop. Bridget thought her successful blog would be affected. Jennifer couldn't lose any more customers at the salon. Astrid took in the stall. It was all small enough to be packed away and carried off in a big sports bag. 'Are you worried about your business?'

'No, no – I'll be fine. My customers are people wandering along the promenade. I'm not lucky enough to have my own salon or blog. Like those two.' Astrid kept completely still. Morgana was on to a more delicate part of the design, filling in the turtle's shell with tight swirls. 'The thing is, I've had a big tragedy in my life. It brings back all that pain.'

Morgana let a yawning silence open up between them. Astrid stayed silent. Jennifer had warned her about setting Morgana off on her big tragic story. She waited until it became almost painful, then cracked. 'A tragedy?'

'Yes. A trrragedy.' Morgana looked into Astrid's eyes. 'I've not told that many people about it. You know... it's still so raw, even after all these years.'

'Right, well, I won't put you through it again.'

'No, no. I have to keep talking about it.' She sniffed weakly. 'That's how I'll heal.'

'Even so, you don't—' But there was no escape.

Morgana turned and gazed out to sea, staring blankly at

the horizon. Choking back the emotion. Then she brought a curled knuckle up to her lower lip and began her story from the very start. Well before she arrived in Spain, Morgana had been married to a carpet fitter called Keith, a local man from her hometown of Swansea. The marriage was variously described as 'humdrum' and 'moribund', which sounded more satisfying and fruitful in a Welsh accent than she no doubt realised.

By the time Morgana and Keith arrived in Estepona, the turtle's shell had been filled in and a lopsided smile added to the side of its head, from which trailed a line of bubbles. Astrid couldn't look any more. She stared up towards a nearby streetlight. The sun had dipped below the waves and a swarm of flying beetles had gathered round the halogen bulb and were beating themselves tirelessly against the glass fitting. Which was as good an analogy of Morgana's hopeless marriage as any. 'Sometimes you can be with someone and be entirely lost. Do you know what I mean?'

Astrid nodded. It wasn't the time to tell Morgana about her own failed marriage. This was Morgana's story and there was no stopping her. She soon picked up the flow again. 'The thing is, I changed – and he didn't. That's what made it hard. I wanted to do other things in life. Read poetry. Cook. Learn samba. Express myself through pottery. But Keith didn't change. He still wanted to sit on the sofa watching the footie. And that is why I'm here...' She put her hands on her hips, nodding. 'On my own, in the land of the grape, as Shirley Valentine said in that film – what was it called?'

'*Shirley Valentine*?'

'That's the one.'

'But I would never have been here if it wasn't for...' Her

voice trailed off. 'If it wasn't for Alonzo. My darling Alonzo.'
She wiped at the corner of her eye.

'Honestly, you don't have to tell me about it,' said Astrid.

'No, no. It's fine.'

And so came the rest of the story. In a flood. Halfway
through their holiday in Estepona, Morgana had decided to
go for an evening stroll. That's when she met a local fisherman
called Alonzo at the harbour. Their eyes met over the lobster
pots. 'It was electric,' she said, rubbing her forearms as if she
had goosebumps. 'Something passed between us. We both
knew it.'

'Passed between you?'

Morgana ploughed on. 'We both knew what it was, even
if we couldn't express it in words.' She gazed out across the
beach. The man Astrid had seen with the metal detector
waved at her. But Morgana didn't see him. 'It was like…' She
drew a long breath. 'It was like arriving in a different country.
Without a valid passport, but still knowing this was home. At
six in the morning when the sun came up, I went back and
told Keith I was leaving him.'

'Wow – how did he react?'

'He was gutted, obviously. But he agreed not to stand in
my way. He moved onto the sofa. Although I didn't stay at the
apartment after that. I was lodging at Alonzo's fisherman's
cottage.' She scrunched the hem of her wrap. 'We may not
have had a shared language, Astrid, but we'd found another
way of communicating… with our bodies. If you know what
I mean?'

Astrid nodded. Hoping she wouldn't dwell on this bit.
Which she didn't. The story was nearing its tragic conclusion,
as Jennifer had said it would.

Morgana steeled herself to push through. 'Then, at the end of the week, he went out at night on the boat. And he didn't... come back.' Her voice cracked. 'His shipmate wasn't sure what happened. One minute he was on board. Then he was caught in the nets and there was no saving him.' She tightened the wrap across her chest against a cold breeze that wasn't there.

'I'm so sorry,' said Astrid. 'At least you had, for even just a short time, a true connection.'

'I know, I know...' breathed Morgana. 'For just one summer, I found heaven on earth.' She shook her head. 'I know I'll never find love like that again. Not in that way. I mean, my, shall we say...' She glanced down at her midriff. 'My womanly area is a closed book these days. If you get my meaning?'

Astrid nodded for the second time.

'You see. Once you've had caviar, why would you have...' Morgana stalled on the analogy. 'Some other—'

The man with the metal detector piped up from behind a rack of bangles. 'Lump fish caviar? It's a cheaper alternative, and just as tasty, apparently.'

'Hello, Fenwick,' said Morgana, with a hint of annoyance. 'How long have you been there?'

'Oh, from the "womanly area" bit,' said Fenwick, picking at a new mark on his Hobbit T-shirt. 'But don't worry. I've heard the story. We all have – amazing stuff.'

'*Amazing?*' asked Morgana.

'Mmm...? Not amazing then. Terrible... yes, a terrible business.' Fenwick put down a bracelet. 'But hey, I'm sure wherever your fisherman friend is, he's looking up at you now, Morgana.'

'*Up* at me?' Morgana sounded shocked. 'You mean *down*… he's not in hell, Fenwick.'

'Maybe, I mean, I never met the guy.' Fenwick reached for a wicker circle on the stand. It had feathers and netting across it. 'These are nice. What are they?'

'Dreamcatchers,' said Morgana sternly. 'They bring good luck.'

'Clearly not,' mumbled Fenwick.

Morgana stared at him.

Astrid decided to step in and put the conversation out of its misery. 'So, how is the tattoo looking, Morgana?'

'Um, yes.' She picked up another tube of henna from the table, which had an even finer point to it. 'I just need to add a baby turtle behind it.'

'Honestly, you don't want to spoil it,' said Astrid, through gritted teeth. The turtle looked up at her with bulging eyes.

'What's that?' said Fenwick, pointing at Astrid's hand.

'What do you think it is?' said Morgana tersely.

'I'm not sure. A drowning tortoise?'

'No, Fenwick – it's a turtle.'

'Oh, right… sorry.' Fenwick reached into a plastic bag and brought out three sandy paperbacks. 'Just found these – a Janice Hallett and two Osmans. Not a bad haul.' He put the books into a cardboard box on the wall that had 'Lost Property' written on the side in marker pen. 'Right, I'll be off.' He wiped the sweat from his brow with a tissue from his bum bag and set off down the beach.

Morgana composed herself and quickly added a smaller turtle trailing behind the larger one. 'There you go,' she said. 'Try not to wash your hand for twelve hours or you'll smudge it.'

Astrid brought her hand closer and mustered her best smile. 'Beautiful. Thanks, Morgana.'

'My pleasure,' said Morgana.

Astrid paid her and got her things together. Morgana tucked the money in her purse and started tidying up the dreamcatchers that Fenwick had touched.

'I forgot to ask,' said Astrid, 'have you any idea who is behind the poison tweets?'

Morgana lined up the dreamcatchers, loosening the feathers so they fluttered in the breeze from the sea. 'I've no idea,' she said.

Astrid lay in bed, unable to switch off. The siesta had thrown her out of sync – she'd gained another couple of hours' sleep. So even at midnight she felt fresh and awake. She'd been itching to rub the henna turtle off. Salt water was best – she'd looked it up online. But she knew she was bound to bump into Morgana again, and she might be insulted. Then there were her thoughts about the trolling case, all jostling for attention. She'd now met nearly everyone on the expat list – well, enough to put a face to a name.

She got up, found her jotter and phone on the table and came back to bed. It was time for a new list. First, everyone on the troll's list that she'd met or seen in person, with a few notes from what she could find on the internet. After an hour, it looked like this:

- *Jennifer – stepmother and owner of Classy Costa Cuts. Says she has no secrets or enemies.*
- *Bridget and Sebastian – She's a successful lifestyle blogger.*

He's renovating the farmhouse. Say they have no secrets or enemies.

- *Terry – owner of Shakespeare's. 'A good landlord', according to Pearl.*
- *Zhang – owner of BOBS, Best of British Supermarket. Delivers to Shakespeare's.*
- *Roger and Charlotte Cherry – He's a teacher-turned-waiter at Shakespeare's. She's the chef. Roger doesn't like Pearl (the feeling is mutual).*
- *Morgana – jewellery stall owner. Ended her marriage over an affair with a local fisherman who then drowned. Says she has no idea who's behind the trolling.*

That left two people on the list she'd yet to meet. Wonderful, who ran the Second Chance Animal Rescue Centre, and Declan – she had no more than his first name. It was a decent start, although there wasn't much to go on. She circled Morgana's name a few times. Had there been a slight falter in her voice when she'd said that Jennifer and Bridget were 'lucky' to have their success? Jealousy might be the motive there. Fenwick was certainly a fan of Morgana. Having said that 'people weren't his thing', he'd still come over to speak to her. It had been awkward – no, it had been toe-curling – but he'd made the effort.

She ringed a few more names and added a couple of question marks. Someone was lying, that's all she could be sure of right now. Maybe all of them were? It was early days, though – plenty of time. And the troll was in no rush either. Up until now, they'd only sent the 'I know your secret' reply.

She switched the phone off – the henna turtle leering at her in the light of the screen – tossed the jotter to the floor and felt the first soft currents taking her away.

Ten

Astrid got up and took her coffee up on to the deck. It was eight thirty, and already too hot to spend any more time below. The roasting weather was still showing no signs of breaking. That's what the weather forecaster said on TRE – Talk Radio Europe – an English-speaking station she'd found. Did they even need a weather forecaster, wondered Astrid? They could just record a few options on tape. Hot. Very hot. Hot and breezy. Play those instead.

There might even be some kinds of English weather you never get on the Costa del Sol. A diagonal driving sleet. A damp mist that pools at the base of your neck and beads down your back. A hard overnight frost – so you have to scrape the ice off the car windscreen with a credit card until your fingers are numb. She scanned the sky, up and down the coast – there wasn't a cloud to be seen. The rain in Spain? Did it even exist?

Astrid's phone beeped. A text had popped up. It was from her father.

Hi – Can you meet me at the Church of Our Lady of the Remedies in the old town? 10.30 am? Would be good to chat. Dad

She quickly replied that she'd be there. There would be just enough time to head up to Shakespeare's for breakfast first. See which expats were around and, with a bit of luck, get some more clues.

Roger greeted her on the terrace with a big smile. 'Welcome back,' he said, pulling out a chair for her. His good mood, she guessed, was because Pearl wasn't there to needle him. 'It's lovely up here when it's quiet,' he said, hands on hips, glancing at the empty seat by the wall – Pearl's usual spot.

She ordered coffee and Roger glided off to the kitchen to give her a few minutes to choose from the menu. Instead, she used the time to check out who else was on the terrace. At the table to her right, a woman in her mid-thirties was reading a copy of the *Guardian*. From her T-shirt – 'Save the Whales' emblazoned on the front – and a picture she'd seen on the website for the Second Chance Animal Rescue Centre last night, Astrid knew this was Wonderful.

By the table against the low wall was a man, at least three decades older than Wonderful. He was surprisingly supple for his age. She knew this because, every so often, he got up and swung his leg on to the wall, bringing his head down to his knee. It was one of a number of stretching exercises he performed between bites of toast, his pink polo shirt staying firmly tucked into his tailored white shorts. Leaning against the wall next to him was a white and red golf bag, bristling with clubs.

Terry, the bar's owner, was at his usual table. He had on a tight white T-shirt this time, and was in deep conversation with a man in a shirt and a light grey jacket. *A bit formal?*

This was the only time she'd seen someone in a jacket, other than her father, since she'd arrived in Estepona. She watched the two men closely, unable to read their lips. But from the body language – Terry leaning forward on his elbows, the man in the jacket flipping through a stack of papers between them, nodding now and then – it looked like business.

Roger returned with the coffee and brought out his notepad and pencil. Astrid hurriedly picked up the menu and scanned it. 'Sorry,' she said. 'I haven't had time to take a look.'

'No problem.' Roger came closer, turning the menu over to the back. 'There you go – we have a range of pastries and cereals. Or, if you're feeling hungry, you could go for the all-day full English breakfast.'

There was the scrape of a chair leg on stone behind him. A rasping voice in the same note said, 'nonsense.'

Roger spun round on his heels to see Pearl sitting back in her seat. 'Oh, Christ – you're here,' he groaned. 'You're like a gas leak, aren't you? Silent and noxious.'

Pearl crossed her arms, her expression barely moving. 'It's not breakfast if you can have it all day, is it?'

'Sorry, Pearl.' He stabbed at the notepad. 'I'm serving a customer.'

She ignored him. 'Breakfast is served at a certain time. I remember when I ran my bed and breakfast, I had that sideboard cleared at eight forty-five, sharp. No excuses.'

'You know what,' said Astrid, 'I will have the full English breakfast, thank you.'

'Super – let me tell you what's in it. In case you want anything left off.' Roger listed the ingredients, counting them down on his fingers. 'Sausage, bacon, black pudding, eggs, mushrooms, tomatoes, beans, fried bread, hash browns and toast.' He held up both hands, pleased he'd remembered all the items. 'Now, could you repeat that for me, so I know you've learnt it?'

'Sorry?'

'Oh, right,' Roger laughed. 'Forget it. Old teaching habit, I'm afraid. Making sure the kids have been listening.'

Pearl rocked back in her chair. 'You know what they say about teachers, don't you?'

Roger glared at her. 'Don't you dare say it, Pearl.'

Pearl drew in a long breath over unmoving lips. 'If you can't do, teach. And if you can't teach, teach physical education.'

'Yes, yes… everyone's heard that old cliché before.' He paused. 'Maybe not the physical education bit, but the rest of it.'

'Must be some truth in it then,' said Pearl.

'Listen, one day I'm going to…' He brought his hands up, as if pretending to strangle her by the neck. 'Urggh.'

'Just ignore her, Roger,' interrupted Wonderful. She turned to Pearl. 'That wasn't very nice, was it? Teaching is a very important profession – we need educators more than ever these days.'

Pearl half closed her eyes, chuckling to herself.

'Thank you for saying that, Wonderful,' said Roger, calming down. He got back to Astrid's breakfast order. Not being hungry enough to consume the full English, she went for the 'continental' version, which Roger explained involved removing anything 'meaty or brown' from the plate.

Wonderful sat down next to Astrid and introduced herself. She'd moved to Spain from Bristol five years ago to start a new life. She was on her own, so adopted a stray dog. Then another. Soon she was collecting money to set up a sanctuary to give them a new life. When she talked about the place, she beamed with pride. Not in herself, but the animals. 'The things they've been through… and they're still able to forgive,' she said. 'You must come up and meet them.'

'I will,' said Astrid.

Wonderful rolled up her copy of the *Guardian* and got up. 'Right, I better get back to them.'

'You know what I think about whales?' Pearl piped up from behind them. She was pointing at Wonderful's T-shirt.

Wonderful gave Pearl a patient smile. 'Please, do tell.'

'We need to get rid of them.'

'Is that right?'

'It is,' Pearl said. 'You see – whales are so big. If you get rid of the whales, then sea levels will go down. That's the other thing you lot are always complaining about, isn't it? Sea levels rising.' She cracked her knuckles. 'Lose the whales and your problem's solved.'

'Tell me then…' Wonderful's patience had reached its limit. '…how would you get rid of the whales?'

'That's up to you. But there's a lot of food there – it might even solve world hunger.' She licked her lips. 'Everyone's a winner.'

Wonderful breathed in through her nose, her eyes narrowing. She was about to launch into her defence, but the man in the white shirt picked up the bag of clubs and stepped in. 'Come on now, Wonderful.' He had a strong Irish accent, and a warm deep voice that rattled when he laughed – like gravel pouring over a smooth rock. 'Don't fall for it.' He wagged his finger at Pearl. 'Now you behave yourself.'

Pearl grunted and tipped her eyes down to the menu. She hadn't been defeated, but she had listened to him.

The man pushed back his baseball cap. 'Astrid, right?'

'That's me.'

'I'm Declan.' He held out his hand, the bag of clubs almost sliding off his shoulder.

She pointed at them. 'You playing today?'

'Every day is a good day for golf in Spain. That's why I moved down here – to improve my handicap.' He glanced at his watch. 'Blimey, gotta rush.' He turned to Wonderful. 'I'll head out with you.'

'Let's go,' she said, before turning to Astrid. 'Listen… Jennifer told me about tonight – thanks for agreeing to do it.'

What have I agreed to? 'My pleasure,' Astrid said.

Five minutes later, Roger brought out Astrid's continental breakfast and a glass of orange juice. She ate slowly, watching the terrace. Not much happened. A handful of couples strolled up to the entrance, checked the menu and moved on. Terry was still discussing the documents with the man in the grey jacket. Pearl champed her way through a portion of beans on toast – then seemed to go into 'stand-by' mode, head resting back against the wall.

The only drama was when The Beef, the smell of hot food in his nostrils, ambled over and squeezed under the table. Astrid gripped her glass to keep it steady as The Beef shunted into the table legs. It was like, she laughed to herself, the glass of water on the dashboard scene in *Jurassic Park*. She paid up and gathered her stuff. From the other side of the terrace, Terry gave her a big friendly smile.

'See you tonight, Astrid!' he shouted, his thumb in the air.

Apparently so. She gave him a thumbs-up in return.

At the top of the stairs, she saw Jennifer climbing up towards her. They both stopped halfway.

'Um, Jennifer… am I doing something tonight?'

'Oh, that,' Jennifer said, sheepishly. 'I completely forgot to tell you. We're going to have a meeting tonight – about the trolling. I told the others you'd be giving a little presentation.'

'A presentation?' Astrid's heart sank. There was no point – she had hardly anything she could tell them at this stage. Jennifer wouldn't hear it though. She said they were all so grateful to her, and desperate for any news. So, Astrid agreed.

Behind them, the man in the grey jacket passed them on the stairs. She noted he was much older that she'd first thought. Late seventies, at least. Jennifer greeted him with a 'Hi, Elliot' and offered to help him with his briefcase, which looked heavy. He said he was good, and stepped nimbly down the last couple of stairs.

'Who was that?' asked Astrid as he disappeared out of view.

'That's Elliot Green,' she said. 'He's a retired lawyer. He helps us all with our legal paperwork. You know – visas, permits, driving licences. Sometimes he doesn't even charge us – he says he just likes being busy.'

'I guess there's a lot of paperwork in Spain?'

'You've no idea.' Jennifer rolled her eyes. 'They say – if you're moving to Spain, make sure you bring a photocopier.'

'That's good,' Astrid laughed. 'What time do you need me tonight then?'

'Five o'clock.' She set off up the steps, turning at the last one. 'Don't worry – you'll be great, Astrid.'

Eleven

The Church of Our Lady of the Remedies was a fifteen-minute walk from the marina. First, east along the promenade, then north through the old town, which rose gently from the coast.

The old town was lovely. There was no other word for it – just lovely. The narrow streets were lined with icing-sugar-white buildings. Plant pots – orange, pink, white polka dots on blue – overflowed with geraniums, their heady scent collecting in the still corners. There was no need to check her phone for directions. You couldn't miss it. The church was the tallest building in the old town. Wherever you were, you could always get a glimpse of the peaked bell tower above the rooftops.

Astrid took a flight of steps that opened out into a small square – the Plaza San Francisco. The church was at the back. It was a stocky white building with the bell tower welded to its east flank. It was less showy than most Catholic churches. More like a New Mexico desert church – the kind you see in cowboy movies.

Her father was already inside. He was seated on a pew at the back, away from the central aisle. She thought again how she could greet him affectionately. There wasn't, she thought, for the British anyway, anything between a handshake and a bear hug. The Europeans had a range of air-kissing and embracing. Before she could make a decision, he patted the bench next to him.

'Hi, Astrid.' He crossed his legs.

'It's good you could get away from your desk, Dad.'

'Desk?' There was a flash of confusion. 'Oh, yes – the trading... right. Don't worry, I've left some automatic trade instructions. You can put in sell limit orders and hopefully...' He drew a wavy line with his finger in the air between them. 'It's like...' His voice trailed off. 'To be honest, it's too dull to explain.' He sat back and looked round the church. 'Impressive. Don't you think?'

Astrid agreed. Inside, the church more than made up for lack of glamour on the outside. Set into alcoves by the wall were gilded statues of saints, Jesus and the Virgin Mary. 'I guess you can forget that Spain is a devoutly religious country.'

'I know. Most of the Brits out here stick to the beaches and the bars. They're missing all this.' Her father stretched his arms across the back of the pew. 'There's so much history in these walls.'

'Is that right?' Astrid encouraged him, and he told her all about the different churches in the town. How, over centuries, they'd been destroyed by earthquakes and religious wars and rebuilt in different styles. She didn't really log much of it away. She was just happy to hear him talk so freely. It had been a long time since it had been just the two of them.

'Oh.' He sat up, remembering why they were here. 'Jennifer?'

'What about her?' said Astrid, her mood curdling.

'I wondered if you'd made any breakthroughs with your investigation?'

She told him there wasn't much to report. It was 'early days'. Until she'd spoken to all the expats on the list, she couldn't narrow down the suspects. Maybe, she said, there would be some progress at the meeting.

'Shakespeare's, right?' he said, without much enthusiasm. 'Jennifer mentioned it.'

She nodded. 'You going?'

'Nope – it's not my cup of tea. Jennifer likes the place though – she adores the mojitos, and the expat gossip.'

'Right, well, I'll leave you to it.' She picked up her bag and got to her feet.

'Hang on.' He held out his arm and caught her elbow. 'Don't go.'

Her good mood switched back on.

'I want to ask you something.' He rose to his feet and led the way down the side of the church. There was still nobody else there. It was silent. There was only the smell of candle smoke and cold stone. She followed him round to the altar. A statue of the Virgin Mary, dressed in purple and gold, gazed down at her. Astrid's neck itched. Churches – they weren't her thing.

Her father stood, arms folded, looking up at the paintings on the wall. They covered the life of Jesus, from his birth to resurrection. 'You're an expert on fine art, Astrid. What do you make of this?'

Astrid felt a glow of pride. He was asking her opinion. She moved closer and studied the nearest canvas. It showed Jesus stepping out of a marble tomb, three sleeping soldiers at his feet. 'It's Early Renaissance. Most people would be illiterate, so there's going to be some heavy visual clues here.' She pointed at Jesus's red robes. 'Like here. Instead of white robes, he's wearing red robes. It's a symbol of royalty – Christ the King, and all that. And here—'

'No, no… that's all very impressive, Astrid. What I meant was – what do you think of all this?' He spread his hands out to take in the whole collection of paintings. 'Do you think it's fair?'

'Fair?'

'That the Catholic Church should own so much incredible art.'

Astrid checked again to see if they were alone. They were. Even so, it didn't feel like she should be talking about this in church. There were in the eyeline of at least two Jesuses and a Virgin Mary. Her neck started itching again. 'If it's on display for everyone to enjoy, I guess that's fair.'

'But they own so much. Did you know the Vatican Museums alone have over seventy thousand works of art?' Astrid thought that maybe she did. But she kept quiet – her father had more to say. 'Only a third of this art is on display. The rest is in private houses and monasteries. In vaults where nobody can see it.'

'If the Church owns it, they can do what they want, surely?' Astrid knew her father was right. It was good to take the other side, though. To hear him being so passionate about something, other than Jennifer.

'The thing is, dear Astrid,' – he jabbed a finger in the air – 'if people don't get to see it, then it's invisible. It's as bad as if someone stole it.'

'That's one way of looking at it,' she said, seeing him smile at her in agreement. When he did, he looked very much like his brother, her Uncle Henry. Astrid breathed in. She might as well ask – this was the other reason she'd come to Spain. To find out, once and for all, why her father had fallen out so badly with his brother. 'I guess Uncle Henry would have said the same thing.'

Her father's chin dropped slightly. He seemed sad. Annoyed, maybe? At her, for mentioning his brother's name? Or at himself, for what happened between them? She couldn't tell. An elderly lady dressed in black shuffled into view to their right. She pushed a coin or two into a collection box and took a votive candle. 'Dad?'

He didn't reply. He was staring at the woman, who was lighting the candle and placing it on a black metal rack. Astrid repeated herself. Louder this time. 'Dad?'

'It's complicated,' he said, avoiding her gaze.

'In what way?'

'In a way that would take too long to explain.' He turned away and squeezed between the end of the pew and a pillar.

'I've got time.' Astrid circled round the pillar and boxed him in. 'You know that I inherited his boat? That's all he had when he died, and he gave it to me.'

'Yes, I know.'

'Which is amazing – but I feel bad that he didn't leave you anything. I just want to know what happened.'

He stared at her, gathering his thoughts. Which she never heard, because his phone beeped and his eyes darted down to it. He read the screen, a sombre expression forming. 'Oh, dear. Lulu won't eat her lunch. Jennifer's a bit concerned.'

'I'm sure the dog will be fine.' *Great – now Furball was ruining the moment.* 'Dogs can be fussy.'

'No, no. I better go.' He pocketed the phone and sidestepped her. 'Sorry, I need to give Jennifer some support. See you later, Astrid.'

She watched him leave. 'Bye, Dad.'

Twelve

Astrid went for a swim in the afternoon. There had been an offshore breeze and she'd been surprised to find how quickly, floating on her back and not paying much attention, she drifted out to sea. A stiff wind and you could end up on another continent. Now it was four thirty. She'd showered the salt from her hair and was feeling sharp as a tack. Ready to give her presentation to the expats – although there was still not much to tell them.

'Afternoon!' came a sunny voice over the rail. Nelson was standing there, a round white coffee cup in each hand. She pulled open another chair and helped him aboard.

'*Café con leche*,' he said, handing over a cup.

'Ooh, thanks, Nelson,' she said, sitting down again.

Nelson glanced at her hand. 'Nice tattoo, Astrid.'

'Thanks – it's a turtle.'

'Is it really?' He raised an eyebrow.

She took a sip of the coffee. It had a silky bitterness that her regular coffee didn't. 'Gorgeous,' she sighed.

'And I'll tell you what. One day I'll make you an even better drink: Spanish hot chocolate. It's so good it's like...' He paused to find the phrase. '...like a balm for the soul. A hot chocolate to heal a heartbreak.'

As he sipped his coffee, she told him her theory about the weather on the Costa del Sol. That there were weather conditions you got in England, but not here. He agreed with her. It worked both ways though. There was a rare phenomenon here, he said, called a calima, that happened now and then. It's caused by sandstorms over the Sahara. The dust is thrown high into the atmosphere, turning the sky orange. It was rare, and incredibly beautiful. He squinted in the sun, then got up and started fiddling with the sheets of the mainsail. In a few seconds he had the sail half up, which cast a cool shade over the chairs.

'Why didn't I think of that?' she groaned.

He sat back down and sipped his coffee. Astrid checked her watch. 'Listen, do you know about this trolling business?'

'Yeah, a few of the expats have mentioned it.'

'Right, well, I have to get up to Shakespeare's in a few minutes to give everyone my theories about who's behind it.'

'Good for you.' He sipped his coffee. 'I might pop in later then. I've just got a few things to do first.' He told her that his wife was coming back from the UK today, and he wanted to get a lot done before she did. Tidy the boat. Buy flowers. He was, he said, a bit of an 'old romantic'.

'Okay, so can I ask you, why do you think people become internet trolls?'

'Mmm... that's hard to say.' He drained his cup. 'It's not really my area of psychology, but I've read a few papers. If you're interested?'

'Of course.' She listened intently as he went over some of the theories.

Internet trolls, he said, tended to have a cluster of personality traits known as the 'dark triad'. This included narcissism – 'there's a lot of that around at the moment,' he laughed. Machiavellianism – the ability to manipulate people. And finally, psychopathy – a cruelness or lack of empathy. Social media gave these people a chance to express all three of these traits with little consequence.

'The dark triad? That all sounds a bit malevolent,' said Astrid.

'It can be, for the very committed troll. But we don't know that's what we're dealing with.'

'You're right – there's only been one message so far.'

'Correct.' Nelson folded his hands across his knees, as if he was in one of his therapy sessions. 'We don't really know what this person wants. Are they just being mischievous? Or do they really have a grudge against the expats on their list? Until they tweet something else, it's impossible to tell.'

Astrid was enjoying the conversation. She was fascinated by psychology and would have studied it at university, if she hadn't loved art.

'There's another aspect to internet trolls that's important to understand,' Nelson added.

'Go on?'

'They have a lot of cognitive intelligence. They do understand how others feel – that's how they know how to hurt people's feelings.'

'Then why do they do it?'

'Because it's all about getting attention. In the real world, the troll often feels lost or ignored. Under-appreciated. But online – it's different. People are finally listening to them. Even if it's for all the wrong reasons.'

'Yeah, that makes sense. And I guess if they're just doing it for the attention—'

'Exactly.' Nelson knew what she was going to say. 'If you want a troll to disappear, you ignore them. If you don't give them attention, they'll go away and find someone who will.'

'It's the most important rule, isn't it – don't feed the troll.'

Nelson nodded sagely. 'It's the number one rule.'

When Astrid used the word 'troll', she found it impossible to conjure up an image of a person. She just visualised a dark shape under a bridge. Glowing yellow eyes. Long claws. Waiting to lash out. Odd, maybe? But didn't everyone do that when they heard the word 'troll'?

She finished her coffee and handed Nelson the cup. As they got up, she took a quick peep at her phone. There was a notification on Twitter. @*TheAllSeeingEye7* had sent a new tweet.

She read it. Then held up the phone to Nelson.

'Hey – the troll has sent the "I know your secret" message to your wife, Talia.

He peered at the phone, reading it slowly. 'There you go then,' he said, unconcerned. 'She's on the list.'

'You're not worried.'

'Of course not.' He laughed. 'I can assure you, my wife doesn't have any dreadful secrets. It shows how desperate they are.' Then he stepped over the rail and sauntered back to his boat.

By five o'clock, nearly everyone on the troll's list had arrived at Shakespeare's. Roger was at the bar serving drinks to Jennifer and Morgana. On the end, Terry was sitting in front of a stack of receipts and punching numbers into a big calculator. At the table in the centre of the room was Wonderful, who was now wearing a Greenpeace T-shirt. On the table next to Astrid's were Bridget and her husband, Sebastian, whom she'd seen working on the roof. Their daughter, Miller, was sitting cross-legged on a chair, hunched over a phone.

The only person there who wasn't on the list was Pearl. She was seated by the wall, swirling the ice in her drink and tuning in to everyone's conversations. This was presumably her favoured spot indoors. Centre of the wall, between a pillar and the fruit machine – where she could cover all the angles. A sniper would have chosen this position.

To be fair to Pearl, Astrid was also eavesdropping. In front of her, a tense conversation was playing out between Bridget and her daughter, who wanted a glass of wine. But wasn't getting one.

Miller huffed, 'What about all that Mediterranean café culture we came here for?'

Bridget soothed, 'Sorry, darling. You're fifteen, remember?'

The rest of the conversation went like this.

Miller – 'But Spanish kids are allowed wine.'

Sebastian – 'That's why their GDP is a third of the UK's.'

Miller – 'How fascinating.'

Bridget – 'Come on, Miller, what else do you want to drink?'

Miller – 'Orangina.'

Bridget – 'What's the magic word?'

Miller – 'Abracadabra?'

Sebastian – 'No, the word that gets you something straight away.'

Miller – 'Now?'

Bridget – 'No, Miller… it's *please*.'

Halfway through this exchange, Astrid noticed Pearl

back-heel the plug of the fruit machine, switching it off so she could hear better. Bridget and Sebastian waited for Miller to put her air buds in her ears, then Bridget said something like – 'I'm sure it's just a phase.'

Declan came into the bar. He was wearing another pink golf shirt, tucked into the same pair of white shorts. There were three people on the list who weren't there. Charlotte, who was probably in the kitchen. Zhang, who was possibly working late at his shop. And Talia, the latest addition to the list, who was out having a romantic reunion with Nelson.

'Astrid!' Bridget had spotted her sitting on her own. She waved her over. Sebastian got up and pulled out a chair. 'Pleased to meet you,' he said, in an accent that Astrid placed somewhere in West London.

'Hi there,' said Astrid. 'I think I saw you working on the roof.'

'Yeah, yeah.' He flicked his hair back. 'A lot to do. We're trying to restore it to its original condition using authentic materials. The place must honour its heritage... suit the vernacular of the region. You know... right?'

'Right.' Astrid nodded confidently.

'I'm pretty much doing the construction on my own. A lot of the good freelance builders had to leave after, you know...' He dropped his voice. 'Brexit.'

Pearl caught it though. 'Hard cheese, I'm afraid. We had a vote to stay or leave and that was the result.'

Astrid had been waiting for the subject of Brexit to come up. It was only a matter of time. She heard Bridget whisper something like, 'Don't rise to it, Sebastian.' But he carried on anyway.

'Come on, have some sympathy, Pearl.' Sebastian turned

his seat to face her. 'A lot of people had set up their lives here. Then the rug was pulled from under them.'

'They should have applied for a residency visa a long time ago.' Pearl crunched down on an ice cube. 'That's what I did.'

Now Bridget couldn't hold back. 'Not everyone is lucky enough to have a Golden Visa, you know.' She glared at Pearl. 'And those that do shouldn't have pulled up the drawbridge for the others.'

Wonderful, who'd caught the gist of the argument, shuffled her chair closer. 'It's true. Why would any expat living in Spain vote to get out of Europe?' She turned up her palms. 'It's like a turkey voting for Christmas, isn't it, Pearl?'

Pearl ignored her, a tiny crescent of a smile at the corner of her mouth.

'It's worse than that,' said Sebastian. 'It's the old turkey who's too gamey to eat, voting for Christmas for all the other turkeys.'

Terry and Declan came over from the bar, both holding their drinks. Pearl turned to Terry. 'I was just saying, Terry – the Brexit vote. It was all fair and square, wasn't it?'

'Yeah, it was,' he said cheerily. 'The people of Britain spoke – they didn't want any more immigrants.'

Declan piped up. 'I hate to tell you, Terry – in this country, we are the immigrants.'

Wonderful gave a round of applause. 'Well said, Declan.'

'I dunno about that,' said Terry. 'The way I see it... the British abroad are never immigrants – they're expats.'

There was some muttering of disagreement. Pearl tried to silence it with a stream of 'Blah, blah, blah...'

Eventually, Bridget held up her hands. 'I know, why don't

we ask someone who's not got a vested interest.' She turned to Astrid. 'What do you think, Astrid?'

'Mmm… me… oh, no,' Astrid squirmed. A debate on Brexit was worth avoiding at the best of times. But here, in Spain, with every expat having to leave or fight to stay, it was a minefield.

'Astrid?' Bridget was staring at her. They all were.

Then she was struck by an image of the street vendors last night – gathering their goods in a blanket and escaping the police. How sad that was. 'Right, well, this is my humble opinion.' She swallowed. 'I guess you've got to ask – who is more of a foreigner here? The African migrant who travelled a few miles on an inflatable or the British expat who's travelled a thousand miles on easyJet?'

'Hah!' roared Declan, wagging his finger at Terry. 'How do you like them apples?'

'Alright, alright… let's not fall out about it. We're all mates here,' Terry said calmly. He walk over to the handwritten sign on the door. 'That's why I wrote these house rules.' He pointed at the first line. 'And number one is: no discussing Brexit.' When he said it, a few of the expats wearily repeated the Brexit line. They'd heard it many times before – the discussion was closed. It was Terry's bar, and his rules.

'Tell you what.' Terry clapped his hands and walked back towards the group. 'Everyone can have a drink on the house tonight.'

Declan raised his pint. 'Cheers, Terry.'

'Good, good…' Roger let out a relieved sigh, then turned to Astrid. 'Now, what can I get you?'

Sebastian leant over to Astrid and said, 'You simply must try the sangria.'

'It's san-gree-haah, darling,' Bridget corrected him, her fingers pinched near her mouth, the way top chefs are supposed to do when they've sampled delicious food.

Sebastian rolled up a bit of spit and said it again a few times as Miller shrank further into her chair with embarrassment.

Roger took the order down in his notepad and said he'd bring all their drinks into the games room. That was the cue for Bridget, Sebastian and Miller to get up and wander towards a door by the far corner. They were soon followed by Declan, Pearl, Jennifer, Wonderful and Morgana. Terry finished pouring himself a pint of lager and joined the end of the line. The Beef hauled himself up from the floor and followed him.

The term 'games room' suggested to Astrid a private room in a grand English Trust mansion. A billiard table in the middle. Wood-panelled walls. Shelves crammed with leather-bound books. The games room of Shakespeare's was a less stately affair. It was about the size of a two-car garage. At the back was a tatty dartboard and a rack of pool cues. The pool table was in the middle of the room. Scuffed yellow and red balls were scattered over the green baize. In front of it were two rows of white plastic chairs, nearly all taken by the expats, who were waiting quietly for her to address them. Alright, she thought, this wasn't going to be the TED talk she'd dreamt of, but there was no turning back now.

Jennifer ushered Astrid over to the pool table and made a short speech to the others that included the line 'my brilliant stepdaughter is going to use her considerable skills to expose our troll.' Jennifer was certain – if anyone could sort this out, it was Astrid.

Astrid took in the two rows of expectant faces. 'Okay, then,' she said, running her tongue over her dry lips. 'I'm really flattered that you're all trusting me to get to the bottom of this.'

Sebastian raised his hand.

Astrid pointed to him. 'Yes, Sebastian?'

'Do you think we should be discussing this only with people who are on the troll's list?' He thumbed down the line to Pearl. There was some muttering of agreement.

'Sorry, Pearl,' said Terry. 'You better go.'

'I think you'll find that if I've been served a drink.' She held up her half-full glass. 'I have the legal right to consume it on the premises.'

Terry got up from his seat.

'I've worked in hospitality for forty years – them's the rules.' Pearl gripped her glass with both hands. 'Up to you though, Terry – it's your drinks licence.'

'Fair enough.' He sat back down again. 'You can stay.'

'Anyway, Sebastian,' said Pearl. 'What about your daughter?' She pointed over to Miller, who was seated in the far corner, hunched over her phone. '*She's* not on the list.'

'Don't worry,' Bridget piped up. 'She's got her air buds in – can't hear a thing.' Bridget called over a couple of times to Miller, who didn't look up. 'See? It's fine.' She turned to Astrid. 'Please continue.'

'Okay then,' said Astrid. 'I promise I'll do my best to sort this out. But at the moment, I haven't made much of a breakthrough.'

There was a communal shiver of disappointment. They wanted answers – now. Roger came in with the tray of drinks and handed them out. He was joined by a woman in a white chef's jacket, her hair drawn up tightly into a hairnet. This must be Charlotte. They took the spare seats on the end of the row.

'Right, so the first thing I want to do is double-check with you all.' Astrid leant back against the pool table. 'Is there anyone here who believes that someone is out to get them? An enemy? Anyone with a grudge?' She scanned the room. Everyone was shaking their heads. 'Alright. And has anybody noticed they've been followed, or had any other messages sent to them?' Again, they all shook their heads.

'This is pointless,' muttered Pearl.

Astrid mutely agreed – she wasn't getting anywhere. She told them a bit about Nelson's theory of the 'dark triad' of troll personality traits, but she could tell she was losing everyone's attention. Morgana was whispering to Jennifer about something. Declan had taken out a scorecard, presumably from his last game of golf, and was going over his performance. Even The Beef, who had been sitting up on his haunches, his beady eyes trained on her, slumped down at Terry's feet. She was grateful when Charlotte raised her hand and started talking.

'Sorry to interrupt, but what I want to know…' She slipped off her hairnet, letting her curly hair fall to her shoulders. '… Why have all of us been sent the same message?'

It was, thought Astrid, a good question. She picked up a red ball from the table. There were more than enough balls left to make a visual metaphor out of this. A bit of drama. 'Because you all have the same secret.'

There was a ripple of laughter. Roger said it was 'ridiculous', and that was the consensus. The expats insisted they didn't have any secrets, let alone the same one. 'Okay, let's forget that.' Astrid dropped the ball in the pocket and waited for it to rattle around inside the table before coming to a rest with a *clunnng* in the far corner. 'I guess then,' – she picked up a yellow ball and turned it in her hand – 'there's nothing we can do but wait and see if they go away.' This didn't go down well either. There was some grumbling from the room.

Wonderful spoke for all of them. 'This thing is like a cloud hanging over us. We need to sort it out.'

'What do you want to do then?' said Astrid.

'I know,' said Bridget. 'We call their bluff.'

The others turned to her, confused.

'It's obvious,' she carried on. 'We send them a message now – tell them to reveal what they know or shut up.'

'Good idea.' Pearl rubbed her hands. 'Let's find out what grubby little secrets you all have.'

Roger turned to Pearl and went '*Shush!*'

Astrid remembered something else that Nelson had said. The number one rule: don't give the troll any attention. She told the others it was a bad idea, but they couldn't be talked out of it. This was the plan – they were going to challenge the troll. Astrid stole a glance at Jennifer. She was calm. All the other expats who were on the list – Morgana, Wonderful, Bridget, Sebastian, Roger, Charlotte, Declan and Terry – were just as relaxed. It was settled then. She put the yellow ball to one side and got out her phone. Everyone else reached for theirs. Except Terry and Pearl, who didn't have their phones with them. 'I'll reply to their latest message to Talia. Call them out in public.'

When they were all logged on and looking at the *@TheAllSeeingEye7* account on Twitter, she started typing, reading out slowly what she'd put in. 'Prove... it... or... go....

away.' Astrid hit send, then picked up the yellow ball again. All the expats, except Terry and Pearl, stared at their phones. After a minute, there was no reply.

Declan broke the silence, 'Looks like we're right, Astrid. They've got feck all.'

'All hot air,' echoed Bridget.

Some people started to get up. A wave of relief passed through the room.

'Okay,' said Astrid, rolling the ball down the table. 'I'm guessing we're not going to hear from our little troll ever again.'

There was a beep from her phone. Other beeps from the expats' phones. Astrid read out the message from @*TheAllSeeingEye7*. 'Watch this!' Below that was a line of emoji eyes, then a video clip. Everyone tapped it to get it started.

It was a beach, filmed from a low angle. On a phone, probably – the scene was unsteady. Then it settled, and you could make out a headland in the background. The top of a lighthouse. The camera swung away from the sand and up to a short flight of concrete steps between the rocks. It homed in on two people. They were holding hands, their backs to the camera. He was wearing shorts and a T-shirt. She was wearing a light summer dress. The man put his arm around the woman's waist, gathering her closer and kissing her on the lips.

Wonderful whispered, 'Why have they sent us this?'

Nobody answered. Everyone was studying their phone, trying to see if they recognised the couple being filmed. The camera focused in as the couple turned and strolled down the steps.

Most of the people in the room gasped. Morgana said in an incredulous voice, 'That's Talia.'

Jennifer said, 'So what? It's rather romantic, isn't it?'

The others looked down the line at her. Bridget spoke for all of them. 'Jennifer, take a closer look. The man... it's not Nelson.'

Everyone returned to their phones and restarted the video. Shaking their heads in disbelief. Except Pearl, who sat back and said smugly, 'Told you so.' Nobody replied to her. Another message had appeared on @TheAllSeeingEye7.

Morgana stood up and read it out in a slow, shocked drawl. 'You are all on my hit list and I am going to expose you one by one.'

The atmosphere in the room had changed. A cold draught had swept in from somewhere, and nobody knew where. The sunny, carefree lives of the expats were over – the game had become real. They'd poked the troll under the bridge. Fed it something. And it had come out to bite them. In public. It hadn't been bluffing. The list of expats was now a 'hit list' for the troll. Question was – who was going to be next? That was the part that nobody mentioned as everyone silently gathered their things.

There were footsteps from outside the games room. They turned to the doorway and there was Nelson.

'So then,' he said. 'What have I missed?'

Thirteen

Astrid woke up just before seven, after a long and fitful sleep. She'd only stayed at Shakespeare's for a few more minutes. Nobody had hung around – everyone shuffled to the door, avoiding eye contact with Nelson. Except Jennifer, who went over and put her arm around his shoulders – the first to put him out of his misery. She showed him the video on her phone. His shoulders sank, the despair dragging him down to a nearby seat.

Astrid sat up in bed and checked the video the troll had sent the night before. It had already had over 600 views – over 600 people had watched Nelson's painful betrayal. One of them, no doubt, his own wife. It seemed she hadn't rushed back from the UK to see *him*, but someone else. At least, thought Astrid, when Simon had betrayed her, there was no video for strangers to pore over, again and again, whenever they wanted.

She scrolled away from Twitter and searched for a recipe for Spanish hot chocolate. Then she went to the supermarket to get the ingredients. The recipe asked for:

2 cups of whole milk
300 grams of good-quality dark chocolate

2 tbsp of cornflour
2 tbsp of white sugar
A pinch of nutmeg

When she'd got everything she needed, she headed into the old town. On the way to the church to meet her father, she'd seen a bakery down a side street. It wasn't hard to find again. A few locals, elderly women with shawls drawn tight across their shoulders, were wandering down the hill. They had wheeled shopping trolleys with loaves poking out. For the last hundred yards, Astrid homed in on the smell of fresh bread.

The bakery was a small dark room with black and white tiles on the floor. A metal counter divided the space in two. There were two women in the queue. The first spoke quickly in Spanish to the man behind the counter. He passed over her order and wrote something down on a small pad. Then he did the same for the second woman. No money changed hands.

Astrid ordered a loaf of bread and a dozen churros. The transaction involved a bit of choppy Spanish and some pointing at a tray at the back. The server handed over the loaf, then dropped the churros into a paper bag and spun it round by the corners. He took Astrid's ten-euro note and gave back a few coins that smelt of sugar and dough.

When she got back to the boat, the marina had woken up. A couple of fishing boats were chugging into dock by the far harbour wall. Some old men were carrying fishing rods and plastic bags to the end of the breakwater.

In the cabin, she put the bag of churros in the oven and set it at a low heat. She checked the hot chocolate recipe on her phone and got started.

First, she poured the milk into a small red enamel pan. As it warmed on the hob, she stirred in the cornflour with a wooden spoon. Then the sugar. Then a pinch of nutmeg. She kept stirring so it wouldn't burn. Eventually, the milk boiled up, a small ring of bubbles grasping for the rim of the pan. She turned down the heat until the foam settled back. Now the chocolate, which was dark and bitter – closer to black than brown. She snapped the bars into squares and dropped the pieces into the pan. A dark marbled slick appeared on the surface. A bit more stirring and the mixture turned a velvety plum colour.

From the porthole above the sink, she could see over the next two smaller boats into the living area of Nelson's yacht. He was packing a few things into a suitcase on the table. She quickly turned off the oven and took out the bag of churros. They were chubby golden fingers, about five inches long, with dark brown ridges running down their sides. She arranged them on a plate. Then she put two deep bowls of hot chocolate on a wooden tray that she found at the back of a cupboard.

Astrid carefully carried the tray up the gangplank of Nelson's boat. He came out, his suitcase in his hand. Then he saw the tray of hot chocolate and churros and said weakly, 'For me?'

'Yes. Something for your soul, Nelson.' She went over and put them down on a circular table.

He went to the table and sat down. She sat down next to him and watched him take a long sip of the chocolate. His eyes slowly closed, as if he'd been filled up with joy. 'Just what I needed, thank you.' He dipped a churro in the hot chocolate and wolfed it down. 'Perfect.' He wiped the sugar off his finger on his Hawaiian shirt and picked up another.

'You going away for long, Nelson?' said Astrid, pointing at his suitcase.

'A few days. I've booked a hotel down the coast. We need to spend a bit of time together. A long way from here.'

They drank the hot chocolate and ate the churros, and he explained some theories about their origin. Churros, he said, got their name because of the distinctive ridges. They looked like the markings on the horns of the Spanish churra sheep. They'd started out as a humble shepherd's food, fried in a pan over an open fire. Nelson rattled through the explanation and she could see he was telling her to distract himself. Not wanting to think about his wife's infidelity for a moment. When they'd finished the churros, the subject stole up on him again.

'The troll then—'

'You don't have to talk about it if you don't want to.'

'No, no...' He brushed some crumbs from the table. 'I want to know what you think, Astrid. Releasing this video...' He winced. 'What does it tell us about them?'

Astrid had given it a lot of thought. She set out her ideas and he listened intently. They had all underestimated the troll. This person had gone out of their way to investigate Nelson's marriage. To follow and secretly film his wife. This morning they'd be feeling pretty pleased with themselves. 'Right?'

Nelson nodded. 'Yes, this is going to be pretty exciting for them and they'll want to get that feeling of power again. To get that attention. So, we can pretty much assume they'll release someone else's secret soon.'

'You think they've discovered everyone has a secret?'

'I'd say, almost definitely. That was a pretty bold message.' He hooked his fingers up. '"You are all on my hit list and I'm going to expose you one by one." I don't think they're joking.'

'I agree. This is just the start.' Astrid sipped her hot

chocolate. 'In which case, they have spent a lot of time with the expats. They know their routines. They could even be someone on the hit list.'

'Hang on.' Nelson held up his hand. 'But when you challenged the troll on Twitter last night, most of the people on the hit list were in that room?'

'Sure, and they were looking at their phones.'

Nelson was still confused.

Astrid drained her cup. 'The point is, we don't know what people were doing on their phones. Anyone in the games room could have loaded up the video and posted it there and then.'

'Did everyone have their phones with them?'

'Let me think.' Astrid paused, rewinding some of the evening. 'No, Terry didn't have his phone. Neither did Pearl.'

Nelson sat back. It had dawned on him, as it had with Astrid, that the release of the video at the meeting hadn't narrowed things down that much. The troll could be anyone else on the hit list. Or someone who was close to the group.

Nelson finished his hot chocolate and Astrid put the plate and cups back on the tray. When they both reached the bottom of the gangplank, Nelson stopped. He said, 'I still love her, you know.'

'Best of luck then,' replied Astrid.

'It's this place.' He gazed into the middle distance. 'People come to live in Spain and kind of lose it. It's like they're on holiday all the time. They do crazy things they'd never do at home.'

'You might be right.'

He turned without saying goodbye, deep in thought, and she watched him as he wheeled his suitcase towards a taxi that was waiting by the harbour office.

Fourteen

Astrid refilled her water bottle and unpacked the bike from the deck. It would be good to get out into the hills – to get some height and views. Forget the trolling case for a few hours.

She found a rough track to the north of the town. It started out gently uphill, in a direct line to the peak of the Sierra Bermeja. There were some half-built apartment complexes behind high wire fences. Silent cranes watched over them. It soon got steeper – the path narrower with small houses on either side, some rendered in peach or cream, the rest bare brick. The plots of land in front of them were either grey baked earth or green grass – watered by the *kiss, kiss, kiss, kiss* of a lawn sprinkler. The verges were dusted with bright yellow flowers, as if someone had taken pinches of cadmium yellow and dropped them here and there. She carried on cycling until it was too steep. Then she got off and pushed the bike ahead of her.

It was hot now. A dog lying on the porch of a farmhouse raised its head as she passed. It was tied at the collar to a long rope. When she was level with the gate, it sprang to its feet and ran out at her. The rope jammed, and the dog span in the dust. It gave three urgent barks, then padded back to the porch.

After another half an hour of pushing her bike up the track, it became clear that the summit of the Sierra Bermeja was still a long way away. The peak of the mountain didn't look much bigger than when she'd left the dog – too far to reach in half a day. She sat down on a rock in the shade of a pine tree and drank half of the water in the bottle, her back against the warm stone.

Another childhood memory stole up on her. They were becoming more frequent. Seeing her father again. Hearing his voice, the mannerisms, the smell of his aftershave – vanilla and new leather. It had opened old neural pathways, winkling out memories from crevices deep in her long-term memory.

Here she was, eleven years old, standing in her parents' bedroom. It was a place she did her best to avoid because of the strange smells of perfumes and creams. Odours that never seemed to percolate beyond the bedroom door. There was the big bed, with the mushroom-coloured nylon valance that draped down to the carpet and gave your shins little electric prickles if you got too close. Her mother was perched on the end, legs crossed, a white handkerchief balled in her hand.

'You know that things have been a bit tense between your father and me recently?' Her mother was referring to what Astrid called the 'Cold War of 42 Barrington Avenue' – a brief three months when they barely spoke to each other, during the day, at least. At night she'd lie awake, listening to them argue. Raised voices would drift up from the kitchen. Not loud enough to make out more than a few lines. 'It's not my fault.' – her father. 'Well, it's not mine, is it?'– her mother. But there was never enough to patch together the whole argument.

At breakfast, their voices were quiet and weary. There was nothing in between – as if the volume settings weren't working between '3' and '7'.

'Astrid?'

'Yes?' She was staring at her mother's shoes. They were green patent leather, buffed to a high sheen. Her mother always wore smart shoes, even around the house. 'Your father and I...' She paused to dab a damp ball of tissue to her eye. 'It's not working.'

'Okay.'

'Do you understand, Astrid?' she said, mistaking Astrid's indifference for confusion. 'Do you want me to spell it out for you? – we're getting a divorce.'

She knew she was supposed to say how shocked she was. Instead, she thought about the Tammy Wynette song 'D-I-V-O-R-C-E', the chorus jangling through her head. She wanted to hum it out loud because she liked it. Instead, she said something vague, like 'A divorce... that's a shame.'

Her mother told her how bad things had been. That they'd reached 'the end of the road' and that was that. The news had already been broken to Clare.

'Clare?' protested Astrid. 'But I'm older.'

Her mother brushed her complaint away and carried on with the announcement. It was going to be a 'no-fault divorce', which, from painful recent experience, Astrid knew probably meant one of them was more to blame than the other – and she was pretty sure who.

There was a large black suitcase in the middle of the bed. Her mother reached over and worked the zip shut. This day was bound to arrive. It had been booked in years ago. Even at eleven years old, she knew that it was better for all of them.

They'd all be happier. Her father would be his old cheerful self again.

Her mother stood up, heaved the suitcase from the bed and set it down on the carpet.

'So, Mum. Where will you go?'

'Oh, no.' Her mother tipped her head to one side. 'This is your father's suitcase.'

Astrid opened her eyes and shook the memory away. The sadness of it still clung to her for a while. It was horrible to remember how sad her parents had been back then – when their marriage was in its death throes. Now, though, her father was the happiest she'd ever seen him. Here in Spain, with Jennifer. She had to admit it: Jennifer was a big part of his happiness.

She took another sip from the water bottle and tightened the cap. The decision had been made – *No...* She couldn't be responsible for splitting them up. Whatever Jennifer's secret was, she shouldn't be the one to reveal it. She'd keep up her investigation – with even more determination. But now it was because she wanted to catch the troll *before* they exposed Jennifer. She got up, feeling better about herself. Not exactly saintly. Jennifer was still a bit annoying. And as for Furball... But she knew she was doing the right thing.

She turned her phone on. There was a notification waiting for her from Twitter. *@TheAllSeeingEye7* had posted a new message:

You're next Zhang!!!

Up ahead, a sandy path veered off west from the main track. She could see it glint between the bushes as it rode the valleys, then carved down towards the foothills behind her father's house, on past Eduardo's bar and into the town. She pushed her bike up to the path, climbed into the saddle and freewheeled downhill.

Fifteen

Zhang's store was on the western end of the Avenida España. Not a bad location, thought Astrid. If you were walking along the promenade, you couldn't miss the sign – *'BOBS – Best of British Supermarket'* written in big red, white and blue letters.

She parked the bike outside and took a trolley from a line at the entrance. The first thing that greeted her was a shelf filled with British magazines: *Take a Break*, *Puzzler*, *Chat*... This must be where Jennifer got her magazines from for the salon. Astrid carried on past a teenage cashier, who didn't look up from her copy of *Hello!* Why the exclamation mark, wondered Astrid? What was the shouting for? Was someone trapped down a well?

Astrid searched the aisles looking for Zhang, admiring how well stocked the place was. There was aisle upon aisle of tins, packets and boxes, every one of them a familiar British brand. She found him halfway down a long section of tins of soup. He was on his knees, fiddling with a red price label gun, a nearly empty pallet of tins at his feet. When she got close, he got to his feet and pointed the price gun at her, like a cowboy drawing their pistol. 'Stick 'em up, kid,' he said in an American accent.

Astrid raised her hands, palms facing him. 'You got me.'

'Don't mind me. I'm just muckin' aboot,' he said, reverting to his Geordie accent, the vowels clotting into something that sounded like the start of a folk song.

'My name's Astrid. Maybe one of the regulars at Shakespeare's mentioned me?' She brought her hands down.

'Yeah, they did. Nice to meet you, Astrid.' He spun the price gun on his finger and plunged it into the front pocket of his work apron. 'And welcome to BOBS.' He held out his hands and beamed.

Astrid looked round the shop. Everything was neat and tidy. All the tins were facing forwards. The signs hanging over the aisles were bold and bright. The floors sparkling clean. 'I like it, Zhang. It all looks very enticing.'

'Cheers. A lot of thought has gone into the layout.' He tapped the side of his nose. 'I've got a few tricks to get the punters buying.'

'Yes, I think I know a bit about this.' Astrid cast her mind back to an article she'd read somewhere. It was about how the layout of supermarkets is designed to wring the most money out of customers. It was a science and Zhang had a name for it: 'trolleyology'. The way he said it – the vowels bouncing off his tongue – it was one of the loveliest words she'd ever heard.

'Trolleyology,' she repeated slowly.

'Exactly. Take this shelf then.' He stood back from the tins. 'You've got your budget food – tomato soup, mushy peas – on the bottom section. But then the prices go up.' He slowly raised his hand. 'Now here's your sweet spot.' His hand was up to his nose. 'The shelves at eye level. That's where you put your big profit-makers. Like this...' He eased out a tin and presented it to her, as wine waiters do when they show you the label on the bottle. 'Baked beans with pork sausages. How about that? A complete meal in a tin.'

'I'm impressed,' she said.

Zhang put the can into her shopping trolley. 'I've got some more trade secrets for you – if you can keep them to yourself?'

Astrid crossed her chest with her thumb. 'I'll take it to the grave, Zhang.'

'Right then, follow me.' He walked backwards, talking as he went. 'The three basics are eggs, bread, milk. Trick is to keep moving them round the shop.'

'Why?'

'Cos then people have to go searching for them. And on the way they might see some other stuff they like the look of. For example...' He brought his fingers up to his lips, his mouth forming an 'O'. 'They look good!' He shot his hand out and grabbed a box of Yorkshire Tea. He tossed it into Astrid's trolley. 'To be honest, I've never worked out where the tea plantations are in Yorkshire. Makes no sense, right?'

Astrid nodded. It was a good point.

Zhang was now darting around, like a boxer warming up. 'Where's them eggs? They were here last week.' He pretended to look confused. 'Okay – we better try another aisle.'

They ducked round the corner, squeezing past a knot of customers. 'But hang on.' He stopped at the dairy chiller. 'It can't be... can it?' He put his hands up, acting out a scene of a happily surprised shopper. 'Yes, it is. You little beauty – Cathedral City Cheddar cheese.' He dropped it into her trolley. 'But which cathedral city is it? I've no idea. Winchester? Ely?'

'Durham?'

'Nobody knows, Astrid.' He hurried on, stopping now and then to put other items into her trolley.

'But you're not giving up, are you?' Zhang was back in character. 'You want that eggy bread for breakfast.' Astrid had no idea what 'eggy bread' was, but she wasn't going to prompt him for a recipe. The shopping was costing her a fortune as it was, and the longer she walked and talked, mostly him doing the talking, the fuller her shopping trolley became. In it went: Sunpat peanut butter, Findus fish fingers, a bag of pickled-onion flavoured Monster Munch as big as a travel pillow.

'Let me show you something.' He gripped her trolley and pushed it down the aisle. 'You hear that? The wheels?'

She listened. The wheels clacked slowly over the tiles. Then the clacking suddenly got faster. 'I don't understand.' She looked down. 'How does that work?'

'Ah, you see,' Zhang pointed at the floor, 'in this section, the tiles are smaller. So the wheels sound like they're moving faster... and guess what?'

Astrid studied the tiles. They were half the size of the ones further up the aisle. 'You slow down?'

'Exactly – you want to slow the shoppers down because this is where I stock the most expensive stuff. Biscuits, chocolates, pudding mix.' He reached out, grabbed a couple of bright pink packets of Angel Delight and carried on. 'There they are.' He pointed to a stack of egg boxes on the corner of the aisle. The marketing lecture wasn't over yet. 'You've finally found the eggs. But... hey presto!' He pointed at the almost full trolley. 'Your trolley is crammed with other stuff you didn't come for.'

'Clever,' said Astrid. 'Keep them moving round the store. The longer they're searching, the more chance they'll buy.'

'That's it – troll-ee-ology… now, where's that bread?'

Zhang's sales strategy appeared to be working. Not too far from them, a middle-aged man, as pink as the Angel Delight, had just walked into the store. He gazed in wonder at the shelves as, imagined Astrid, the Earl of Carnarvon might have felt breaking into the inner tomb of Tutankhamun and seeing the treasures inside. She watched the man pick up a multi-pack of KitKats and shake his head in disbelief. *Why was he surprised?* The supermarkets in Britain were full of produce shipped in from distant locations. Green beans from Ethiopia. Blueberries from South America. And yet, the thought that a KitKat had made its way from York – as she recalled from a school trip to the factory – was somehow inconceivable. It was a mystery that Zhang had tapped into. Above them hung a sign that said: *We Have Bovril!!!*

It had been an entertaining if expensive trip so far. But Astrid was here to find out what Zhang thought about the troll and being named as the next to be exposed. As they strolled back to the checkout, she said, 'Shame about Nelson, don't you think?'

'Yeah, poor bloke.' He shook his head. 'Nobody wants their dirty laundry washed in public. But that was the full boil wash, wasn't it?'

'It sure was.' She wheeled the trolley to the back of the queue. 'Did you see their message this morning – that you're next?'

'Yeah… yeah. I saw it.' He shook his head dismissively. 'Rubbish – I've got nowt to hide. They're just trying to wind us all up and I'm not falling for it.'

'Right...' It was hard to tell, but Zhang looked like he didn't have a care in the world. 'So, who do you think is behind this?'

'Well,' he sighed. 'It's someone local, isn't it? They know Nelson and his missus. They have enough time on their hands to follow her around.'

Astrid said she agreed. She told him her theory that it could be someone who regularly went to Shakespeare's. Even someone on the hit list.

'That would be a shame,' he said. 'We Brits need to stick together.'

Astrid remembered that this was what Roger had said in Shakespeare's when she'd first met him. However much they rubbed each other up, the expats needed each other. 'Do you know if there's any grudges between anyone?'

'Well, there's Pearl and Roger, obviously. But then Pearl seems to have a problem with the whole world. She's a reet mean bugger,' he said, which needed no translation.

'You know why she's so bitter?'

'Dunno. Some people are just like that, aren't they?' He edged forward. 'But I don't think she's behind all this.'

'I agree,' said Astrid. 'Anyway, she tells people what she thinks of them to their face.'

'Good point,' Zhang snorted.

The queue at the till had receded. There was only one customer now, a young man who was buying a couple of energy drinks. He paid up and Zhang started emptying the items from Astrid's trolley on to the conveyor belt. The cashier swept them down into the bagging area, where Astrid loaded them into bags. When it was all packed away, the cashier pointed to the till. The total was exactly thirty-nine euros. Astrid tried not to flinch, and calmly dug out her purse from her shopping bag. Zhang waved his hand. 'Don't worry, it's on me.'

'I couldn't possibly,' protested Astrid.

But Zhang was having none of it, tucking Astrid's purse back into her bag. He gave a thumbs-up to the assistant, who waved and said, '*Que tengas un buen dia.*'

'Oh, Sofia.' Zhang stopped. 'Remember…' he said slowly. 'It's "thank you for shopping at BOBS".'

She cleared her throat. 'Thank you for shopping at BOBS,' she said, even slower and in a perfect Geordie accent.

'Magic!' Zhang gave her another thumbs-up. 'You're getting the hang of it.'

Outside, Astrid stood in the shade of the awning, summoning the energy to step out into the scorching heat. 'So, Zhang – if you had to bet on who was the troll. Who would you go for?'

'I guess it would be Terry.'

'Terry?'

'Thing is…' Zhang sucked in a breath. 'I shouldn't say this because he's a big customer – Shakespeare's takes a lot of stock from us.'

'Don't worry – you can trust me,' she said.

'Okay… well, a couple of times, when he's had too much to drink, he's hinted about some dark criminal past. You know, how he had to leave the UK in a hurry. Like he's on the run, or something.'

'I suppose he could be one of those gangsters you hear about?' Astrid was warming to Zhang's theory. 'I've seen a few documentaries about British criminals hiding on the Costas. In fact, one was called something like *Villains in Villas.*'

Zhang laughed. '*Villains in Villas*... yeah, I've seen it.'

They'd been fascinating shows, she remembered. British criminals, mostly from London, had been hiding out in Spain for decades. The 'Costa del Crime', that's what the programme called it. They'd buy property and local businesses. The UK notes rinsed into euros. Identities changed. New passports, new faces thanks to plastic surgery. That's what the programme said. She made a note to check Terry's face if she got close enough next time.

'You think it's true?'

'I dunno... probably just the drink talking. You know what people are like when they leave home and come to Spain. They make all sorts of things up. Nobody checks.'

Zhang might just have struck on something, thought Astrid. People could make up anything about their past lives in the UK. They could make themselves seem more successful, richer, more dangerous. Completely reinvent themselves, knowing that nobody would be bothered to dig into their past.

She put on her sun hat and levelled the brim. 'And what about you, Zhang? What did you do before you came here?'

Zhang mulled it over, then he gave a quick sketch of his background. He'd been born in China. His parents emigrated to Newcastle when he was a toddler, too young to remember much about the place of his birth. He stayed in the north-east until his late twenties. Built up a few small businesses, which he'd sold about ten years ago because he wanted a change of scene. Then he came out to Estepona on holiday and fell in love with a local Spanish woman. He settled here and started a family – two kids, a boy and a girl. Every few months, he went back to Newcastle for a few weeks to see friends and parents. But Spain... 'Is it home?' He let out a satisfied sigh. 'Home is where the heart is, right?'

'That's what they say.'

'So yes, then. I have my family here, so it probably is.' He smiled. 'What about you, Astrid? Where's home for you?'

Astrid picked up the plastic bags and loaded them on to the handlebars of the bike. She sighed. 'I'm not sure. It depends on family, doesn't it? And I'm still trying to work out what that means.'

'Good luck with that then.'

She thanked Zhang for the groceries and offered him some money for the second time – to be absolutely sure.

'No, no...' There was no persuading him. 'My pleasure – a little taste of Britain, on me.'

Sixteen

There wasn't a whisper of a breeze down in the marina. Astrid raised the mainsail halfway and sat back in her chair. She brought up the plate of cheese and crackers she'd made and put it on her lap. It was delicious. The cheese, and the gossip. Terry just might be a former gangster. He might be... her mind raced... on the run. Holed up in Estepona. Spying on the other expats.

'Ugh, hang on.' She remembered – Terry didn't have his phone. He couldn't be the troll. Could he?

She ate the rest of the crackers – they didn't taste quite as delicious now – and put the plate down at her feet. She brought up Twitter on her phone and searched out the *@TheAllSeeingEye7* account. The video of Nelson's wife in a clinch with her lover had over 2,000 views now. People had watched it 2,000 times – but was there anything they'd all missed, herself included?

Astrid studied the video, pausing it every few seconds. Nelson's wife and the man were casting shadows on the path. Shadows that fell behind them up the steps, away from the beach. It had been filmed late in the day then, when the sun was setting in the west, obviously. That meant the troll would have been positioned up the beach to the west.

There was another clue that confirmed it. She swiped back a couple of times. For a brief second or two, you could see the tip of a lighthouse in the distance. This had to be the lighthouse Punta Doncella, just to the east of the marina. It had a distinctive white dome with a metal cage over the top. Definitely – she caught the frame just where she wanted it. So, the beach where the video had been filmed was further up the coast, beyond the Playa del Cristo. The next beach on from that, maybe?

The troll had lain down in the sand and filmed them. When she thought about the troll now, they'd become more human – a faceless figure shivering with excitement, because they had their moment to shame Nelson. To ruin his life.

She took the plate downstairs and locked up. It was time for an early evening walk to find the troll's beach. Not on her own, though; she'd need Fenwick to come along, if he was around.

She found him a couple of hundred yards up the Playa de la Rada, only a few yards from the promenade. He was kicking a trench of sand with a Croc, then sweeping the hoop of his metal detector over the area to home in on the loudest beeping. He reached down and picked something up, holding it up to Astrid.

'Another bottle top,' he said miserably.

'Keep searching, Fenwick, you'll get lucky.'

'I know, you've just got to put in the hours.' He popped the bottle top in his bum bag and carried on sweeping the sand ahead of him. She followed slowly, wondering how to get him to open up. 'This piece of kit then, Fenwick. It looks very professional.'

Fenwick patted the metal detector, smiling appreciatively. As if he was a racehorse owner patting his favourite horse in the winning circle. 'The Treasuremaster 7000X Pro. It's a thoroughbred among metal detectors.' This was the start of a long description of all its features that took them almost to the west end of the beach. On the way, Astrid learnt it had four settings. *Field*, *Park*, *Gold* and *Beach*. He was on *Beach*, of course. It showed up on a digital screen towards the top handle. There were other readings – for volume, sensitivity and battery levels. The Treasuremaster 7000X Pro could find everything from jewellery to coins. Although today, the haul of treasure had been seventeen bottle tops, six nails, and two spoons from the beachside restaurants.

Astrid pretended to listen intently, encouraging him with the odd 'wow' and 'no way'. Because he was enjoying showing off his pride and joy. Plus, she had a favour to ask of him.

'It's even waterproof to a depth of three metres.' Fenwick shook his head. 'I mean, that's impressive. But why would you need that?'

'Listen, Fenwick. Are you busy?'

'Never,' he replied.

As they walked back past the marina, she told him about the video the troll had posted on Twitter. He wasn't on social media, so hadn't seen it. She told him her plan – that she was going to try and find the exact position where it had been filmed. And, if he didn't mind, use his metal detector to search the sand – the troll might have left something behind. It was a long shot, she said. But there were no shorter ones.

'Okay, I guess we could,' he said reluctantly. 'You want to go now?'

'If that's alright?'

'Sure... I mean, that beach, it's not my kind of thing, Astrid... Each to their own, I guess.'

'Rrright,' she said, confused.

He tucked the metal detector under his arm and shambled ahead.

They were there in half an hour. Round the back of the marina, a straight line across the Playa del Cristo, then over a headland that funnelled down to a wooden boardwalk. Along the way, Fenwick talked about his former career as an insurance actuary. It took a bit of persuasion, but once he got going, he became quite animated. 'There's risk everywhere,' he said, throwing out his hands. 'From the moment you get out of bed—' He checked himself. '—even when you're in your bed, bad things can happen.'

He told her that his job was to work out the chances of those bad things happening. The insurance company would know how much to charge for a policy that paid out when they did. To get it right involved maths, statistics and as much information as you can get. 'That's why there are so many questions on insurance applications,' he said. 'For home insurance, for example... what kind of locks do you have? Do you have smoke alarms? A deep-fat fryer?'

'Got it,' she said, wondering if it was time to renew the insurance on her boat. 'And do you miss the job?'

'Nope,' he said, without hesitation. 'I'm out here, in the fresh air, instead of a tower block on a roundabout in Bournemouth.' He gazed back down the coast. 'Best decision I ever made.'

Astrid was looking back to the marina too, to check when the tip of the lighthouse was the same size as it was in the troll's video. She nodded. It was about here. There were some concrete steps heading down to a beach. She took the first couple of steps. Fenwick stayed where he was.

'Listen, Astrid.' He fiddled with the sensitivity dial on the metal detector. 'When we go down on to the beach. Do you mind if I keep my clothes on?'

'Sorry?' Astrid gulped. 'I mean, I'm more than happy with that.'

'Phew. I guess if you want to take yours off, then that's okay.'

'Sorry?' Higher this time.

He went over to a sign on the railing. It said 'Playa Nudista'. 'You do know this is a nudist beach?'

Astrid laughed, out of sheer relief. Then it sank in. 'Hang on, Fenwick. I know this is obvious, but this beach is going to be full of naked people.'

'Yup. Everyone. Completely starkers.'

Astrid didn't want to appear prudish. Nobody did. But there was something about naturism – *wasn't there?* Something a bit odd. She'd heard naturists say the same things. Getting in touch with nature – wind in the hair, and all that. Just as God intended. But still… It was as if Fenwick had read her mind.

'The thing I don't get…' he said.

'Go on.'

'Whenever I've accidentally ended up on a nudist beach…' He stressed 'accidentally', although for someone who never took his socks off while wearing sandals, there was no doubt that naturism wasn't Fenwick's thing. '…they're always bending over to pick up shells.'

'Is that a fact?'

'It is. Or pebbles. But why? They don't even have pockets.'

'Good point.'

'And badminton.' Fenwick was on a roll. 'Naturists play a lot of badminton. You never see people with clothes on playing badminton on the beach. It's all a bit unusual, if you ask me.'

'I guess.' She carefully took the last few steps. 'Or maybe we're being too British about this?'

'Maybe,' he said. 'The thing is. I'm not that good with people with their clothes on. So dozens of naked people...' He gave a little shudder. 'Ugh.'

'Come on.' Astrid waited for him to catch up with her. 'Listen, we won't know anyone, so it's going to be fine.'

The beach was busy. All the sun loungers under the straw parasols were taken. A steady flow of people ambled along the shoreline. They were all naked, all deeply tanned. Fenwick stood still, gazing at the scene.

'You okay, Fenwick?' said Astrid out of the corner of her mouth.

'I know what this reminds me of.'

'Go on.'

'A leather furniture warehouse I used to drive past in Bournemouth. All that dark brown leather.' He gave another shudder.

They set off down the beach. Fenwick staring at the sand in front of him. Astrid checking the video on her phone. After fifty yards, turning back to the lighthouse now, she found the rough position the video had been taken from. It was high up on the beach, just before it turned into a jumble of big sandstone blocks.

A path weaved between the blocks towards a holiday complex. Hundreds of people, she thought, would have disturbed the sand. There was no point checking footprints.

But they could still give the area a thorough sweep. Get it done quick, before anyone asked them what they were doing.

Fenwick adjusted the dials of his metal detector. He set off in a straight line, fanning the ground ahead of him. After ten yards, he took a sharp U-turn back – as if he was mowing a lawn. Astrid was on 'trowel duty', digging up anything that caused a *beep*. After four turns, they only had two bottle tops to show for their efforts.

A handful of people wandered down the path, beach towels across their shoulders. It was the only fabric touching their bodies. One of them stopped and shouted to Astrid and Fenwick. 'Hey, it's you two!'

Fenwick glanced at Astrid. 'Oh, no,' he whispered. 'It's Roger Cherry.'

Roger gambolled up to them. 'Fancy seeing you two here.'

'Hullo,' said Astrid awkwardly. His body was covered in curly, dark hair. From ankle to chest. Fenwick was bewitched.

'You alright, Fenwick?' said Roger.

'I'm just staring at your body, it's so… um, fascinating. With all the hair and that.'

'Oh, right.' Roger put his hands on his hips and set his feet apart. As if he was about to launch into some star jumps, which mercifully, to Astrid and Fenwick's relief, he didn't. 'Anyway, welcome to Costa Natura. Spain's oldest naturist beach.'

Fenwick turned to Astrid and mimed the word 'help'. As his metal detector swung past Roger at hip height, it *beeped*. Fenwick repeated the motion a few times. There was a *beep* each time. After years of searching with the metal detector, his actions were automatic. He couldn't help homing in on the source of any beeping – which, this time, was slap bang in the middle of Roger's groin. 'That's strange – I'm getting a very strong signal.'

'Oh, that?' said Roger breezily. 'It's my adornment, shall we say.'

Astrid caught a glint of something silver and stared off into the horizon to empty her mind.

Roger laughed. 'Well, if it's good enough for Prince Albert, it's good enough for me.'

Fenwick gave Roger another couple of sweeps. *Beep. BEEEP.* 'Is it real silver?'

'Actually, no,' said Roger. 'It's chrome. Silver tends to tarnish in the sea air.'

'Interesting.' Fenwick changed the setting on the dials. 'This detector isn't usually good at picking up chrome...' He suddenly realised what he'd been doing. He looked at his watch. 'Gosh, is it that late?' He made a surprised expression.

It took a second, then Astrid twigged. 'Oh, yes, we should get on and leave you to it, Roger—'

'Hang on, guys.' Roger was waving over at the path. 'Here comes my wife.' Charlotte Cherry was heading their way. The only thing she was wearing was a large sun hat. She had two badminton rackets under one arm and a tube of shuttlecocks in her hand. 'Over here, darling,' Roger shouted. 'Fenwick and Astrid are here.'

Charlotte veered off the path and hurried over the sand. Fenwick hooked a finger into the neckline of his Lord of the Rings T-shirt – on the front was a picture of the flaming Mount Doom. He was sweating profusely, even though a cooling breeze had picked up.

Charlotte arrived and told them that she was about to have a game of badminton with some of the other members. Which caused Fenwick to say 'Told you so' under his breath, though it was loud enough for everyone to hear.

Charlotte pointed at Fenwick's metal detector. 'What are you searching for, Fenwick?'

'Oh, Astrid has lost something,' he said, before she could signal him not to.

'That's a shame,' said Charlotte. 'What have you lost?'

'Um… it was a necklace. Yes, a necklace.' Astrid thought it best not to tell them they were checking last night's troll video. They were still suspects. 'Last night. I was leaving the beach and I must have dropped it around here.'

'How wonderful – there's nothing like it, is there, Astrid? Being in the sun, *au naturel*, as they say in France.'

'Oh, hang on, no…' Astrid protested. 'I'm not a naturist.'

'Don't worry, there's no shame in it,' whispered Roger, as if they now had a shared secret.

Before Astrid could say anything else, Charlotte said, 'Come on, let's see if we can find your necklace. She dug the tube of shuttlecocks into the sand, then dropped the rackets either side. 'Where shall we search?'

'No, honestly,' blustered Astrid. 'Thinking about it, we'll never find it.'

'No, no. Let's give it a go. There's more of us now,' she said, turning to Roger. 'Right, darling?'

'Absolutely,' said Roger. 'We'll find that necklace for you – you'll see.'

'No, really.' Astrid twisted in the sand. 'The necklace is worthless. I'll just buy another one.'

But Roger and Charlotte had made up their minds. They were going to help, and nobody was going to stop them. 'Here's the plan.' Roger slipped his towel from his shoulders and tossed it down next to the badminton gear. 'Charlotte and I will get down on our knees and do a hand search. You two can follow behind.'

They got on all fours in front of them. The neck of Fenwick's T-shirt was soaked in sweat. It looked like it was going to extinguish Mount Doom. Fenwick took his head in a high arc over the horizon to avoid seeing the naked Charlotte and Roger below him. He mimed 'Let's go.' But it was too late. Roger was up again.

'You know what? We could do this faster if we had a few more people,' he said excitedly. 'There's a naturist family resort up there. I can go and get some others.'

'Families?' said Fenwick.

'Yes – families. There's lots of kids up there. We can all get down in a long line, like they do when the police are searching for a piece of evidence.'

'Good idea,' chimed in Charlotte. 'I bet we could get at least a couple of dozen people down here.'

'Oh, sweet Jesus… no,' moaned Fenwick, almost hysterical.

Roger looked a bit deflated. 'Right, well, just a thought.'

'That's very kind.' Astrid came to the rescue. 'But I don't want to put your friends out. I'm sure us four can sort it out.'

Roger smiled again. He got down on his knees and he and his wife set off slowly, skimming the sand with the palms of their hands. Fenwick turned down the detector's sensitivity to its lowest setting and followed at a safe distance, wiping his forehead with the back of his hand at increasingly regular intervals.

After five minutes, which felt like an hour at least, they'd not found anything of any significance. Just a few more bottle tops and a pronged piece of metal, which Fenwick dropped in his bum bag without much thought.

They thanked the Cherrys, who both said 'Any time' in unison, although Fenwick made it clear that a naked search of the beach would never happen again. Ever. He walked back in silence to the steps and slumped down on the nearest bench. His T-shirt and face were drenched in sweat now. His eyes were wide – as if he'd opened a dishwasher mid-cycle and been caught with an updraught of hot steam, but been too shocked to move. It took him a couple of minutes before he spoke. 'That was horrendous... just horrendous.' He rubbed his eyes with his knuckles, working them into the sockets. As if to grind the images from his retinas.

Astrid hadn't been quite as squeamish as Fenwick. But she agreed, she'd seen some things today that would be hard to scrub from her memory. 'The British aren't designed to be naked in public, are they?'

'No, the men especially. It's like a vacuum cleaner that was built on the Friday afternoon of a bank holiday. Someone was in a rush to finish – all the loose bits, tubes and what have you – just hanging off.'

'That's a very specific analogy, Fenwick, but I get the image.' Astrid sat down on the bench next to him.

She watched Fenwick unzip his bum bag and start sorting out the debris he'd collected. The bottle tops were dropped into a bin to the side of the bench. He brought out the metal fork and studied it. 'Any ideas?' He passed it over.

Astrid turned it over in her fingers. It was about three inches long and the shape of an elongated teardrop, with the end divided in a 'V'. It was made of a flat metal that was grey from the salt and sun. It wasn't precious – a tool of some sort.

There was a circle of words stamped roughly into the metal. She rubbed the dirt away until she could read what it said:

El Paradiso GC

'Okay.' Astrid turned up her lower lip. 'GC? Any ideas?'

'That'll be "Golf Club". There's a course not far from here called the El Paradiso.'

'You played there, Fenwick?'

'No. Never played golf in my life.' Fenwick sat up. 'Which I consider something of a personal achievement.'

'You know anyone who does play there?'

Fenwick thought for a moment. 'Declan – I think he might be a member there.'

Astrid turned the fork in her fingers again. This was a solid clue – it held some truth, she thought, and she wanted to know what that was.

She thanked Fenwick and he said he'd go ahead. He wanted to have some time on his own, to clear his mind. As he stepped away, she called after him, and he turned back.

'Listen, Fenwick. Do you ever go to Shakespeare's?'

'Not really. As you know, there's just…' He fiddled with a wire on the metal detector and mumbled, 'too many people.'

'Okay, well, if you change your mind. It would be good to see you there.'

He shook his head.

'I think Morgana goes there a lot.'

He didn't look up, but she caught the edge of a smile. 'I'll think about it.'

When he'd gone, she went back to where he'd found the metal fork on the beach. She took out her phone and checked the video again.

'Gotcha,' she said, under her breath.

How had she watched the video a dozen times and missed it? For less than a second, you could make out the edge of a rock jutting into frame. She scrolled back through the video, pausing at the right moment. Then she got down on her knees in the sand, until she had the exact position where the troll had taken the video. The exact place Fenwick had found the prong. The prong was now a key.

Seventeen

Astrid walked slowly back to the marina. It was cooler now. The sun had slipped low in the sky, taking the dry itchy heat of the day with it. As Astrid passed the terrace of Shakespeare's, a shrill voice echoed out. 'Astrid!'

She looked up and saw Jennifer leaning over the rail, a glass in her hand. She shook the glass and waved for her to come up.

The main bar was closed – there was a handwritten notice on the door apologising for the inconvenience. A few of the expats on the list were on the terrace – Morgana, Declan and Bridget, with Pearl in her usual spot, back against the wall. The rest of the customers were smarter couples and families she hadn't seen before. They were lined up at the front of the terrace, watching the sun set over the Strait of Gibraltar.

Jennifer greeted Astrid at the entrance and ushered her to the last available table, in the far corner. 'I'm afraid we haven't got the terrace to ourselves tonight,' she said, thumbing at the other customers. 'Roger and Charlotte have got the day off, so Terry shut the main bar and told us to share with the holidaymakers.'

Astrid mentioned she'd seen the Cherrys on the beach earlier, but didn't go into too much detail.

'Good for them, they deserve some time off.' Jennifer raised her empty glass. 'Fancy a sundowner?' And before Astrid could reply, she floated off to the bar.

Astrid looked around the terrace. Since leaving London, she'd realised that the British had different drinking habits, depending on where they were. In Hanbury, back in Dorset, it was the pub and pints, usually warm real ales. On the Isle of Wight, during Cowes Week, it was more refined. Gin and tonics in the sailing club bars, champagne on the lawn. Squirrel beer for the locals. Here on the Costa del Sol, people seemed to drink anything, as long as it had alcohol in.

She looked at the tables. There were pints of lager, shot glasses of tequila, jugs of sangria, stemmed wine glasses for red and white – Pearl's tumbler of Dubonnet and lemonade. It was holiday drinking. The sun's shining and there's no rules. No alarm clocks. No boss to breathe away from in the morning. The expats drank as if they were on holiday as well. And they were on holiday all the time. If they weren't careful, it would be the bank manager or the doctor (English-speaking) calling time.

Jennifer returned from the bar and set a mojito in front of her.

'Cheers,' said Astrid, clinking glasses.

Jennifer pulled her chair into the table and lowered her voice. 'Poor old Nelson. That video must have been so embarrassing for him?'

'I know, just horrible,' Astrid said, pushing the sprig of mint to one side of her glass and taking a long gulp. 'They're going to release Zhang's secret next, aren't they? I saw their latest message.'

'Yes, I think they will – if he has a secret.'

Jennifer looked close to tears. 'That's the worst thing, isn't it? The waiting.'

'I'm afraid it is, Jennifer. But that's what the troll wants – for you to lose sleep. Don't give them the satisfaction.'

'Yes, yes…' Jennifer reached out and squeezed her hand. 'You're right, I'll try not to worry.'

Morgana and Bridget came over and sat either side of them, so they were all facing out to sea. 'Poor old Nelson,' said Morgana, which set up a Mexican wave of agreement down the row. 'I guess the only good thing is, it narrows down the suspects. We can now tick Nelson off the list.'

Bridget, who had been lining up a photo of the sunset through Jennifer's drink, turned to the others and said, 'Not necessarily. Nelson could still be the troll?'

'Sorry?' said Astrid. 'Why would Nelson troll himself?'

'Because…' Bridget sat back and wove her fingers together. '…it's the perfect alibi.' For the next few minutes, Bridget outlined her theory. Nelson's wife had been cheating on him. But it was Nelson who'd discovered the affair, not the troll. He'd filmed her on the beach, weeks, maybe months ago. Since then, they'd worked through their problems and decided to stay together. And now he can start his campaign of revenge against the expats. At this moment, with everyone feeling sorry for him, he could be in a hotel somewhere, tweeting away as @*TheAllSeeingEye7*. 'You've got to admit,' she said, 'it's rather clever.'

'But why is he out for revenge?' said Jennifer in disbelief.

'That,' Bridget sighed, 'I don't know.'

'You know, I don't think it's Nelson.' Morgana angled herself to the others. 'I think Roger and Charlotte are behind the trolling.'

Astrid's head spun. First Nelson, now the Cherrys. But Morgana was sure – and her theory went like this. Apparently, a few months back, an anonymous restaurant review of Shakespeare's appeared online. It trashed the place. This was a while back, when Charlotte Cherry was just trying to find her feet in the kitchen. She'd no training as a chef and the food and service at the start weren't great. All fingers pointed at Nelson because he was the part-time restaurant reviewer. He denied it – said anyone could have written the review. 'But maybe the Cherrys didn't believe him and still bear a grudge?' said Morgana. 'They could be behind the trolling.'

Bridget and Jennifer didn't say anything. All three of them sat there in silence, trying to work it out. It was that perfect moment that landscape painters wait for. The sun – six degrees above the horizon. The light – soft and generous. Astrid studied the expats. Even with the flattering light, they looked tired and drawn. The stress of the trolling was dragging them down. The accusations – the rumours, it was pulling the expats apart.

Bridget broke the silence. 'Look at us.' Her chest heaved. 'We're turning on each other. Pointing the finger at Nelson, or Roger… when there's no proof.'

'It's true,' Morgana agreed. 'The troll wants to split us up.'

'Yes, they do,' said Bridget. 'But why?'

'Who knows?' said Jennifer mournfully. 'Who knows?'

They drank their drinks and watched the sun melt into a molten pool of itself. Nobody said anything. Even Bridget didn't have the energy to take any more photos. Then, out of the corner of her eye, Astrid noticed Declan pick up his golf clubs and set off towards the exit. Astrid got up.

'It's been a long day.' She half yawned. 'I better go.' She picked up her bag and told them she'd redouble her efforts to find the troll, and she'd catch them in the end. They thanked her – although she could tell they weren't convinced.

She caught up with Declan at the bottom of the stairs.

'Hey, Astrid.' He seemed pleased to see her. 'How's it going?'

'Good, thanks.' She pointed at his golf clubs. 'Which club were you playing at?'

'El Paradiso.'

'Oh, right – El Paradiso.' She nodded knowingly.

'It's a tough little course. But with a bit of local knowledge,' – he rubbed his chin – 'you can put a good score together.'

'Is that right?' She put her hand in her pocket and gripped the metal fork. 'I've never played before, but I'd love to give it a go. Seeing as we're in Spain – the home of golf.'

'The home of golf is Scotland.'

'Is it?'

'It is.' He smiled. 'Spain is as great place to learn though, and I'm more than happy to teach you.' He ran his hand across the clubs in his bag. 'I don't mind telling you, I'm a bit of an expert.'

It turned out that Declan played golf nearly every day of the year. He had a one o'clock 'tee time' tomorrow and was more than happy to add her to the booking. She thanked him and he picked up his golf bag and rattled off towards the taxi rank.

There were footsteps behind her. Jennifer was hurrying down the stairs towards her, phone in hand.

'Are you alright, Jennifer?'

Jennifer shook her head. She passed over the phone. It was showing the latest tweet from *@TheAllSeeingEye7*.

Astrid read the message. It was hard to make out what it meant at first. There was a photo of a pack of British teabags. Another, closer up this time, just on the barcode. The text said:

Hah – hah! The barcode is fake. You're selling fake British products Zhang!! Do these companies know?

Below, the troll had attached the Twitter addresses of a handful of big British food distributors. Tea, coffee, biscuits – all well-known brands in the UK. They'd definitely notice. Astrid turned to Jennifer.

'Let's get this straight – BOBS, the Best of British Supermarket, is selling products that aren't from Britain?'

'It seems that way,' said Jennifer. 'He must be printing his own packaging and labels somewhere.'

'Yes, it must be cheaper than importing the real stuff.' Astrid focused in on the photos. It was convincing, at a glance. But looking closer, you could see the writing on the packaging wasn't sharp. The barcode was a little hazy. So far, Zhang had fooled everyone, except the troll.

'Astrid?' Jennifer was staring at something else on her phone. She held up the message for Astrid to read.

You're next WONDERFUL!!! LOL

Eighteen

Astrid woke up to a text from Declan.

> Tailored shorts. Matching belt. Short sleeve shirt with collar. White sports socks (no logos)

Which made little sense until she saw another text from him.

> Strict dress code. Sorry. Some of the members are fussy.

If she wasn't going to fall foul of the members, she'd have to do some shopping later.

She checked Twitter as she ate her breakfast up on deck. There was nothing new on her account. The tiny synaptic storm of likes and follows had drifted by. Twitter was happening for everyone else right now. She felt ignored, and it was a relief.

Zhang wouldn't be feeling the same way. Or Wonderful – her secret was going to be revealed. But by whom? And why were they doing it? Lots to think about – and with the morning free, she might as well do it while she mended the painting.

Below deck, she found her work case. She took out a green velvet cloth, which she smoothed over the table. Then she laid the painting of *The Last Supper* on it, face up. Next, an examination of the cross-shaped rip with a magnifying glass. She'd seen this pattern of damage before. The rip was neat, with sharp edges. A rip like this was usually made when someone took down a painting in a hurry – they'd catch the canvas on the hook in the wall. This might only be a copy of an original Perugino, but it was still precious. Why would someone be so clumsy with it?

Astrid let her eyes wander over the painting, finding its rhythm and flow. It was a beautifully balanced scene, anchored by Judas in the centre foreground, his head turned to the viewer – guilty as sin. Hanging from his hand, out of sight of the others, was a small purse. In it would be thirty pieces of silver – the reward for his betrayal. That night, he'd point out Jesus to the Roman soldiers in the Garden of Gethsemane. Betrayed by a kiss. The expats had their own Judas. Was their motive money? Maybe it was that simple – it usually came down to money, didn't it?

Astrid turned the painting over and squared it up on the velvet cloth. A few more things from the work case – a pot of white gesso glue, sharp-point tweezers and a patch of canvas that was large enough to cover the damage by some way. She started picking out any grit and stray fibres with the tweezers. It was like cleaning a wound. *Revenge? Could that be the motive?* As she worked, she went over what Morgana had said – that Roger and Charlotte Cherry were behind it. They were getting their own back on Nelson for writing a horrible review of Shakespeare's. That might explain why they were so keen to search the nudist beach with her and Fenwick.

To find some evidence they'd left behind before anyone else did. She teased out a loose fibre. But then again, if Bridget wanted to be the most successful blogger in town, of course she'd say Nelson was guilty. Wouldn't she? Although Astrid's hunch was that Pearl had written the review. It had to be Pearl. Surely? She could almost see her, late at night, dripping acid on to the keyboard. But then there was Zhang – someone was trying to ruin his business too.

Next was the patch. She pasted the gesso carefully around the damage with a medium brush, applied more of the glue to the patch. Bridget had been convinced Nelson was still around. Holed up in some hotel so he could secretly taunt the expats. She slid the patch on with the tweezers. 'No, no,' she said under her breath. It couldn't be Nelson. He was a decent guy, she was sure of it. There was no way she was that bad a judge of character – apart from her ex-husband, Simon, obviously. It was impossible. Anyway, Bridget might have a grudge of her own and wanted to keep him in the frame. And then there was Morgana – was she jealous of Bridget and Jennifer's success?

Astrid put down the tweezers, her head spinning. She could see how the troll had rattled the expats. Making them think the worst of each other – imagining all sorts of sordid things. Maybe that was the reason they were doing it? To make them paranoid and suspicious of each other. To split them up. So far, it was working.

She pasted more gesso over the top of the patch. A vague sense of failure had crept up on her – on the case, at least. She wasn't any nearer finding the troll. Thankfully, the repair was going well. The patch looked good. The next stage, restoring the paint on the surface, would have to wait until the glue was dry. She laid a small block of wood on the back of the patch. Then weighed it down with a glass tumbler. Twenty-four hours should do it – to be on the safe side. She checked her watch. It was time to get ready for golf.

The clothes shopping took the rest of the morning. She bought the white socks – no logo – from the supermarket. Everything else was from backstreet shops, including one gloomy place that had two dead wasps in the window and was manned by an old woman who brought down a minty polo shirt from high on the wall with a long, hooked pole and exclaimed '*Bonita! Bonita!*' before plucking two ten-euro notes out of Astrid's purse.

Declan was waiting for her on a bench in front of the clubhouse, a white ranch-style building that faced the course. He had a little wire brush in his hand and was scraping away at the grooves of one of his clubs. She waved over to him. He stopped scrubbing, got up and slid the club back into his golf bag.

'You look grand, Astrid.'

Astrid knew that she didn't. She looked absurd. The pale green polo shirt. The white tailored shorts with the white belt. The socks.

He scanned her, checking for anything that might break the club rules. 'Great – that shouldn't set off any alarm bells,' he said, tightening up the matching belt of his own white shorts.

'Right,' she said. 'Let's go and play some golf.'

'What about golf clubs, Astrid?'

'Of course.' She snapped her fingers. 'I probably need those, don't I?'

He laughed, then set off round the side of the clubhouse. At the corner was a small island of very flat grass. It bristled with little flags. This was the 'Putting Practice Green', according to the sign. A handful of people were stalking across it, tapping balls towards the flagsticks. They were all men – all in similar outfits to Astrid and Declan's. White and pastels, their shirts tucked into their belts. The way they were bent over, it was as if a flock of budgerigars had descended on a lawn. Astrid was beginning to feel she didn't stand out after all. This was a kind of uniform. It wasn't clear who chose it, but everyone knew it had to be worn.

They went in through a side door marked 'Pro Shop'. It was full of golf gear. Racks of shoes on the wall. Golf clubs in all shapes and sizes. Pastel tops and shorts – *so that's where everyone gets them?* A young man – slim, tanned, with his sunglasses pushed up on to the crown of his head – spotted Declan at the door. He turned to an older man who was sitting behind him, wrestling a golf club into a vice. They exchanged a couple of words. She couldn't hear what they were. But when he turned back to them, he was doing his best to keep a straight face. 'Declan. Good to see you.'

Declan introduced the man to Astrid. This was the club 'pro', which Astrid imagined meant he made his money playing golf – a professional. Declan told him Astrid was a complete beginner and needed some clubs. He sized her up and started asking a lot of questions. If she was right- or left-handed. Her height. Shoe size. It was the kind of questions, she thought, that you might ask someone before you go deep-sea diving for the first time. Or on the space shuttle. Not tootling around a golf course in the sunshine.

'Listen,' she said. 'I'm going to be hopeless. Just give me any old clubs.'

'Don't worry,' added Declan. 'I'll be teaching her how to play.'

There was a snigger from the man sitting down, and the club pro clamped his lips shut, trying not to laugh. 'Right then,' he said finally, letting out ten seconds of held-in breath. 'Let's find you some clubs… and some shoes.'

The older man got up and went to a cupboard, avoiding eye contact with the club pro. While he was rummaging around in there, the club pro tapped the price of the 'green fees' and the hire of the equipment into the till. Then he said, 'What about some extra balls, Declan? Just in case you lose some.' There was a muffled giggle from inside the cupboard. The clatter of dropped clubs.

Declan picked out a pack of three new balls in a cardboard sleeve. Then he reached for another pack. 'Mmm… maybe another three.'

There was more giggling from the cupboard. The club pro rang up the bill, his eyes watering. There was an in-joke between the two men, but Astrid couldn't work out what it was, and Declan hadn't noticed.

Outside, Astrid wheeled her bag of clubs on a trolley towards a bench. She tried on the white golf shoes. They were like trainers with grippy plastic spikes on the bottom. They smelt of school beef stew and slipped around at the heel until she did the laces up as tightly as possible.

Declan gave her golf bag a thorough inspection. Zipping open pockets and checking for golf balls and little wooden tees. He zipped them all shut again – the full MOT passed.

Astrid put her trainers in a side pocket and brought out her purse.

'How much do I owe you, Declan?'

'No, no… my treat.' He waved her away.

'Okay, then. I'll get the drinks afterwards.'

'Anyway, I'm a member so it's not too much for a guest. Only twenty euros, which is about par for the course.'

This was the first time Astrid had thought about the meaning of the phrase – 'par for the course'. As Declan explained on the way to the first tee, it was the very crux of the sport. It went like this… each hole had a degree of difficulty – a specific number of shots you were supposed to take to get the ball into the cup at the base of the flagstick. The shortest holes were par threes. Medium-length holes, par fours. The longest, and there were only a handful of these, were par fives. They were usually over five hundred yards from the tee box – where you gave the ball the first hit – all the way to the flag.

Declan handed over a scorecard. 'You put in your score for each hole and add them up at the end.' He gave her a tiny green pencil, the type plumbers are supposed to pluck from behind their ears and start chewing on when you ask them how bad a leak is. Your 'handicap', Declan explained, was the number of extra shots over the par for the course, which, in this case, was seventy-two.

'Got it,' said Astrid. 'And I'm guessing there's a lot more jargon and rules to come.'

'Oh yes. Lots of rules,' he said sombrely. 'You've got to have rules or there's no point playing.'

Declan set off down the path, his chest puffed out. They

walked past a terrace in front of the clubhouse. A few golfers were sitting at tables, having a drink. Two men – yellow shirt, blue shirt – about Declan's age, saw him walking past. Yellow Shirt raised his pint and shouted. 'Hey, Declan. You back for more punishment then?'

'Oh, yes, boys.' Declan pulled up at the low wall. 'I have a good feeling about today. I'm going to have the round of my life.'

'That so?' said Blue Shirt. 'What's your handicap at the moment?'

'His clubs!' shouted Yellow Shirt, and they both roared with laughter.

'Now, now, boys. Don't jinx it.' Declan patted the side of his golf bag. 'Today's the day I shoot under ninety.'

'What?' Blue Shirt took a swig. 'If you shoot under ninety, I'll shoot myself.'

They both laughed again. Declan seemed a bit flustered, but still in a good mood. 'Alright, let's put a bet on it then.'

Both the men sat up, rubbing their hands. 'Right. Twenty euros says you don't?' Yellow Shirt looked to Blue Shirt, who nodded vigorously. 'I'm in.'

Declan got out his wallet and checked the contents. 'Make it fifty… each.'

'Fine by us.' They clinked glasses. 'Easiest money we'll ever make.'

'No chance,' scoffed Declan. 'I'll see you in the clubhouse. Make sure you have the money.' He set off down the path again, supremely confident one hundred euros was coming his way.

The sniggering in the pro shop now made sense to Astrid.

Everyone at the club thought Declan was an awful golfer. Were they right, though? He certainly had all the kit. He knew the jargon and all the rules.

The first tee had a view over the whole of the course. Ahead of them, fingers of bright green turf searched between banks of olive trees and crystal-clear lakes. In the distance was the parched Sierra Bermeja. It was an impressive feat of landscaping. A whole valley sculpted and manicured for one sport: golf. And here was Declan, looking out over it all – a king about to go into battle. He reached into his bag and took out a small pair of binoculars. This was a 'rangefinder', he said, which could estimate the distance to the hole. He bent down and plucked some grass between his thumb and forefinger. Held it out and watched it float away in the soft breeze. Now he knew the wind direction as well.

He picked out the biggest club in his bag – the driver – and gave Astrid a quick tutorial on how to swing it. First the grip, then posture – 'straight back, wide stance, weight settled on the arch of your feet'. He placed his golf ball on a wooden tee in the ground and stepped back. In super slow motion, he showed her what the perfect swing should look like. An easy draw away from the ball, the club reaching up over his shoulders. A sideways bump of the knees to start the club's downward motion. Each part of the swing had been studied on YouTube. Practised over and over again until it was, he said, burnt into his 'muscle memory'.

He stepped forward and took a deep breath, levelled the club face behind the back of the ball and played the shot.

Declan may have known every element of the perfect golf swing. In slow motion, he could put them all together in one silky-smooth action. But at speed – it all went horribly wrong. He started badly, the club jerking out too wide. So, he stuck out a knee to get it back on the right line, which only slowed the club down. That meant he had to rush to catch up. An elbow shot out. He raised the club – straight up, like a lightning rod, then brought it hissing down and smashing into the ground a few inches behind the ball. A clump of turf flew up and the ball, caught with a glancing blow across the top, skidded over the ground, trundling to a stop only eighty yards away.

'Oh, for feck's sake!' shouted Declan. Astrid kept quiet. There wasn't much to add. It was a terrible shot. 'First shot – a feckin' worm-burner.' Declan picked up the clod of earth, which was the size of a small hedgehog, and tamped it down with his shoe into the scar in the ground.

'Don't worry, I'm sure the next one will be better,' said Astrid.

'Yes, first-tee nerves. I'll be fine.'

Astrid stepped forward and pushed a wooden tee into the ground. She balanced her ball on top – which was trickier than it looked. Declan was already walking ahead with his trolley. 'Declan?' she called after him.

He came back. 'You're off the ladies' tee, Astrid. It's further up the fairway.'

'Ladies' tee?'

'Yes, the ladies' tee is thirty yards nearer the hole.'

'And why's that then, Declan?' She crossed her arms, rooted to the spot.

'Oh, well… you see. Ladies being not as strong…' he mumbled '…and not being able to…'

Astrid shook her head. 'I don't think so, Declan.' She picked out the driver from her bag.

'Of course, ridiculous rule,' Declan spluttered. 'Away you go, Astrid.'

Astrid remembered she'd been quite good at hockey at school. *It's the same kind of thing, isn't it? Focus on the ball. Hit it. Simple as that.*

Declan's demonstration on how to swing the club – in slow motion, at least – made sense. She stepped forward, drew back the club without much thought, and smacked the ball. It made a satisfying *clink* off the face of the club and soared off down the middle of the fairway, bounding past Declan's ball. 'Not too bad,' she said, striding after it.

Declan gripped his trolley and followed, head down.

Over the next half a dozen holes, Declan's swing rapidly deteriorated. He became more and more stiff and mechanical. Like a robot on the blink. Every club he picked up was worse than the last. Off the tee, the low grass-cutting 'worm-burner' had turned into a raking hook that sent the ball curling wildly to the left. When he did manage to get back on to the fairway, after chipping out of the long grass, his 'irons' – clubs to play mid-range shots – let him down as well. Every time, the ball was magnetically drawn into the trees on the right.

Astrid was beginning to feel sorry for him. He wasn't the king of the course, but the court jester. The butt of a clubhouse joke and about to be one hundred euros poorer by the end of it. To make matters worse, she was playing well, for a beginner. She'd even got a couple of pars, which she was very pleased with. As Declan trudged off down the fairway, she remembered why she was here. She caught him up and brought out the metal fork that she'd found on the nudist beach.

'Declan... I don't suppose you know what this is?'

He stopped short of the green and studied the fork. 'Yes, it's a pitch repairer.' Golf had a lot of gadgets as well as rules. This, Declan explained, was one of the essential ones. It was used to repair the scrapes in the green made when the ball landed. That was it. It might look like a small weapon, but it was just a fiddly tool.

'Is it yours, Declan?'

'Mine?' He seemed amused by the question. 'No, no.' He reached into his back pocket and brought out a similar tool. 'They sell them in the pro shop. Everyone carries one. Why do you ask?'

'I found it on a beach,' she said. 'I didn't know what it was.'

'Rrright,' he said, distracted. But it wasn't because of the pitch repairer. They were on the ninth green, and he had a difficult chip ahead of him, in full view of the clubhouse. Yellow Shirt and Blue Shirt were watching him and laughing. Declan composed himself, then proceeded to fudge the chip, then putt three times. He walked off the green, his head held high – although she could see his heart was breaking.

Astrid totted up the scorecard. He was already fourteen over par and there was half the course to go. He could only drop another three more shots if he was going to have his dream round of golf and shoot under ninety.

'Listen, Declan,' she said as they arrived on the tenth tee box. 'Those two guys at the clubhouse – they're idiots. Why don't I fill in your scorecard with pars. Say you did it.'

'No, no...' He shook his head, shocked at the idea. 'Absolutely not.'

'They don't deserve your money.'

Declan was having none of it. 'But that would be cheating – you can't cheat in golf. It's the worst thing in the world.'

Astrid thought there were a lot of things that were worse than cheating at golf. Electoral fraud. Ice-cream headaches. Diphtheria. But she kept quiet. It was clearly sacrilege to cheat in golf. She decided not to say anything.

Declan lined up his drive. He took a long breath... then swung viciously at the ball, taking the tee clean out from under it and sending it whistling and twisting in the air like a cheap firework. It landed with a thump at the front of the tee box.

'Feck.'

'Don't worry, Declan,' said Astrid. 'I'm sure your game will improve.'

'Thanks for trying to cheer me up,' he muttered, glaring at his ball. 'But I don't think this is going to be my day.'

Astrid set her ball up on the tee. He waited for her to play the shot. It was another good strike, down to the right but nearly one hundred and eighty yards, which seemed to be her maximum distance.

'At least you're playing well today.' Declan stepped forward to take his second shot. He thrashed at the ball with the driver, and worm-burner number twelve fizzed off down the fairway. 'Honestly, I might as well kick the ball. It would go further.'

Over the next couple of holes, Declan's mood hit a new low. Not only had he played awful golf, but he noticed that a few players had been breaking the course rules. Which infuriated him. There were divots – the chunks of turf dug up by golf swings – that hadn't been placed back. There were pitch marks on the greens. At the side of each bunker was a wooden rake that you used to smooth out the sand after you'd played a shot. Some players – Declan shook his head, unable to find words that were harsh enough – had left the rakes in the sand.

By the time they reached the thirteenth tee box, Astrid thought Declan might as well walk to the clubhouse and hand over the one hundred euros. She totted up his score. He was already seventeen over par – one shot under ninety. She told him the score and he nodded blankly. He'd also been counting up his shots and knew there was almost no chance of winning the bet. He sat down on a bench with a gold plaque that said '*RIP Peter – he loved this hole*', put his head in his hands and sighed through his fingers.

Astrid stood next to him. 'Listen, Declan. I'll pay those guys the money. It's fine.'

He brought his hands away from his face. 'No, no… that's very kind. But it's not about the money.'

She sat down next to him.

'I just want to play one good round of golf in my life. Just once in my life.' His shoulders slumped. 'This is the reason I came to Spain – to get better at golf. I thought the weather might help, but it didn't. I bought new clubs, took some lessons, spent hours and hours on the driving range… and I'm still a load of crap.'

Astrid offered her hand. 'Come on.' He took it and she heaved him off the bench. 'Let's get this over with.'

He nodded. Then he stepped forward, and without giving it too much thought, slashed at the ball, striking it with a mighty *thwack*. The ball hurtled through the air. He stared at it as it flew over the ridge in the fairway, a twinkle of hope in his eyes. Then the wind picked up, pushing it out to the left. They watched it peel off into a dense clump of palm trees. 'That's that then,' he said, resigned to the humiliation ahead.

Astrid took her shot, guiltily watching it fly straight as an arrow. She put the driver away and caught him up at the ridge. In front of them were both their balls, slap-bang in the middle of the fairway. Declan went over to his ball to check. 'Yup, that's mine,' he said, smiling for the first time in two hours and twenty-seven minutes. 'It's got my initials on – DF. It must have bounced off one of those palms.' He looked to the trees to their left. 'First bit of luck of the day.'

Declan's next shot was his best so far. Which wasn't saying much. But it was straight, and high, and on a direct line with the flag. 'Come on, be good,' he muttered. The wind picked up again. Declan moaned softly as the ball stalled in the air and fell just short of the green. 'Bugger.' Then the ball bounced up again, twenty feet in the air, and landed about ten feet from the flag.

'What happened there?' said Astrid.

'Must have hit a sprinkler head.'

'Huh?'

'The plastic lids on the water sprinkler system. You get a wild bounce. My second bit of luck today,' he said, breezily.

Declan strolled up and made two putts for a four. He went off to the next tee box with a spring in his step. It was almost impossible to keep it up, but at least he'd managed to get a 'par' on his scorecard.

The next hole was a par three. There was a small lake with a fountain in the middle, which he managed to get across thanks to a puff of breeze that buffeted his ball over to the other side and into a deep bunker. From there he made a stab with a sand wedge. It caught the ball thinly on the side, sending it knifing over the green into a bunker on the other side. 'Damn. A Saddam Hussein.'

'A Saddam Hussein?' said Astrid.

'It's when you go from bunker to bunker.'

Astrid laughed. 'Nice.'

Declan's third shot from the next bunker was almost identical to the first one. Struck on the edge of the blade, the ball zipped across the green towards the water. They both held their breath, and watched it strike the flagstick plum in the middle, jump up in the air, and land in the hole. Another par.

The next couple of holes and it seemed that something was in the air. However bad a shot Declan hit, he somehow got away with it. His drive on the fifteenth – a narrow fairway lined on the left by new-build apartment blocks – always gave him the 'heebie-jeebies', he said, with all those glass windows and patio doors. Yet again, his ball went hard left. All seemed lost. Then they heard a tinny *pinggg*, as the ball hit a mobile phone mast and ricocheted out on to the fairway.

At one point, someone out on the course shouted 'fore!' – this was a warning of a badly hit ball. Someone was having a bad day, and for once it wasn't Declan. No, Declan was having the luckiest round of his life. Between the fifteenth tee box and the seventeenth fairway, he managed to hit all the inanimate objects on the course – bins, sprinkler heads, bunker rakes – and got a fortuitous deflection every time.

'I can't believe it,' he said, the scorecard shaking in his hand. 'I'm still on eighty-nine. I could do this.'

Astrid had decided to pack in her game. She'd had enough – sport shouldn't take over three and a half hours, *should it*? She also wanted to settle Declan's nerves. 'You're doing well,' she told him. 'Now try and keep calm.'

'Yes, yes... stay calm,' he said, walking up and checking his ball. It was sitting up on a fluffy patch of turf, just asking to be struck. They both stared at the green ahead. It was nestled in an alcove of olive trees. There was a bunker either side, with a narrow sloping gap between them up to a lozenge of short grass.

He brought his rangefinder up to his eyes. 'That's strange,' he said softly, passing it over to Astrid. 'There's something in the left bunker. Can you tell what it is?'

Astrid peered through the rangefinder. But she couldn't make it out either. The bunker had a high lip at the front and all she could see was a hump of pink material poking up.

Declan had already decided it wasn't worth much more thought. He quickly took his next shot – a low scud that looked like it was going to make the gap between the bunkers. But at the last second, it skipped to the left and rolled into the sand.

'Don't worry, Declan, you've got this,' said Astrid.

As they approached the green, Astrid noticed a golf trolley parked up in the shade of a tree to the left. Declan made a beeline for the bunker. A few steps short of it, he stopped in his tracks. 'Hey, Astrid!'

She hurried to his side. In front of them, flat on his back in the sand, was an elderly man. He was staring at the sky, a serene expression on his face. Arms out at his side, palms up, as if he was soaking up the sun on a beach. He wasn't moving.

Astrid recognised him. It was the retired lawyer who helped some of the expats with their legal paperwork. She'd seen him on her second visit to Shakespeare's. Astrid turned to Declan. 'It's Elliot, right?'

'That's him.' Declan edged nearer. 'He's one of the senior members here. A real stickler for the rules.'

There were two golf balls near Elliot. One of them was by his shoulder, the other a few inches from his left shoe. A wooden rake was lying in the sand, its handle close to his head. Astrid knelt by the edge of the bunker, avoiding touching the sand. She took his wrist and tried to find a pulse. Nothing. She stood up again. 'Well, we better go back to the clubhouse. They can call the police.'

Declan stepped forward. 'Let me just check.'

'Honestly,' said Astrid. 'There's no need. He's definitely dead.'

Declan ignored her. He strode up to the ball by the dead man's shoe, leant over and studied it. 'Yup, that's mine. There's the initials, DF – Declan Foley.' He hopped out of the bunker and took his sand wedge from his bag.

'Declan?' she gasped.

'What?'

'You're not going to play your shot, are you?'

He avoided her gaze, his eyes on the green, working out the distance to the hole. 'I'm sorry, Astrid. I'm having the round of my life. I can't finish now.'

'You're joking!'

'No. I'm deadly serious.'

'Declan?'

But he was already in the bunker, making a practice swing.

'There's no way you can play that shot without hitting his foot,' said Astrid. 'Then you'd have to explain to the police why you clubbed a dead body with a sand wedge.'

He thought about it, his smile fading as he realised the shot he'd have to take. Astrid was right. He didn't have a clear swing at the ball. 'Hang on.' He brightened. 'You sure he's dead?'

'Definitely.'

'Great.' He gave a mini fist punch. 'Then the body is technically an immovable obstruction. And you know what that means?'

'No idea.'

'An immovable obstruction – in this case, a dead senior member – is something that interferes with a player's swing or stance. I have a rule book in my bag. I can show you if you want?'

'Don't worry, I believe you,' she said, her arms folded.

'What it means is – I'm allowed to drop the ball away from the body. No more than one club's length and no nearer the hole.'

There was no point arguing – Declan had made up his mind. He picked up the ball and dropped it back in the sand a club's length from Elliot's shoe. Then he quickly took a swing. The ball shot up through a puff of sand and landed on the green, rolling to about six inches from the hole. Another par for Declan.

Astrid was still scowling at him.

'I know, I know…' he said sheepishly. 'I just need a par on the last… and it's an easy par three. Then I've done it.'

'Okay, Declan. If you must.'

'Right. I'll be off then.' He grabbed his trolley and hurried forward. Then made a U-turn back to her. 'Oh, would you rake the bunker and leave the rake to the side when you're done, please, Astrid?'

'Really?'

'If you don't mind,' he said, hurrying off to the final tee box. 'It's what Elliot would have wanted.'

She watched him take his shot from the eighteenth tee box.

It was the first really good swing he'd made all day. The ball climbed up into the sky, heading straight for the flag. It kept its line, for once, bouncing five yards short of the green and rolling up over a gentle hip of short grass to within six feet of the hole. Declan marched off – a swagger in his stride – towards the clubhouse and sweet, sweet victory.

Nineteen

Astrid knew exactly what to do. She'd been here before – standing in front of a dead body in Dorset and the Isle of Wight, knowing the clues would quickly evaporate. This was a precious window of time – to record the facts, before they became muddy from opinion and sharing. In a few minutes, Declan would reach the clubhouse and tell them what had happened. The club pro would call the police. Everyone would have to leave the golf course – and that would be that.

Right – check the time: 4.16 p.m.

Next – pictures.

Astrid took out her phone from a side pocket of her golf bag and started taking photos from the edge of the bunker. A few different angles – from the front and the back. For the first time, she noticed there was a golf club lying along Elliot's left side. It was a sand wedge. Elliot must have taken it into the bunker to play his shot. Must have – there were a few footprints in the sand that matched his shoes. The other set of footprints had been made by Declan when he went in to play his shot.

She stepped carefully into the bunker and took some more photos. First, she zoomed in on Elliot's feet. There was a shallow pit at both heels. By each, a handful of sand had been thrown sideways. In her mind, she created a reconstruction of what might have happened. Elliot had stood over his ball, club in hand, ready to take his shot. Then for some reason he'd collapsed, spinning round on his heels and falling backwards. There was a dusting of sand up the side of his pink shirt. It must have puffed up there when he landed flat in the sand. The same effect as a baker slapping down a slab of dough on a floured board. Next was a photo of Elliot's golf ball. It was a Titleist Pro V1, with the initials 'EG' in green ink pen.

She inspected what she could see of Elliot's body above the sand. There were no marks or blood. No indication of violence. She took a quick picture – this bit never felt good. Then she stepped out of the sand and collected the rake that was lying on the grass next to the other bunker. She used it to smooth over her own and Declan's footprints. Not because of golfing etiquette, but because she didn't want the police to know she'd been nosing around.

She gave Elliot's golf bag a thorough search and found a water bottle (half drunk – smelt like water), a bar of cherry flapjack in a clear wrapper, a pair of light waterproof trousers and the usual golfing accessories: tools, brushes, tees, pencils and spare balls – unmarked Titleist Pro V1s. There was a scorecard tucked into a clip on the trolley handle. She pulled it out and checked his score – seventy-five for sixteen holes. Elliot had had an excellent day on the course... well, apart from the dying bit.

She was about to put her phone in her pocket but realised that Declan's rangefinder was there – he'd rushed off before she could give it back. She brought it up to her right eye and turned slowly round. To the right of the green was a high wire fence that ran behind a flank of olive trees. There was nobody on the sixteenth tee box, or the couple of holes behind. Then it was over the lake, and back to the clubhouse. She'd come full circle without seeing any other players. She put the rangefinder in her pocket and set off towards the eighteenth hole. It was surprising that nobody had come out to see her – better check what was going on.

The clubhouse terrace was still busy. A few of the members stood up and watched her drag her trolley up the path. They seemed excited – ready to greet her. The news must be out, she thought. When she was ten yards away, Yellow Shirt and Blue Shirt pushed their seats back from their table. It was cluttered with empty pint glasses. They got up unsteadily and weaved down to the low wall.

'We heard,' said Yellow Shirt mournfully. 'Is it true?'

'I'm afraid so,' said Astrid.

Blue Shirt took his visor off and waved it in front of his face. 'Unbelievable. I mean—'

'Just unbelievable.' Yellow Shirt finished his sentence. He shook his head in utter disbelief. 'We never thought it would happen.'

'Uh, sorry…?' said Astrid, now confused.

'Declan… He shot under ninety.'

Twenty

Astrid woke up the next day with an annoying twinge in her right shoulder. It was worse at certain angles. Turning too quickly or lifting the kettle sent a sharp pain firing between her shoulder blades. It must be the golf, she thought. There were so many moving parts in a golf swing, and many of those parts of her hadn't moved that way before.

She knelt down on the Persian rug and did a couple of exercises she remembered from her yoga class back in London. An 'upward facing dog' pose – which involved lying on her stomach and pushing her arms straight to create an arched back. Then a 'downward dog', which was sort of the opposite – bum high in the air, head between her arms. She couldn't imagine The Beef performing these two. It seemed to work. Sitting up on deck with her coffee, she found that the pain had almost gone.

She went over the events of yesterday. It had been, by any standards, an unusual introduction to the sport. The game itself, with Declan defying the odds to get a personal best, had been something. But then finding a body in a bunker, on the same day... She thought about Declan's reaction. He'd been so blasé about the death. So keen to carry on with his game. She didn't understand the grip golf could have on you, sure. But shouldn't he have been more shocked that Elliot was dead? Obviously, she was with him for the previous three hours, so he had that as an alibi. But was there some bad blood between the men?

After talking to Yellow Shirt and Blue Shirt, she'd gone into the members' bar and found Declan doing a victory lap. He was waving his one hundred euros in the air and giving a blow-by-blow account of his round to anyone who asked. And a few who didn't. Ten minutes later, two officers with *Policia Municipal* written across the back of their gilets arrived. The pro drove them down to the seventeenth green in an electric golf buggy. Declan stayed at the bar and bought a big round of drinks with his winnings. That's when Astrid decided to bail out. She left her details with Declan and told him to pass them on to the police, if they needed to contact her – which, as yet, they hadn't.

It was hard to see how Elliot dying in the bunker linked up with the trolling case. The only connective tissue was the golf repair tool Fenwick had found on the beach. It *could have* been dropped by the troll when they were spying on Nelson's wife. They *may have* got it from the El Paradiso golf course. It was, thinking about it, a thin strand of gristle – not strong enough to pull everything together.

She got her phone and powered it up. There was something she'd forgotten to do – read that damning restaurant review of Shakespeare's Bar and Grill.

She took a while to find it – Roger must have got it taken down from the main review sites. She'd heard that bad things never completely disappear on social media – they hang around in eddies, swirling round for ever, like that whirlpool of plastic and rubbish in the Pacific Ocean. Sure enough, thanks to numerous retweets, she found the review on Twitter, as fresh as the day it was typed.

The review didn't hold its punches.

The menu at Shakespeare's is less a list of food options and more a series of life-threatening dares. Anyone eating there might consider leaving some of their food to one side, in case doctors need it to create an antidote.

So far, so awful. Astrid read on.

I visited Shakespeare's on a quiet Tuesday evening and opted for the three-course deal with a glass of wine. The waiter, Roger, who, as it turned out, was married to the chef, pointed me in the direction of the seafood starters – or 'catch of the day'. But which day? I had a plate of whitebait that did not appear to be fresh off any boat. 'Long time no sea!' as I jokingly remarked to the couple on the next table.

I dutifully ploughed through the generous pyramid of whitebait, which smelt like a bucket of damp cats and had a tangy afterburn that refused to budge even by sucking hard on the wedge of lemon that accompanied this dish.

The quality of the main course, according to the reviewer, didn't improve. They opted for the Coronation Chicken Paella, described on the menu as a 'fusion' of Spanish and British cuisine. A dish so horrid, the reviewer said it *could set British/Spanish relations back to the Franco years.* The only positive comment was aimed at the service – *brisk and cheerful*, it said, with Roger singled out for praise for sticking with a restaurant that was clearly doomed... *as a loyal Roman waiter from Pompeii might have done, dishing up a final meal as the lava licks his sandals.* This led smoothly into a description of the raspberry meringue as having *all the flavour and consistency of a lump of volcanic rock.*

The reviewer did accept that Shakespeare's was under new management and may have had some *teething problems.* But it wasn't enough of an excuse to hold back with the payoff.

> *It may be worth going to Shakespeare's out of sheer morbid curiosity, or just to say you got there before United Nations weapons inspectors swooped in to collect evidence.*

It was one of the harshest restaurant reviews Astrid had ever read. Exaggerated for effect, no doubt, but still hurtful. She could see how the Cherrys, or Terry, might be upset. Enough to take revenge and expose Nelson's wife's affair? Even if they weren't sure he was behind it? That was impossible to know.

There was still no sign of Nelson. He was obviously still trying to patch up his marriage. Or, as Bridget had suggested, sitting back on a sun lounger and laughing at them all. There hadn't been anything else from @*TheAllSeeingEye7*, whoever they were. She checked. The 'You're next Wonderful' message was the last thing they'd posted.

She sat back and took in the view. The still, white villas dotting the hillside. The boats nodding in the marina. It was the definition of a sleepy Mediterranean town. That didn't mean it wasn't a hotbed of scandal... *maybe murder?*

Twenty-one

The Second Chance Animal Rescue Centre was signposted at the bottom of a dry ravine behind a flank of apartments. A dirt-track road circled round to the east. Instead, Astrid took a sparse path that ran directly uphill. It was hard going. She was glad she hadn't brought the bike.

After twenty minutes, the path had almost run out. She lifted her bag and edged through a thin section hemmed in by thorny bushes. Not many people took this route, she thought. It might only be used by goats. There were cloven footprints in the dust. She pressed on and clambered out and rejoined the dirt-track road.

Looking back over the edge, she realised how steep the path had been. Below her was the town, the marina and the open sea. To the west, only a few hundred yards at the other side of the valley, was Bridget and Sebastian's farmhouse, the El Paridiso golf course in the distance.

Astrid carried on towards the sanctuary, which was just ahead. In the first field, a donkey was lying in the shade of a tree. It raised its head, flicked its ears at a small cloud of flies, then slumped back into the dust. After that was a big pen made from metal poles and chicken wire. There were around two dozen dogs in there. All shapes and sizes – the largest was a lurcher of some sort. The smallest, a brown terrier with patchy white fur. As she passed, they bundled down to the wire and started yelping for her attention.

Wonderful must have heard the barking because she appeared at the door of the main building before Astrid reached it. She was wearing a shapeless boiler suit and dusty work boots. 'Hey, Astrid.' She leant against the door frame and looked her up and down. 'You took the path – I'm impressed.'

Astrid picked a couple of thorns from her shorts. 'There's no stopping me,' she said.

Wonderful seemed pleased to see her. After the troll's tweet, thought Astrid, she might just be happy to see any friendly face. They both knew that that was why she was there. 'I've got to feed the dogs. You mind tagging along?'

'Sure, you do what you have to,' Astrid said.

Wonderful went over to an outhouse that wasn't in a much better state than the main building. Both were made from grey breezeblock, with shutters that didn't quite fit. She emerged with a sack of dried dog biscuits, which she carried over to the dog pen. Astrid got ahead and opened the door for her. Wonderful tipped the biscuits into the first of a line of steel bowls. The dogs chowed down, snapping and jostling for more room.

'You ever have pets?' asked Wonderful.

'I had a dog for a short time recently. And when I was a kid, there was a family cat. I called it Chairman Meow.'

'Good name.'

Wonderful finished pouring out the biscuits and stepped back out of the pen, shutting the door behind her. 'Dogs… they ask so little, don't they? But they give so much back.'

Astrid surveyed the knot of dogs. None of them would get into Crufts. They were all a bit thin. Some had pinkish knees or tattered ears. But they were lively, with bright eyes. 'Where do they all come from, Wonderful?'

'They're nearly all strays. People find them on the street, or in the hills. We get a lot of *galgos* – they're hunting dogs. They get lost, or abandoned at the end of the hunting season.'

'These ones?' Astrid pointed to a couple of wiry lurchers. Their ribs heaved through their coats as they wolfed down the food.

'That's them. Lovely dogs.' Wonderful folded up the sack. One meal, and it was empty. It must cost a fortune to feed them, Astrid thought. She wasn't wrong. Without prompting, Wonderful gave her a breakdown of her expenses. Food, water, electricity, vet bills – they were the biggest outlay. The dogs came to her with everything from tick fever to broken legs. In total, it cost over thirty thousand euros a year to run the sanctuary. Which was hard to find. 'We rely entirely on donations,' she said. 'And there's never enough money to go round.'

They headed to the field. On the way, Astrid noticed a tin mailbox on a pole by the road. It was probably there to save the postal driver a walk up to the door. There was a small padlock attached to the flap.

Wonderful found a bale of hay by the fence. She snapped the twine holding it in shape and broke it up into a feed box on the other side. The donkey hauled itself to its feet and lumbered over. 'That's what worries me about this troll. I do some fund-raising in the market. But it's mostly online. I don't need anyone giving the sanctuary a bad name.'

'That's what a lot of people are telling me. They don't need the bad publicity.'

What was this bad publicity? thought Astrid. Wonderful's less-than-wonderful secret? She watched her stroke the donkey's forehead and her eyes filled with pity. It was hard to believe she could do anything bad.

'There you go,' said Wonderful, patting the donkey's flank, then turning back to the main building.

Astrid walked alongside her. 'Wonderful... have you noticed anyone behaving strangely recently?'

Wonderful hesitated. Then shook her head. 'No, I haven't.'

'Anyone hanging around the sanctuary?'

She shook her head. 'Nope – nobody comes up here.'

'You sure?'

Wonderful shook her head again, then went inside. Astrid found another bale of hay next to the wall and sat down. The sanctuary wasn't in much better condition than Bridget and Sebastian's farmhouse below them. Every bit of paint was peeling. Every frame and beam was dry and twisted. The money was clearly all spent on the animals.

'You want one?' Wonderful was at the door, holding out a can of cola.

Astrid brought out her water bottle and told her she was fine. They sat in silence for a while, watching the heat shimmer over the valley. Then Astrid went through the rest of her checklist of questions as Wonderful emptied her can in steady sips. Like all the other expats she'd spoken to, Wonderful claimed she didn't know who the troll was, or why she was being targeted. 'Wonderful... I can't sort this out if you don't tell me the truth.'

'Truth?' She raised an eyebrow. 'What do you mean?'

Astrid pointed to the mailbox on the pole. 'The lock on your mailbox.'

'I don't understand.'

'If nobody comes up here, why do you need to lock it?'

Wonderful bowed her head. 'Well spotted, Astrid.'

'So, someone stole your mail?'

'Yeah, a couple of days ago.'

'What did they take?'

'A letter.'

'How do you know it was a letter?'

Wonderful crushed the empty can in her hand. 'They left the envelope. I guess to let me know they had it.'

'Something incriminating?'

'Yeah. From the envelope, I know exactly what it is.' Wonderful got up and tossed the can into the bin. 'I'd rather not tell you. If that's okay?'

'Sure.'

Wonderful stood with her back against the wall and stared at the dog pen. 'It's too late, isn't it? The troll's going to expose me.'

'Not if I get to them first.'

Wonderful shook her head. 'Really? Come on, Astrid... you have to admit it,' she said firmly. 'You're no closer, are you?'

Astrid got up. She was about to bluster something about her closing in on the troll. That the death of Elliot was a big breakthrough. But she couldn't talk about Elliot, not until his family had been informed. And she wasn't even sure his death had anything to do with the trolling campaign. Only Pearl and Terry had been ruled out as suspects. That was all she had, and it wasn't enough to save Wonderful. 'Okay, I admit it. But I promise you – I will catch them.'

'I know you will… just not in time to save me.'

Astrid found her purse and gave Wonderful a couple of ten-euro notes for the sanctuary.

Wonderful thanked her for the money and stuck the notes into a top pocket on her boiler suit.

'Whatever it is,' said Astrid, 'I'm sure nobody will think any the worse of you.'

Wonderful smiled weakly. 'I hope that's true.'

Twenty-two

Astrid had been expecting to find a note from the local police tucked under the cabin door. They hadn't called her. So, she'd assumed they were going to come round and speak to her in person. There was nothing. She refilled her water bottle. They'd be in touch soon enough.

Half an hour later – a quick detour into town to buy some flowers (yellow roses), and a clammy taxi ride, even with the windows fully down – she arrived at her father's house for lunch. There was no sign of Jennifer's car. The Triumph was there, gleaming in the sunshine.

Astrid remembered another of his cars from her childhood. It was a maroon Volvo estate, the car before he bought the classic Jag. That would place her at around nine years old. On Sunday afternoons he'd take the whole family out for a mini road trip. There was a generation of men who did that – they'd clean and polish the car in the morning, then go out for a drive straight after lunch, not knowing where they would end up. In this memory, thanks to some poor map-reading on her mother's part, it was a town to the west of London called Staines.

She sat in the back seat, gazing out of the window as they took one wrong turn after another. Off the motorway straight into a disused industrial park. Then into a warren of concrete tower blocks. She thought it was exciting. Her mother thought it was appalling. At a junction, she told everybody to push down the locks. She pointed at a queue at a bus stop. 'They're all wearing tracksuits,' she said. 'It's like we've wandered into an Olympic village.'

Admittedly, there were a lot of people wearing tracksuits. 'What I don't understand,' her mother continued, 'is why sports clothing is worn by people who are unlikely to do any sport?' She shook her head as a woman in a green velour tracksuit, can of beer in hand, trundled across a zebra crossing. 'You see?' said her mother.

The nine-year-old Astrid remembered saying that people could do what they wanted, and it wasn't anyone else's business. But nobody else in the car joined in. This wasn't a joining-in kind of conversation. It was her mother pointing out the clear lines between the people outside the car and the people inside the car, who belonged to some other class. What exactly that class was, was never expressed, then or since. She remembered once, at a Christmas party at their house, overhearing a male relative describe her mother as 'nouveau riche'. Her mother, who was just in earshot, leant in and said, 'Better late than never, Alan.' Then she drifted off for a refill of eggnog from the drinks table. That was the only time she heard her mother talk about money, and what it meant to her.

Her father eventually found a way out of the town. Her mother watched the *Welcome to Staines* sign recede in her side mirror, popped up the locks again and relaxed in her seat. 'Peter, we need to get a corner bath,' she said, for no apparent reason, entirely unaware that in a few short years, the house would be sold, and everything in it.

Astrid snapped back to the present. She gripped the flowers and headed round the side of the house to the garden. Nobody there either. The patio doors were open, so she stepped into the living room. Shouted 'Hullo?' a couple of times. But nobody came.

It was a nice room. Tastefully furnished, with a big dark wooden table in the middle of a stone tile floor. Arranged around the walls were: a brown leather Chesterfield sofa; a matching armchair that had seen a lot of use; a side table; a carved oak sideboard; and a standard lamp with an ivory linen shade. Hanging on the walls were around a dozen oil paintings. They were mostly coastal scenes and still lifes – jugs of flowers, bowls of fruit. It was a decent collection. Nothing sensational though.

In the corner, Astrid spotted something that looked like a tiny Bedouin tent. There were gold tassels hanging along the edge. The doors were tied back by tiny ropes of the same material. Two tiny eyes stared out. Jennifer's dog got up and tiptoed out on to the tiles, baring its needly teeth.

'Hullo, Furball.'

The dog yapped at her. Then it went back into the tent and lay down, its head on its paws. It didn't take its eyes off her as she climbed the stairs up to the first floor. Well, she thought. She might as well have a snoop around while she had the chance.

The first room off the landing was a bathroom. It had a white marble floor with Spanish blue and white tiles on the walls, and a copper showerhead and taps. *Very classy.* She trod quietly along the line of bright Moroccan rugs on the landing. Halfway along, it became a bridge overlooking the living room. She leant over the rail and saw Furball staring up from her tent.

She decided not to go into either of the two large bedrooms, which were next. Just peer in from the doorway. It felt icky enough creeping around upstairs. That meant there was only one room left to investigate – her father's trading room at the end of the landing. There was a key sticking out of the lock. She turned it and pushed the door open.

It was exactly what she'd expect for her father's bolthole. It was cluttered with patriotic memorabilia. On the wall were framed regimental flags, diagrams of tanks, and sets of coins and stamps. There was a painting of Queen Elizabeth II in a powder-blue suit, arms folded across her handbag. The rest of the space was taken up by bookshelves and a modern desk on which were two large computer screens. This must be her father's trading desk. There was nothing on it except a pen pot with a pack of unused biros stuffed into it. The screens were off. She pushed the swivel chair out of the way and looked more closely. They were covered with a very thin layer of dust. She ran her finger gently across the surface. It came back grey. These computers – her breath jammed in her throat – hadn't been used for a long time. If at all.

Getting down on her knees, she moved under the desk. At the back was a handful of cables winding down from the computers. She followed them to the wall socket, which was tucked away in the corner, too far to reach. They were unplugged. Astrid reversed out. It made no sense – other than her father had lied to her. He'd said he was up here every day to do his trading. That's what he'd told her. Twice. *Why would you say that, Dad?*

From the front of the house, she heard the sound of the big metal gate swinging out. The yapping started downstairs. They were back. Astrid quickly put the swivel chair exactly where she'd found it, making sure the castors settled into the indentations in the carpet. She hurried to the door and padded back across the landing, the floorboards creaking under her step.

She could hear the car parking up in the gravel, the engine grumbling to a halt. There was a crunch as the big metal gates were swung back into place. They weren't automatic. So that meant Jennifer had got out to open and shut them. And, right now, she'd be making her way down the side of the house.

She gingerly took the stairs.

Jennifer's heels were clacking on the flagstones down the side passage.

Lulu was glaring at Astrid from the bottom of the stairs. 'Yeah, yeah…' Astrid muttered. The dog wheeled in tight circles, letting out sharp, high barks. Calling out to Jennifer.

When Astrid was halfway down the stairs, Jennifer called out from the patio – 'Lulu? What is it?'

The dog shuttled back and forth in front of the bottom step, trying to trap Astrid. But she brushed past, ran across the living room, and slumped onto the sofa, grabbing a magazine from the side table. A split second later and Jennifer strode in.

Astrid peered over the magazine. 'I let myself in,' she said calmly. 'Hope you don't mind.'

'Of course not.' Jennifer put a shopping bag on the table. Then she turned to Lulu, who was still barking, her head swivelling from Astrid to the stairs, then back to Jennifer.

'Dogs, eh?' she said, bundling Lulu up in her arms. 'If only they could talk.'

Good job they can't, thought Astrid. Right now, Lulu would be blabbing away how she'd found her skulking around in her father's office. No, dogs couldn't talk. And that's why, she thought, none of them get to read the news on the radio, police dogs don't give evidence in court, and she was sitting down, a big fat secret in the palm of her hand. 'I know,' she said. 'What stories they'd tell.'

They'd gone to get fresh bread. That's why they were late. The rest of the lunch had been prepared earlier by Jennifer. Astrid gave her the yellow roses. Jennifer 'loved them' and found a vase for them in the sideboard. Then Astrid helped her bring the food from the kitchen as her father went upstairs.

There were a dozen plates covered in tinfoil, which they arranged on the patio table. There were plates of hams and cheeses. Bowls of olives, couscous, roasted peppers and salads. A jug of iced water. Two bottles of wine, one red, one white. Jennifer cut the bread into thick slices and poured some olive oil and balsamic vinegar into a shallow terracotta dish. It was a colourful spread. Jennifer had made an effort – just to thank Astrid for investigating the trolling campaign. Little did she know, Astrid was also about to investigate her own father.

Jennifer chatted about the dog and the weather. Astrid nodded along, one eye on the patio doors. 'Sounds like you're still busy... wine? No, thank you... I'll have water.' Jennifer topped up her glass. *Best to stay sharp.*

Eventually, her father appeared from the living room and took a seat at the head of the table. 'Sorry to keep you waiting. There were a couple of trades I had to make before switching off for an hour. I'll get back to it after lunch.'

'So, Dad,' Astrid said, scrutinising his face. 'Tell me a bit about the day trading. How does it all work?'

'Honestly?' he said, reaching out and picking a few things on to his plate. 'It's too tedious. I'll spare you the details.'

'No, I'm interested,' Astrid persisted.

'Why?'

'Because, with my divorce, I have a bit of spare cash. If you have any hot stock-market tips, I'd love to know.'

He swirled a slice of bread in the olive oil and chewed the crust. 'I better not, Astrid – in case it didn't work out.'

'I'd forgive you.' She couldn't catch his eye.

'But could I forgive myself?' He prodded a piece of ham on his fork and smacked his lips. 'Serrano ham... my favourite.'

Jennifer fussed around with the dishes. 'Yes, it's probably best left to the experts, Astrid.'

Does she know? It was possible that Jennifer had no idea her father hadn't even switched on the computer screens.

Astrid turned to Jennifer. 'Has he shown you how it all works?'

'No, no.' She looked under the table. 'Are you under there, Lulu?' she said, changing the subject. 'There you are.' Lulu peered up – still fuming that she hadn't trapped Astrid. 'Are you sure you don't want wine, Astrid?'

'No, I'm fine.' She covered the top of her glass with her hand. 'The trading – you've never seen him in action then?'

'Mmm? No, no, he locks the door and nobody is allowed in.'

There was the smallest lightning strike of panic in Astrid's chest. *He locks the door.* She quickly rewound the memory on the landing. The key in the lock. Her shutting the door of his office. Yes, she'd walked away without locking the door. *Had he noticed?*

'You know what I was thinking about today?' he said cheerily. 'Attempted murder.'

Astrid bit down on an olive. 'What?'

'Yes, I was listening to the radio in the car and there was an item in the news.' There were a few seconds of eye-rolling from Jennifer. 'And this report said,' he continued, 'that some criminal has been given four years in jail for *attempted* murder.' He turned up his palms, looking between the two of them.

'Sorry, dear,' Jennifer said hesitantly.

'Four years,' he stressed. 'The chap had tried to kill someone and he was only given four years because he *hadn't* succeeded.' He prodded at another slice of ham. 'My point is, he should have got twenty years for the murder bit and an extra six, seven maybe, for making a hash of it. Otherwise, you're just rewarding incompetence.' And in went the ham, his eyes tipping back to the ceiling.

He hadn't changed, thought Astrid. For as long as she could remember, he'd sat at the head of the table, complaining about a general decline in standards. The dying art of etiquette and manners… that things, in his eyes, were getting worse and worse. Still, this was nice. Like the best of the old times. *This* was why she'd come all this way.

Her father's anecdote about the radio report had shut down any discussion on the day trading. It was hard to tell if that was deliberate. But there were going to be no answers about that today.

The conversation moved on to the painting Astrid was repairing. She told him she'd started, and it shouldn't take too long. He seemed delighted and again offered to pay. As she brushed the offer away, Jennifer asked how the trolling case was going. Then she quickly decided she didn't want an answer. 'No, let's not. It's too distressing and we're having a lovely lunch.' They could discuss it at Shakespeare's later

– she'd organised a Caribbean night, which Astrid 'definitely had to pop down to'.

Astrid agreed. 'A Caribbean night? That sounds unmissable.'

'It is,' said Jennifer. 'It's only fifteen euros and there's a "bottomless rum punch".' She turned to Astrid's father and said firmly. 'You're going, aren't you, Peter?'

He gave a thumbs-up. 'As long as I don't have to dress up, I'll be there.'

Jennifer then talked affectionately about some of the customers at the salon – she was heading back there in about an hour to see a couple more 'clients'. Which, to Astrid, sounded a bit grandiose. *Clients?* She was cutting people's hair, not running a top law firm. But she kept it to herself. They were all getting on so well.

Her father found a couple of other things to gripe about – how modern washing machines only last for years not decades, and how hard it was to find a good shaving brush these days. Astrid smiled along, enjoying the food and rhythm of the chatter. He was relaxed, she thought. She could relax too. The chances were, he'd not noticed the unlocked office door. Or he did, and assumed he'd forgotten to lock it.

Jennifer started to clear away the plates – which was Astrid's cue to get up and leave. It had been a lovely lunch. A very revealing one, too. She hugged them both and set off down the hill.

Twenty-three

Astrid was halfway down the hill when a text pinged on her phone – it was from Jennifer. She thought maybe she'd left something at the house – but then she read it.

Did you see the tweet about Wonderful? Not sure what it means.

Astrid tucked into the shade of a palm and brought up @*TheAllSeeingEye7*. The troll had posted a couple of photos – pictures of a document. Was this the letter that Wonderful said had been stolen? *Must be.* It was a legal demand of some sort – the phrase *comparecencia ante el tribunal* came up a couple of times. And the word *hurto*, which she thought had something to do with stealing. The message from the troll cleared that up.

You're a thief Wonderful!!!

But what had Wonderful stolen? Eduardo's bar wasn't too far away. Maybe he could translate for her.

Eduardo was sitting on a high wicker stool behind the bar, reading a Spanish newspaper. He was the only person there.

'*Hola!*' Astrid settled into a chair opposite him. 'How's things, Eduardo?'

'Good, very good…' he said, folding up the newspaper and gazing round the empty bar. There was nobody there, or in the garden. '*Cerveza?*'

'Sure.'

He picked up a square beer mat from under the bar and slapped it down in front of her. 'I bring you Cruzcampo. It's the best beer for thirst.'

He was right. The beer, served in a frosted goblet, was the most thirst-quenching beer she'd ever had. She drank it down in three long draughts and held the empty glass to the side of her neck, absorbing the last of its coldness.

Eduardo picked up another goblet from the ice tray under the counter. Without asking, he poured a second beer from the silver pump. 'Another, yes?'

She gave a little thumbs-up, although it was too late to refuse. Then she held up the photo on her phone. 'Eduardo – would you take a look at a document for me? My Spanish isn't up to scratch.'

'Sure, sure…' he said, swapping the beer for the phone.

Eduardo speed-read it, then gave her a summary. It was a court summons. It appeared that Wonderful had been caught shoplifting from a supermarket in town earlier in the summer. It was serious enough to go up in front of a judge. The document laid out the dates, times and Wonderful's rights under Spanish law. He passed the phone back. 'Wonderful is your friend, yes?'

Astrid nodded. 'Is she in big trouble?'

He shrugged. 'I dunno. It doesn't say what she stole. But if it's a judge, then it's not good.'

Eduardo wiped his hands and went back to the kitchen. Astrid brought her jotter out from her bag and opened it on the hit list. She took out a pen and wrote 'Shakespeare's expats' at the top. Then she read it again.

- *Jennifer – stepmother and owner of Classy Costa Cuts. Says she has no secrets or enemies.*
- *Bridget and Sebastian – she's a successful lifestyle blogger. He's renovating the farmhouse. Say they have no secrets or enemies.*
- *Terry – owner of Shakespeare's. 'A good landlord', according to Pearl.*
- *Zhang – owner of BOBS, Best of British Supermarket. Delivers to Shakespeare's.*
- *Roger and Charlotte Cherry – he's a teacher-turned-waiter at Shakespeare's. She's the chef. Roger doesn't like Pearl (the feeling is mutual).*
- *Morgana – jewellery stall owner. Ended her marriage over an affair with a local fisherman who then drowned. Says she has no idea who's behind the trolling.*
- *Wonderful – runs the Second Chance Animal Rescue Centre.*
- *Declan – moved to Spain to improve his golf. Member of the El Paradiso Golf Club.*
- *Talia – Nelson's wife. Spends her time between the UK and Spain. Had an affair behind Nelson's back.*

Astrid scored out three names on the hit list – the expats who'd had their secrets exposed. That was Wonderful, Zhang and Talia, though it wasn't clear if revealing Talia's affair was aimed at hurting Nelson. She read over the page again – three down, six to go. The hit list was getting smaller by the day. Wonderful was right. Astrid couldn't save her in time. And if she was right about bad publicity and fundraising, she couldn't save Wonderful's beloved sanctuary either. It felt like she'd failed. Not only that – there was still the mystery of the body in the bunker to solve. Plus, find out whatever her father got up to when he was supposed to be day trading.

Eduardo came over with a small plate of fat green olives, which he put down next to Astrid's jotter. 'Shakespeare's?' he read from the jotter.

She closed the jotter. 'You know it?'

'Sure. Your expats go there. I don't know why.'

He pushed the small plate towards her. She'd just had lunch, but these looked too good to miss. She teased a cocktail stick from a bundle on the edge of the plate, stabbed at a fat olive and put it in her mouth. 'I'm not sure why they go there either… wow.' The flavours exploded on her tongue. Lemon zest, a crackle of rock salt, syrupy olive oil. 'These are really delicious… sorry, yeah – Shakespeare's. Maybe it reminds them of home.'

'Maybe, yes?' He shrugged. 'But if there was so much they liked about home, why did they come here?'

She took another olive. 'It's a good point, Eduardo.' Today, she imagined, the expats would shuttle between the British hairdressers, shops and golf courses, with little in between that would remind them they were in Spain. Then they'd go to Shakespeare's Bar and Grill for a Caribbean-themed evening.

Eduardo pulled up a bar stool at the other side of the bar and helped himself to an olive. 'Don't get me wrong. Spain has welcomed the British, everyone in Europe, for many decades. You are our guests, and we are very glad you're here. Every one of you. But I wonder…' He shook his head, bailing out of the rest of the sentence. 'No, it's good.'

'Come on, Eduardo. What were you going to say?'

He chewed the olive down. 'Okay. Maybe some of your friends happier if they saw more of Spain.'

'You could be right.'

'I think so.' He smiled faintly, looking around the bar. 'And maybe they would like this bar too. No?'

'I'm sure they would.'

The door swung open and a boy and a girl, each pushing a mountain bike, came in. The girl was taller than the boy by a good couple of inches, only a bit shorter than her father, who was average height. The fresh air was doing them good. Eduardo hurried round the bar and hugged them both. Then he checked his watch and scalded them. '*Que hora es?*' He shooed them out to the terrace, telling them to put the bikes away and do their chores and how he loved them – from the few words of Spanish she could translate. They laughed and ignored him. Propping their bikes against the far fence, they unloaded a plastic carrier bag of old golf balls at their feet. Then they began examining each one, placing them in different piles. Eduardo went over to the back of the bar and picked up two packets of crisps.

'Take care, Eduardo,' Astrid said, getting up from her seat.

'You too,' he said, taking the crisps over to his kids.

Twenty-four

Astrid went for a swim to lose the last of the pain in her shoulder and burn off the couple of mid-afternoon beers. It worked a treat. When she got back to the boat, she was feeling fresh again. Declan was waiting for her. He was standing at the rail, reading the name on the side of the boat. She went over to him. 'You okay?'

'The *Curlew's Rest*? You don't get a lot of curlews down here.'

'Maybe you do? I've got a book of birds in the cabin. I can check, if you're interested.'

'No, you're alright,' he said, climbing aboard and plumping down in the nearest seat. 'I'm in a bit of a hurry. I've got a tee time in forty minutes. Just wanted to give you an update on yesterday.'

'Oh, now I'm interested.' She pulled up a chair next to him and sat down. 'What's the news?'

He was wearing his golfing gear – a new polo shirt with the logo of the El Paradiso Golf Club on the chest. 'Well, after my triumph yesterday, there's rumours in the clubhouse that I might be made club secretary next year.'

'Declan, I meant news about Elliot Green...'

'Mmm?'

'Who we found dead in the bunker. Remember?'

'Oh right, that.' Declan sat up. 'Elliot Green. Lovely fella. He was seventy-eight, they reckon. Not a bad innings... although that's cricket, isn't it?'

At least, thought Astrid, Declan was being a bit more sympathetic about Elliot than when they found him.

He carried on. 'I just hope they don't buy a memorial bench for him. There's too many of them on the course as it is.'

'Declan... what did the police—'

'Far too many memorial benches on the course. It's all a bit depressing. And why golf? You don't see crown green bowlers having to roll their bowls around a bunch of headstones. No, sir.'

'Declan.' She leant forwards. 'The police?'

'Sorry.' Declan sat up and began to tell Astrid what had happened after she'd left the golf club. The two police officers had stayed at the seventeenth green and ordered the pro to go back and close the course for the rest of the day. Half an hour later, a few more vans and police cars arrived. Some had their lights flashing. Declan wasn't sure who these people were – one might have been a doctor – but they all trooped off to the seventeenth green. An hour after that, Elliot was wheeled off to a van, and everyone slowly left.

Declan rolled his shoulders, limbering up for the round ahead. Then he continued the story. The club pro, who'd been liaising with the police, had rushed into the members' bar. He said that the course would be open tomorrow as normal, and a cheer had gone up. The annual club competition had been arranged in the morning, and nobody wanted to miss it. The police, according to the pro, were pretty sure what had happened. Elliot had collapsed in the bunker from heat exhaustion and struck his head on the bunker rake.

'Struck his head on the bunker rake?'

'That's what they said.' Declan rummaged in his pockets, checking he had enough golf tees and a small pencil. 'When they turned him over, they found a wound on the back of his head.'

'They don't want to speak to me then?' said Astrid.

'Nope.'

Astrid was a bit crestfallen. She was more than prepared to speak to the police. Maybe show them the photos on her phone. At least make a statement. 'They're honestly not going to investigate this? It could be a murder.'

'Murder?' Declan looked shocked. 'Are you serious?'

'I don't see why not,' Astrid blustered. 'The wound on the back of his head – someone could have hit him with that rake. The police shouldn't rule it out straight away.'

'Thing is, Astrid. The police said they'd seen this kind of thing before. You know, people retiring to Spain and… let's say, overdoing it. A generation ago, when you retired, they gave you a carriage clock and subscription to the *Radio Times*. Now they give you a mountain bike, or a paddle board. You're asking for trouble.'

'But dying on a golf course? In a bunker? How often does that happen?'

'Statistically, I guess… maybe more than you think. But then, I'm not an expert.' He slapped his knees and got up.

'One more minute.' She got up. 'I think the regulars at Shakespeare's knew Elliot. He sorted out their legal documents. Do you think we should tell them?'

'Probably best to wait until it's officially announced. You know – when it's on the news.'

'Good idea – if it doesn't get out there sooner.'

He checked his other pocket, bringing out a pitch repairer. Now he was all set for his game. That's all she had as evidence, she thought, as he hurried off the boat: a pitch repairer, found on the beach where the troll filmed Nelson's wife, that led to the El Paradiso golf course, where a dead man in a bunker was an unremarkable statistic. Not murder. According to Declan. He wasn't an expert on accident statistics, though. *Was he?*

Neither was she – but she knew someone who was.

Fenwick was sitting on a bench in the shade of one of the sailcloth awnings, his back to a raised bed of stumpy palms. There was no sign of his metal detector. As he explained, the events on the nudist beach had put him off metal detecting for a while. 'I'm having flashbacks,' he said, blinking hard. 'Even in the middle of the day.'

Astrid's phone beeped in her bag. She fished it out, apologising to Fenwick. 'Sorry. Terrible habit.' There was a new message from the troll. A new victim. Declan, the troll said, was 'going to be next.' The troll had moved up a gear. An expat's secret had been revealed, and another threatened within a few hours. She dropped her phone back into her bag.

A few yards down the boardwalk, a man was setting up a metal frame. There were two tripods, about hip height, and a wire that ran between them. A chalkboard was propped up on the walkway – it said *Papagayo Show* next to a chalk sketch of a little parrot. A small crowd was gathering, waiting for the show to start.

Astrid decided to see what would happen if she didn't say anything else to Fenwick. Would he talk to her? He sat there, leaning forward, watching the shadows of the people on the promenade. Not saying a word. That was her answer, then – he didn't feel any pressure to keep up a conversation. Didn't care much for small talk or know the rules of it. It was refreshing.

She broke the silence and asked him if he knew the chances of dying on a golf course. She didn't say why she wanted to know. Just that she was interested in how you measure the risk.

'Yes, yes, Astrid. That's what I was saying, it's all about risk.' He bounced upright on the bench. 'To measure it, you need to apply some complex statistical and mathematical formulas. It's quite hard to explain.' He kept going, though, barely pausing for breath. He said it was all about putting in as much data as possible on one side of the equation – with the risk appearing on the other side.

'Okay, so let me give you a hypothetical example,' said Astrid. 'Just for fun.'

Fenwick beamed. This was going to be his kind of fun.

'Right… so let's say we have a man in his late seventies. It's a hot day – very hot, thirty degrees. He's near the end of his round, so he's been exercising for around three hours.'

'What's his general health?'

'Not sure.'

'Which we'd need to know,' Fenwick tutted. 'If I was calculating a life insurance policy, I'd want to see a medical. But I'm not – I'm sitting on a bench trying to tell you how common this kind of thing is. To do that, we could start by comparing the risk of death in golf compared to other sports.

Oh, look... how lovely,' said Fenwick, swivelling on the bench to face the show.

The man had pulled back a cloth that had been draped over a wire cage. Inside was a small green parrot. He reached in, brought it out on his finger and carried it over to a perch by one of the tripods. A few other people joined at the back of the crowd.

'Is golf a dangerous sport then?'

'Dangerous?' Fenwick turned round to her again. 'There are worse.'

'Like base jumping?'

'That's at the very top of the table. Not a surprise, though. If you jump off a cliff attached to a tent, things are more likely to go wrong.'

'Where is golf on this risk table?'

'If I remember correctly, it's sixth, with an annual rate of injury of one point eight per hundred-thousand persons a year. Which actually makes it more dangerous than rugby or snow sports.'

This surprised Astrid. But then Fenwick explained there were reasons for it. The golf swing was quite a violent movement and could lead to muscle and back injuries. There were crashes with golf carts. People drank too much on the course. 'In your example, had this man been drinking?' said Fenwick.

Astrid rewound to when she'd searched Elliot's golf bag. There was only a half-drunk bottle of water in there. 'Let's say he wasn't.'

He continued the list of bad things that could happen on a golf course. It included breaking clubs, being hit by a golf ball, lightning strikes and falling into lakes. It was quite a list.

But it wasn't, said Fenwick, enough of a reason *not* to play the game. 'As I said, there's a risk in everything we do, Astrid. In fact, did you know that around two people in the United States are killed by vending machines every year?'

'Really?'

'Yes, sometimes an item they've bought jams on the edge of the shelf. They pull the machine towards them to shake it down and arrrgh...' Fenwick mimed something falling on him, his arms flailing like a trapped beetle.

It was the first time Astrid had seen Fenwick talk quickly and easily – insurance was a subject that clearly relaxed him. The only subject, maybe. Now he became distracted again; his eyes had trailed over to the parrot show. The man slipped the parrot on the end of the tightrope. The bird rocked up and down then slowly shuffled along the wire. Some of the kids at the front of the crowd were clapping.

Astrid brought Fenwick back on track. There was one last detail to add: the bunker rake. Declan had said the police believed the man had died because he'd hit his head on the wooden handle. 'Okay, just for a bit more fun. I'm going to add another detail to the example.'

'Go on then.' Fenwick rubbed his hands together.

'Let's say our imaginary golfer collapsed in a bunker and struck his head on a wooden rake.'

'How many rakes were on the course?'

'No idea.'

Fenwick shrugged. 'It's probably the same for most courses, so appears in the general risk for the sport.' He fidgeted on the bench, then turned back to the show.

Astrid knew she should wrap this up. 'Okay, so finally... if you were working in life insurance and someone put in a claim for a death on a golf course. With all the details I've given you – would you think it was suspicious?'

Fenwick put his hands up as if they were scales. Dropping his right one down, the left one up, he went over the risk factors – a hot climate, the man's age and the whole list of risks specific to golf. When he finished, his right hand was at waist height. His left, by his ear. 'In my expert opinion, I'd say what happened to our golfer isn't extraordinary. It's sad, but it's not suspicious.'

Astrid sat back. The door of the Elliot Green case had just closed – before she could get her foot in there and investigate further. It might be for the best, she thought. There was more than enough to keep her mind busy.

They both watched a bit more of the show. The man had brought out a small silver metal bicycle and lined it up on the wire. It had a weight on a stick underneath, to keep the bike stable. The bird edged over and gripped the tiny handlebars with its beak. Its little pink legs whirred round and the bicycle trundled forward. There was some 'oohing' and 'aahing' from the crowd, then a big round of applause as the parrot reached the safety of the far tripod.

Astrid stared at the performance. 'The thing I don't get about that, Fenwick… parrots can fly, right?'

'Yes, they can, Astrid.'

'So, if the bike falls off the wire, that bird isn't going to plunge to its doom. It's just going to sort of… well, sort of hover in the air.'

'I guess it would.'

'In which case, where's the dramatic tension?'

Fenwick smiled. 'You're right, Astrid – where's the risk?'

Twenty-five

'So...' Jennifer held her arms out in front of her, like a preacher inviting the audience to get to their feet. 'What do you think?'

Astrid took in the scene in front of her, trying to find the right word. 'It's um...' The Jamaican theme had the upper hand. There were strings of small yellow, green and black flags of Jamaica across the entrance. Steel drums in the corner. The sound of reggae drifted from a small speaker high on the wall. But the decor had also taken inspiration from a number of other distant cultures. There were a couple of tiki lamps by the wall – Polynesia, if she remembered correctly – and the dress code seemed to be Hawaiian shirts for the men, raffia skirts for the women, with floral garlands for both. 'It's extraordinary.'

'Thank you.' Jennifer's face was rapt with pride.

'You've really made an effort, Jennifer. Well done.'

'I'm glad you like it. We usually have a "curry night" on a Monday. But we thought we'd do something a bit different. Let our hair down, and forget all about this ghastly trolling business.' She reached down to a foldout table, picked up a garland from a pile and placed it over Astrid's head. '*Aloha.*'

'Lovely,' said Astrid, twirling the fabric flowers in her fingers.

'I came up with the ideas and decorations. Roger and Charlotte have really pushed the boat out with the food. He's even having a go at the barbecue himself.' She wove her fingers into Astrid's hand and steered her over to the far wall. There was a barbecue, made from what appeared to be half an oil drum. Roger was flipping some burgers and chicken legs on a grill, his face underlit by the glowing coals. He was wearing a hat with corks dangling from strings around the brim. Charlotte was behind a table next to him. In front of her was a stack of buns and a collection of relishes and salad items to construct the burgers.

Roger pinched a blackened burger with his prongs and held it up. 'Burger,' he said, intonation rising, as if it was a question, and he was asking for identification.

'Yes, please,' gushed Astrid. 'With everything on. It looks great.'

'Thanks,' he said, whistling along to the chorus of Bob Marley's 'No Woman, No Cry', which was rattling from the speaker. Roger was in a good mood. And she knew why. 'So, there's no sign of Pearl then?'

'Nope.' Roger pressed the other side of the burger on the grill, which sizzled and spat. 'She's busy.'

'Where is she?' said Astrid.

'She's finishing building the Death Star.' He laughed at his own joke. 'No, she'll probably be at church Mass.' He passed the burger down to Charlotte, who started heaping on clumps of salad and a whole pineapple ring.

'I think there's a reason she's so bitter,' said Charlotte. 'There must be.'

'Probably,' Roger replied. 'But it doesn't mean she has to be rude to everyone else. Does it, dear?'

'I guess so,' said Charlotte.

Jennifer jumped in with her order. It was the same burger as Astrid's, with all the trimmings. They shuffled down the line as Roger began putting out a series of small flames that leapt up from the coals, hitting them with his prongs like a fairground whack-a-mole game.

Most of the expats were milling around a tin bathtub on a table. It was filled with ice cubes and cans of drink. Morgana was talking to Declan. Bridget and Sebastian were talking to Astrid's father, who was wearing a Hawaiian shirt. He'd obviously given in to the dressing-up rule.

Jennifer led Astrid over to the tin bath and explained the drinks options. There was a choice of a can of Red Stripe lager or Lilt. The latter had been bought from Zhang's, said Jennifer. All the expats were keen to keep up their support for BOBS, despite what he'd done. 'We have to stick together, don't we?' said Jennifer, picking up a half coconut shell from the table.

'Yes, it's tough for you expats at the moment, isn't it?' Astrid sympathised. She realised this would be a good time to announce that another of their group, Elliot Green, wouldn't be making it along tonight. But they seemed to be in such a good mood, and she didn't want to spoil that.

Jennifer picked out a ladle from a big bowl of punch and filled up the half coconut. She added a straw and a tiny umbrella and passed it over to Astrid. Then she served herself and clinked coconuts. 'Cheers.'

They both went over to the other groups, which merged to greet them. There was a lot of praise for Jennifer, who absorbed it bashfully. 'Thank you – I can't take all the credit. The Cherrys got here early too. Oh...' She pointed to a bamboo cane that was laid across two tables. '...and if anyone is feeling up for it, we can try the limbo later.' There were a few takers. Not Jennifer, though. 'I might not risk it – my back is a bit stiff.' She sighed. 'I'm not getting any younger, you know.'

'Nobody is getting younger,' said Astrid's father. 'That's how time works.' There was a ripple of laughter, Jennifer the loudest.

'Very witty, darling.' She squeezed his hand. It was the kind of act of affection between them that would, before Astrid came here, have set off an involuntary spasm of nausea. Now, it was just sweet. Her father had done up the top button of his Hawaiian shirt as an act of mild protest. He'd no doubt prefer to be at his house in a leather chair, reading some art catalogue or other. But he was here – for Jennifer. Admiring her as she held court, carefully deflecting the conversation away from the trolling campaign to the usual expat topics – property prices, the best beaches up and down the coast, and what was a fair price for a removal van from the UK.

However hard Jennifer tried, the trolling campaign kept circling back – much like The Beef, who all this time had been making a steady trundle round the barbecue area and tables.

'What a shame about Wonderful,' said Bridget. 'I was thinking—'

'I forgot to say,' Jennifer interrupted. 'Has anyone seen that lovely new shop that's opened on the Avenida de España?'

But it was no good. There was no distracting them.

'Does anyone know what she stole?' said Morgana, sipping hard on her straw.

There were blank faces. Then speculation. 'I'm betting it was booze,' said Declan.

'Does she have a drink problem?' said Sebastian.

Terry arrived and plucked out a Red Stripe. 'Only drink problem I have is you lot not buying enough.' That earned a big laugh from the others. 'So, what do we think this troll wants then?' he said.

'Sorry, Terry,' said Jennifer. 'We're trying to have a night off from the troll. That's why I asked everyone to switch off their phones.'

'Yeah, yeah... I'm just interested.' So were the others. Jennifer's pleas to change the subject were drowned out.

'I think it's pure mischief,' said Morgana. 'They're toying with us.'

'No, no – it's probably revenge,' said Sebastian. 'One of us might have done something bad to them.'

'One of *us*?' gasped Jennifer. 'That can't be true.'

Roger wandered over from the barbecue. He'd caught the last comment and slotted smoothly into the conversation. 'One may smile, and smile, and be a villain,' he said theatrically.

Everyone stared at him. Except Astrid and her father. 'Very good.' He gave Roger a round of applause. '*Hamlet*.'

There were a few more blank stares.

'It's a quote from Shakespeare,' said Astrid's father.

Morgana looked up at the Shakespeare's Bar and Grill sign over the door of the main bar. 'How appropriate,' she said, wistfully. 'Someone here could be smiling away right now, but secretly plotting to ruin us.'

There was a silence between them, filled only by Bob Marley, who'd moved on to a live version of 'Jamming', which was doing nothing to lift the mood.

Declan stepped towards the ice bath. 'Come on, let's have a drink and forget it. It will all blow over. You'll see.' He handed out a couple of cans of beer. Grabbed one himself.

Astrid watched him. He was remarkably relaxed – for someone who was next on the troll's hit list. 'I've got to say, Declan.' Astrid sipped from her coconut. 'You're very calm about this. Are you not worried about what they're going to reveal?'

Declan cranked off the ring-pull. *Fussst*. He made a similar noise, dismissing the idea. 'No way. I don't know how they can harm me.' He started ladling out the punch to whoever wanted it. 'I'm going to be club secretary at the El Paradiso. Nobody can take that away. And I have an Irish passport, so I'm technically a European citizen. They can't throw me out if they tried.' He took a long drag from his can. 'I'm bulletproof.'

'You see,' – Sebastian crossed his arms – 'that's what I never understood about Brexit. The special arrangement with Ireland.'

Declan was just about to explain, but Terry clapped his hands. 'Listen, you lot,' he barked. 'Let me just remind you, one more time.' The others stepped out of his way as he marched over to the door. He pointed at the handwritten sign. 'These are the house rules. Right here.' He jabbed at the first line. 'No. Discussing. Brexit.' He looked to each of them for a moment, his face reddening.

Sebastian mumbled, 'Sorry, Terry, we were just—'

'Listen,' Terry cut him off. 'Cos I'm not saying this again. I own this place. If you don't like the rules, you know what you can do?'

There was an awkward silence. The expats sipped their

drinks, shuffling on the spot. Then Terry seemed to snap out of wherever his mind had taken him. He smiled – easily, it seemed. 'Sorry about that.' He waved his hands as if swatting a fly in front of him. 'I'm a bit stressed out.'

'We all are,' Jennifer said. 'And it's what the troll wants. But they're not going to win, right?' She looked at each of them in turn, until they'd nodded in agreement. Then she held out her drink into the middle of the circle and they all reached out and clinked their drinks together – the coconuts and the cans – and it sounded like a small horse running over a cattle grid.

'Cheers!' she said, and they all repeated it.

Astrid wasn't sure if the expats were going to win. The troll had the upper hand, and it was gripped on their necks. They didn't have any idea who they were, or why they were doing it. Or if anyone would be spared. She peeled off towards the main bar. Once inside, she veered off into the games room. She took out her phone and loaded up Twitter. There was a new post from @TheAllSeeingEye7. An emoji face blowing a kiss. Then, below it, a video.

It started with a blurred view of a line of trees. You could just make out a golf course beyond them. The picture jerked into focus, then swung round to find a man in golfing gear. It was Declan. He had his golf bag over his shoulder and was searching the ground at his feet. The focus moved in tighter. Declan checked back at the trees then quickly reached into his golf bag and brought out a new ball. He dropped it at his feet and walked away. After a few yards, he turned back and stopped at the ball he'd just dropped. 'Got it!' he shouted towards the trees. Then he brought out a club from his bag, made a couple of practice swings, and hit the ball high over the trees and back on to the fairway. Club in bag. Head down – off to play the rest of the round.

When Astrid had played golf with Declan, he'd been a stickler for the rules. She remembered what he'd said: '*You've got to have rules or there's no point playing.*' She guessed that pretending to find your ball was breaking a big rule. The troll had replied to their own video, and confirmed it.

They're not going to like that at the clubhouse, Declan!

Laughing emoji.

The troll had also added the Twitter address of the El Paradiso golf club – so they'd definitely notice.

This was going to hurt him. Playing the wrong ball might not seem a big deal – but up at the clubhouse, they weren't going to see it that way. Declan would be back to being a laughing stock. He wasn't going to be club secretary, that's for sure. She turned off the phone and went back to join the others.

The party had warmed up. Jennifer's rousing speech. The fruit punch – which Astrid suspected was just sangria with added rum – it was hard to know what had made the difference. But the expats were having fun. Sebastian, Bridget, Terry and the Cherrys were dancing. Morgana was spinning around, her grass skirt rising up to knee height. Jennifer was bending under the limbo bar. Stiff as a deckchair. Laughing uncontrollably. Declan was bashing out a tinny tune on the steel drums. Poor old Declan. They were going to hear that a lot in the next few days. Not now, though. He was enjoying himself. They all were. He'd find out soon enough.

Astrid went over to her father. He took her hand, and they danced.

Twenty-six

Long walks, a trip to an art gallery, a sail round the bay. These were the sort of things she'd come to Spain to do with her father. Spying on him was definitely not on the list. But here she was. Ten in the morning – tucked in behind some rocks, high above his back garden, the rangefinder poised for any sign of movement. Then again, she hadn't come to Spain to go to a Caribbean night at a British-themed bar, where some people were dressed in Hawaiian shirts. The previous evening had yet to sink in. It had all been so odd. A handful of cultures thrown into a blender.

It had been a memorable night, though. Especially for Declan. *And what a humiliation.* The troll had found him cheating at golf – just once, Declan said after seeing the message at the end of the night. But the troll had used it to take away everything he'd dreamt of. There was no way they'd make him club secretary now. They might ban him from any more competitions.

She checked her watch. Five past ten – nearly two hours up here and still no sign of Jennifer or her father. She scanned the hillside. The paths connected everything – the El Paradiso Golf Club, Eduardo's bar, Wonderful's animal sanctuary,

Bridget and Sebastian's farmstead. The troll knew these tracks. They'd been spying up here too.

Astrid took out her phone. She'd promised to check out Bridget's blog sometime, but not got round to it. It might help pass the time.

On the opening page were the words 'Walking on Orange Blossom' in a swirly font wound through a cloudless blue sky. Under that, in the same font but smaller, was 'Sunkissed stories from the Costa del Sol – how a regular family from England followed their dream of a new life in Southern Spain'.

Then there was the rest of the photo beneath the sky. Bridget and Sebastian were holding hands on a deserted beach and gambolling towards the camera. All smiles and swooshy hair. The kind of photo that's already in a new picture frame when you buy it. Miller was just out of shot. Her father was holding her hand and you could make out the arm of her black hoodie.

Astrid scrolled down the page. There was a list of past blogs, each with a tasteful photo. 'Thirst-quenching recipes from the orchard', 'El Olivo – the tree of Spanish life!', 'A roof over our heads!'

It was all very professional. Astrid opened a blog from earlier in the year, titled 'Meeting the locals', and began to read.

It didn't take long to meet our new neighbours. No sooner had we taken the winding path up through the orchard than a very old lady in a black dress came rushing out of her simple stone house. I have no idea how old she was. Maybe she didn't either? '*Por favor, tome,*' she said. It means 'please take' in English. In her hands were a bunch of fat ripe plums. *'Comer! Comer!'* (Eat! Eat!), she cried. Then she pushed the plums in her mouth and chewed, her eyes smiling, a trickle of dark purple juice running out from a gap in her lower teeth, which she wiped away with the sleeve of her simple black dress. Pretty soon we were joined by her husband, who was riding an ancient donkey.

There was some lively description of the rustic meal that was then prepared before their eyes. It involved the husband making an open fire on the rocks by a crystal-clear stream. A black iron skillet was brought out from the house along with a slab of fatty ham, which the husband cut up into cubes and fried over the fire. *Hunks of pan-fried ham, caramelised to perfection*, opined Bridget. *Who needs a five-star restaurant?!* Question mark *and* exclamation mark? It was all washed down with a dark, viscous wine that was jetted directly into their mouths from a goatskin bag. At the end of the meal, the old Spanish couple washed up the skillet in the stream then wandered back into their house, waving from the door.

The end of the article was rounded off with the question: *Do we have any regrets? Yes – just one. That we didn't move to Spain sooner!!*

Astrid had enjoyed reading the blog. It was warm and fruity, if a little smug. Still, she could imagine that anyone back home on a wet, drizzly day in England would love it. And many people apparently did, by Bridget's numerous references to her 'thousands of subscribers'.

Astrid turned off the phone and tossed it into her bag. There was still no sign of Jennifer and her father, and the whole morning to fill. She rummaged in the bag and brought out the *Field Guide to Spanish Birds* – she was right, there was a copy on the boat. That might kill a bit of time.

She flicked through the pages, stopping now and then to aim the rangefinder at anything that moved in the brush below her. Within ten minutes, she'd seen three starlings, a goldfinch, a wagtail and a… *ooh, that's exotic*. The bird had a peachy chest and a comb in the same colour, with black dots on the end. Back to the book. It must be a… *hoop… hang on, there's Dad*.

She dropped the bird book and used both hands to steady the rangefinder. Her father had come out to the garden and placed his cup of coffee on the table. Jennifer appeared soon after. It didn't look like she was staying. She pulled her handbag high on to her shoulder and they exchanged a few words. From his body language – weary, thumbing back towards the house – she guessed he was telling her he'd be back in his office soon. He glugged down his coffee and she leant over and pecked him on the check. Then she turned for the side alley.

He waited for her to get out of sight, then paced slowly to the corner, checking that she was definitely leaving. After about thirty seconds, Astrid saw Jennifer's car pass between a gap in the houses. Her father had heard it leave too. He scuttled back into the house with the coffee mug, then soon reappeared and sauntered down the side alley and out on to the road.

Astrid threw all her stuff into her bag and rushed down the path towards him. When her father reached the entrance to Bridget and Sebastian's plot, he peeled off down the short cut into town. Astrid broke into a slow jog, taking a steeper way down the hill. Trying to close the gap.

The short cut ran alongside a high white wall. There

must be holiday apartments on the other side. She could hear the sound of splashing and laughter behind the wall. The path began to shelve out as it reached the town. Astrid slowed – she had her father in her sights. Now it was about holding back far enough not to be seen. But not too far that she'd lose him in the maze of narrow streets. When he reached a turn, she ducked into the nearest doorway, in case he looked back. He wasn't moving that fast, but there was something purposeful in his stride. As if he didn't want to be late.

In the heart of the old town, he turned into a pretty, open square. The sign said Plaza de las Flores. In the middle of the square was a stone fountain shaped like a goblet. The water overflowed into a round pool bordered by bright red geraniums. It was like the hub of a wheel, with paths radiating out to other hedges and gardens. Astrid hung back and watched her father take a seat at a café behind a low hedge.

She sunk down on a bench in the far corner, her eyes still trained on her father. A waiter came over and took his order. A minute later, a glass of red wine was placed in front of him, which he sipped between checking his watch and straightening his shirt. *Why so nervous, Dad?*

A woman approached from the other side of the fountain and headed straight to his table. She was wearing a white silk shirt and dark blue trousers. Her hair was silver-grey, cut to shoulder length. Astrid placed her in her mid to late fifties. Her father didn't get up. He just turned his head and blinked in the sunshine as she stood over him and said a few words. They knew each other, but it was frosty. Again, she could tell from their body language. The woman's arms clamped by her side. His folded across his chest. If this was an affair, it was over. They'd reached the bitter dregs.

The woman sat down in the chair next to him. A flock of pigeons swooped low over the roofs of the buildings and settled on the edge of the fountain, obscuring Astrid's view. She shuffled to the edge of the bench for a better angle. All she could see was her father's back. The woman was side-on and doing most of the talking. Then the woman took out a piece of paper from her pocket and unfolded it on the table. She pushed it over to him. Her father glanced at it and shrugged. A few more words were exchanged. He brought out his wallet, tucked a note under the plate, got up, and nonchalantly walked away across the square without saying anything more. The woman stayed at the table and watched him walk away, a sour expression on her face. There was something deeply personal going on here. Had to be.

Astrid realised there was more to her memory of her mother announcing her father was leaving. When she'd left her mother's bedroom and gone downstairs, she noticed how tidy the house was. Tidier than usual. The carpets were vacuumed. There were flowers in a vase on the table. Biscuits on a plate – the best ones, orange chocolate – she remembered it clearly, as she was supposed to. Her mother's idea, no doubt. The backdrop had been perfectly staged. The clean carpets. The flowers. The biscuits. Her mother knew that Astrid and Clare would always remember this moment. That they had come from a good home, before it was broken. Astrid's father and Clare arrived half an hour later. He'd collected her in the car from some after-school club. He talked about his day at the gallery. Asked her about school. It was as if everything was normal. Then he went upstairs to get his suitcase. No blame for the split was handed out that day. Or since. Exactly why they'd divorced remained a mystery, like his falling-out with his brother. There must have been a reason. Her mother and father seemed to get on okay – then, after a 'tense' three months, as her mother said, it was over. An affair on his part – that might account for the suddenness of it all. Was she watching the end of another affair? Played out in a sunny square in Spain, this time.

Astrid stared at the ground between her feet. Trying to leave that kitchen all those years ago. She got up from the bench and almost bumped into the woman.

'Sorry, I mean…' Astrid stammered. '*Lo siento.*'

The woman forced a smile. 'It's okay,' she said in a Spanish accent. She stepped to one side to get past, but Astrid blocked her way.

'Would you mind?' Astrid brought out her phone from her bag.

'Of course.'

Astrid pretended to have trouble finding the camera setting on her phone so she could get a good look at the woman. There was no softness to her. She had sharp eyebrows, with hard shadows around her eyes. Picasso would have painted her and found even more angles. 'Goddesses or doormats' – that's what Picasso had called women. Was this her father's goddess?

'Are you ready?' said the woman.

'Um… yes, sorry.' Astrid passed over the phone. 'If you could get the square behind, that would be great. And you need to press it firmly.' Astrid crabbed out into the middle of the path and struck a pose.

The woman aimed the phone and took the picture. Then she handed the phone back.

'Thank you,' said Astrid, very carefully putting the phone into her bag.

Astrid waited until the woman had left the gardens and turned the corner up the hill. Then she hurried after her. There was no harm, she realised, in following the woman as well. Soon, Astrid was just the right distance behind her – sidestepping into doorways and keeping to the shadows.

The woman took a flight of stairs up towards the church. Astrid waited until she'd climbed some way ahead of her and set off again. Halfway up the stairs, Astrid noticed an elderly woman who was gripping the handrail and dragging herself up a step at a time. In her other hand was a thin blue plastic bag, which bulged with shopping. As Astrid got closer, she heard the elderly woman release a volley of swear words – in English. It was Pearl.

'Aargh…' Astrid groaned under her breath. She couldn't leave anyone to struggle up the hill with their shopping, even Pearl. She watched as the woman took the last few steps and disappeared from view. Then she turned 180 degrees and headed back down. 'Hi, Pearl – do you need a hand?' she said, as cheerfully as she could muster.

'Oh, it's you,' she grunted. 'Yeah, you can take the bag. I'm sweating like a glassblower's arse here.'

Astrid took the bag. It was heavy, and peeping into it, she could see it was filled with big yellow potatoes and tins of tomato soup.

Pearl pulled out a handkerchief from the sleeve of her summer dress and pressed it against her brow. 'Why do they always stick churches on the top of hills?'

Astrid knew this one. The church would usually come first, built on a high point where everyone could see it, and where it was best defended. Then the town would expand around it. But she didn't say that, because Pearl wasn't really asking for an answer. She was, as usual, complaining.

'They should have put my shopping in two bags.' She rubbed the fingers of her left hand, which had yellowed lines where the plastic bag had dug in. 'Right, chop chop – let's get going.' She set off again and Astrid followed alongside her.

'Are you off to church again, Pearl?'

Pearl squinted at her. 'Yup – I go as often as I can. Have done for the past six months.' As they took the next flight of stairs, Pearl told Astrid how she'd ended up in Estepona. For many years she'd visited the Costa del Sol for holidays with her late husband, Mitch. Then one winter in Britain they watched a TV show called *A Home in the Sunshine*. Astrid had seen it. Couples were flown to foreign countries to look at properties to buy. At the end of the show, they could put in an offer for their favourite. Although this rarely happened.

Astrid had always wondered if the couples on the show had any intention of buying a place, or were just there to get a free holiday, all expenses paid. Pearl confirmed it. Once she and Mitch had heard there were free flights, they signed up for a Costa del Sol edition. Unfortunately, Mitch – 'the daft sod,' breathed Pearl – ended up offering just under the asking price for a two-bed apartment in a new-build block near the promenade. 'She was very persuasive,' said Pearl. 'The TV presenter... all tropical tan and overhanging bosom, and Mitch got carried away. He was showing off.'

To Mitch's surprise, the offer was accepted. And to avoid ruining the happy ending to series 19 – an episode called

'Mitch and Pearl search for paradise in Estepona' – they went ahead with it. They sold up the bed and breakfast in Blackpool and moved out to Spain. Which was the best thing they'd ever done. Pearl didn't miss the grinding routine of the B&B. Getting up at 6 a.m. to put out twenty different breakfast cereals and tinned grapefruit that nobody ate. Scrubbing red-wine stains out of duvet covers. No, it had been, she said, 'a brilliant decision'. For a while, at least.

Pearl stopped with one flight to go. Then she explained that Mitch had suddenly died. She worked the handkerchief around her eyes. A woman dressed all in black overtook them and headed towards the church. Pearl set off again, carrying on with her story.

With Mitch gone, she thought about moving back to the UK. But she was enjoying living in Spain. The weather, the food, most people spoke English... it was the usual expat checklists. Plus, she still got to see her family. Her only daughter, Kelly-Anne, now in her late thirties with two kids, came out to stay every summer holiday. There was a pull-out sofa for Kelly-Anne in the living room and inflatable camp beds on the balcony for the 'little uns', as Pearl called them, even though they were almost teenagers. They reached the top of the stairs. The church loomed over them.

'So, when did you become interested in Catholicism?' Astrid rowed back on their conversation.

'Oh, yeah, that.' Pearl wandered into the shade of a tree. 'I just want some answers really.'

'What kind of answers?'

'For starters, I'd like to know if God exists.'

'I guess that would be a good place to start.' Astrid put the bag down between them.

'Then I'd want to know why Mitch isn't here.'

'Sorry, I don't—'

'You see, we'd worked hard all our lives, serving other people. Now it was our turn in the sun. Our golden years out here in Spain. It was perfect and,' – she snapped her fingers – 'he was taken away. I'm here on my own now. If there is a God, they've got a lot of explaining to do.'

It took a moment for Astrid to process what Pearl was saying. She wanted to find out if there was a God, but only because she wanted to give them a rollicking for taking Mitch away from her. Knowing Pearl, if God existed, they weren't going to win this one. All Astrid could do was nod sympathetically.

'I come down here every day,' said Pearl. 'I'm trying to get through to him… her, whatever. Just one sign that they exist… that's all I'm asking. And then they're getting an earful.'

'You're looking for a sign, then?'

'Exactly.' She shook out her fingers, getting ready to pick up the bag again. 'A sign – that's all I want.' She craned her head up to the ornate cross over the doorway. 'I know he's busy. But we all are, to be honest. Just a sign… is it too much to ask?'

'A miracle?'

She picked up the bag. 'Yeah – all I want is a miracle.'

Twenty-seven

In the cabin, Astrid gently held the phone by its edges and laid it down, face up, on the cloth, away from the painting. Then she rooted around in her work case and found the six things she needed.

A soft puffy brush

A square of clear acetate – about the size of a small postcard

A small wide-mouthed jar of titanium dioxide power

A pen torch

Scissors

A roll of clear sticky tape

When she'd bumped into the woman in the square, the plan had come to her in a flash. She didn't want a photo of herself against the fountain. She wanted to get a clear fingerprint from the woman. She wasn't sure what use it would be. *You needed access to some criminal database to get a name. Didn't you?* There was little chance of that. Still, it was a skill worth practising.

In all her work as an art conservator, Astrid had never lifted a fingerprint from a painting. It had been in her training though. Artists' fingerprints occasionally turn up on paintings or frames. Van Gogh had a habit of accidentally adding his fingerprints to his work. In 1889, he was admitted to an asylum in Saint-Rémy-de-Provence. He painted a lot there, including a series on the surrounding groves of olive trees. On one of these paintings is his fingerprint. It's just above a pulsing mustard-coloured sun – right in the middle, which suggests that Van Gogh lifted the painting off the easel when the paint was still wet. Balancing it in one hand, he would have walked back to the asylum, to put it with his others. Unsold and unappreciated.

Degas made a series of monochrome paintings on metal plates – wiping the black ink from the surface with his hands. The fingerprints he left behind are used to authenticate the rest of his work. The same for Leonardo da Vinci, who left careless thumb marks on his drawings. A fingerprint, the right one, can make art collectors faint with happiness.

She went round the cabin and drew the curtains across all the portholes. At the table, she unscrewed the lid of the powder. In went the brush – gently, only using the tips of the fibres. The pen torch was held at a forty-five-degree angle over the surface of the phone until she could locate the woman's fingerprint. There it was – a distinctive horseshoe pattern, swirling tightly in the middle. She carefully traced the flow of the contours with the brush, circling into the centre until the ridges had all picked up some powder.

Next, she pulled out a four-inch length of sticky tape and snipped it off with the scissors. She smoothed the tape over the fingerprint with the side of her thumb, making sure there were no air pockets. Then she peeled it back and applied it in exactly the same way to the acetate card. When she unpeeled it for the second time, the woman's fingerprint was etched clearly on the card. She ran the torch beam over it, pleased with the result. It was sharp and clear. It still didn't get her any closer to working out who this woman was. Or what she had whispered in her father's ear. That's what she really wanted to know. All this time, she'd been wondering what Jennifer's big secret was – and her father had one too.

Astrid opened all the curtains and began packing the equipment away, placing the acetate card with the print in the top tray. Astrid's stomach turned – the horns of a dilemma were digging in. If her father was having an affair, didn't Jennifer deserve to know? Would she have wanted to be told about Simon's affair? The idea caught her off-guard – because this was the first time she'd given much thought to her ex-husband since she'd arrived in Estepona. And this was exactly the sort of place he'd love. He'd book them a late-season break to 'recharge his batteries'. Then he'd spend his time exploring the backstreets, lingering at reflective surfaces, ordering her food and chuntering on about his career, or how he'd buy a place here if it wasn't for the 'red tape', or some achingly pretentious film he wanted to see, and just anything to avoid admitting he was having an affair and their marriage was toast.

She ran the water from the tap over her palms, then rubbed it into the back of her neck. It was stifling hot in the cabin. 'Damn right,' she whispered. She would have wanted someone to tell her that Simon was cheating on her. But would Jennifer want to hear that her father was having an affair? That was impossible to know… unless she asked her.

Twenty-eight

When Astrid arrived at the salon, Jennifer was helping a customer out of the door – steadying her by the elbow as she stepped out on to the pavement. Astrid watched the woman check her reflection in the nearest shop window, and wink at herself. Another satisfied customer.

Jennifer waved Astrid in, closed the door behind her and turned over the 'Closed' card. 'I'll make us some coffee – black coffee. That's what we need right now,' she said, heading into the back room.

Astrid wandered over to the 'magic eye' poster by the coat stand. It was a blurry picture that magically turned into a clear image if you stared at it in the right way. She stopped a couple of feet from it, then focused beyond the picture. Squinted. Pinched the top of her nose and tried again. And again, until she felt a prickly headache coming on. Nothing swam into focus.

'It's Neptune riding a white horse through the waves.' Jennifer was at her side with a glass cup of black coffee in each hand. 'Apparently… I mean, I can't do it myself.'

'Me too, never have.'

'Something else we have in common,' she said. 'Right, let's grab a seat.' They went over to the leather sofa by the window and sat down. Jennifer put the coffees on the low table in front of them. 'It's awful, isn't it? That's four of us now.'

'I know. Nelson's wife, Zhang, Wonderful and now Declan.'

'Poor guy. I think his name will be mud at that golf course of his.' Jennifer sipped her coffee. 'And I spoke to Wonderful on the phone this morning. She's so upset by it. She can't bear to see anyone right now.'

'Do you know what it was she'd stolen?'

'Dog food, apparently.' Jennifer neatened up the magazines. 'A few sacks of dog biscuits from the supermarket in town. She loaded up her trolley and wheeled it out of the exit without paying. They caught her in the car park. She admitted it all on her website this morning and apologised.'

'She must have been desperate.'

'I know.' Jennifer linked her hands and squeezed them together. 'It does feel like the troll is tightening their grip, doesn't it?'

Astrid agreed. Two people from the list exposed in one day – something had stirred them up.

'The thing is – am I next, Astrid? That's all I can think of.'

Astrid put her hand on Jennifer's shoulder. 'Try and relax. I'm going to do my best to find them before that happens.'

Jennifer mouthed 'Thank you' and took a long swig of coffee.

Astrid took out her jotter and a pen from her bag. 'Okay, let's narrow down the suspects.' She turned the page to the hit list and crossed out Declan and Wonderful. Obviously, they'd never expose their own secrets. They were far too embarrassing. Astrid asked Jennifer for her thoughts on everyone else on the list, starting with Bridget and Sebastian.

'Gosh, no… they're such a lovely couple,' she said.

'Morgana?'

'Impossible... she's a marvellous person. And after everything she's been through.'

'The Cherrys?'

Jennifer shook her head in disbelief. Everyone on the list was given a free pass. She really couldn't see the bad in anyone. Which made Astrid feel bad about seeing the worst in her in the past.

Jennifer got up and took the empty cups away. She returned with a metal tray – a souvenir of the engagement of Prince Charles and Lady Diana. On it were the two cups, refilled, and a small square plate heaped with pink and yellow circular biscuits that she said were Party Rings. They had a nice snap to them, and a jolt of sweetness from the icing that made you want to immediately have another one. Then another.

'Astrid, I want to tell you something.' Jennifer rubbed the crumbs from her fingers and took a deep breath. 'It's why we didn't visit you in London, as much as we should.'

Astrid fumbled biscuit number four off the plate. 'Go on.'

'It was Simon... We didn't really like him.'

Crunch. 'Oh?'

'I'm so sorry, Astrid. You see, if it had been just you, then we'd have visited all the time. But Simon was always there.' She made a face as if she'd bitten into an onion. 'And he rather dominated the conversation, to be fair.'

This was fair. When she thought about it now, Simon had been overbearing on the few times her father and Jennifer had visited their flat. Lots of long stories, from which he'd emerged bathed in glory. Even Jennifer, who liked everybody, had found him unbearable. Astrid shrugged. 'Maybe you could have told me?'

'Maybe we should have. But then…'

'No, it's fine.' Astrid knew Jennifer was right. She would have found a way of defending him. 'I guess sometimes you can't see the forest because there's a big tree in the way.' She took a sip of the fresh coffee. 'No, that's not the expression, is it? But hey, you know what I mean?'

'I do.' Jennifer shuffled closer. 'Anyway, I know this doesn't sound right, but I'm glad you and Simon have split up. Even though it was painful because…' She glanced at the tray of Prince Charles and Lady Diana.

'Yeah.' Astrid got there first. 'There were three people in our marriage.' She moved her coffee cup so it obscured Prince Charles's face. 'Looking back, I think the worst thing was that Simon hid the truth about that. For months. Years, maybe. He let me think everything was alright – but it wasn't. And other people must have known too.' Astrid realised that the conversation had steered itself to where she wanted it: her father's possible adultery. 'Listen, Jennifer. I'm sure it would never happen, but if my father was seeing another woman – would you want to know?'

Jennifer tipped her head to one side. She thought for a while. 'You know, I think I would.'

'Is that right?'

'Definitely. And I'd hope someone would have the courage to tell me.'

'Okay.' It was time to leave – before she said anything else. She thanked Jennifer for the coffee and biscuits and headed for the door. On the way, she stopped in front of the magic eye poster. She stood back a bit further this time and narrowed her eyes. Waited.

'Nope. Still can't see it.'

Twenty-nine

A couple of birds of prey wheeled in the cloudless sky above her. Even if she had her field guide, they were too high to identify. They were like flecks of dust, rising up in the thermals above the valley. She'd decided to go for a walk in the hills – to think some things over. She still couldn't decide if she should tell Jennifer about the woman her father had met in the town square. People, she thought, often say they want to hear the truth. But when they hear what the truth is, they wish they hadn't asked. Did Jennifer really want to know? And who was this woman? All she had was her fingerprint, which was worth nothing right now. She couldn't ask her father, or he'd know she'd been spying on him.

She turned back down to the top of her father's road, to take the short cut into the town. As she reached the gates of Bridget and Sebastian's plot, she heard footsteps behind her.

'Astrid.' Bridget caught her up. 'What great timing – I was about to call you.'

Astrid was hoping to get back to the boat. It was getting late. The sun had started to turn pink. She could do with an early night. But Bridget wasn't going to let her go. She hooked her arm through Astrid's elbow and steered her down the path. 'You must speak to Sebastian. He has a theory he wants to tell you – about the troll.'

'Right, well, any theories at this stage would be great.'

They carried on past the caravan towards the farmhouse. Sebastian was at the top of a wooden ladder propped up against the wall. In his hand was a clod of yellowy mud, which he pushed into the gaps of the jumbled stones. He dipped his hand into a bucket that was hanging on the ladder.

Bridget called up to him. 'It's looking good, darling.'

He clambered down the ladder. When he reached the second bottom rung, he jumped down to the ground and stood there with his hands on his hips, smiling – as if he'd just landed a high-tariff vault in a gymnastics competition. 'I know, I know…' He rubbed his hands on his shorts, which were stiff with dried mud. 'It's so amazing,' he drawled. 'To think… a year ago I was working in an open-plan office in Hoxton. And now—' He nodded in a half circle, taking in the wall. 'I'm here – fingers deep in the tierra of Spain. We use the earth back there.' He pointed to a muddy bank. 'Just add water. It's so, so… natural?' He wiggled his fingers. 'Are you handy, Astrid?'

'Well, I guess…' She studied him. He reminded her a bit of Simon, whenever he fixed anything in the flat. He needed lots of praise. Her dad was the same. He'd lock the door and all you'd hear was banging and shouting. That's what the family said DIY stood for – 'Dad Is Yelling'. Then he'd emerge, triumphant, like a dog that had fetched a log – waiting to be patted on the head. 'I renovated my boat.'

'Good for you,' Sebastian said absent-mindedly. He was standing back from the wall, admiring his handiwork. Then he slid into a monologue about traditional Spanish building techniques, 'honouring the landscape', 'artisan mortar'…

which was about as dry as the hillside, and made her very grateful when Bridget piped up, 'Darling, why don't you explain your theory about the troll to Astrid?'

'Oh, yeah.' He looked at his muddy hands. 'Let me just freshen up in the orchard. We can talk on the way.'

As they walked, Sebastian outlined his theory. Well, it wasn't his theory, exactly. He'd read an article in an online magazine. Men and women tend to text and tweet differently. For example, women are more likely to use multiple exclamation marks. As well as abbreviations, emojis and words all in capitals. Basically, women are usually more effusive with texts. More colourful.

The more Sebastian talked, the more intrigued Astrid became. This was a fascinating theory – backed up by some solid research, according to Sebastian. In fact, it was part of a growing discipline known as digital forensics. He wound up with a description of a recent criminal case. A man had murdered his wife. Then he continued to send texts from her phone, so it looked like she was still alive. But investigators managed to prove his text style wasn't the same as hers, and he was duly arrested.

'I have to say, this is really good, Sebastian,' said Astrid.

'Thanks.' Sebastian flicked his hair back.

'Because, of course,' continued Astrid, 'the troll's tweets have included nearly all the things women tend to do.' She counted the details. 'LOL. The face emojis. Multiple exclamation marks.'

'Sooo,' drawled Bridget, 'the troll is a female?'

'Not necessarily.' Astrid shook her head. 'We can only say it's more *likely* that the troll is a woman, not that they definitely are. Right?'

Sebastian nodded.

They'd reached the orchard. It was roughly the size of two tennis courts. There were a few rows of older olive trees at the back. In front were younger trees – lemons and oranges that had almost outgrown their wooden stakes. Astrid noticed that under the trees were pools of green grass, as bright green as Centre Court at Wimbledon. The surrounding land was parched and dusty. 'So why is the orchard so green?'

Bridget laughed. 'Now you've done it. Sebastian!'

He was rubbing his hands, delighted the question had come up. 'Follow me!'

They trooped off towards the edge of the valley to the east, stopping at a circle of green grass. In the middle was a square stone pillar that came to hip height. A black iron handle curled out next to a thick pipe.

Sebastian stepped forward. 'I discovered an artesian well and built a traditional hand pump so we can irrigate the orchard. Let me show you.' He slipped a bucket underneath the pipe and cranked the handle. There was a gurgling noise deep at the base of the pillar. After half a dozen hard cranks, the pipe spluttered and coughed. Clear water exploded out, then became a steady flow. Sebastian filled the bucket. He cupped his hands in it and splashed water over his face. 'Cool, clean aqua.' He ran his fingers through his hair. 'Beautiful.'

'That was really good, Sebastian,' said Bridget. 'Do it again and I'll post it on Insta.' She got out her phone, scrolled to the camera and aimed it at Sebastian.

Miller appeared on a mountain bike. She braked next to them and stared at her parents. 'Ugh… that's all Instagram needs. More photos of you two.'

Bridget lowered her phone. 'Oh, hello, darling.'

'I'm off on my bike.'

'No, no… it's getting too late.'

'I won't be long.'

'Okay,' Bridget sighed. 'But just be sociable for a minute. Say hi to Astrid.'

'Yeah, hi.' Miller smiled at Astrid, who gave her a big smile back.

Bridget aimed her phone at Sebastian again and shuffled round the pillar. 'We want to get the right background… obviously.'

Obviously? Astrid looked out over the valley. On the other side was Wonderful's animal sanctuary. It looked even scruffier from over here. Bridget was going to make sure it didn't ruin her photo. When she'd found the right angle, she nodded at Sebastian. 'Get ready… three, two, one…' She waved her hand down and Sebastian pumped at the handle, filling the bucket up to the top.

'Hang on,' interrupted Miller. 'Dad's hair's already soaking wet. It looks like he's trying to drown himself.'

'Thank you for the input, Miller.' Bridget clicked off the phone and tucked it into her bag. 'Actually, why don't you go cycling, darling?'

'I'm fine here. Keen to see how the photoshoot works out.'

'No, really – you enjoy your bike ride, darling. I'll have dinner ready for you when you get back,' she said cheerily.

'What's it going to be?' said Miller. 'A photogenic sardine on a piece of hard toast?'

'Hah, very good.' Bridget gave a taut laugh. 'See you later, darling.' Miller pedalled off past the house and tracked up the path into the hills.

Thirty

Was there anyone else right now reading a research paper about the 'gender differences in text and social media posts'? thought Astrid. In bed. On a boat in Spain, second glass into a bottle of supermarket Rioja. No. She was sure of that. And it was good to be sure of something tonight.

This was the background to the article Sebastian had referred to. It was a serious paper – well researched. And Sebastian had summed it up well. It said you couldn't be certain if someone was male or female from their media posts, but there were strong clues.

Astrid brought up the *@TheAllSeeingEye7* account and scrolled through the last dozen tweets. There was something about the style – all those capitals, the emojis and GIFs. According to the research, women were almost three times as likely to use emojis and GIFs than men. Then there was her own hunch – she just felt that a female hand was behind the messages. She sat up in bed – a brainwave had struck. She could send them a message. Why not? What was the worst that could happen?

She quickly typed a direct message, before she could overthink it.

Have I met you?

Astrid took a glug of wine, her eyes glued to the screen. A reply came ten seconds later.

Yes

The troll was up. Astrid arranged her pillow behind her, to get comfortable.

Are you on the hit list?

No chance – you think I'm stupid?

I think you're a woman.

That right?

I know it

What else do you know?

That you're doing it for attention. Because you're lonely.

Astrid waited, cradling her wine glass in her hand, the tension mounting. She was talking to the troll. Finally. They couldn't just leave now? 'Come on, come on…' she breathed. 'Yusss.' They'd replied.

You wanna know why I'm doing it?

Go on

Money

Money?

It was Astrid's turn to wait. This was getting interesting. She'd already found out that she'd met the troll in real life. Now they'd revealed what the trolling was all about – money, it *was* that simple.

I want 30K euros in cash

I don't understand

But she did. This wasn't just a mischievous troll – it was a blackmailer. Their next message settled it.

Everyone left on the list needs to pay up then I go away for good

30K is a lot of money

It will be worth it… I know what they've done… I could ruin them all

When do you want the money?

Soon

You're a scumbag. You know that right?

There was a pause. Longer this time. Had she pushed them too hard? It had to be said, though. They were a scumbag. She was about to turn off her phone when the message came in.

I was going to save this for later…But now you've been rude… Check my account Astrid – this one is on you

Astrid brought up *@TheAllSeeingEye7*.

You're next Charlotte

Thirty-one

The next morning, Astrid went straight to Shakespeare's without even having a cup of coffee on the boat. Roger came straight over and said he'd get Charlotte from the kitchen. He didn't need to ask why she was there. She looked around – it was even quieter than usual. A couple of customers tucked into the corner. Terry at his usual table.

Charlotte and Roger came back. He took her order – a Danish pastry, the coffee she'd held out for – and left her with Charlotte. 'You okay?' said Astrid.

'Not really.' She looked up and noticed the Jamaican flag bunting was still up. 'I need to take that down,' she said vaguely. There were deep bags under her eyes. Astrid doubted if she'd had any sleep last night.

'Listen. I've got to tell you – last night the troll DM'd me. We had a chat.'

'What did they say?'

'They want money. That's what this is all about, I'm afraid – blackmail.' She told Charlotte that everyone who was left on the list had to come up with thirty thousand euros between them – in cash – if they wanted to keep their secrets safe. Astrid said she'd arrange the drop-off if that's what they wanted, but she knew what Charlotte was going to say.

'We can't pay,' she said, loosening a top button on her chef's jacket. 'No way. We have some savings left, but it's not going to cover it.'

'Sure, I just had to pass on the news,' Astrid said. 'I'll let the others know too.'

Charlotte pulled her chair in closer. 'I've got some news as well. Something happened last night. It was…' She shivered. 'Sorry, I'm still thinking about it. It was so creepy.'

'What happened?' Astrid took out her jotter.

Charlotte took a deep breath, then started talking in bursts, stopping now and then to go over the facts in her head. To get it right. At around nine thirty, she'd gone back to their apartment after closing the kitchen at Shakespeare's. She got a glass of wine and went to sit out on the balcony. After a few minutes, she noticed a figure on a balcony on the opposite apartment block. They were hiding in the shadows. In front of them was a telescope on a tripod – it was trained in her direction. 'They were spying on me – I'm sure of it,' Charlotte said, rubbing her wrists. 'I went to the rail and waved at them. I wanted them to know I'd seen them. But they slunk deeper into the shadows.'

'Okay.' Astrid turned a new page of her jotter. 'Can you give me a description of them?'

Charlotte didn't have any details. They were average height, maybe. That was it. Most of the apartments in the other block were unoccupied – in fact, the apartment opposite was for sale – so it was too dark to make out anything but an indistinct shape. 'Roger had stayed on in Shakespeare's for a drink, so I took matters into my own hands,' she said proudly. 'I went back into the apartment and found a torch. Then I put on my clothes and marched over there to confront them.

But when I got there, they'd gone.' She sighed. 'I was going to report it to the police but what's the point, I mean—'

'Mmm... sorry. What was that bit?'

'The police?'

'No, the lack of clothes.'

'Oh, yes... I was naked,' Charlotte said, as if Astrid had asked a stupid question.

'Naked?'

'Of course. When we're back at the apartment, Roger and I don't wear any clothes. That's what's so creepy about this. Having our privacy invaded.'

Astrid struggled with a few thoughts. Not least, how Charlotte and Roger weren't bothered who saw them on a nudist beach. But people watching them naked in their apartment – that was strange? There was almost too much irony to process.

'Unfortunately,' said Charlotte, 'I think the troll might be a bit of a weirdo.'

'I'll add it to my notes,' said Astrid, doodling in the corner of the page instead. 'Although,' – she tapped the pen on the table – 'we don't know this is the troll who was watching you.'

'Oh, but we do.' Charlotte reached into her sports holdall and brought out her phone, tapped the screen a few times and passed it over. It was open on @TheAllSeeingEye7.

Astrid checked the screen.

Good to see you last night Charlotte – love The Costa del Troll
XXXX

The Costa del Troll? – that was new, thought Astrid. *Very snappy.*

'It was posted about ten minutes ago.' Charlotte took her phone back and put it in her bag. 'It was definitely them.'

'Right, well, I'll look into it.'

Astrid took down the address of Charlotte's flat: number 16, Block A, Sol Dorado Apartments. The one opposite with the telescope was 16, Block B. Both apartments were on the corner of their blocks. Charlotte thanked her and said she'd go to the kitchen and see how Roger was getting on with the order. Even he, she said, couldn't mess up putting a pastry on a plate.

'Before you go,' said Astrid, 'can I ask you something?'

'Anything.'

'Are you glad you gave up teaching and moved to Spain?'

Charlotte crossed her arms, weighing up her answer. 'I really miss the kids – it was amazing to see them absorb all that knowledge. But there was too much paperwork – assessments and targets. We'd always had this dream of running our own restaurant abroad. So, we thought we might as well take the plunge.'

'But you've ended up running someone else's place.'

'Exactly. We didn't have enough money to do it ourselves.' She shrugged. 'And I'll be honest, it's taken a while for me to get the hang of the cooking – I'm sure you saw that review?'

'I did, yes.'

'It was a bit harsh, wasn't it?' Charlotte said.

Astrid shook her head. 'It sure was.'

Charlotte did up the top button of her uniform and left.

Astrid sat on the town beach, in the shade of a palm tree. A few minutes. That's all she needed, to let what Charlotte had told her sink in. To plan her next move. The Cherrys weren't able to pay off the troll. It was a bad idea, even if they did have the money. The troll might take the cash and expose them anyway. These latest developments were good news in another way. The troll was getting bolder – the direct messages, the spying on Charlotte from the opposite apartment. Sooner or later, they'd get careless, and she'd be ready for them.

She closed her eyes and slowed her breathing in time with the waves. The water heaved back, then rushed at the sand. Over and over – the rhythm was soothing. Drowsy. There were other distant sounds: the high *fizzz* and *slappp* of a jet ski hopping over the waves; the roar of a speedboat; the cry of a seagull. Her mind began to clear of all her thoughts. The troll. Her father. Jennifer. All there was were the noises of the beach and the warmth of the sun on her eyelids.

A shadow passed over her. She felt a cold flutter in her chest. It was as if she'd walked through a spider's web in the dark. Had she been asleep? A few minutes? Longer? She sat up and shielded her eyes. Terry was standing over her.

'Don't get up.' He sat down next to her, his wrists on his knees. He was wearing white trainers. The usual pink shorts. 'I've been thinking.'

'Has that happened before?'

He levelled his eyes at her. 'Very funny.' But he wasn't laughing.

And she didn't care. 'What do you want?'

'You need to stop investigating the troll,' he growled. 'It's bad for my business. You've seen how quiet Shakespeare's is now.'

'I'm not stopping,' Astrid said flatly.

'You're just making it worse – you've made them angry.'

'I'm getting closer.'

'The thing is.' He rubbed the corner of flesh at the base of his thumb and first finger, drawing attention to a small blue swallow tattoo. It had been there a long time – the ink was muddy and it looked home-made. She'd read that it was a sign someone had done time in prison – done 'bird'. When he was sure she'd seen the mark, he put his palms in the sand. 'I just spoke to Charlotte. She says the troll wants thirty thousand, and they'll go away. That right?'

'Yes, they DM'd me last night.'

'I think we should pay it.'

'That's a bad idea.'

She looked up and down the beach. There were enough people around her for him not to try anything. It still didn't feel comfortable. But she wasn't going to be pushed around. 'Terry, I've made a promise to a few people that I'll catch this Costa del Troll, and I'm not going back on my promise.'

'Then we've got a problem.' He worked his fist into the sand and his voice cracked with rage. 'A big problem.'

'I'm not scared of you, Terry,' she said, as calmly as she could.

'Doesn't matter if you are,' he hissed. 'You're going to persuade the others to pay up and stop winding the troll up.'

She shook her head.

He stared dead ahead. A speedboat was coursing across the bay. Behind it, on a short rope, was a yellow inflatable in the shape of a huge banana. Four young women were gripping on for dear life as it bounced over the waves. Their screams cut above the whine of the engine. Terry's mood suddenly changed, like a switch had been flicked. He smiled. 'It's good fun that. You should try it.'

'Maybe I will.'

The boat slowed and turned for the shore. A man in red shorts walked down to the water's edge and dragged the banana inflatable on to the sand. 'Yeah... better than some of the other inflatables that get washed up round here.'

'I don't understand,' said Astrid.

'You know. The ones that come over from Africa.' Under his breath he added, 'Bloody immigrants.' Then he got up and dusted the sand off the back of his shorts. 'It's nice here, isn't it, Astrid?' he said casually, as if they'd just had a chat about the beach and the weather. Then he walked off down the beach in the direction of Shakespeare's.

She sat on the sand a bit longer, rewinding their conversation. The 'immigrant' comment – it was terrible. She felt bad she didn't challenge him, but what would be the point? She wouldn't change his mind. There was a choice now. To stay and carry on her investigation. Or to give up and leave Estepona. *Not happening*. She'd come here to get closer to her father, and a dodgy bar owner wasn't going to stop her. It meant she'd have to keep away from Shakespeare's for the time being.

Thirty-two

The window of Elite Estate Agents was filled with a grid of A4 pages describing nearby villas and apartments. Only a couple had a red SOLD stamp branded across the photo. Inside were two people. A thin man in his late twenties was sitting on the corner of the desk, leaning over a younger woman, five years younger maybe, who was playing solitaire on her computer. The man heard the door click shut behind Astrid and hopped down from the desk. The woman scrambled to bring up a new page on the screen.

'Seen anything you like in the window?' he said in an accent that Astrid placed somewhere in the Midlands.

'Yes, actually... I'm interested in the Sol Dorado Apartments.'

'Very desirable,' he said, squeezing past her to the window. Behind each A4 sheet pinned to the window was a Perspex box full of copies. He started plucking out a few sheets.

'Actually, I'm only interested in corner apartments, if you have one?'

The man checked the sheets. 'Yes, you're in luck. We have one left – number 16.'

'Great... can I see it?'

'When?'

'Now.'

The man sucked his lower lip, taking in the empty room. 'Yeah, I think I can take a break,' he said, aiming his finger in a trigger action and firing at the younger woman at the desk. 'Mandy, you okay to hold the fort?'

The woman snapped her gum in her mouth and nodded.

'Right then.' He held the door open. 'Let's go.'

It took about five minutes to reach the Sol Dorado Apartments. In that time the estate agent, Bashir, mentioned three times that the property market was still holding up well. 'Brexit was a bit of a shock, but prices are defying gravity at the moment.' He paused at a busy road junction and pressed the button to change the traffic lights. 'And you can see why.' He gazed round with an air of wonder. 'Who wouldn't want a place in the Garden of the Costa del Sol?' He stood there watching the traffic grind past, realising he'd completely mistimed his welcome-to-the-green-and-pleasant-town-of-Estepona pitch by two hundred yards. 'Well, not all of it's a garden, but you know...' he said, irritably pressing the button again and again.

The Sol Dorado Apartments were two identical whitewashed blocks separated from the main road by a high wire fence and a strip of scrubby grass. There was a red-brick path that ran round the front to the side of the building. They followed it, arriving at an iron gate that was half open. Bashir stepped in front of Astrid, trying to shield her view of the broken security code lock. 'Twenty-four-hour security... for peace of mind.' He swung the gate open for her. 'Are you investing or buying a place for yourself?'

'Oh, um.' Astrid knew that she was doing neither. She was

just nosing around to see how someone could break in. It would be easy, she thought. To get up to a first-floor balcony though? That might be the hard bit. 'It's for myself. A little holiday place.'

'Lovely stuff... and this' – arms outstretched – 'is the pool.'

Ahead of them, in between the two apartment blocks, was a sizeable pool. It was about thirty feet long and twenty feet wide. Wide enough that even if you took a run-up you wouldn't reach the middle. Not that that was encouraged. There was a sign by the gate that had a list of 'pool rules' in English, with 'running' and 'divebombing' right at the top. There was also a ban on littering, alcohol, food, water guns, inflatables and shouting, the latter illustrated by a crossed-out loudhailer. The management, thought Astrid, weren't just expecting bad behaviour – but complete drunken chaos.

They carried on past a row of white plastic sun loungers. Nearly all of them had damp towels hung over the end. Pearl was lying on the last one, angled towards the sun. She was wearing a one-piece swimsuit with large pink flowers. There was a red cardboard food box between her knees. When Bashir walked past her, she grunted, 'You the new janitor?'

He shook his head and carried on.

Then she saw Astrid. 'What you doing here?'

Astrid came over to the side of her lounger. 'Oh, hi... yes, I'm just having a look around the complex. I might invest in a property.'

'Ugh,' she grunted. 'Didn't know you were staying.'

Bashir came over and introduced himself. She didn't move a muscle – she just lay there, tanned and sinewy. A strange thought flashed into Astrid's mind – she and Bashir were government scientists about to perform an alien autopsy. The probing was all done by Pearl, though.

'What you going to do about the pool then?' she said, directly to Bashir.

'Sorry?'

'It's always out of order. A verruca sock got stuck in the filter last week – we weren't allowed in there for days. Then there's the big bins at the back of the car park – they're overflowing.'

'I'm just an estate agent,' he said, all his confidence drained in less than twenty seconds in Pearl's company.

'You can still have a word, right? And as for those flippin' disposable barbecues. People use them on the lawn.' Pearl pointed at a couple of square patches of burnt grass. 'The coals stay hot for ages.' She reached into the red carton and ate the last of her burger. Then she licked her fingers, scrunched up the box and dropped it into the middle of an inflatable rubber ring by the side of the lounger. 'They want to put "no barbecues" on the sign,' she said, without a flicker of shame that she'd just broken, Astrid totted it up, yes... three of the rules on the sign in one single motion.

Pearl ran through a few more complaints – towels left out to book sun loungers, kids running around after 9 p.m., moths at the lights. Bashir nodded sympathetically and backed off towards the building. When they were through the door, he said, 'Lovely lady. A real community spirit in the Sol Dorado, don't you think?'

Apartment number 16 was at the end of the corridor on the first floor. It was nice and bright, with a faint smell of pancakes and old socks, even though the owners – a nice couple from Cheltenham, according to Bashir – hadn't visited for at least three months.

'Are you sure about that?' said Astrid as she walked through the hall towards the front of the apartment.

'Definitely.' He held up the key. 'This is the only spare key and I haven't shown anyone around... not that,' he corrected himself, 'there hasn't been a lot of interest. There has. A lot of interest.'

Astrid mulled it over. How did someone get in here? They must have climbed up, or down. She pressed on towards the balcony, which she could see ahead of her through the living room. But Bashir held his arm straight out, filtering her into the kitchen. 'And this...' He looked around to check which room it was. '...is the kitchen.'

'Very nice,' said Astrid. It was spotlessly clean, with grey marble worktops and glass-fronted cupboards revealing neatly stacked cups and glasses.

Bashir circled the room, pointing at various features – 'You have your genuine marble... your overhead cupboards... your double fridge.' Astrid suddenly realised that a big part of being an estate agent was describing things other people could clearly see. Like a tour guide who was as lost as everyone else.

They moved on to the two small bedrooms, which were both neat and tidy – the bedding folded up and left at the end of the mattresses. Then finally, to the living room, which was almost filled by a pair of cream sofas that faced each other over a coffee table. 'And that's your living room,' said Bashir, going over to the glass balcony doors and working a key into the lock. He slid them back, allowing Astrid to step out.

'The apartment is "pool view", as you can see.' Bashir explained that the most expensive properties were at the front of the building – these were 'sea view'. Then it was 'pool view', then 'mountain view', which he volunteered really meant 'car park view'. Which was why the apartment they were in was much more desirable. He then began to run through the maintenance costs – but Astrid had tuned out. She was assessing the view out to the other block. The Cherrys' apartment was on the opposite corner, on the first floor. Below them, Pearl was making slow progress across the pool. She was on her front, the inflatable round her midriff, arms swooshing down by her side. Each stroke set flickering hoops of light fluttering over the surface of the pool. It was like one of Hockney's 'splash' paintings. Astrid leant out over the balcony. It was ten feet to the ground, roughly – a struggle to climb up, but possible.

To her left were two wicker chairs. To her right, tucked in the corner, was a black telescope on a tripod. It was the kind you use to gaze at the night sky. This wasn't aimed upwards, over the Sierra Bermeja, though. It was level – pointing at the opposite apartments. Astrid went over. 'You mind?' she said, squeezing behind the telescope.

Bashir shrugged. 'Sure, knock yourself out.'

Astrid brought her right eye up to the viewfinder, making sure she didn't budge the position of the telescope. It was lined up directly at the Cherrys' apartment, and in perfect focus. Charlotte was right – someone had been spying on her.

'You okay?' Bashir had noticed that Astrid was smiling to herself.

'Yeah, thanks.' She stepped back from the telescope. Checked that there was a screw on the tripod to adjust the height – there was. Then she squared up to it again. This time she made a note of how much she had to lean down to find a comfortable eyeline. It was no more than an inch or so. She turned to Bashir. 'Can I ask you... the owners of the apartment, how tall are they?'

Bashir looked confused. But he was here to answer any question thrown at him. 'They're both pretty tall – five eleven, maybe.'

He didn't notice her smile again, a bigger one this time, as she'd turned her back on him. The case was finally opening up. *Click*. One more number in the digital security lock – and this one was working. Bashir continued the sales pitch behind her.

'Great view, right? Imagine sitting out here in the evening... a chilled glass of your favourite tipple.' He breathed in deeply. 'Heaven.'

Astrid glanced down to her right. Running down the corner of the building was an iron gutter pipe. It looked strong enough to take someone's weight. This must have been how the troll scaled up here. They were strong and agile enough to shimmy up a ten-foot drainpipe, reach out and haul themselves on to the balcony. Then scale back down.

Pearl was taking a breather. Her chin was resting on the edge of the pool, legs dangling limply behind the inflatable. Not Pearl then. But who?

It was a question that took up much of her walk back to the marina. She started with a reconstruction of what had happened last night. The troll had walked in through the broken gate. They'd climbed up to the balcony and trained the telescope on Charlotte. But not before adjusting the tripod to a comfortable height. That placed them at around five feet seven, an inch or so shorter than she was. But then – Astrid stopped herself – who knows what shoes they were wearing?

They might be even shorter. Certainly not taller, though. She latched back on to her train of thought. Charlotte had waved at them and rushed back into the apartment. The troll decided to make a break for it. Down the pipe, out through the gate – and they were gone before Charlotte reached the pool.

If the troll wasn't lying when they spoke last night, Astrid's new list of suspects should only include people she'd met. They'd have to be at least an inch shorter than her. Plus they'd have to be fairly athletic. Female suspects first, that would now include Bridget and Morgana. Then Sebastian. The Cherrys were in the clear – Charlotte's story panned out, and Roger was too tall. Or it was someone else she'd met. The thought nagged at her – had she missed anyone?

Her phone beeped, jolting her back to reality. It was a text from her father. She hadn't thought about him for a while. On purpose. She still hadn't come to terms with him meeting a woman behind Jennifer's back. Then he sends a text like this.

Just to say. It's lovely having you around, Astrid. Dad x

A kiss? That's a first, Dad. Astrid read the text a couple more times. A warm glow in the pit of her stomach. Then frustration. *Why are families so complicated?*

Astrid decided to work on the painting for a while. It would be good thinking time, if she could steer her thoughts away from her father. She first checked the back of the painting. The canvas patch had bound well. She turned it over and was pleased to see the rip had drawn tightly together. There would be no need to fill it with white putty. She could now get on with matching the paint colour.

She set up a lamp and aimed the light over the damage. Then she brought out her collection of conservator's paints from her work case. They were all soluble, in case the work needed to be reversed. She chose a range of blues and squeezed out beads of each around a circular palette. Taking a brush, she carefully mixed the different shades, glancing back and forth between the sky above Jesus and the palette. These days, computers could do this kind of thing. But Astrid liked to do it by eye.

She chose a very fine brush and picked up a tiny amount of paint. Not much more than a poppy seed of colour on the tip. Stippling it into the crack. Running the magnifying glass over it. Viewing from different angles. Then remixing on the palette until she had the perfect match. And relax... she'd done it. This was the joy of the conservator – knowing history was in safe hands.

As she carefully inpainted the crack, her mind drifted back to her childhood, and her father. There was no getting away from him. There had been a year, she remembered, when the family had felt truly settled. Just a year. It was between her father's business almost going bust and him leaving the house. The calm before the storm – and it was all down to her uncle.

She only had bits of the jigsaw – snippets of overheard conversations. But it was enough to get the picture. After she was taken out of school, her father's business continued to struggle. There were the usual clues. Unopened bills, phone calls he didn't answer. Her mother never got the corner bath. Then Uncle Henry showed up one day and unloaded some paintings from his car. Her father helped him carry them into his office and the door was locked. Cigar smoke and laughter leached out from under the door.

A week later, Dad was wearing a smart new suit – 'Jermyn Street,' he said, opening out the jacket to reveal a silk square in the lining. After that, Uncle Henry came back every month to drop off a new painting. From the paint marks on his hands, these were his artworks. She never got to see what they were.

By the end of the year, the dealership was booming. Paintings appeared on the walls of the house again. Not Uncle Henry's, though – these were the pick of his gallery. The car was upgraded to a newer Jag. Life was good. There was even talk about her and Clare going back to their old schools. But as suddenly as Uncle Henry had arrived, he disappeared. The last time he visited, he came to see her in her bedroom, to say goodbye. He hugged her longer than he usually did. And the way he stopped on the pavement outside and looked back at the house – it was as if he knew he was seeing it for the last time. He was right – he never came back, and his name was never mentioned again. Her parents split up soon after. But this time, her father's business kept going. Her uncle had bailed him out somehow, and now he'd found a way to survive without him. Exactly why they'd fallen out – only her father knew, and he wasn't telling.

Thirty-three

The inpainting took a couple of hours to finish. She stood back, pleased with her work. Only an expert could tell the painting had been damaged. With a coat of varnish, she'd fool them too. She threw the brushes and palette in the sink, and packed away her work case. It was too hot to spend any more time below deck.

She'd only got a few yards down the boardwalk when she noticed Nelson standing at the glass doors of his boat. He saw her and gave her one of his jaunty salutes. 'Come aboard,' he shouted.

She parked the bike up against a pillar and climbed the gangplank. 'Nelson,' she laughed, 'you have returned.'

'I have indeed,' he said, taking her hand in both of his and squeezing. 'And it's marvellous to see you. Come, come...' He led the way through the open glass doors, ushering her to a cream sofa. It was a beautiful space. Bright and airy, with big smoked-glass windows running down both sides. 'Now sit down, I've got a lot to tell you.'

'Me too,' she said, although it was best to let him tell her his news first. Which he did – calmly, without rising to melodrama. The past few days, he said, had been both the hardest and the most rewarding of his marriage. After seeing the troll's video of his wife with another man, he'd confronted her. She told him everything.

Her lover was another expat – a property developer who worked on projects up and down the coast. They'd first met when they shared a taxi to the airport. They got on well – there was a spark, she'd said, and she couldn't put it out. They texted each other for weeks afterwards. Then met for drinks. Created an alibi – a visit to see her mother in the UK – and began their affair. Nelson hadn't asked for any more details. There was no point, he said. The affair had happened and now it was over. It was her decision – he'd made no ultimatums. What mattered now if they were going to save their relationship – and they'd decided they were going to try – was forgiveness. On his part.

Astrid leant back into the sofa. 'You just forgave her?'

'Yes.' He shifted round to face her. 'People don't realise that one of the most important things you can do if you want to be happy is forgive people.'

'Sure, but this affair. It was so planned... behind your back.'

'It was, yes. But it's not a good idea holding on to that anger. It's a natural thing to do – but it will only make you unhappy and often unhealthy. Anxiety, stress – bearing a grudge can make you ill.'

Astrid knew he was probably right. He was a relationship psychotherapist, so he should know. But still... He saw she wasn't convinced.

'Listen, Astrid, if you're betrayed by someone, you have a choice. And it is *your* choice – you can forgive them or not. It doesn't mean you accept what they did was right. Or you approve. But it's the only way to move forward with your life.'

Astrid thought about her ex-husband. After nearly six months since she'd discovered his affair, she still hadn't dealt with her anger. Properly, anyway. There were feelings deep within her, wrapped so tightly in a clenched fist she didn't know what they were. No, he was right, she had to release that grip. The grip Simon had over her. 'It takes time, I guess,' she said quietly.

'It does. And it's hard. But it's for the best. In fact,' – he became more animated – 'if you want to be competitive about it, it's the way *you* get to win. Not them. Remember – every time you have a negative thought, it denies in that instant your chance to feel something positive. Like joy, or ecstasy, or love.' He got up. 'Don't rule out forgiveness in your life, Astrid. It's so good for you, it's almost selfish.' He clapped his hands. 'Now, I've been very rude. I've not offered you anything to eat or drink.'

Astrid protested. 'No, honestly… I couldn't.'

He waved her away. 'Please, stop being so British. I'm going to make a late lunch, and that's what's happening.'

They both wandered through to a smart dining area. Astrid sat on a stool by a kitchen island as he went to a big silver fridge and took out a handful of packages, laying them on a marble worktop next to the sink. He told her that his wife was in the UK visiting her mother – and this time he knew it was true. He was on his own for a few days and was glad of the company. 'Right, change of subject,' he said. 'What's been happening with the troll?'

Astrid told him everything that had happened since he'd left. How, by luck and elimination, she'd managed to narrow down the list of suspects to a handful of people. Although she still couldn't be sure that was all of them.

'Am I a suspect?' he said.

'No, you're well over five foot seven.'

'Sorry?'

'It's a long story.'

'Rrright, maybe later then,' he said, distracted by the packages. He began opening them and leaning in to sniff the contents – cheeses, hams, olives, figs – all from a local grocer somewhere.

'And did you take my advice and ignore the troll?'

'Well…' She grimaced. 'About that.' She told him that she'd been DM'ing the troll. He tutted, then carried on unwrapping the food. 'Sorry, Nelson. But anyway, it turns out the troll wants money.'

He looked up. 'It's not about attention then – it's blackmail?'

'It seems so. They want thirty thousand euros from the remaining expats on the hit list. In cash.'

'Woo…' He whistled. 'That's a lot of money – I hope they're not going to pay.'

Astrid said she was going to pass it on to the others, it was up to them. But the two of them agreed it was a bad idea to pay a blackmailer when all you were buying was a promise. He took a wooden chopping board out from an overhead cupboard, and a small sharp knife from a drawer.

'At least it wasn't just you and your wife that the troll was after.'

'I suppose so.' He laid the figs on the board and began chopping them into quarters. 'But you know, I really wasn't bothered.'

'Really?'

'Absolutely. I don't care about what other people think of me – there's another mental well-being tip for you, Astrid.

Having the troll expose my wife's affair in public – it did me a favour. It's allowed me to save my marriage.'

'Good for you.' She got down from the stool and went over to the worktop. 'I'm not sure how Wonderful is feeling about being exposed, though. Or Zhang. As for Declan, I doubt he'll play golf at that club ever again.'

He swept the cut figs to the corner of the board with the side of his knife. 'Hey, I heard on the radio someone died a couple of days ago at Declan's golf club.'

'I know… Declan and I found him in the bunker.'

'Jeez,' Nelson gasped. 'Was he dead when you discovered him?'

'Yeah, very. They're saying he collapsed and hit his head on a wooden rake. Did the report mention that?'

'No, it just said there were no suspicious circumstances.' He curled up a bit of ham and fixed a quarter of a fig to it with a cocktail stick. 'They gave their name: Elliot Green.'

'That's right – Elliot Green. He did the legal paperwork, visas mostly, for the expats at Shakespeare's.'

Nelson said he didn't know him. His visas were all sorted out a long time ago, so he hadn't needed any legal advice.

Astrid churned over a couple of thoughts. The expats would now know that Elliot Green had died. That was bound to stress them out even more. Secondly, there was something about Elliot's death that still didn't feel right. Again, it was a hunch, and she'd been wrong before. But she was going to pay the golf club one more visit after lunch.

Nelson held up the chopping board. He was more interested in the juicy food on it than the recent crimewave. 'Come on… let's eat.'

Thirty-four

Astrid browsed the clothes rails of the pro shop, waiting for a couple of golfers to pay their green fees. It would be good to know who else was out on the course that day. Maybe someone who wanted to do Elliot harm? She'd just have to be careful how she got the information. The couple left the shop. Astrid slid the pair of pink and green paisley trousers she was holding back into the rack and went over to the golf pro.

'Back again? You must have enjoyed it,' he said cheerfully. 'Apart from the body in the bunker, obviously.' He pinned on a sombre expression that seemed painful to keep up.

'What a shame. Poor old Elliot.'

'A real shame – some of the members are going to have a few drinks in his honour in the Faldo Bar this Friday, if you're interested?'

Astrid said she'd try and make it. The pro started checking his computer screen, mumbling about finding a tee time for her.

'No, I'm not playing today.' She leant casually on the counter. 'I'm trying to find out who was on the course behind us when we played on Sunday.'

'Why do you need to know?' he said suspiciously.

'I'm trying to find something I left on the course.'

'What'd you lose?'

'Um, I lost…' She remembered the nudist beach. 'I lost a necklace.' The imaginary necklace was proving very useful.

'I'll check if it's been handed in.' The pro walked over to a cardboard box behind him that had *Lost Property* written on the side. He rummaged around, then shook his head and went back to the computer. 'Maybe they hung on to it.' He started typing. 'Let me check who was on the course behind you.' More typing. 'Sunday… Declaaan… and Astrid.' He paused, scrolling up and down around her booking. 'It seems you were the only people out there that afternoon. It was scorching, wasn't it?'

'Yes, it was – as usual,' she said gloomily.

'Don't worry, the weather will break soon.'

But she wasn't despondent about the weather. Another of her theories was falling apart before her eyes – that another player had followed Elliot on the golf course and finished him off with the wooden rake. There was a clear Perspex box on the counter filled with maps of the course. She plucked one out and studied it. It showed the tee boxes and the greens. All the water features. And around the edge was a dotted line – the boundary fence. 'Listen – is there any way someone could have sneaked on to the course through the fence?'

'You really want that necklace back, don't you?' he said.

'Yes, it means a lot to me.'

He tidied up the maps in the box. 'There's a few gaps in the fence. According to the players, some kid gets in sometimes. They nick the golf balls. And anything else lying around – might have been them?'

'What kid?' She tried to hide her excitement.

'I dunno. Local kid.'

Just like that, the case had sprung open again. She picked up a pitch repairer from a tray. 'How much?' She held it up. He said they were free. She was now sure the troll had sneaked on to the course. They'd found a pitch repairer on the green and kept it. And she was sure she'd find them at Bar Finca.

Astrid waited at the bar, sipping her rosemary lemonade and making small talk with Eduardo, one eye on the door. He was on good form. Yet again, they were the only ones there. He seemed unconcerned about the lack of customers – or was good at hiding it. His kids were happy – that's all that mattered, he said. *You can only be as happy as your least happy child, no?*

She nodded in agreement, checking the door again. The last time she was here, Eduardo's two kids had come in with a bag of golf balls. They must, she assumed, have found them at the El Paradiso, which was across the valley to the west. Ten minutes later, the door swung open and the two kids came in, pushing their bikes ahead of them. Astrid gave a sigh of relief. Hanging from the handlebar of the boy's bike was a plastic bag. It was weighed down by what looked like a dozen golf balls.

Eduardo went through his routine of admonishing them, then hugging and kissing them, before shooing them out to the back garden. When he came back round the bar, Astrid asked, 'The golf balls – do they get them from the El Paradiso course?'

'Yes, yes… the kids find them – they sell them back to golfers. Extra money for summer.'

'You know, I play a bit of golf.' She sipped her drink. 'Could I buy some?'

'Of course. Please, this way.'

He led her out to the garden. Then he spoke to the kids in Spanish, too fast to work out exactly what he'd said. The girl shouted '*vamos, vamos*' at the boy, and he rushed off down the garden. The girl stayed where she was and unloaded the contents of the plastic bag – eight golf balls in total, which she laid out in a neat line, the brand facing up. She smiled at Astrid, waiting for her brother to return. How tall was she? thought Astrid. Five feet five? Six?

Her brother hurried over. In his hands was a box brimming with bright white balls.

Eduardo said, 'These are the ones they've cleaned.' He turned to his kids. 'Yes?'

'*Si, si*,' the girl said.

'Maybe you practise your English now,' said their father.

They got down on their knees and the boy started to line up the other balls. The girl was in charge of the sales patter. 'Best quality. Best brands,' she said excitedly. 'You won't find a better deal in Estepona.'

'How much?' asked Astrid.

'Two for one euro. Twelve for five euros,' said the girl. Her English was as good as her father's. But was it good enough, she thought, to write those tweets? Why would she do it? To ruin Shakespeare's for her father – so his business would do better?

'Do you go on to the course to get them?' asked Astrid.

'No, no,' the boy piped up. 'We never would.'

'Oh, right.' Astrid's heart sank. 'You've never been through the fence to pick up a ball?'

'Never,' said the boy. 'That would be stealing.' He looked at his father, who was nodding and smiling. 'We only take balls that are hit over the fence, then they are lost.'

Astrid brought out the pitch repairer from her pocket and held it up, studying the girl's face for any flicker of recognition. 'You've never found one of these on the course?' They stood there, shaking their heads, in confusion this time.

'Sorry, forget that. Come on.' She got down on her knees. 'Let's see these golf balls.'

The girl swept her hand over the lines of balls. 'What do you like? Srixon? Callaway? Titleist?' She pushed back her fringe and grinned. 'Titleist the best, yes?'

'Yes, they're good,' said Astrid, fighting back the disappointment. Yet another theory had unravelled before her eyes. Eduardo's daughter wasn't The Costa del Troll. She told the kids to pick out a dozen golf balls for her – they could decide which ones. They packed them up in the plastic bag. Astrid got up and handed over five euros, which the girl stuffed into the front of her dungarees.

'Thank you,' she said. 'Sorry, we don't have as many this time.' The girl looked at the boy, who shook his head gravely. There was an understanding between them.

'Okay, you guys.' Eduardo stepped in. 'Time for homework.'

'Hang on,' said Astrid. She turned to the kids. 'Why don't you have so many?'

'Because…' the boy scowled, '*she* gets there first.'

'Yes, *she* goes through the fence and on to the course,' said the girl.

'Sorry.' Astrid's head spun. 'Who goes through the fence?'

'The girl,' they both said in unison.

The boy carried on. 'She waits for the players to hit their shot to the green, then she runs out and steals their ball. Whatever she can find.'

'Which girl?' said Astrid.

The boy spoke. 'The British girl. From the farm on the hill.'
The shock prickled through her veins like static on silk.
It was Miller.
The Costa del Troll was Miller.

Thirty-five

Miller was sitting on a flat boulder on the lip of the valley, her feet hanging out into space. She reached out to the dirt next to her, selected a stone and idly flicked it out to the rocks below.

Astrid slowly approached. She was annoyed with herself. How hadn't she seen it before? Miller – she'd been hiding in plain sight. Plotting her next move. The other clues held up too. The style of her tweets – all those emojis, and GIFs... more likely to be a female hand behind them. She was just under five foot seven, and athletic – strong enough to get up to the balcony of a first-floor apartment. And then there was Nelson's professional assessment. Deep down, she was lonely. Astrid watched Miller throw out another stone.

'How's it going, *Miller*?' Astrid's voice betrayed her. The way she emphasised Miller's name – it spelt bad news. Miller stiffened, not yet ready to make eye contact. But she knew in that moment the game was up. That all the spying and trolling had come to an end. She was cornered.

Astrid sat down on another rock next to her. She picked up a handful of stones from the dirt and began sifting through them. 'Why did you do it, Miller?'

Miller put her head in her hands and whimpered. Astrid waited until she was calm enough to speak. 'I did it because of this.' She held out her hand and swept it over the valley and up to the caravan and farmhouse. 'Why did they bring me here?'

'Is it that awful?'

'Yuh,' she huffed. 'It's the worst.'

'They'll finish the house soon. Then it won't be so bad.'

'But I had friends. School. My life. At home.' Her words tumbled over each other in a jagged stream. 'And they didn't ask me if it was okay. They just said, we're going. Like that!' She clicked her fingers. 'Because Dad got fired and he decided to drag us all out here. And Mum pretends like it's the dream life… and it's not. That blog of hers – it's a joke. If only people could see what our life out here is really like.'

Astrid waited again until Miller composed herself. She wanted some clear answers to a few things. She picked up a stone and handed it to Miller, who threw it out. They watched it *skitter* and *clatter* on the rocks below. 'Okay – I get it. You're angry with your parents and you want to troll them online. But you can't just target them – because it would be obvious it was you. So you troll a few of the expats down at Shakespeare's.'

Miller nodded. 'Thing is, I had no idea.' She pulled her legs up from the edge. 'I had no idea they had all these secrets. I mean, what in the actual… and they call themselves grown-ups.'

'Good point.' Astrid got out her water bottle and offered it to Miller, who shook her head. 'I don't think anyone ever grows up really.' She looked out at the blue sea and the blue sky that merged into it. 'Everyone has secrets. The older you get, the more you have.'

'You?'

'Sure – did you follow me around too?'

'No, just the others.'

Miller explained how it began.

One day she'd been out on the hill trails on her bike. She'd found a hole in the fence at the golf club and worked out that if you were quick, you could nip on to the course and steal the players' golf balls. It was just for fun. Then, a week later, she'd seen Declan dropping a fresh golf ball behind the trees. He was cheating. Maybe the other expats, she'd thought, had secrets too? That's when she had the idea to follow them and expose them if they did. It was the perfect smokescreen for her to troll her own parents. That was the master plan – to make them so stressed and paranoid they'd decide to sell up and take her back to the UK.

'Declan was the first person you filmed?'

'Yeah. But, as you know, Nelson's wife was the first person I exposed on Twitter.'

Miller explained how she'd watched Nelson saying goodbye to his wife at the marina. She'd followed her to the taxi rank. But instead of getting a cab, she'd hurried round the corner and got into another car with another man. They'd kissed. Now Miller had a number plate, then a name, then, on the naturist beach, video proof of the affair.

Astrid reached into her pocket and brought out the pitch repairer. She passed it to Miller. 'You dropped one of these on the beach?'

Miller turned it in her hands. 'Yeah, I found one on the

course.' She handed it back. 'It must have fallen out of my pocket.'

'You know, Miller,' Astrid sighed, 'you do realise how much you've hurt people?'

Miller hung her head. The first time she'd shown any remorse. 'I know... I went too far,' Miller stuttered. 'I guess I was bored. You know – I mean, it's not like I've got any friends out here.'

'Yup, I know what it's like. But hey... let's not feel sorry for ourselves. The point is you knew how mean you were being,' Astrid said sternly. 'At those meetings in Shakespeare's, you were sitting at the back, and you heard everything, because your headphones were turned off, weren't they?' Miller nodded. 'And you could see how upset people were. But you kept on going.'

'I get it... but —'

'No buts, Miller. You have to say sorry on Twitter. Then shut down The All-Seeing Eye.'

Miller put her head in her hands again. This time she sobbed. The tears came in short bursts, Miller rasping for breath between them. Astrid looked down at her. Online, Miller had been menacing. In real life, she was sad and desperate. A lonely outsider. When she got her breath back, she said quietly, 'I can't stop.'

'What?'

'I can't stop.'

'Miller—'

'You don't understand. Terry won't let me stop.'

'Terry? I don't...' Astrid's voice faltered.

'He found out I was the troll. I was about to give up, but he wants me to keep going.' The whole story spilled out.

That first meeting in Shakespeare's, Terry had noticed Miller posting the video of Nelson's wife on the beach. He'd been sitting behind her and seen her phone screen. A few days later, after she'd posted the video of Declan, he told her he knew she was the troll. By this stage, Miller realised she had to give up. It was hurting too many people. But he wouldn't let her. He took over The All-Seeing Eye account and told her to keep digging up dirt on the expats.

'Let me check,' interrupted Astrid. 'So that DM conversation I had. That wasn't you?'

Miller shrugged. 'Not me.'

'Okay, well, he's after money. That's why he's trolling the others – it's blackmail.' Astrid paused. 'I don't suppose he told you about that?'

'No, he just said he was in charge now, and he was going to make them suffer.'

Astrid let her carry on with the story. She said that Terry had threatened to expose her as the troll if she didn't help him. So she went along with it. Next was Wonderful. She'd waited until Wonderful had driven down the valley, then cycled over and rifled through her mailbox. One morning, there was a court summons for shoplifting in there. 'It was easy,' she said. 'Zhang, too.' She'd noticed the packaging seemed badly printed on some of his British goods, so she'd run the barcodes through a price-checker app. It didn't work – they weren't genuine products. After that was Charlotte – although she hadn't found her secret yet. She'd just spied on her from the other balcony and seen her wandering around in the nude, which she agreed with Astrid was hardly a major crime.

'Okay, here's what we're going to do—'

'You're not going to tell my parents, are you?' Miller started to sob again.

Astrid sighed. 'Don't worry, I'm not going to tell anyone.'

Miller sniffled. 'You serious?' The tears began to dry up.

'Come on.' Astrid held out her hand.

'Where we going?'

Astrid pulled Miller to her feet and led her to the caravan. She told her to go inside and get her iPad. When she came back out, Astrid said, 'Right. Terry. I want you to find out everything about him.'

Miller nodded. 'I'll have a dig around.'

'Good,' Astrid said firmly. 'I want to know everything about that guy. His business interests. His criminal past. His enemies. All the dirt you can find.'

'I'll get on it.' Miller switched on the iPad. Then she looked up. 'What are you going to do with the information?'

'You know, I've no idea.' Astrid took out her water bottle, took a swig, screwed the lid back on and stuffed it into her bag. 'Soon as you can, please, Miller.'

As Astrid reached the brow of the ridge, the breeze picked up. A tiny whirlwind of dust chased back down the path towards the farmhouse. It was a good spot, the farmhouse tucked into a pleat in the hillside. The green orchard behind. Of course, there was no weather-beaten old woman. Or husband on a donkey who cooked rustic meals over open fires. No crystal-clear stream either. The only thing that was crystal-clear was that Bridget's blog was an illusion. A carefully crafted one – assembled from flattering photos and fake anecdotes. A fantasy of a rural life on a Costa del Sol that no longer existed. Or never did.

Astrid could see why readers loved it and Miller hated it. Hated it so much, and the new life that had been thrust on her, that she'd decided to troll her own parents. The dust whirlwind died out in the courtyard of the farmhouse. One day, she thought, it would make a good home. Miller just didn't know that yet.

Way before that, Astrid was going to bring Terry down – that was going to start now.

Thirty-six

When Astrid got back to the boat, she sent Jennifer a message. She had some important news for the expats who were still on the hit list – that was Jennifer, Bridget and Sebastian, the Cherrys, Morgana and Terry – they were being blackmailed. Astrid had already told Charlotte. And, of course, Terry knew… because he was the blackmailer. Astrid suggested a meeting, as soon as possible. Jennifer said she'd set it up at Shakespeare's in an hour's time. Just enough time for Astrid to shower, change and work out what exactly she was going to tell them.

On the way to Shakespeare's, she decided to drop into BOBS, to see how Zhang was doing. He was out front, a plastic spray bottle in his hand. She wandered up.

'There you go.' He spritzed a fine mist over a box of watermelons. 'Make it look like they're still covered in morning dew.'

Zhang was in as good a mood as ever. His public shame about selling dodgy groceries didn't seem to have bothered him. In fact, Astrid had to jog his memory. 'The troll… when they put those pictures up of the fake goods.'

'Oh, that, yeah.' He carried on down the row of boxes. 'Hasn't made much difference really. I mean, I got a slap on the wrist from a couple of the brands. No legal threats, though.' He gave a cheery wave to a handful of customers going into the store. 'So, I just started filling the gaps in the shelves with some Spanish products. They've gone down pretty well.'

'That's great news, Zhang.' She checked her watch. Told him she was in a rush, but they'd catch up soon.

'Aye, see you later,' he said, turning back to his spritzing.

At the entrance to Shakespeare's was a sign saying 'Private Function'. Astrid carried on into the main bar and found everyone waiting for her. Their chairs were arranged under the big-screen TV, which had been turned off. There were two rows – Jennifer and the Cherrys at the front; Morgana, Bridget and Sebastian in the second tier. Pearl was tucked in by the fruit machine, nursing a large Dubonnet and lemonade. She must have been there anyway and wasn't going to budge.

There was an empty chair at the front. Astrid went over and sat down, not bothering about getting a drink, even though her mouth was dry. Terry was behind the bar, going over some paperwork – and she'd rather not speak to him.

'Okay, everyone. I've got some news for you,' she said, pleased her voice didn't sound too tense. The expats were watching her expectantly. 'I had a conversation on Twitter with The Costa del Troll – that's what they're calling themselves now. They say they want you to pay some money and they won't expose your secrets.'

Jennifer crossed her arms. 'How much?'

'Thirty thousand euros – between all of you.'

There was a collective intake of breath from the two rows.

Except the Cherrys. Astrid turned to Charlotte. 'I've spoken to Charlotte, and I know she's decided not to pay. But I thought I should tell everyone else.'

Sebastian stood up. 'Hang on, we're being blackmailed?'

'I'm afraid so,' said Astrid.

'Well, we're not paying.' Sebastian stayed on his feet. 'I've sunk most of our funds into the build.' He glanced down at Bridget, who was nodding. 'Until we can Airbnb the old stable, we can't spare the cash.'

Out of the corner of her eye, Astrid saw Terry's expression harden. He balled up the piece of paper he'd been looking at and tossed it into the bin. Then he got up and wandered round the bar. Morgana, who'd been anxiously twirling the beads of a bracelet, spoke next. 'I have some savings, but this is a lot of money for me.'

'Me too,' Jennifer jumped in. 'I've got some savings too. But it's the principle, isn't it? You can't pay blackmailers.'

Terry stepped in front of the rows of chairs. 'Hang on, hang on,' he soothed. 'Way I look at it – it's not that much when you split it between all five of us. That's six grand each—'

'But Terry,' interrupted Bridget, 'we haven't got the money.'

'Then bloody find it.' His voice went up an octave. He breathed in slowly through his nose, then when he was calm, he said, 'Look. We make a few savings and get the cash together – I'll arrange to hand it over myself if you want.' He turned his hands over, palms up. 'Then it's over, and we can get on with our lives.'

The mood in the room had begun to change. There were some resigned shrugs. Someone muttered, 'I guess we've got no choice…' Terry was drawing them in. 'Six grand, that's all, and we can get on with living the dream.' He turned to Astrid.

Everyone else was looking at her too. 'I'm sure Astrid would agree. Right, Astrid?'

Astrid looked him squarely in the eyes. She wanted to enjoy this. 'Well, the thing is.' She smacked her lips. 'I think paying them would be a truly terrible idea.'

He stared at her, the corner of his left eye twitching. He placed one hand over the other to stop it trembling. Then said, 'It's none of your business, Astrid.'

'Come, come… that's not fair, Terry.' Jennifer leapt to Astrid's defence. 'Astrid has spent a lot of her valuable time investigating this. So it is her business.'

'Thank you, Jennifer,' said Astrid breezily. She *was* enjoying herself. 'And you're right, Jennifer – you don't pay blackmailers. They don't deserve a penny.' She aimed that one at Terry.

'Now what?' Terry grunted. 'We just sit around, waiting for them to destroy our lives?' He looked in desperation at the others. They ignored him.

'No, Terry,' said Astrid. 'They won't ruin your lives. Unless you let them.'

'I don't understand,' said Morgana.

Astrid said that she'd spoken to Nelson. He'd said having his secret revealed wasn't so bad. It gave him a chance to rebuild his marriage. Zhang hadn't noticed any difference in sales. She'd checked the website for Wonderful's sanctuary – since people had found out she'd been stealing dog food, the donations had flooded in. She couldn't vouch for Declan, but for the other three, having their secret out there had been a weight off their mind. This was her idea – they all shared their secrets right now. Here in Shakespeare's. 'You may find it's a relief too,' she said. 'And then The Costa del Troll has no power over you.'

Bridget was the first to agree. 'Why don't we? We're all friends here, right? Then we're finally free.'

The others nodded in agreement. Except Terry. He got up and barked, 'You lot can do what you want. I'm not sitting around sharing anything.' Then he marched off to the kitchen, glaring at Astrid on the way.

'Right, who's going first?' said Charlotte.

'Get on with it,' Pearl piped up from the back.

'What?' Charlotte startled. 'How long have you been there, Pearl?'

'All night,' she said. 'Now come on, let's hear what filth you've been up to.'

'You know what you're like?' said Roger. 'Those old ladies who used to knit on the front row of executions in the French Revolution – the tricoteuses, that's it.'

'Chop chop...' Pearl tapped a bony finger on her watch. 'Let's get a head on the block.'

'Right, I'm going to ignore you, Pearl.' Charlotte stepped forward and faced the others. 'Okay, here goes. I'm here in Spain because I was suspended from my teaching job. I forgot to give some money back from a geography field trip.'

'Embezzler?' croaked Pearl. 'That's a surprise. I assumed you'd hit a pupil.'

'Just ignore her, Charlotte,' said Roger.

'I gave that money back, Pearl.'

'Course you did.' Pearl crunched down on an ice cube.

'Okay, you're leaving.' Roger marched over and escorted Pearl to the door. She protested, reminding him that she'd bought a drink so was legally allowed to stay. 'It's a private function... and you're not invited,' he said, taking the drink from her hand and shutting the door behind her.

When he got back to his seat, Sebastian had decided to go next. 'Same sort of thing. I stole a lot of company money,' he said, looking down the line at Charlotte. 'Except I didn't give the money back.'

'What did you do with it?' said Roger.

'Internet gambling,' he said. 'About fifty grand. Gone – just like that!' He snapped his fingers. 'It's a mug's game, Roger – don't get involved.'

'I won't,' said Roger.

The energy in the room had changed. It was a subtle shift – from negative to positive. Now, nearly all the expats had revealed their secrets. And nobody had been shocked. Bridget was right – it was setting them free.

Morgana was next to take the floor. She heaved in a deep breath. 'You're not going to believe this, but…' She clutched at the neckline of her floral wrap dress. 'Alonzo didn't exist – I made him up.'

'Well, fancy that,' said Roger. 'Who's next then?'

Everyone darted stares at him. They'd all heard Morgana's tragic story before, and knew it was nonsense. But this was her big moment, and she was going to take her time. That time was over fifteen minutes. She explained in detail the drudgery of her marriage. That much was true. And that she'd split up with Keith on a holiday to Estepona. It was all very amicable, though, with Morgana staying on for a couple more weeks. As she moved on to the second act of the drama, Roger took a drinks order and tiptoed over to the bar.

'I guess I wanted my life to sound more exciting than it was.' Morgana began to pace the room. 'So, I invented this affair with a gorgeous fisherman. It was ridiculous. But friends at home believed it. They started to ask me when they could come over and meet him. I couldn't keep making up excuses – so I told them he'd drowned at sea – it seemed like the only way out.' For no apparent reason, The Beef got up from the corner of the bar, wandered between Morgana and the front row, then on to the games room, where he sniffed the leg of the pool table, then wandered back out. Morgana waited for him to slump back down in the corner. 'I was like Alice in Wonderland,' she said. 'I got lost in a fantasy world.'

Astrid sat up in her chair. 'Well, I think you've been very brave, Morgana. You all have.' She looked towards Jennifer, who was already getting up.

'Yes, I guess it's my turn,' she said.

Astrid realised that this was the moment she'd been waiting for – Jennifer's secret. It was the reason she'd agreed to find the troll. Now it was here, there was no excitement. She felt nervous, that it would be too awful or sad.

'Okay, so back in the UK, I had a hairdressing salon that went bankrupt.'

Nobody batted an eyelid. Not even Astrid – this wasn't too bad after all. In fact, she could imagine why Jennifer's business failed. She'd seen how generous she was with her 'regular ladies' – hardly charging them for haircuts. Jennifer was too kind – that was her downfall.

Jennifer continued, 'I ran up a lot of debts with the banks. Which meant I couldn't set up a new business for years. That's why I came out here, to start a new life... with Astrid's father, who's been my rock. I can always rely on him.'

Jennifer nodded at Astrid, who smiled weakly. Her father still had some explaining to do about meeting the woman in the square *and* his lie about the day trading. When Jennifer sat back down, a communal sigh of relief seemed to pass through the room. The expats were unburdened of their lies and secrets. They'd laid them out in the open for everyone to see, and nobody judged them.

They chatted and laughed as they finished their drinks, then gradually made their way to the door. Each of them thanked Astrid for her help. She told them it was no problem – she'd been happy to help. Which was true – it had been a challenging case, but it was over now. Almost.

Terry began to switch the lights off. Astrid realised she was the last to leave. She picked up her bag and walked quickly to the door. As she reached for the handle, Terry's arm jutted out and blocked her way.

'Not so quick, Astrid.'

Astrid stepped back. She knew how this worked. Don't show any fear. Breathe slowly. Settle the heart rate. 'It's over, Terry.'

'You worked out I was the Costa del Troll… very clever.'

'Thanks.'

'Why didn't you tell them the others?'

'Because I'd have to reveal Miller was involved. And I promised her I wouldn't.'

'Aren't you a saint.'

She glanced at the door handle. He was a second ahead of her, his hand grabbing the lock as she stepped forward. He turned it over with a dull *clink* and rested with his back against the door frame. 'I still need that thirty thousand.'

'Twenty-four thousand,' she corrected him. 'It's not like you were handing over your share.'

'Alright – seeing as I'm a gentleman, let's call it twenty-four grand,' he sneered. 'I don't care where you get it from, but you're going to bring it to me.'

'What do you need it for?'

'That's my business.'

She reached for the lock. He caught her by the wrist and squeezed hard.

'You've got forty-eight hours.'

Astrid twisted her hand out of his grip, pulling it sharply back. 'You mind?' She saw the muscles at the side of his neck tighten, a flash of his gold chain in the V of his T-shirt. She reached out – to show him she wasn't scared – and teased out the chain. She held the shark's tooth pendant between her fingers and rubbed it with the side of her thumb. 'Bet it's not real gold, is it?'

He stared at her. She wondered if he'd blinked since they started talking.

'Bet it's fake. Like you, Terry... a fake gangster.'

'That right?'

'A billionaire tried to threaten me once – and they came off worse. You're not in their league, Terry.' She pulled the door open and squeezed past him, her bag brushing his chest.

He called after her. 'Forty-eight hours, Astrid. Clock's ticking.'

She didn't look back.

Thirty-seven

There was a handful of direct messages on Twitter waiting for Astrid in the morning. They were from the expats at the meeting last night, thanking her for making it all go away. She searched for *@TheAllSeeingEye7* – it had been taken down. That was it, then – the end of the Costa del Troll.

As she put her phone down, she noticed a mark on her wrist. It was a slight bruise – from when Terry had grabbed her. *How dare he?* Miller was on the case, but she could still do some investigating of her own. Last night, Terry had been at the end of the bar, hunched over a stack of papers. He didn't seem happy. He'd scrunched up one of the letters and thrown it into the bin. Astrid hoped they hadn't collected the refuse this morning.

The alley down the side of Shakespeare's smelt of cooking oil and potato peelings. Astrid edged up to the side door. It was locked. The lights were off inside. Lined up along the wall were three big square bins on castors. The lids were orange, yellow and blue. From the stickers on the side, she could tell they were meant for general waste, plastic and glass, and paper. *Huh…* Terry might be a sociopath, but at least he recycled.

She went over to the blue bin, her espadrilles crunching on

bits of broken glass, and lifted the lid. It was full of packaging and cardboard. No sign of any documents. She rummaged around, pushing aside the cardboard. There it was, the balled-up piece of paper, tucked down the side. The light went on in the kitchen. Astrid fished out the paper and shoved it into her bag. There was the slap of feet on the kitchen tiles – getting louder. The scrape of a key in the lock. She let the bin lid slowly drop and turned to face the door as it opened. Charlotte came out, holding a black plastic bag.

'Aargh!' Charlotte dropped the bag at her feet. 'You shocked me... what are you doing back here?'

'Oh, I um...' Astrid pointed down the alley. 'I thought I saw something.'

'What was it?'

'A dog.' *A dog?*

'What dog?'

Astrid realised she'd committed to this – she had to see it through. 'Jennifer's dog. It's missing. I've been looking for it all morning. I thought I saw it turn in here.'

'Why didn't you say?' Charlotte lifted the orange bin lid and dropped in her bag. At the bottom of the alley was a metal gate. Beyond it were some concrete stairs to the street. Charlotte walked over and looked through the bars, left then right. She rattled the gate. 'It must have got through the bars.'

'Well, there you go.' Astrid rubbed her hands. 'That explains it.'

'Where did it go missing?'

'Missing? Yes... in the old town.'

'You got a photo? I'll keep an eye out.'

Astrid said there was no need. It was a clever dog and would probably find its way back home. But Charlotte insisted. She got out her phone and told Astrid to airdrop a picture over. She'd send it to Wonderful too, in case someone handed the dog in at the sanctuary. Astrid was near panicking. Then she remembered she did have a picture. The first time she went to see her father, she'd taken a photo because it was the strangest dog she'd ever seen. Astrid showed the picture to Charlotte.

'Lovely,' she cooed. Then she got Astrid to send it over.

'Right, well, I better keep looking.' Astrid sidestepped her and set off up the alley.

Charlotte called after her. 'Astrid?'

'Yup?' She spun on her heels.

'What's the name of the dog?'

'The name of the dog?' Her mind raced. What was Furball's real name? Jennifer had said it a few times. *M – it began with M. There were a couple of vowels. A… no, E. Hang on, there was no M.*

'You do know the dog's name?'

'Of course. The name of the dog is… Lulu.' *Thank you, brain.*

Astrid had just reached the bottom of the stairs when her phone rang. It was Jennifer. She went over to an awning on the corner and took the call. Jennifer spoke so quickly Astrid had to ask her to slow down, then go over it again. It took a few minutes to get a clear story. Jennifer said that she'd just come in from shopping and found that the house had been broken into. Right now, she was standing on the lawn, too afraid to go back inside. She'd tried calling Astrid's father, but couldn't get through.

'Don't worry, Jennifer. It's going to be fine,' Astrid reassured her. 'Stay calm and I'll be there as soon as I can.'

'Bless you, Astrid,' Jennifer's voice crackled back.

Astrid jogged back to the boat, picked up the bike and cycled as fast as she could up to the house. When she got there, Jennifer was in the middle of the lawn, Lulu clutched to her chest. She didn't take her eyes off the open patio doors as Astrid walked over. 'Do you think they're still in there, Astrid?'

'I'd say they'll be long gone.' Astrid set off to the house.

Jennifer put Lulu down on the grass and the two of them followed a few yards behind Astrid, stopping on the patio. 'Careful, Astrid.'

Astrid went inside and stood in the middle of the living room. She was listening for any noise. The creak of a floorboard. The sound of voices. But there was nothing – the room was perfectly silent. Except for a high *buzzz* and *thrippp* as a fly bounced against the patio glass, then found the gap.

She scanned the living room. It was a mess. The furniture had been dragged away from the wall. The drawers of the cabinets and sideboards were pulled out, their contents – cutlery, papers, pens – tipped out on to the floor. All the paintings had been taken down and left on the table, face down, their backing papers ripped out. She listened again. Nothing. She called out 'Hullo?' Still nothing.

Astrid waved at Jennifer, who was still standing on the patio. 'It's fine.'

Jennifer stepped cautiously into the living room. Lulu made a beeline for her little tent by the wall. 'Thank you so much, Astrid.' Jennifer clutched Astrid's hand. 'I didn't know who else to call.'

'I'm glad you did. Now try and relax.'

Jennifer released her grip. 'Thank goodness they didn't take Lulu.'

'Why would they?'

'Sorry?'

'I mean...' Astrid looked over at the tent. Lulu was now snoring, head on her paws, her tongue lolling out of the side of her mouth. 'Is there a market for, errr, dogs like that?'

'Of course,' Jennifer gasped. 'Lulu's a pedigree dog. Ninety per cent, anyway. These dog smugglers would love to get their hands on her.'

'Right then,' Astrid said briskly. 'Why don't we check the rest of the house?' Astrid suggested that Jennifer have a look around downstairs, while she went upstairs. But Jennifer was still feeling jumpy and insisted they stick together.

Astrid went first, pushing the doors open with her foot to avoiding touching the doorknobs. The intruder had ransacked every room. Clothes had been taken from wardrobes and scattered on the floor. Suitcases pulled out from under beds. Like the living room, the paintings were off the walls, their backing papers torn open. The only room they didn't check was Astrid's father's study. It was locked and there was no sign of a key. No sign of her father either. Where was he right now? thought Astrid.

Downstairs, they did an inspection of the kitchen and the rest of the rooms. The intruder had visited those as well. When they got back to the living room, Jennifer, now satisfied that nobody was going to leap out from a wardrobe, replaced the cushions on the sofa and collapsed back with a sigh. 'You know what? I don't think they've taken anything.'

'You sure?'

'Pretty sure. Everything seems to be here. My jewellery was still in the boxes on the dresser. Why would they leave that?'

'Strange.' It was very strange. Astrid went over to an

upturned drawer. All the drawers had been flipped over. They'd been looking underneath them, not in them. Whoever had broken in – well, just walked in; Jennifer had admitted that they rarely locked up as they'd felt so safe up here – was making a thorough search for something. *But what?*

She went to the table and examined the back of a painting. The brown paper had been pulled away to reveal the back of the canvas. They'd been looking *inside* the paintings, thought Astrid. She didn't tell Jennifer though. She just said, 'I don't know. Maybe someone has just vandalised the place for kicks? Hard to say.'

'That's the awful thing… not knowing who's been in your house. Going through your most personal things.' Jennifer dabbed at the corner of her eye. Then she took out her phone and left an urgent message for Astrid's father to get back to the house. The way she curled her lip when he didn't answer suggested she'd been calling all morning.

Astrid used two pieces of torn paper and carefully turned one of the paintings over by the corners. It was a landscape – a Mediterranean hillside. Framed behind glass. She moved her head until the light caught the glass at the right angle. 'Aha…' she whispered. Now she could see some fingerprints. Four on each side of the glass. They must have been left when the intruder gripped the painting and turned it over. Even without her magnifying glass, she could see the fingerprints were sharply defined. And they were small – *a woman's?*

'Jennifer?'

'Yes?'

'I'm just going to pop to the boat to get something.' She went to the patio doors, then turned back. 'Oh, and Jennifer… don't touch anything.'

It took about half an hour to get to the boat and back to the house. It was tricky to cycle with one hand, her work case in the other. She got off and pushed the bike for the last bit up her father's road. As she approached the house, her stride dragged. She was weighed down by a single thought – could she really do this? If *this* was what she thought it was?

In her work case was the fingerprint she'd taken from her phone – it belonged to the woman her father had met in the square. She was about to check if it matched a fingerprint on the painting. And if it did? She pushed the bike ahead of her on to the gravel drive... If it did – he'd have to explain why she'd trashed their house. Had she come back to get something that belonged to her? Or was it revenge? A woman scorned, and all that. It was a saying she hated. It wasn't just women who behaved badly when they were rejected. Men too. Rage and passion were different sides of the same coin.

She parked the bike up against the corner of the house, her thoughts tumbling ahead of her. What about Jennifer? She deserved to know... *right*? Astrid remembered the last time she was at the salon. They'd discussed Simon's affair, and Jennifer had said she'd hate to be left in the dark. That's what she said. Astrid gripped her work case and marched down the side alley.

When she got to the living room, her father was sitting on the sofa, his arms outstretched across the back. Jennifer was seated stiffly in an armchair by the wall. There was a brittle atmosphere between them, as if someone had turned up the air conditioning and it was sucking too much oxygen out of the room. Had they had an argument? wondered Astrid. About where he'd been?

Her father greeted Astrid without getting up. 'Thanks for

coming to the rescue,' he said. Jennifer rolled her eyes behind him.

Nothing had been put back in place. The contents of the drawers were still on the floor. The painting still face up on the table. Astrid put her work case down next to it. She explained she'd noticed some fingerprints on the glass and was sure they'd been left by the intruder. She told them she knew how to lift them from the surface.

Jennifer wasn't keen. 'That kind of thing is best left to the police. They're the professionals, Astrid.'

'Hang on.' Her father brought his hands down to his knees and sat up. 'I don't think we want to involve the police.'

Jennifer swivelled her head round the room. 'But look what they did, Peter.'

Astrid began to take out a few things from the work case, listening to them arguing, focusing on the tone of their voices – her father's patronising, Jennifer's increasingly shrill. 'Well, I want to call the police, Peter. They might have some suspects. A local crime gang or something.'

'But they didn't take anything, did they?'

'No, but the damage... it's awful.' The tears weren't far behind.

Her father held out his hand and brought it slowly down while making a shushing sound, as if he was trying to calm a lively horse. 'Let's not overreact, Jennifer. We'll tidy up... I'll get some proper locks.'

'About time too, Peter.'

The argument rumbled along, eventually reaching a stalemate of pleading and shushing. It gave Astrid time to set everything up and get on with collecting a fingerprint. She had the titanium dust brushed over the glass before Jennifer noticed and came over. Astrid stretched out the length of tape and ran it over the print of the forefinger. Then she transferred the print on to a clear acetate card. *Now for the moment of truth*. She brought out the acetate card that held the mystery woman's fingerprint and put it next to the one from the painting. Then she held the big magnifying glass over both of them. Astrid's breath tightened.

'What is it?' said Jennifer in a hushed voice.

'I need to be sure.' Astrid laid the first acetate card over the second one. She nudged the cards ever so slightly until the prints were perfectly lined up on top of each other. Last check with the magnifying glass.

Jennifer read her expression of shock. 'What is it?' she repeated.

Now that she had the truth, she wasn't sure what to do with it. Out of the corner of her eye, she caught her father shifting uneasily on the sofa. She began to pack up the equipment. 'Maybe you're right. It's best left to the professionals.'

Jennifer wasn't letting it go. 'But I don't understand. Who does the first print belong to?'

Astrid clipped up the work case. 'You know, it's not really my business.'

Jennifer went over to the patio doors and slid them shut. 'Astrid... please. What's going on?'

Astrid glanced at her father, who looked away. Jennifer saw the exchange – her voice deepened. 'You have to tell me, Astrid.'

'Okay, then.' Astrid pulled out a chair at the end of the table and sat down. 'The first print was taken from my phone. I'd given it to a woman to take a photo of me. She left her fingerprint on the screen.'

'What woman?' snapped Jennifer.

'Right, well...' She turned to her father. He was staring at her, an eyebrow raised. Astrid knew there was no going back. 'I followed you into the Plaza de las Flores, Dad.'

'Why?'

'Because...' She was digging deeper and faster than she wanted to. 'Because I kind of went into your office and noticed that the screens hadn't been turned on for a while.'

'The computer screens?' Jennifer interrupted. 'For Peter's day trading?' She said this to Astrid, but her eyes were trained on her husband. He didn't flinch.

'Go on, Astrid,' he said flatly. 'We might as well hear it all.'

Astrid took a deep breath. 'There's no day trading, is there, Dad?' He shrugged, not a flicker of emotion. 'That's why I followed you, to find out what you really do all day.'

Jennifer went over to a sofa and slumped down. Astrid continued. 'When I caught up with you in the town square, you met someone. A woman. I waited, and when she left, I stepped out and got her to take a picture of me. Like a tourist.' She held up the top acetate card. 'I lifted her fingerprint on this card and kept it... just in case.'

'Is this true?' Jennifer said softly to Astrid's father. 'There's no day trading? And you've been meeting another woman?'

'It's not that simple, Jennifer.'

Astrid picked up her work case.

Jennifer turned to her. 'And Astrid. Why would you tell me this?' she said angrily.

'In the salon, remember?' Astrid protested. 'We were talking about Simon being unfaithful – and you said you'd want to know if my father was seeing another woman.'

'You're right...' Jennifer said softly. 'But maybe I didn't mean it.'

'Then how was I supposed to know?'

Jennifer turned her back on her.

Astrid's father got up and walked over to the patio doors, his hands jammed into the pockets of his shorts. 'You know, Astrid...' he sighed. 'We don't see you for ages and then you start interfering in our lives.'

'Oh, come on, Dad – this one is down to you.'

'Sure, I've got a lot of explaining to do. But the snooping around in my office. Following me into town... taking fingerprints?' He shook his head. 'Is that why you really came here, Astrid?'

'Course not. I—'

He held the patio door handle and raked it back. 'If it is, then it's best you move on, Astrid.'

'Fine by me,' she said, stepping out into the sunshine.

Thirty-eight

Bar Finca. Astrid was sitting out in the garden, a rosemary lemonade on the table in front of her. No beer – her thoughts were spiralling down as it was. Beer would only chase them into the abyss. She stared out at the hillside. It was a disaster. A 24-carat catastrophe. Right now, if she was asked to score how successful her trip to reconnect with her father had been – where 10 was 'you feel closer than you ever have' and 1 was 'dumpster fire' – she'd have to put it at a solid 2.

She went over the lowlights – she'd been caught spying on her father and accused him of meeting another woman – in front of Jennifer, who now wasn't speaking to her. Was it really her fault? She sipped the lemonade. Had her nosiness got the better of her again? When she thought about it, she didn't have to follow her father. Or take the woman's fingerprint. He didn't have to meet her – that was on him – but she could have minded her own business. There again – she was who she was.

Eduardo came over and sat next to her. He put his feet up on an opposite chair. 'You want to talk about it?' he said, keeping his eyes forward.

'Well, Eduardo. I do and I don't.' She put her feet up too, now that it was allowed. 'I've screwed up – big time. But I don't want to go into the details. There's no point – because I can't change them. And I'm still confused about what happened. So no.' She took another sip. 'It's a kind offer, but I'd rather just pretend we talked about it. If that makes sense?'

'It doesn't.' He laughed. 'But to be honest, I'm not good at giving advice anyway. You know – I'd love to be the wise barman, solving people's problems. I'm not. I've got my own trouble.' He glanced back at the empty bar – this was her third visit, and again, she had the place to herself.

'You want to talk about it?'

'No, thanks.' Although he summoned up a few short sentences. 'Maybe I survive until the next year. Maybe I don't. Maybe I'll pray. It could help, no?'

They sat in silence for a while. Astrid wasn't sure what they'd talked about, but she felt a bit happier now. Then she noticed Miller riding her bike down the track towards the farmhouse. She got up and picked up her bag.

'Take care, Astrid,' he said.

'You too, Eduardo.'

Astrid cycled through the farmhouse gates at the same time as Miller appeared over the brow of the hill. Miller swung her bike round in the dust and waited for Astrid to catch up.

'Hey, Astrid, I was going to the marina to see you.' She rubbed her hands together – a devilish grin.

'Ooh, someone's got some news.'

'You've no idea.' Miller got off her bike and told Astrid about her investigation of Terry. It had taken a while to 'hit dirt', she said. At first, the usual internet searches came up with very little. He had no social media accounts. No business profiles, in Britain or Spain. The only thing that came up after the first few hours of digging was a blurry photo of him wearing a green football kit. He was on the edge of a team line-up. Miller had 'reverse searched' the photo – a technical trick that revealed a bit more about when and where the photo was taken. In this case, it was from the news section of a website belonging to a builders' merchant in Wolverhampton. From other news posts from the website, Miller worked out that Terry had been employed in the warehouse there until at least six years ago. Then he disappeared.

'Disappeared?' said Astrid.

'Yeah – that's the strange thing. There is no mention of him online after that.'

'Did he go to jail?'

Miller scuffed the path with her training shoe. 'No – nothing in any local papers or court reports from the UK.'

'What about in Spain?'

Miller had checked thoroughly. There were no news articles or criminal records in Spain either.

'Yes – I knew it,' Astrid whooped. 'All that chat about his dangerous past – it was rubbish. He's not a gangster – he's just some bloke who owns a bar.'

Miller shook her head, smiling. Enjoying holding back the big reveal.

'Come on, Miller… let's hear it,' said Astrid.

'He doesn't own the bar.'

'Wow.' Astrid reached out for a high five. 'Nice work, Miller.'

Miller explained how she'd found this piece of the jigsaw. She'd checked something called *Registro Mercantil*. It's the database of Spanish companies. Shakespeare's was one of a number of bars along the coast owned by a Spanish consortium. Terry wasn't even down as the manager – which meant he must be running it as a favour. 'And there's another thing,' Miller said gleefully, 'he's not on the Padrón.'

'The Padrón…' Astrid remembered Nelson had explained this to her. 'If you're not on the Padrón, you're not living here legally. Right?'

'Right.'

Astrid was now reeling. 'Let me just get this straight.' She counted down on her fingers. 'He's not got a criminal past. He doesn't own Shakespeare's. And he has no right to be living in Spain.'

'You got it, Astrid – he's an illegal immigrant.'

As soon as Astrid reached the marina, she found a bench and searched her bag for the scrunched-up piece of paper she'd dug out of the bin behind Shakespeare's. She'd almost forgotten about it. It was still there, formed into a tight ball by Terry's hand, a hand which also held a swallow tattoo that meant nothing. She carefully picked the creases loose, then smoothed the sheet on the bench with the heel of her hand. It was an official reply from the *Oficina de Extranjeros* – which Astrid thought must be the Spanish immigration department. Her knowledge of Spanish could only get her so far with the rest of the document. But it was enough. This was almost definitely a reply to Terry's application for residency. And not the reply he wanted. There was a stamp at the bottom, a red square with '*RECHAZADO*' in the middle. '*Refused*' – *had to be?*

There were two names at the bottom. Terry Gallagher and

Elliot Green, who was down as the *agente*. Now it all made sense. Terry had been living illegally in Spain for the past six years, as Miller had said. This letter confirmed it. He was applying for residency, and he wasn't getting it. Elliot Green had helped him with the paperwork as the agent, as he had with a few of the expats. Then Terry's application reaches a dead end, and so does Elliot Green. That, she thought, carefully folding up the document and tucking it back into her bag, was too much of a coincidence. The plan formed almost instantly in her mind – like breath turning to frost on glass. This could be her chance to get rid of him, for good. It just depended on the weather, and if she could buy the right things in Estepona.

There would be too much to handle on her bike, so she dropped it off at the boat and U-turned back into town. First stop was a boat supply store up near the harbour office. There she bought a good-quality life jacket, a foil emergency blanket and a flashlight. At the supermarket, she bought a 10-litre drum of water and some energy bars. That was everything. It was more than she'd wanted to spend, but she knew it was going to be worth every euro.

Astrid carried her purchases back to the boat and stowed them in a cupboard. But not before locating the emergency whistle on the life jacket and cutting it off. Last thing – check the weather for the next few days on her phone. It was looking good.

She went over to the bookshelves and teased out a sailing chart of the Mediterranean. The painting was still on the table, so she pushed it to one side and spread out the map next to it. She was paid up for another week at the marina. But after that? Was there any reason to stay now? She could just get up early and sail off up the coast. No regrets – well, probably lots. But she'd just have to live with them.

There was the sound of footsteps on the stairs down to the cabin, hard heels gingerly finding each tread. Her father stepped through the doorway and looked around, nodding. 'Well... this is rather nice.'

'Tea, coffee?'

'No. Brandy. If you have it.'

Astrid went to the rack of glasses and pulled out two small tumblers. She found the bottle of brandy at the back of the cupboard and poured each of them a double. Her father was sitting at the table, his hat still on. He tapped a finger on the map. 'Are you leaving, Astrid?'

'Depends.'

'On what?'

She slipped into the opposite bench and passed a brandy over to him. 'If you're going to tell me the truth.'

He swirled his drink, watching the amber liquid cling to the sides of the tumbler. He brought it to his lips, tipped half the contents down, then settled the tumbler on the map, just to the west of Cyprus. 'Alright, if you're ready to hear it.'

Astrid knocked her brandy back. Now she was ready.

'Right, then.' Her father sat back. 'For the last year, I haven't been doing any financial trading in my office. I took the course in Marbella, but it didn't make a lot of sense. So, I just decided to potter about, really... walk up in the hills, explore the town. I'm very good at keeping busy.'

'And Jennifer didn't know?'

'No idea. She'd go to the salon, and I'd lock the door and nip out.' He wagged his finger at her. 'I'd leave the key in the lock.'

'Key?'

'Please...' he scoffed. 'You forgot to lock the door behind you, didn't you? That's how I knew you'd been in there.'

Astrid shrugged. 'Well done – you got me.'

'Thank you.' He leant back and weaved his fingers together. A faintly smug expression that faded away when Astrid asked, 'And the woman you met in the square. Who was that?'

'Do you need to know?'

'No, but I want to.'

'Fine.' He took off his hat, set it down on the bench and drew a breath through flared nostrils. As he told the rest of the story, Astrid tried not to appear shocked – in case he held back. The woman he'd met, he said, was from a special department of the Catholic Church. Her job was to retrieve stolen paintings and artefacts that had disappeared into private hands. They'd met on two occasions, 'for professional reasons'. There had been no affair.

'What professional reasons?'

'Well, the thing...' His voice dried up. Astrid stared him down until he spoke again. 'The thing is... I do happen to have an artwork that the Church is very keen to get back.'

'What artwork?' But she noticed his eyes drift to the painting *The Last Supper* on the table. 'Really? This belongs to the Catholic Church?'

'It does indeed,' he said – guilt mixed with pride. He was like a boy who's been caught getting up early on Christmas Day and opening all the presents.

'So that discussion we had, about the morality of the Catholic Church owning too much art. It was because you've stolen some of it?'

'Stolen?' He raised an eyebrow. 'That's a matter of opinion.'

'Sure, Dad.' She folded her arms. 'And in the opinion of the Catholic art-theft department, it's a firm yes. Which is why this woman broke into your house to try and get it back.'

'Correct.' He held up his hands, as if he was a bank clerk in an armed robbery. 'But to be fair, I didn't take it myself.'

'Oh, well, that's something,' she said dryly.

'I came into possession through a third party, along with some other Catholic antiquities. I didn't ask too many questions about where they'd come from.'

'The rip I repaired?'

'What about it?'

'The shape of it – a cross. It could have come from someone taking the painting off the wall in a hurry and catching the hook?'

'That sounds possible.' That was as good as admitting it. The painting had been stolen, by a clumsy thief. Her father leant over the painting and gently swept his finger over the blue sky, trying to find where the tear had been. He smiled. 'I must say, you've done a brilliant job, Astrid.'

'Thanks,' she said. 'So, what will you do with it now?'

'Well, I sold everything back in the UK except this piece. I'm holding on to it as a sort of retirement plan.'

Retirement plan? Astrid was confused. This was a copy of a Perugino, by one of his assistants. It would be worth tens of thousands – not enough for a very comfortable retirement, given her father's tastes. The way he got up and drifted over to the bookshelf, avoiding her gaze – there was more. She stood back and viewed the painting, letting her eyes roam across the canvas. There was something about it – a flow of energy between the disciples. The way their heads and hands twisted towards each other. Their natural expressions. They appeared as real people – alive, weighed down by gravity. Judas weighed down by guilt. It was a much more remarkable painting than she'd first thought. This was the work of an apprentice, but they were someone who would become a master painter. 'It's a Raphael, isn't it?'

'Well done,' he said. 'You got there in the end.'

'Thanks.' Astrid folded the cloth carefully over the painting. Raphael was Perugino's most famous pupil. He would have been only a teenager when he painted this in Perugino's workshop. Not at the height of his powers. But it would still be worth a fortune, even on the black market. 'How much do you think you'd get for it then. A million?'

'Something like that.'

This felt bizarre. As a kid, she'd been regularly hauled into his office to face the music about some misdemeanour or other. A poor grade. A mysteriously broken pane of glass. That was small beer – her father was fencing priceless religious art. 'There's a couple of things I don't understand.'

'Fire away.'

'Why didn't you tell me it was a masterpiece? I could have made the damage worse.'

'No, no, you never would. I had complete faith in you.'

It was good to hear. But he wasn't off the hook just yet – he still had some explaining to do. 'Another thing – if you knew the Catholic Church would do anything to get their painting back, why did you leave the back doors of your house unlocked?'

'A bluff.' He grinned. 'The best way to alert them to the fact I had it would be to lock up the house. They'd break in anyway, but they'd be more determined and really trash the place.' He flipped a book out from the shelf with a hooked finger, opening the cover page.

'Have you told Jennifer about all this?'

'Yes, I just told her.' He slid the book back. 'Let's just say she was a little… no, she was absolutely furious with me. You too, I'm afraid.' He paused. 'Don't worry, Jennifer is a very kind soul. She'll forgive me – she always does.'

He moved down the bookshelves and noticed a small watercolour that Uncle Henry had painted. It was a view from the mooring at Hanbury. Astrid had found it at the back of a drawer on the voyage over and pinned it up for good luck. She watched her father run his finger across the signature, his eyes starting to glaze.

'He was a wonderful man, wasn't he?' she said.

'He was,' her father said softly, angling his back to her so she couldn't see him rub his eyes. When he'd composed himself, he turned to her and carried on, as if nothing had happened.

Astrid got up and stood next to her father. She straightened the picture. 'A very complex man, too?'

'Yes – we made a lot of money from his art, but he gave it all away. All he had at the end was this boat – which he gave to you.'

'That was all there was in his will.'

'I don't suppose…' – he swallowed – '…he left me a note… or a letter?'

'Sorry, Dad, there was nothing.'

'Not to worry.' He shuddered away the dark cloud. 'It is what it is.'

'Listen,' she said. 'I still want to know why you and your brother fell out. Please?'

He shook his head. 'I will explain... just not now.' He checked his watch and said he should probably head off. Astrid knew that's all he'd tell her, for now. Which had been more than he'd revealed to her in his life.

He picked up the painting without asking and headed up the steps. On the deck, she took his hand to steady him as he stepped over the rail. 'What's going to happen to the painting now?'

'They've given me a bit of a deadline. I've got until eight o'clock tomorrow night to return it.'

'Or else?'

'I'm led to believe it will be very bad for me if I don't. The retribution of God, all that.'

'Are you going to give it back then?'

He pinched the brim of his Panama hat and tipped it at an angle. 'Who knows, Astrid? Who knows?'

Thirty-nine

It had rained overnight. A light drizzly rain, not much more than a wet fog, had rolled down from the hills. For most of the next morning, grey clouds hung over the town, threatening to rain again. The tourists, the few of them that were around, weren't happy. They'd been promised sunshine. They lingered outside the shops at the back of the promenade. Checking the sky. Wondering if they should go inside and buy umbrellas. Or wait it out until the clouds cleared and they could go back to the beach.

Astrid was enjoying the cool weather. She found an old sweatshirt that she hadn't worn for a long time. She'd missed that feeling. The weight, draped around her shoulders – it was like a hug. She spent most of the day in the hills, walking the trails. Going over in her mind what her father had told her. Her father, the art fencer – it was still a shock. The sun came out at around one o'clock. The light seemed fainter though. There was the slightest pink blush to the sky – it had started.

She looked at her phone for the twentieth time – there were still no messages from Jennifer. She'd been hoping that her father might have smoothed things over with her. Clearly not. A message pinged in... from Terry. It was only a matter of time before he got in touch.

You got that money yet?

Astrid checked the weather on her phone. Smiled to herself. Then she tapped in a reply.

Of course

There was a pause. He couldn't believe it. Then:

Good. Bring it to me by 9pm. CASH

No problem – nine o'clock. Meet me at the harbour breakwater

A few seconds later.

You better show up

She typed:

I'll be there

She stuffed her phone back into her bag. Nine o'clock. Now she and her father both had deadlines.

She reached the old town and stopped to weigh up her options. A late lunch at a café, or something from the bakery. Café? Bakery? Café? *Huh?* Her train of thought pulled into a siding. Something on a telegraph post had caught her eye. *No – it can't be?* But it was – a picture of Lulu.

Astrid walked slowly up to the post, trying to process what she was looking at. It was a white piece of paper. A4 size. Printed in the middle, in black and white, was the photo of Lulu that she'd given Charlotte in the alleyway next to Shakespeare's. There were some words above it, in big print – *LOST DOG*. Then, below the photo, in smaller print – *Has anyone seen Lulu? Missing in the old town. Reward.* Underneath was the translation in Spanish.

She stepped closer. There was a phone number to ring at the bottom of the page. It was for the Second Chance Animal Rescue Centre. It didn't take long to work out what had happened. Charlotte must have told Wonderful that Lulu was missing. Wonderful, being her kind-hearted self, had leapt into action and printed up a missing-dog poster. The problem was, Lulu wasn't missing. The poster had to come down before anyone saw it. Astrid checked nobody was looking, then carefully teased out the drawing pins from the corners. The poster was quickly rolled up and bundled into her bag.

At the next corner, Astrid's heart sank again. Deeper this time. To her right, stuck to some railings, was another picture of Lulu. There was another further down the street. She dashed between them, pulling them down and stuffing them into her bag. Wonderful had been busy. Very busy. In the next street – there was a total of twelve posters. On posts, railings, pinned to a noticeboard. She knew it was the same photo – but Lulu seemed to be laughing now.

There were a few people milling around on the street. Too many to take the posters down in broad daylight. *What would people think?* Someone ripping down posters of a sweet missing dog. They'd think she hated dogs – that's what

– or she'd lost her mind. Astrid carried on zigzagging through the old town, hoping to find just one street that didn't have a poster. But she couldn't. Lulu was all over town.

Eventually, she sat down on a bench, her head in her hands. Yet again, she thought, she'd been caught out by one of her lies. There would be no more lying, she promised herself. And she was going to own up to this one. Jennifer was already furious with her. But she had to do it – she got up and headed to Classy Costa Cuts.

Before she reached the door, she took out a poster from her bag and unrolled it. When she looked up, Jennifer was standing in the doorway, staring at her. Astrid held up the crumpled poster. 'I know,' she said sheepishly.

Jennifer walked over and threw her arms around her. Astrid stood there, rigid, as Jennifer clamped her in a tight embrace. 'Astrid, Astrid… thank you – I can't believe you did this.'

'Me too,' whispered Astrid. Her mouth was almost touching Jennifer's ear, so she didn't have to talk too loudly.

'I was so worried. When Lulu disappeared, I didn't know what to do.'

Disappeared?

'Yes, disappeared.'

Astrid realised she'd said it out loud.

'I'd brought Lulu to the salon. I left her in her tent, and when I came out of the kitchen…' – she hugged tighter – 'she was gone. Gone. My baby is out on the streets.'

Astrid pulled away. Jennifer's perfume was about to make her sneeze, which wouldn't help. 'Don't worry, Jennifer. People will see the posters. They'll find her.'

Jennifer reached out and took the poster from Astrid's hand. She held it up. 'I can't believe you did this, Astrid.' She mouthed the words 'Bless you', unable to summon any more energy.

'Phufff!' Astrid waved away her thanks. 'I think Wonderful is behind the posters. I bumped into Charlotte, she must—'

'Yes, I know – it was Wonderful. She called me this morning. But the point is, you searched for Lulu on your own.' Jennifer took Astrid's hands in hers. 'You cared, Astrid. You cared...' Her voice trailed away.

'It was nothing – don't say any more about it.'

'No, no.' Jennifer hadn't finished. 'And here's the crazy thing,' – she shook her head, as if she couldn't believe what she was about to say – 'I actually thought you didn't like Lulu.'

'Didn't like Lulu?' *Just one more lie then.* 'That's ridiculous. Who couldn't love that dog?'

'I know, what a crazy idea?' Jennifer released her grip. 'Oh, I was wondering. How did you know Lulu had gone missing?'

'Missing? Oh, well... Dad came down to the boat and told me.' *That's the last one – definitely.*

'Right – got it.'

Astrid tightened up her bag so Jennifer couldn't see the other crushed posters in there and turned to leave. But Jennifer caught her hand and steered her into the salon. There was, she said, a lot of planning to do. A fair amount, it seemed, had been done already. On the coffee table was a clipboard with a list of names. Next to it was a stack of photocopied maps of the old town. This was, Jennifer explained, the game plan for this evening's big hunt for Lulu.

'This evening?' Astrid checked.

'Yes, this evening.' Jennifer squared the stack of maps. 'We're going to sweep the town for Lulu.'

Astrid stood there. 'And it has to be this evening?'

It did, Jennifer said, her voice high and urgent. Tonight was one of the most important nights on the Estepona calendar. A procession was going to take place in honour of Santa María de los Remedios. The statue of her was to be taken from the church in the old town and paraded through the streets. Everyone would come out to celebrate, and that's why Jennifer was so worried. 'Poor Lulu', wherever she was, would be 'scared and confused'. She had to be found this evening. Most of the expats were going to meet at the salon at half past six and set off from there. Jennifer picked up the clipboard and teased a pen out from under the clip. 'Can you make it, Astrid?'

'Oh, yes,' said Astrid, 'you can rely on me.'

Over the next hour, Astrid got everything ready. She made a quick sandwich, had a shower, and headed out to the harbour breakwater. Nelson was on the deck of his boat. He saw her carrying the drum of water and bag of things from the boat supply store and called down, asking what she was doing. Astrid smiled, pretended not to hear him, and hurried on. When she got back to the boat, an hour later, he'd gone. A last check of the weather. Then she set the alarm for five forty-five. She was tired, the siesta would work this time. It needed to. It was going to be a long night.

Forty

By six thirty, everyone had assembled at Jennifer's salon. Declan had been the last to arrive. He wheeled a brand-new racing bike up the hill and chained it up outside. Astrid went out to meet him. 'That looks smart, Declan.'

'Yup – new hobby.' He patted the saddle proudly. 'You know, I'm not sure if I was ever going to be brilliant at golf.'

'You think?' said Astrid.

'I do. But cycling... wooo.' He puffed out his chest, stretching the name INEOS across his replica cycling top. 'I don't know, I just have a feeling I could be incredible at cycling. Maybe break a few local records.'

'You never know,' she said, holding the door open for him. 'Oh, I almost forgot.' She reached into her bag and handed over his rangefinder. 'Your golf rangefinder.'

He held up his hand. 'You keep it, Astrid. I don't need it now.'

'Aw, thanks, Declan.'

Only Zhang couldn't make it. BOBS was opening late, and he needed to man the tills. That was according to Nelson, who'd dropped in and picked up a box of torches that Zhang had donated, in case the dog search went on into the dark.

'They're water-damaged, apparently. You have to slap them on the end. That's what Zhang said.'

'Still, that's very kind of him,' said Jennifer. 'And all of you.' She pressed her hands together as if she was praying and nodded round the room.

Nelson thumped the base of each torch with his palm like a bottle of ketchup, and handed out the ones that worked.

Declan brought his finger up to a black band round his forehead. 'Don't worry, I have my new cycling head torch.' He pressed the button on the side of a light at the front. 'Five hundred lumens. Very powerful.' Then he revolved very slowly, like a tiny lighthouse fashioned into the shape of a middle-aged man.

The expats ducked as the beam of light swung past them. Sebastian wasn't quick enough. 'Jeez…' he winced. 'Declan!'

'Sorry,' said Declan, pressing the button on the light.

'You okay, darling?' hushed Bridget.

'I don't know,' said Sebastian, rubbing his eyes with the heels of his hands. 'All I can see is this white square of light.'

'Sorry,' repeated Declan.

As Sebastian carried on blinking, Wonderful went round and gave everyone a photocopy of the map of the town. She'd decided that they should work in pairs. Each couple would search a handful of streets. She'd marked them out with a fluorescent pen. 'We'll cover more ground that way,' she said, pressing a map into Pearl's hand.

'Right – well, good luck everyone,' said Jennifer. 'Let's hope we can find Lulu before…' She didn't have the strength to finish her sentence.

Fenwick turned his map up the right way and smiled at Jennifer. 'I'm sure Lulu is going to be fine.'

'Thank you,' said Jennifer.

'If you think about it,' Fenwick carried on, 'it's nice and warm. There are plenty of alleys to explore. Bins to raid for food.' Jennifer was staring at him. But he carried on. 'In many ways, he may well be happier on the streets. Much happier – having fun with other dogs... doing what dogs are supposed to do.'

'Sorry, um, Fenwick,' Wonderful interrupted. 'I think you might be underestimating the very real plight of street dogs.'

'You might be right. Sorry,' he said, eyes downcast.

'Come on,' Morgana nudged him. 'Let's search together.' Fenwick perked up again. 'Urrr... yeah, great.'

Astrid waited until everyone had drifted out into the streets. Her father had hung back on the pavement, Lulu's empty travel tent at his feet. Astrid tapped her watch.

Her father didn't miss the hint. 'I know – eight o'clock.'

'You have to give that painting back, Dad. Wherever it is.'

'Relax, Astrid. Plenty of time.' He picked up the travel tent and set off up the hill.

For the next hour, Astrid and her father searched the streets they'd been assigned by Wonderful. They checked down alleyways and over fences, calling out Lulu's name. There was no sign of her, or any other animals, except a black cat sleeping on the top of a wall. It hissed at them, its tail flicking angrily down the side of the wall.

They soon began to notice the sound of a band – high trumpets rising above the steady beat of drums. It must be the start of the religious procession, she thought. For most of the time it seemed distant. Then they'd walk past a junction and the band would sound closer. Another junction, a different direction. The music was ricocheting through the narrow streets of the town. Astrid asked her father if he knew about the event. He did – of course. The celebration of Santa María de los Remedios was the second-biggest procession of the year. The first was for the Virgen del Carmen, earlier in the summer. A statue of her was taken down from her church and carried to the beach, where a blessing was made to the sea. Forty years ago, he said, few locals would swim until this blessing was made. Tonight was a smaller event, but the whole town would come out.

They stopped to tick off another street on the map. Astrid leant in and whispered to her father, 'Did you see them?'

'Yes, I did,' her father said quietly, not looking up from the map.

At the last turn, a man and a woman, both in suits, had appeared round the corner, then tucked back into the shadows. It was the same woman her father had met in the square. He said he didn't know the man, and that he would have definitely remembered. The man was tall – over six feet – and heavily built. In his hand was a black briefcase. He was taking orders, judging by the way the woman held out her arm and he quickly stopped in his tracks.

'They want the painting back, you need—'

'Yes, yes...' he snapped. 'Trust me, Astrid.' He folded the map, picked up Lulu's travel tent and strode off up another street.

They turned right, then left, then right again, hurrying up the hill. But they couldn't shake off their followers. At each junction, Astrid glanced back and saw the man and woman edge out from the corner of a building. After a while, the pair realised they'd been spotted. She said something to him, and they both stepped out into the middle of the road and carried on towards them.

Astrid's father stopped at a four-way crossing and listened down each street.

'Come on, Dad,' Astrid muttered, looking back at the man and the woman. They were about fifty yards away and getting closer.

'Give me a second,' he said. She heard it too, above the music. The murmur of a crowd. 'This way,' he said, pointing to a cobbled stairway.

A few flights from the top, they could hear raised voices. A cheer went up, then there was clapping. Astrid glanced back down the stairs. Her breath quickened. The pair were only thirty yards away. The man saw she'd stopped. He gripped the briefcase in both hands and strode up the steps, two at a time. Astrid took her father's hand and they hurried on, up over the last step and into a wide street.

They'd timed it well, arriving just ahead of the procession. At the front was a handful of young boys in red and white vestments. One of them was swinging a silver incense burner. Behind the boys were four rows of men in maroon shirts. They were shouldering the weight of an ornate silver float on which balanced the statue of Santa María. She was wearing a sweeping white and gold dress and a gold crown topped with an explosion of stars.

Astrid and her father weaved through the boys and reached the far pavement. They turned and watched the float edge forwards. Astrid muttered 'Come on...' A bit further and the crowds would block the top of the steps. The men toiled on, heads down. Then someone shouted, and they ground to a halt. The statue's headpiece was about to get tangled in a wire that crossed the road.

'Holy…' Astrid caught herself.

A man with a long pole emerged from behind the float. He hooked the wire, raising it up so the statue could pass underneath. They were off again – the crowd surging forward, filling the street. Ten feet ahead of Astrid and her father, held back by a river of people, were their pursuers. They scowled at them through the incense smoke. Then they looked up, then down the street, and realised there was no way of getting through.

Astrid and her father took the nearest alley, pulled a sharp right, and found themselves in a quiet boulevard. Astrid slumped against a wall, getting her breath back. 'That was close.'

'Too close,' said her father.

Nelson wandered round the corner. Pearl was close behind him. 'Any luck?' he said.

'With what exactly?' said Astrid's father. Then, reading their blank expressions, he added, 'Oh, finding the dog. Err… no. You?'

'No sign, I'm afraid,' said Nelson.

Pearl folded her arms. 'It's a wild goose chase, if you ask me. I'm going to join the procession – see what they're up to.' She pushed past them and carried on in the direction of the music.

Nelson held up his map. 'I'll finish off then, Pearl,' he shouted after her. Then he noticed the sky over the sea. It was a peachy orange. Astrid and her father were already staring at it.

'It's the calima,' said Astrid.

'Yes, must be,' said Nelson. 'I heard on the weather forecast that one was sweeping in.' He went back to his map. 'Right, looks like I've got a few more streets to do. I'll see you later.'

Astrid waited until he was out of sight, then checked her watch. 'Dad, it's seven forty.'

'I know,' he said. 'Let's go.' He set off up a flight of stairs towards the tower of the old church. When they reached the square, he carried on through the open church doors without saying anything.

The church was empty. Everyone was out following the procession. Astrid finally caught up with her father at the marble steps in front of the altar. He put down the travel tent and stared up at the carved wooden panel on the back wall. It was huge, about thirty feet tall. On either side were alcoves that held figures of saints. In the middle was a bright red archway. It was empty, now the statue of Santa María was out for the evening.

'Impressive, isn't it?' said her father. 'Shall I tell you a bit about it?'

'Maybe another time, Dad.' Astrid glanced at the church doors. 'They're going to be here soon. We should get out of here.'

'Just a second.' A smirk flashed across his face. He knelt down next to Lulu's tent and carefully removed the square cushion from the base, putting it to one side. Underneath was the painting of *The Last Supper*. He brought it out, propped it up against the top step, and sat down on the step below.

Astrid joined him. 'Really?'

'I told you to trust me.'

'You know you have to give it back, Dad?' He couldn't

take his eyes off it. Because it was beautiful, or valuable, she'd couldn't tell. 'Dad?'

'Yes, you're right, Astrid,' he said softly. 'It doesn't belong to me.'

'No, Dad,' Astrid whispered. She was looking back down the church. Two shadows were crawling down the aisle. 'They're here.'

Astrid's father grabbed the tent and they crept down the side of the church, stopping behind a pillar. The footsteps grew louder. Astrid pointed to the confessional box against the wall. Her father nodded. They tiptoed over to it. Her father opened the nearest slatted door. Astrid took the other.

It took a few seconds to get accustomed to the dark. Along the back wall was a wooden bench. A dividing grille ran down the middle of the stall. She could just make out the shape of her father on the other side. He was peering through the slats of the door. Astrid turned back to her door and did the same. She'd just got the right angle when the man and the woman appeared in front of the altar steps. The man held back as the woman stepped forward and gazed at the painting. Her left hand reached up to the side of her face. Her right made the sign of the cross.

She stood back and the man came forward. He laid the briefcase down on the bottom step, opened it and brought out a red cloth. Pinching the upper corners of the frame, he laid the painting on the cloth. Then he folded the fabric around it and stowed it back in the briefcase. The pair waited a moment, listening for the slightest noise. Astrid held her breath. Then they marched back down the aisle, and out into the square.

Astrid slumped on the bench and exhaled. 'That was all a bit tense, wasn't it?'

'It was indeed.' His voice was loud in the silence. 'Very exciting though... hiding in churches, stolen art... well, um, *borrowed* art,' he backtracked. 'Right then...' There was the slap of his hands on his knees. She could imagine his expression, the brittle smile of the politician wanting to 'draw a line' under some scandal or other and carry on as normal. Which Astrid wasn't going to allow. The door on his side gently creaked open.

'Hang on, Dad,' she said sternly. 'Not so fast.'

The door creaked shut again.

'Seeing as we're both in a confessional box, which will probably never happen again, you might as well tell me the rest of the story.'

She heard him settle on his bench. 'What do you want to know?'

'Your brother – what happened between you?'

Astrid looked around the wooden booth, waiting for him to start. Over the decades, thousands of people must have shared their secrets here. Her father's couldn't be any worse. *Could it?* 'Come on – let's hear it.'

'Alright then.' He sighed. 'You remember that time you had to be taken out of school?'

'Yeah, I do.'

'Well, it was because my business was going badly.' His usual bluster had gone. His voice was quiet, and stained with sadness. 'We were about to lose the house, and I felt a failure.'

'I guessed it was – but losing the house?'

'I was almost bankrupt, Astrid. Everything was crashing

around me. And that's when your uncle and I worked out a little scheme.'

'Uh huh. What scheme?'

'Henry was such a good artist. And nobody appreciated his talents. So, I suggested that I'd lend him one or two paintings from the dealership. I had a couple of major works left. He could make a few copies, then I'd pass them off as the real thing to... shall we say, less discerning buyers.'

'Right... I've got it now.' She shuffled down the bench towards the grille. 'Uncle Henry was forging paintings and you were fencing them?'

'Mmm... fencing. I guess that's one way of putting it. I'd prefer to see it as dealing without provenance.'

The way her father explained it, it all sounded fairly innocent. Like relabelling supermarket jam as 'home-made' and selling it at the local village fete. But then he mentioned how much they made. It was a staggering amount of money. Enough to pay off his mortgage and save his business, with plenty to spare.

'Anyway, it was going very well, then your uncle... well, he had some qualms about another business opportunity I'd decided to invest in. He didn't think it was moral. You know what he was like.'

'This would be you dealing religious art? No questions asked. Like the painting you were about to sell?'

'That's pretty much it.'

'And Uncle Henry never forgave you?'

'Yes – unfortunately, Henry passed away before I could make it right between us.' She could hear the hurt in his voice. It was time to leave – it wasn't fair to push him any further.

'Maybe we should go,' she said, getting to her feet.

Her father drawled, 'Not so fast, Astrid. I think you've got a confession for me.'

'Have I?' But she knew a sermon was about to start.

'Be honest – the reason you agreed to investigate the internet troll was because you wanted to discover Jennifer's secret. Right?'

The confession box was open at the back to the bare walls. She pressed her shoulders against the cold stone and closed her eyes. 'Yes.'

'And you were hoping her secret would be so bad it would split us up.'

Astrid squirmed on the bench. 'Yes… I mean – at the start, maybe. I just wanted to get to spend some time with you again – on your own.'

'I thought so.'

'But please, Dad,' she pleaded. 'You've got to believe me. Now I've got to know Jennifer, I think she's fantastic. She's sweet and kind, and you two are perfect for each other.'

'It's true,' he said brightly. 'She and I work well together. And as for the physical side… I realise you won't be interested.'

'I'm not.'

'But let's just say, it's firing on all cylinders in that department.'

'Daaad…' she moaned.

'Fine, let's say no more.'

And they didn't. About the inner workings of his marriage. Or anything else. They sat there for a while, both of them knowing that when the confessional box doors closed behind them, he wouldn't be able to be so honest with her again. Sure enough, when they stepped out into the light, he turned to her and simply said 'Jolly good' and wandered off towards the front doors, the tent swinging by his side.

Astrid caught up with him as he came to a halt in the doorway. He was staring ahead at the orange sky. It was a haze of colour, as if the sun had exploded and dissolved into the atmosphere. They walked out into the square. The dust hung in the air – she could taste it, chalky and sour, on her tongue. The music of the band rolled up over the front of the steps – the procession was approaching.

On the balconies of the buildings either side of the steps, people threw out handfuls of red petals. They fluttered and trembled slowly to the ground, like glitter in a lava lamp. The headdress of the statue of Santa María appeared over the top step. Then her dress, which was streaked with dust. The men carried the float over the top step and waited, swaying from side to side. Gathering their strength for the final push back into the church.

The crowd – women, children, old men – were fixed on Santa María. Some fell to their knees and made the sign of the cross. Astrid knew she didn't see what they did. This wasn't a statue – but a living saint. The embodiment of all beauty and all love. In this cobbled square they made their promise to her, and she to them. That in return for goodness, her face would be the last they saw as their lives petered out like a dying flame.

The search team from Shakespeare's appeared from a side street, their torch beams milky yellow in the thick air. Jennifer was at the front. Then a white furry shape appeared from between the legs of the men. It scampered forward and looked around – not sure where it was.

'Lulu!' It was half a cry, half a question. Jennifer ran across the square and scooped up Lulu, pulling her to her chest. She ruffled her fur, petting then scolding her. 'I was so worried... where were you, Lulu?'

Astrid's father walked over with the tent and put it on the ground without saying anything. Jennifer knelt down and carefully placed Lulu inside. She tied up the door with the tasselled ropes and reached out for Peter's hand.

The men held the float still for a moment, waiting for Jennifer and her father to step aside. The expats gathered around Jennifer, congratulating her, saying how incredible it was that Lulu had appeared now. On the steps of a church under a blood orange sunset, as the Santa María gazed serenely down. It was almost impossible to believe... it was, as Pearl, walking out from the crowd and shaking her head in disbelief, said – 'a miracle'.

In all the excitement, Astrid had almost forgotten about Terry. She still needed to sort him out, once and for all. She chatted with the expats for a while, then slipped away, heading back down through the town. The dust seemed to fall back ahead of her. The calima had pushed up into the foothills and come to a halt. The Sierra Bermeja, it seemed, had taken a great dusty breath and exhaled, sending it back to where it came from. Every street she took, Astrid could taste less dust on her tongue. By the time she reached the harbour the night air was fresh and clean.

The breakwater looped out round the marina like a protective arm. It was made of huge jumbled rocks, with a cobbled walkway on the harbour inside. At the elbow of the arm, she checked her phone. There was a bit of time before

Terry was due to meet her on the far point. The weather forecast was right – a warm breeze, flowing directly south. She waited on a rock, going over her plan in her mind. Steeling herself. Although she knew she already had the better of him – because he was greedy, and cruel, and stupid. Three Achilles' heels in one person, if that was possible.

She carried on along the outward arm, stepping between the fishermen's nets that had been laid out to dry. The blue wooden fishing boats were black in the moonlight, huddled up against the harbour wall, like dogs sleeping by a fire. Eventually she reached the far point. There was a raised cobbled terrace. In the middle was a small beacon about twelve feet tall. Terry was leaning against the side. He stepped out into the light and walked slowly over to her. He was wearing a red tracksuit with white stripes down the side of the arms and legs.

'Have you got the money?' he said, seeing that she didn't have a bag.

'Relax, Terry.'

He looked past her down the breakwater. There was nobody there. 'I told you to bring the money.'

'I know, but you think I'd walk down here in the dark with twenty-four grand in cash? I'm not stupid.'

'So where is it?' He cracked his knuckles.

'Don't worry. I was here earlier – I've stashed it somewhere safe.'

'Where?'

'I'll tell you in a minute. I just want to ask you a couple of questions first.'

'Get on with it then,' he growled.

'Okay – why do you need the money, Terry?'

He looked her up and down, making sure she didn't have a phone on her to record him. She held up her hands to reassure him and he started talking. He admitted that he didn't own the bar. He'd still managed to save a lot of money over the years. 'You know…' he laughed. 'I'm in charge of the till, right?' Astrid didn't waste a question on this one – she knew what he meant – he'd been stealing from the owners. Almost half a million euros, he said, but not quite. That's how much he needed to qualify for a Golden Visa. The twenty-four grand would be enough to cover it and he'd be able to stay in Spain for good.

'And Elliot Green? You killed him because he couldn't sort your visa out?'

'Elliot Green…' He gave a weary groan. 'Elliot told me if I couldn't qualify for a Golden Visa, I had to apply for a temporary visa. I told him I wasn't going to risk it and he said he'd have to tell the authorities.' He played with the zip at the top of his tracksuit. 'Elliot always played by the rules.'

'So, you followed him out on to the golf course and hit him with the rake?'

He gave her a thin smile. 'That's an extra question.' He leant in close to her. She could smell the stale beer on his breath – he'd been at Shakespeare's all evening, celebrating too early. 'But just for you, Astrid… yeah, that's what I did.' His face was inches from hers. 'Right, now where's that money?'

'Okay, let's go then.' She stepped past him. 'This way.' She pointed down at an inflatable that had been tied up on the far side of the rocks. It was one of the boats that had come over from Africa and been impounded by the authorities. There was a yellow police sticker on the side. 'Come on.' She scrambled down over the boulders. The wind had picked up. Terry zipped his tracksuit all the way up and followed her.

Astrid said, 'The money's at the back. It's in a bag that's jammed down the side.'

'Go get it then,' he snapped.

'Really?' She put her hand to her chest, and gasped, mocking him. 'I thought you were a gentleman, Terry?'

'Yeah, yeah,' he grunted, then stepped down the last couple of big rocks. The inflatable's bow was facing the shore, tied by a rope to the rocks. It rose and fell in the waves, straining at its leash. Terry timed a wave and stepped aboard. Astrid watched him crawl over the seat plank towards the stern. 'That's it… right at the back.'

He got down on all fours and pushed aside the water drum and the life jacket, his hands scrabbling in the dark. Astrid went back to the rope that held the boat and untied the knot. It was a knot she'd tied herself, so she knew how to loosen it quickly. She let the rope quietly slip through her fingers and trail into the water.

Terry had found the flashlight and switched it on. He aimed the beam at the sides of the inflatable, pushing his hands into the gap. He swore. Jammed his hand down the other side. When he was sure there was nothing there, he got to his knees and swivelled round. Shouted, 'Where is it!' He pointed the beam of the torch at her, only then realising how far the distance was between them. There was thirty yards of choppy water. Maybe too far to swim in clothes. He desperately searched the rest of the boat for some oars. But there weren't any – because Astrid had taken them out and hidden them on the rocks. And now it was forty yards, and definitely too far to swim.

When she got back to her boat, she looked out beyond the harbour mouth. In the distance was a tiny white light. It blinked again and again but there was nobody to see it. Or hear the shouts, which were carried off by the breeze. Astrid went to bed.

Forty-one

The town woke up and found that it had been repainted in oranges and browns. The dust from the calima was everywhere. It was on the pavements, the cars, the lids of bins, the railings, the shop awnings and the cobbles of the back alleys. It brightened the tiled roofs and dulled the flowers in their pots. The apartment blocks behind the marina that were bright white yesterday were now stained light brown – like sugar cubes that had been dipped in tea.

The locals were out in force. The old women were brushing the steps of the houses. The men – it was mostly the men – had hooked up hosepipes and were spraying the walls and shutters. The water ran down in orange rivulets, over the pavements and into the gutters, where it gathered the red petals and dragged them into the drains.

Astrid turned a corner and chuckled. Ahead of her were the glass domes of the botanical gardens. They were peachy brown – like fancy desserts. A couple of workers in hi-vis yellow waistcoats were standing next to a council cleaning truck. One of them had a high-pressure hose in their hands. Both had forlorn expressions – no doubt trying to work out how long this job was going to take. Or if they could avoid it until the rain came – as it eventually would – and washed all the dust away for them.

By lunchtime, word had got out that Terry was missing. Charlotte had checked in for her morning shift and there was no sign of him. He still wasn't there an hour later, when Shakespeare's was due to open. She'd called him. It was a short and muffled exchange – he said he'd washed up in an inflatable at Ceuta, on the coast of Africa. It was at the other side of the Strait of Gibraltar. He had no idea how and when he was getting back, so told Charlotte to shut down the place.

'Furious' – that's how Charlotte had described his mood to Jennifer, who passed on the news to everyone else via Twitter. Now panic rippled through the expats. It was awful – Shakespeare's was shut. Where were they going to meet up now? Astrid came up with a solution. There was a place on her father's street she knew. It had good food and drink, and a nice courtyard garden. This could be their new base. Everyone seemed excited by the idea, and a meeting was arranged there for four o'clock.

Astrid was the last to arrive. When she went inside, they were all there, lined up along the bar. Eduardo was passing over drinks and small plates of food, happier than she'd ever seen him. Sebastian was nearest to her and sidled up.

'Isn't this marvellous?' He planted his hands on his hips and surveyed the ceiling. 'The original beams really define the room, don't they? And as for this bar top.' He ran his hand over the copper counter. 'I'm stealing this idea for our kitchen.'

'You do that, Sebastian,' said Astrid.

He took out his phone and began lining up a few shots of the furnishings.

Jennifer came over and swept Astrid up in a hug. 'You're so clever. This place is terrific – I had no idea it existed.'

'I know, I spotted it one day, and wandered in. And you've met Eduardo?'

'Yes, yes... he's a little rough diamond, isn't he?' She took Astrid's hand and led her over to the group of expats. She'd interrupted a conversation about Terry, but they were happy to go over the news. Charlotte had managed to speak to him again before the batteries of his phone died. It appeared that he'd made contact with the authorities at a detention centre in Ceuta. It was a Spanish enclave, and a holding point for migrants trying to get across the Mediterranean. They'd run Terry's details into their computers and discovered that he didn't have the proper immigration status to be repatriated to Spain. In fact, they didn't have any record of him on their system. Charlotte had now upped Terry's mood to 'incandescent'. For now, they'd told him, he'd have to wait in the detention centre until he could sort out how he could get back to the UK. That could take a week, maybe months.

'Thing I don't understand,' said Declan. 'How did he end up over there?'

Astrid spoke up. 'I guess he must have been mucking around on an inflatable on the shore. He didn't notice the offshore breeze and then, well, he just drifted off to Africa.'

'Yeah, I think you're right,' said Bridget. 'One thing's for sure. He won't be allowed to come back to Spain.'

The others glanced at Roger and Charlotte. They all knew what this meant – the pair were out of a job. Zhang broached the subject first. 'Listen, I can give you work at BOBS if you're stuck. I'm always looking for cashiers.'

'That's very kind,' said Roger. 'But we've talked about it and we're going to go back into teaching. There's a lot of schools around here that would take us.'

'Yes,' Charlotte agreed. 'I think we've both missed teaching kids.'

Eduardo glided over and took another order for drinks. He made small talk and passed over plates of tapas. Nelson picked at a dish of chubby olives, joy creasing his face. 'These are incredible, Eduardo.' He mimed his legs going wobbly.

Declan sipped his beer. 'There's one thing though, isn't there? We never found out who the Costa del Troll was. Did we?'

Astrid kept a straight face. 'No, I don't think we'll ever know now.'

'Well, I'm not bothered,' said Wonderful. 'I feel better my secret is out there. And the donations for the sanctuary are still pouring in.'

'Good for you,' said Jennifer. 'I'm relieved too... it was hiding the secret. That was the worst part.'

Roger raised his glass. 'And I'd like to thank the Costa del Troll for finding us a much better drinking establishment.' He tipped his glass to Eduardo.

'You are most welcome,' said Eduardo. 'I'm so glad you are here.' When he said this, he put his hand over his heart and smiled at Astrid. She did the same.

Sebastian eased into the group and Astrid took the chance to slip away. She'd seen that Morgana and Fenwick were at the other end of the bar. They were deep in conversation, and she had to say 'hi' a couple of times before they noticed her. 'Oh, hello, Astrid. Sorry...' Morgana spun round. 'Fenwick was just telling me some very funny stories about working in insurance.'

'Was he really?'

'Yes,' said Fenwick. 'I was just explaining that because I was so unsociable at work, my colleagues used to call me The Olympic Flame.'

'Because he never went out,' Morgana finished the anecdote. 'Get it?'

'Yes, that's not a bad one,' said Astrid.

'You know…' Morgana swirled the chopped fruit round in her sangria and batted her eyelashes. 'I'd really love to read your horoscope sometime.'

'Why?' Fenwick took a long glug of beer, leaving a creamy streak across his upper lip. 'I mean, it's utter nonsense.'

Astrid pressed an espadrille firmly on Fenwick's nearest sandal.

He winced. 'According to some… shall we say, less open-minded people.' He'd recovered well. 'Yes, thank you, Morgana. I'd love you to read my horoscope.'

'Oh, Morgana.' Astrid held up her wrist, the henna turtle tattoo facing forwards. It had almost faded away. 'If you have some time, I'd love you to freshen this up for me.'

Morgana looked at the tattoo and beamed. 'Of course – pop round to my stall anytime.'

Astrid moved on towards the garden. On the way, she noticed Pearl. She was sitting in a chair, half-hidden by a large rubber plant in a pot. A prime spot for eavesdropping. This would no doubt be her favourite seat from now on. 'How was church this morning, Pearl?'

'Alright.' Pearl mustered something close to a smile. 'God has offered me an apology, and I've decided to accept.'

'That's great news.' Astrid stopped. 'While we're talking about apologies, it may be worth saying sorry to the Cherrys some time. For that scathing restaurant review of yours.'

They stared at each other for a few seconds. Then Pearl cracked. 'Yes, I probably should.'

Astrid nodded and carried on towards the garden. 'Knew it,' she said, under her breath.

The garden was cool and shady. Eduardo's kids were cleaning their bikes in the far corner by the gate. The Beef was sprawled at the base of the fountain. A low voice to her right said, 'Astrid... grab a pew.' Her father was tucked behind a table in the shade of the fig tree, a glass of red in his hand. He pulled out the chair next to him. Astrid went over and sat down.

Her father pinched the crease in his shorts and crossed his legs. 'I've been doing a bit of thinking.'

'Okay.'

'It's been very nice to spend time with you, Astrid.'

'You too,' she said.

'And I don't want you to leave.' He reached out and patted her on the wrist.

'Good – I don't want to leave either.'

'Which is why I have a proposition.' He swivelled in his chair to face her. 'Your uncle, as you now know, was a rather brilliant forger. I, if I may flatter myself, have the knowledge and the contacts to pass on certain artworks. And you, Astrid... you have your own unique skills.'

'Go on – what are these skills then, Dad?'

'You're smart. You know a lot about fine art and have a good eye for detail.' Astrid didn't stop him. 'You're good at spying, and when you're in a tight spot, you find it easy to lie your way out of trouble.'

She protested vaguely about the lying – but she knew it was true. If needed, she was an excellent liar. Her father picked up his wine glass and swilled it round. 'Art fraud, theft, repossession – whatever you want to call it. It seems to be a bit of a family business. One that I think you and I should continue.'

'Dad? Please... What exactly are you saying?'

'I'm saying there's a lot of beautiful art out there that's in the hands of ugly people. I think you and I should team up and take it back.'

'I'd be doing the stealing, you'd be doing the fencing?'

'Spot on.'

Astrid sat there, shocked.

'Come on, admit it, Astrid.' He chuckled. 'You know how much you enjoy solving crimes. Imagine the fun committing them.'

'Mmm...' She looked out over the hills. 'You know, it's not your worst idea, Dad.'

'Good, good.' He raised his glass.

'But hang on.' She held up her hand. 'It feels like switching sides, doesn't it?'

'Depends who's on the other side.'

'Tell you what – let's say I'll think about it.'

'You do that, Astrid.' He drained his glass.

Astrid got up from her chair – she'd seen Miller cycling past on the lower trail. She hurried to the bottom of the garden, pushed through the gate and waved at her to come over. Miller veered down the path and drew up alongside. 'You coming in, Miller?'

'I'm okay, thanks.' Miller was looking over Astrid's

shoulder. Eduardo's kids were still cleaning their bikes behind her.

Astrid noticed. 'It'll be fine, come on.' She led the way back into the garden, and Miller followed. When they were a few yards from the kids, the boy glanced up and whispered to his sister, '*Es la chica*'. *It's the girl.*

Then they saw Miller's bike and the girl stepped forward. 'How many gears?'

'Eighteen,' said Miller.

'*Dieciocho.*' The boy nodded sagely.

'Good shocks.' The girl leant down and inspected the front shock absorbers.

'Thanks,' said Miller.

Eduardo's kids gave the bike a thorough examination – the wheels, saddle, handlebar – prodding here and there, tutting appreciatively, as if they were middle-aged classic car collectors about to put in an offer.

'Hey, you know what,' Astrid said, as if the idea had just come to her. 'Why don't you all go out on them now? If it's okay with your father.'

The kids looked at Miller, who nodded. 'I guess so,' she said coolly, although Astrid could see she was biting down on a huge grin. 'I found some pretty good jumps off the trail – if you can handle it.'

'Yeah, yeah. We do jumps,' said the girl, rubbing her hands.

The boy rushed into the bar and came out about ten seconds later to tell them their father had said it was okay. They were about to push their bikes out to the gate when Miller said, 'Why don't you try mine?' She handed her bike over to the girl.

'Thanks.' The girl passed her bike to Miller and headed with her brother to the gate. Miller hung back. She rocked the bike back and forth, not sure what to say. The person who'd used words like a scalpel online was lost for them in real life. That must have been another person, thought Astrid. Miller just smiled and turned away. Astrid went over to the fence and watched the three of them climb slowly up the path, over the ridge, and out of sight.

She stood and gazed at the hillside. But she didn't see the Sierra Bermeja. Or the dusty tracks that veined through the scrub. She saw the garden of a cottage they'd stayed at one Easter, when she was a kid. There were daffodils and primroses by the hedge. A damp lawn – more moss than grass. In the distance, a low mist clung to the hills as it had for seven days straight. Her parents had complained about the weather – it was supposed to be a holiday, they'd said. Over the years, they'd said a lot of things that were worth forgetting. Arguments best left for time to wear down to nothing. She saw it now – the past was an illusion. There was only this – the burning edge of the present. This moment under a clear blue sky. The ache of true happiness that comes from knowing that this is enough. Being here, with her family. She rubbed her eyes and walked back to the bar.

Author's Note

The procession of Santa María de los Remedios takes place on August 15th. In the book, this event happens a month later. The author wished to include the celebration to reflect the rich religious traditions of Estepona. Elsewhere in the text, geographical details have been changed or invented for dramatic streamlining.

About the Author

M.H. Eccleston has had a fairly meandering career – starting out as a radio presenter for the BBC, then staying at the Beeb as a journalist and producer for six years. After that, it's a bit of a blur – he spent a couple of decades, at least, freelancing as a foreign correspondent, TV presenter, sketch writer, voice-over artist and film critic. For the last few years, he's been a full-time screenwriter and now novelist. He lives in Ealing with his family, which is ruled by a mischievous Frenchie called George.